UNBRIDLED RAGE

A True Story of Organized Crime,
Corruption, and Murder in Chicago

UNBRIDLED RAGE

GENE O'SHEA

BERKLEY BOOKS, NEW YORK

THE BERKLEY PUBLISHING GROUP
Published by the Penguin Group
Penguin Group (USA) Inc.
375 Hudson Street, New York, New York 10014, USA
Penguin Group (Canada), 90 Eglinton Avenue East, Suite 700, Toronto, Ontario M4P 2Y3, Canada
(a division of Pearson Penguin Canada Inc.)
Penguin Books Ltd., 80 Strand, London WC2R 0RL, England
Penguin Group Ireland, 25 St. Stephen's Green, Dublin 2, Ireland (a division of Penguin Books Ltd.)
Penguin Group (Australia), 250 Camberwell Road, Camberwell, Victoria 3124, Australia
(a division of Pearson Australia Group Pty. Ltd.)
Penguin Books India Pvt. Ltd., 11 Community Centre, Panchsheel Park, New Delhi—110 017, India
Penguin Group (NZ), Cnr. Airborne and Rosedale Roads, Albany, Auckland 1310, New Zealand
(a division of Pearson New Zealand Ltd.)
Penguin Books (South Africa) (Pty.) Ltd., 24 Sturdee Avenue, Rosebank, Johannesburg 2196,
South Africa

Penguin Books Ltd., Registered Offices: 80 Strand, London WC2R 0RL, England

UNBRIDLED RAGE

A Berkley Book / published by arrangement with the author

PRINTING HISTORY
Berkley mass-market edition / September 2005

ISBN: 0-425-20526-6

BERKLEY®
Berkley Books are published by The Berkley Publishing Group,
a division of Penguin Group (USA) Inc.,
375 Hudson Street, New York, New York 10014.
BERKLEY is a registered trademark of Penguin Group (USA) Inc.
The "B" design is a trademark belonging to Penguin Group (USA) Inc.

PRINTED IN THE UNITED STATES OF AMERICA

10 9 8 7 6 5 4 3 2

For Charles G. O'Shea
1928–2003

ACKNOWLEDGMENTS

For their assistance and suggestions regarding the manuscript, I am indebted to my wife, Shannon, as well as to Michael Fries. Others have contributed to this effort directly or indirectly. Among those are Daniel Buckman, Anne Bowhay, and Doug Williams, who provided encouragement and direction in the early stages. The late *Chicago Tribune* crime reporter John O'Brien was also very helpful. Others who must be credited include the late John Konen, as well as Marla Bryan, and James Wagner, retired special agent of the FBI, whose years of experience as supervisor of the FBI's Organized Crime Unit in Chicago proved invaluable.

AUTHOR'S NOTE

Some of the dialogue and situations represented in this book were re-created using documents, courtroom testimony or interviews with the participants.

PREFACE

*The images seen on the 1955 black-and-white film are dis-
turbing, like an old newsreel of soldiers liberating Auschwitz.
The postures of the men gathered around the grass-lined
ditch speak of resignation and sadness. Nothing can be done
here. They are too late. A few smoke nervously. Their shoulders are hunched over, not from age but from the enormity of
what lies before them. The scene changes abruptly, panning
to the remains. Rigor mortis has already set in, leaving the
bodies stiff and lying in unnatural positions. They are naked.
One is lying on his back, his hands folded across his waist.
Another lies on his side, his legs slightly bent, with his arms
to his side. The third is facedown. Parts of the third body
touch the other two as if in some final embrace. A few blades
of grass move slightly from a gentle breeze. The view jumps
several times as the photographer repositions himself to cap-*

ture the scene from different angles. The camera pans the crowd that has begun to grow. The faces of the men gathering at the edge of the picnic meadow are emotionless, grim. Some stand within inches of the crime scene. A middle-aged man in a trench coat and fedora steps into the ditch, and the newspaper reporters begin scribbling in their notebooks as he speaks. He reaches down and moves one victim's head slightly. Whoever committed this crime was cold, brutal and methodical. There's been no effort to conceal the remains. These bodies have been dumped. They've been discarded like garbage along the side of a road. They are the bodies of three boys, not yet fifteen years old.

THE ELDERLY MAN *shuffled about the room. He was uneasy. At first he didn't know why. Then he understood. It was the memory. It was one of those random thoughts that crossed his mind and brought back the nightmare, however so fleetingly. It usually happened at least once a day. He had been living with such intrusions for decades. Sometimes the recollection would simply burst through, uninvited. Other times it was something inconsequential that triggered the anguish. This time it was the baseball game on television. His son had loved baseball, he thought. He took a deep breath and sat down on the couch. His eyes then caught the photograph of his son, who stared back, smiling, with the eternal sparkle of youth and dreams unfulfilled in his bright eyes.*

CHAPTER 1

As he battled the midday traffic on the Eisenhower Expressway, John Rotunno tried to prepare himself mentally for the task at hand. Rotunno was driving from the office of the federal Bureau of Alcohol, Tobacco and Firearms out to one of Chicago's western suburbs. Rotunno swore and braked to avoid a driver who cut him off. The traffic was aggravating even at this hour. Rotunno wasn't in a hurry. In fact, he wished his destination were farther away. At its end he faced the most difficult task he had ever performed in his law enforcement career.

Rotunno knew it was not easy to inform a family that a loved one had been killed in an accident. It's not easy to be the bearer of such significant news, he was told. Any law enforcement professional will admit that one of the hardest tasks for any police officer to perform is to knock on a stranger's door and tell whomever answers that "Daddy" won't be home for dinner. And by the way, you'll need someone to come down to the county morgue to identify and claim the remains.

There is no easy way to do it. Rotunno feared that no matter what words of wisdom he could muster, his abilities would fail him now. He was confident, however, that he and his supervisor James Delorto would handle the situation professionally. The two men, who were traveling in separate cars, were on their way to pay a visit to an elderly couple whose world had been torn apart almost forty years earlier with the murders of their son and two other boys.

Rotunno was thirty-nine years old. He was about five months old when the lifeless bodies of Bobby Peterson, thirteen, and his friends, brothers John and Anton Schuessler, thirteen and eleven, were found thrown in a ditch in the Robinson Woods Forest Preserve on the outskirts of Chicago. Now he and Delorto were on their way to speak to Malcolm and Dorothy Peterson, the parents of the eternally young Bobby.

Rotunno was anxious. He knew the news they were going to pass on to the Petersons would open old wounds. It had been a horrific crime. Rotunno winced the first time he saw the crime scene photographs of the bodies. It was painful for the hardened special agent to think about what horrors had befallen the trio. Rotunno knew that the emotional discomfort he felt in no way compared to the anguish experienced by the Petersons and the parents of the Schuessler boys. In all of his years in law enforcement, including his time with the DuPage County State's Attorney's Office and with the Drug Enforcement Administration, nothing came close to what he had to do now.

When Rotunno pulled up to the apartment complex

where the Petersons lived, Delorto was already waiting for him outside of his car. Rotunno parked and exited and both men walked toward the five-story apartment building in silence. It was a warm, muggy day. Off in the distance two cicadas whined. The two men could hear the roar of gasoline engines as a crew of landscapers began cutting the grass. It was a secure building; they would need to be buzzed in before they could get up to the Petersons' apartment. Rotunno immediately noticed Delorto's serious expression. This wasn't going to be easy for Jim either, he thought.

Rotunno scanned the list of names on the doorbell. Before he pushed the one marked "M. Peterson," he turned to Delorto.

"What do we do if they're not home? Do we wait?" Rotunno asked, knowing full well what Delorto's answer would be.

"We've got to do this today or tomorrow," Delorto responded. "No matter what, they need to know."

Rotunno pushed the buzzer and both men waited. About half a minute later they heard an elderly man's voice through the intercom.

"Who is it?" Malcolm Peterson asked.

Rotunno turned and looked at Delorto before answering. He sighed and pushed the talk button.

"Mr. Peterson, my name's John Rotunno, I'm here with my supervisor Jim Delorto," he said. "We're with the Bureau of Alcohol, Tobacco and Firearms. We need to talk to you. It's important."

"The bureau of what?" Mr. Peterson replied. "I'm not interested in buying anything."

"We're not salesmen, Mr. Peterson, we're federal agents. We're the police," Rotunno replied.

Mr. Peterson didn't respond. After a few minutes the

door buzzed and both men walked into the apartment building. They made their way over to the elevator and pushed the up button. Neither man said a word as they rode up to the Petersons' apartment. When the two men stepped off the elevator, Malcolm Peterson was already waiting for them in the hallway. Dressed in khaki pants and a white-T-shirt, Mr. Peterson stood slightly hunched over. He walked with the aid of a cane and he looked to be about eighty years old. Rotunno quickly spotted the family resemblance between the father and the son. Recalling the photographs of the boy, and earlier news photographs of Mr. Peterson, Rotunno thought the elderly man looked just like Bobby. Both had similar facial features and eyes.

"I know why you are here," Mr. Peterson said in a surprisingly strong voice. "This is about Bobby, isn't it?" he asked.

"Yes, sir, it is," Delorto said, surprised. Before Delorto could introduce himself and Rotunno, Mr. Peterson had taken control of the conversation.

"Let's go down to the laundry room and talk. I don't want my wife to hear any of this. It's been very hard for her," he said. "We put this all behind us years ago. I don't want to upset her."

The old man hobbled down the hall, moving fairly quickly. He led the two agents to the laundry room. It was empty. One of the dryers was on, tumbling some clothes. Mr. Peterson turned and looked at the two men. Though his body was old, bent and tired, his eyes were sharp. He looked intently at the two men.

"What is it you want to tell me?" he said.

"Mr. Peterson," Delorto said, in a calm tone. "We wanted to let you know that within a few days—most definitely by the end of this week—we're going to be arresting a man for the murder of your son and the Schuessler boys. We wanted to tell you in person so you didn't have to read it in the papers or see it on the news."

Delorto's words seemed to hang in the air. Mr. Peterson said nothing. The only sound that could be heard in the room was the tumbling of the dryer. He turned away from the two men, as if in shame, and looked down. His body leaned heavily; he put his elbow on top of a washing machine to support himself.

"Why now? What's different now than it was before?" Mr. Peterson shot back. "I don't understand. Why now, after all these years?"

Delorto began going into the details of the ATF's investigation into the Chicago Horse Syndicate and the murder of candy heiress Helen Brach. It was that investigation that led them to the suspect who was soon to be arrested for the crime, Delorto·said. As he continued speaking, both Delorto and Rotunno noticed that Mr. Peterson's body began to shake almost uncontrollably. His muscles tensed, as if he regained control of his emotions. He began to weep, and wiped the tears from his eyes.

"I'm sorry to have to tell you this, sir," Delorto said, looking to offer some emotional assistance to the man. "Are you going to be all right? Can we get you a chair, a glass of water? Do you need some fresh air?" Delorto asked.

Mr. Peterson turned and looked straight at the agents. Delorto and Rotunno then saw the anger that was there. Delorto could tell Mr. Peterson had been a big man, a "bruiser" at one time, a man whose physical stature sent a strong message. Delorto later assumed Mr. Peterson's anger wasn't directed at the agents but at the cruelty of fate. How cruel to learn the identity of the man who had stolen a large chunk of his life, his dreams, his son and grandchildren who had never been born. How cruel to hear the killer's name, especially in the twilight years of his life, when there was nothing he could do to extract vengeance.

"How come it took you so long?" Mr. Peterson snapped. The agents didn't respond. They didn't know what to say.

Malcolm Peterson then turned and walked away. As he walked back to his apartment, he was alone with his memories. The wall that he had created in his mind that sealed off the nightmare of so many years ago had been fully breached. His thoughts raced back to the day when the world had crumbled around him.

CHAPTER 2

If ever there were "good old days" in Chicago, it was in 1955. The City of Big Shoulders was bursting at the seams. Its tiny suburbs were just promises of subdivisions yet constructed. Chicago was a city of working-class neighborhoods where children ran free. Like parents in other large U.S. cities in the mid fifties, parents in Chicago did not fear for their children.

The intersection of every city block was a ready-made baseball diamond with the sewer caps on each corner serving as makeshift first bases. Alleys were not places to be feared and avoided. Instead, they were for playing hide-and-seek or cowboys and Indians, building forts out of cardboard boxes, or reenacting the Battle of the Bulge. Many a twilight evening in the summer months was filled with the sounds of childhood innocence as kids played kick-the-can and ran through their neighbors' yards. As darkness grew, a hundred mothers and fathers would stick their heads out of their front doors and summon their children home. Whether met with protest or resignation, such orders signaled the end to another seemingly endless day filled with childhood joy.

The good old days, however, had some dark edges. The "Outfit," Chicago's version of La Cosa Nostra, was busy buying off politicians, putting cops on the payroll, and running hookers and numbers rackets throughout the city. One of the biggest hotels north of the Loop was a well-known Outfit brothel protected by Chicago's finest. The Chicago Police Department was one of the most corrupt in the country; mob-connected cops held key positions throughout the department.

Although the days of Al Capone were long gone, remnants of his organization thrived in Chicago in 1955. There was also another criminal organization that existed side by side with the Outfit. It was made up of grizzled cowboys who used riding stables as their main places of operation. If ever there was a time one can point to when Chicago lost its innocence—especially in relation to children—it was October 18, 1955.

From its northern suburbs to the far south, a corridor of public lands abuts a large portion of the city of Chicago. Known as the Cook County Forest Preserves, the area is comprised of picnic groves, woods, lakes, ponds and horseback-riding trails. The forest preserves have long offered Chicago's residents a chance to escape from the daily grind.

The "woods," as many Chicagoans refer to the forest

preserves, are many things to different people. For lovers they are a quiet place to meet; for anglers the ponds and lakes offer fishing; for the equestrian it's a place to ride a horse; and for the working man its wide-open spaces offer the perfect location to hold a family reunion. In 1955 however, the forest preserves were also an ideal place for the quick disposal of bodies.

On October 18, 1955, at about 12:15 P.M. Victor Livingston drove into the parking lot of the Robinson Woods Forest Preserve grove to stop and eat his lunch. It was a common routine for Livingston. He had little desire to frequent one of the numerous roadhouses on the outskirts of the city that made up his territory as a liquor salesman. Since he spent a good part of his day inside taverns, the fresh air and sunshine were a welcomed respite. Weatherwise, October is a transitional month in Chicago. Some October days can be truly miserable, with driving rains and frigid temperatures. But Mother Nature can also be agreeable, granting Chicagoans a few last days of summer. On that day it was overcast. The morning's cool air was beginning to warm. It had drizzled earlier, coating the city with a fine spray of moisture.

Livingston, fifty, had just come from Heur's Tavern, where he had spent about forty-five minutes trying to make a few extra sales to Red Heur, the proprietor. A sociable man, Livingston had also spent some time chitchatting with Don Gudeman, the owner of the nearby Mellow Rust Stable.

Livingston parked his red, 1955 two-door Buick just off a bridle path. He turned to the backseat of the car to grab a bag of sandwiches his wife had prepared for him. He was hungry and looked forward to lunch. At first, Livingston didn't notice the object lying in the ditch several feet behind the car. But then something red caught his eye. He initially thought someone had thrown a store mannequin into a ditch. Then he took a closer look and gasped. "Good God. What the hell is that?"

Livingston knew whoever was lying in the ditch was dead. He had never seen anything like that before in his life. The body's skin was pasty-white. He never considered getting out of his car to see if there was some assistance he could offer. He was far too frightened. Fumbling for his keys, Livingston managed to start his car and gun the engine. Horrified, he drove off, raced back to Heur's tavern, jumped out of his car and burst into the door. "Somebody call the police!" he shouted. "I just found a body in the woods!"

Red wasn't behind the bar; he had gone outside to attend to other business. "Don, Don, call the police," Livingston shouted to Don Gudeman. Gudeman, who was sitting at a table with his wife eating lunch, pushed back his chair and responded to Livingston's cry for help. After he calmed Livingston down, Gudeman reached for the phone and called the Cook County Forest Preserve Ranger to report that a body had been found in the woods. Gudeman spoke to the ranger for a few moments and then handed the phone to Livingston, who was obviously agitated. The ranger on the other end of the line told Livingston to sit tight, that help was on its way.

Within a few minutes Ranger John Byrne arrived at Heur's Tavern, and all three men drove over to Robinson Woods in Byrne's car.

When they arrived at the forest preserve grove, Livingston pointed to the ditch where he had spotted the body.

Byrne got out of the car and started walking toward the spot that Livingston indicated. Livingston refused to budge from the backseat. From his vantage point he could still see the battered corpse. Gudeman didn't venture from the car either. As Byrne got closer, he stopped in his tracks. He turned toward the other two men with a look of shock on his face.

"Hey! It isn't one, it's three," Byrne yelled. Byrne then quickly scanned the woods and nearby groves for anyone else in the area. There were no other cars in the parking lot. Byrne quickly made his way back to his car. "I've got to call headquarters and get the coroner out here right away," he said. "Let's go back to the tavern."

Just a few miles away Richard Ritt was about to sit down to eat lunch. Ritt, twenty-five, was an optometrist; he had come home at the noon hour to see his wife and daughter. Just as he was about to start eating, the telephone rang. Ritt's wife picked up the phone, said a few words, and then handed the receiver to her husband. On the other end of the line was a friend of Ritt's who worked as the assignment editor at WGN-TV, a local television station in Chicago. A camera buff since high school, Ritt worked as a freelance cameraman for WGN and other Chicago stations. He welcomed such calls, no matter what hour, since he enjoyed the work tremendously. Plus Ritt needed the extra money the freelance work provided.

"Listen, Rich. We need you to get out to Robinson Woods right away," his friend said. "We just got a tip that they found a couple of bodies in a depression or ditch near a bridle path somewhere out there. How fast can you get out there and get the film for us? You know where that's at, right?"

Ritt knew exactly where Robinson Woods were located

and had an idea where the bodies might be found. He told the WGN news desk he was on his way and grabbed his camera, a 16mm Bell and Howell 70DL. He was just minutes away from the scene and wanted to get there before anyone else. Ritt sprinted to his car and sped off.

He ignored the speed limit and made it to Robinson Woods in about ten minutes. As he pulled into the parking lot of the forest preserve, he expected to find the scene swarming with police officers. Instead he found only one man, a Cook County Forest Preserve District employee, a groundsman, who was pale and visibly upset. Ritt could tell that the man was shaken up. He looked as if he had gotten sick.

"Hey, I heard there were some bodies out here," Ritt asked as he braked the car and killed the ignition. "Is that true?"

The groundsman didn't respond. Instead he pointed off toward a ditch. Ritt grabbed his camera and started toward the scene.

Though he had seen his share of bodies as part of his medical studies and as a television cameraman, Ritt wasn't prepared for what he saw lying in a depression running just a few feet from the adjacent parking lot. He had never seen the corpses of children. They were three boys. They had been stacked on top of one another and laid in the ditch like rubbish. They were naked, bruised and slightly bloodied. One appeared to have had a portion of skin removed from his thigh, and another boy's eyes remained open, expressionless, staring into the overcast sky. For a moment, Ritt too thought he was going to get sick.

But instead Ritt swore under his breath. The professional persona then came into play. Whereas others would cringe in horror and run away from the scene, Ritt picked up his camera, peered into the viewfinder and began shooting. That was his job. Ritt took close-ups of the boys' faces, those that he could see, since the bodies were stacked on top of one another, and also filmed the overall crime scene. He had been working for several minutes when Cook County Coroner Walter E. McCarron and Coroner's Assistant Harry Glos arrived.

McCarron, the first Republican coroner in Cook County, became furious when he saw Ritt filming. It was uncharacteristic for the usually affable man to explode at any reporter or media representative.

"Get the hell out of there!" McCarron growled. "What are you doing? Get back right now. I'm in charge here!" Ritt quit filming and stepped back, letting McCarron get a close view of the bodies.

McCarron, who was fifty-five at the time, stared down at the bodies and shook his head. He tipped up the brim on his fedora and wiped his brow of sweat. Though it had been a cool fall morning, the sun was breaking through the overcast clouds and it was starting to get warm.

McCarron was in his final year of a four-year term in office. He was facing a tough general election. Ritt suspected the coroner knew he was facing what reporters and police in Chicago referred to as a "heater case." A heater case generates so much media and public interest that it can bring a public servant's career to an abrupt end or advance it, depending on how the case is handled. McCarron didn't want any media coverage that would rankle the voters.

He turned toward Ritt and snapped, "Show some respect. You better not take any close-ups of these boys here. If I catch you doing that, I'll take your film!"

Ritt didn't tell McCarron that he had already taken several close-ups of the bodies. "What can I shoot?" Ritt asked respectfully.

"Anything," he responded. "Just don't take any close-ups of the bodies. These boys have families. I don't want them to see their sons like this," McCarron said.

Ritt continued filming from a respectable distance as more news reporters and police officers began showing up. The crime scene was quickly turning into a chaotic mess. Several daily newspaper photographers gathered around the bodies and started to take photographs. One of them shouted out to Glos. "Hey, Harry. We want to make the late editions. Why don't you come over here and do the roll for us?"

Glos was one of the Chicago media's favorite people. Although McCarron was also well liked—and always quick to offer a quote or basic information to any reporter who asked—Glos was even more accommodating. He would "roll" a victim's body on command and stand over it in whatever pose a photographer requested. In many photographs Glos would be seen pointing to some obvious sign of trauma, like a bullet hole or knife wound.

"Yeah, this looks like a .38," Glos might say, pointing down toward the face of a corpse and the bullet hole between a victim's eyes. "This is definitely a murder."

The photographer would snap the shot and the next day's caption might read, "Cook County Coroner Investigator Harry Glos points to evidence in the murder of . . ."

Without consulting McCarron, Glos scrambled down into the ditch and stood over the remains. The investigator then reached down and pulled the top body over; now all of the boys' faces were exposed. Glos made a motion with his hand for the photographers, to indicate it appeared one of the boys had been struck on the head. Glos had destroyed the crime scene before any police photographers, crime lab technicians or detectives had a chance to examine it for evidence.

Within minutes, several high-ranking Chicago and Cook County sheriffs and police officers arrived at the scene. When they learned what Glos had done, they became furious. Ritt watched silently as Glos was thoroughly chewed out.

More police officers began arriving at the parking lot. There were Cook County Sheriff's deputies, Chicago Police officers and Cook County Forest Preserve rangers. No one knew who controlled the crime scene and which jurisdiction would investigate the case.

Ritt was soon pushed back from the scene by a crowd of other reporters and also by the police. He continued filming, and photographed a group of police officers standing shoulder to shoulder, whom detectives at the scene had organized into one line. The row of officers was sent marching across the adjacent field. They were searching for any evidence that could be found that was related to the murders. A few pieces of clothing were discovered. Ritt then filmed the bodies being taken away by a hearse. By this time, McCarron had let the boys lie in the sun for two hours while he commanded police at the scene.

Years later Ritt would recall how angry he had been that McCarron had let the children lie in the ditch for so long.

"McCarron was too busy telling everyone what to do. But what he was trying to do was get as much exposure as he could get," Ritt said. "Those kids were left lying out there in the sun. That's what made me so mad. For two hours he left them there."

* * *

SEVERAL MILES TO the south, *Chicago Daily News* reporter Jack Lavin had just pulled out of the parking lot at the Cook County Criminal Courts Building located at Twenty-sixth Street and California Avenue. Lavin, who was the investigative reporter for the *Daily News,* had stopped by the courthouse to check on some legal filings. He was on his way back to the newsroom when his two-way radio crackled to life. On the other end was Ritz Fisher, the *Daily News* assistant city editor.

Fisher told Lavin that fellow reporter Buddy Lewis, who was assigned to the Chicago Police Headquarters, had learned that several bodies had been found. Fisher gave Lavin the same news that had been passed on to Ritt by WGN. The word was starting to get out. Someone had found some bodies out at Robinson Woods and Lavin needed to get out to the scene five minutes ago.

Lavin knew how important it was to get out to the crime scene as soon as possible. Other reporters and photographers from the *Daily News,* as well as every other news organization in Chicago, would be mustering their troops and ordering them to descend on the forest preserve grove. Soon the crime scene would be crawling with the media. Every reporter worth his press credentials would be trying to scoop the competition by snaring that one interview or tidbit of information that would make his story better than the competition's. The police would soon be there too. A lot of them, Lavin figured.

Lavin jammed his foot on the accelerator. His 1953 dark-green four-door Ford sedan lurched forward. The fact that Lavin's personal car looked like an unmarked Chicago Police car suited him just fine. He had bought the car just for that purpose. It was all part of the news game in Chicago. Lavin not only drove an automobile that looked like a police car, he also dressed like a member of the Chicago Police Detective Division. "You had to wear a fedora in those days," Lavin would explain years later. "You had to look like a copper; you had to wear the 'uniform.' Whatever the sport coat that was in fashion, whatever the boys in the detective bureau were picking up, you had to get one too."

In Chicago and throughout the country in the 1950s the news business was an overwhelmingly male profession. As such, there were certain unwritten rules that reporters followed. Police officers and reporters shared a much different relationship from the one they do today. It was not adversarial. The son, brother and nephew of Chicago Police officers, Lavin counted many of Chicago's finest as his friends and spent more than a few off-hours with the boys at local taverns.

There were tricks newspaper reporters played to beat the competition. Whenever Lavin was dispatched to a murder scene, he even made sure he wore his fedora cocked the same way as a detective.

"All the bureau guys flipped up the front part of the brim. That's how everyone knew they were detectives from Downtown; that's what they did," Lavin recalled. When Lavin arrived at a crime scene, he would simply stick his notebook inside his jacket pocket and swagger past the uniformed officer working crowd control. Lavin learned early in his career that if you looked like you knew what you were doing, you could get yourself into just about anywhere.

"If you played it right, you could walk right in and get all the good stuff. The guy who shot somebody might be in the corner of the room, crying. Sometimes he would be asking for forgiveness. Some copper would tell the guy to shut up. You'd go about your work and get the information from the dicks at the scene about what happened. Then maybe you'd get some quotes from the suspect while the other reporters would be sitting outside twiddling their thumbs."

Only a handful of people beat Jack Lavin to the crime scene. When Lavin arrived at the Robinson Woods Forest Preserve, he spotted Ritt filming and then looked around for a familiar face, a beat cop or detective who could fill him in on any inside information. He quickly walked over to where the boys' bodies were lying.

Lavin looked into the ditch and then exhaled deeply. He murmured, "Holy shit."

"No kidding," remarked a photographer from another newspaper.

"What sick son of a bitch could do this?" Lavin asked. He began scribbling notes in his notebook. He tried to estimate the boys' ages, heights and weights. He had seen enough bodies in his day that he could tell they had been beaten. The boys' faces and bodies bore bruises. Lavin's eyes were also drawn to the section of skin that had been ripped out of the one boy's leg. In the back of his mind, Lavin recalled reading a missing person's report at the Jefferson Street station a day or two before. The parents of three boys had reported their children missing. Lavin made a mental note to call the desk sergeant at the precinct to get the boys' names off the report as soon as possible. He wanted to confirm if these were the same three missing boys.

When Lavin arrived at the woods, the crime scene had already been destroyed. He noticed Harry Glos posing for pictures and moving the bodies for other photographers. Lavin and other reporters also noticed various impressions and bumps on the bodies. The impressions looked like they'd come from a car mat. The bodies might have been driven to the scene in the trunk of someone's car, Lavin thought.

"Who would have done this? What was the motive to kill them?" he remembers asking himself. "Obviously sex was involved because their clothes were gone. Why did they get rid of the clothes?" Wherever the murders had occurred, Lavin thought, there was something on the boys' clothes that would lead police to the murder scene. Police would later consider the murders as potential sex crimes.

The grass around the bodies was wet, but the remains were dry. It had rained earlier that day, so whoever dumped the bodies had done so sometime in the morning.

Lavin sprinted over to his car, started the engine and called his news desk on the two-way radio. The radio wouldn't work well and Lavin had to move several times to get good reception. He began reciting what facts he had gathered to a rewrite man who would pull the story together for a replate of the *Daily News* "Red-Flash" edition. The Red-Flash edition was the second to the final "Red-Streak" edition. Lavin's city editor told him the *Daily News* was going to put together an "extra" edition, about a 50,000-copy press run for the downtown evening commuters. Lavin's editors were counting on him to deliver.

Several times over the next two hours Lavin ran back to his car and called in snippets of information. These included his observations and the thoughts and theories of the police and others at the scene. Lavin had to move his car a few times to get better reception on his radio. Fellow *Chicago Daily News* reporter Ed Rooney later joined him. Rooney had run a red light to get to the scene and was stopped by a patrolman. When he told the officer where he was going, the officer let him go without a ticket. Rooney also began calling in information to the city desk.

After wrapping up all he could cull from the crime scene, Lavin headed out to the homes of the victims, who by now had been identified.

Lavin, Rooney and other reporters worked feverishly for the next several hours to pull together a series of stories as to who the victims were and what the police knew at that time. Lavin and his colleagues made the Red-Streak edition. Under a 72-point banner headline of "POLICE FIND THREE BOYS SLAIN HERE" with a subheading of "Three Missing Boys Strangled, Left in Woods" the *Daily News* staff put together a package of stories that recounted the events as they had unfolded that day. All of the stories were written in a brief, staccato fashion.

A few assumptions made by officials at the scene that were reported in the *Daily News* main story later proved inaccurate. Such is the price that is paid in deadline journalism. Lavin was instrumental in putting together the main piece of the *News* coverage. Under the subheading "Bodies Found in a Ditch: Youths Dead for 12 Hours, Skulls Fractured, Coroner Says" Lavin and the rewrite men at the *Daily News* reported the following:

> *The nude mutilated bodies of three boys missing since Sunday were found Tuesday in a ditch in the Robinson Woods Forest Preserve in Leyden Township.*
>
> *Coroner McCarron said they had been strangled, apparently with a wire. The bodies were found near a parking lot 150 feet south of Lawrence Avenue between East River Road (an extension of Dee Road) and River Road.*
>
> *The boys were Robert M. Peterson, 13, of 5519 Far-*

ragut; John Schuessler, 13, of 5711 N. Mango, and his brother Anton, 11.

McCarron said the Peterson boy's eyes and lips were taped. His head had been hacked about 12 times with an axe or cleaver, he said. There were also indications that the eyes and faces of the other two boys had been taped.

Skulls of all three boys were fractured, according to McCarron. No attempt had been made to cover the bodies.

BELIEVES BOYS PUT UP FIGHT

He said there was evidence that the youngsters had been held captive "for some time" before they were killed and that they had put up a fight.

Tire marks leading into the parking lot were being studied by the police crime laboratory.

McCarron said he believed the bodies were dumped from a car or truck.

He said apparently they had been dead for about 12 hours.

The spot where the bodies were found is about five miles from their homes.

The bodies were lying side by side in a shallow ditch at the edge of the parking lot.

The soles of the feet of two of them were smudged with a substance that appeared to be grease, police said.

They interpreted this as indicating that the slayer may have stripped the boys in a garage or machine shop where grease smudges could have been picked up by walking across a dirty floor.

Police were puzzled by the waffle-like impressions on the backs of the bodies, apparently made by matting or some kind or springs.

They theorized the boys may have been made to lie on bare bedsprings or a matted rug.

BOYS' MOTHERS HYSTERICAL

Mothers of the boys were reported hysterical in their homes after hearing of the slayings.

The two Schuessler boys were positively identified by a neighbor, John M. O'Donoghue, 43, of North Mango, a lieutenant of the Chicago Fire Department.

Police were attempting to make a positive identification of the Peterson boy.

The bodies were later moved to the county morgue, where an immediate post mortem was ordered to determine whether the boys had been sexually molested.

Forest Preserve rangers and sheriff's deputies fanned out over a square mile area in a search for clues.

Several old pieces of clothing were found but none could be linked to the crime.

The boys were last seen by their parents Sunday when they left home to attend a movie in the Loop.

The bodies were discovered by a wine salesman, Victor Livingston, who pulled his car into the parking lot to eat his lunch.

He went to the Mellow Rust Stables, a saloon in the 5400 block of North River Road, and excitedly began to tell the story to patrons.

Don Gudeman, 63, who operates the saloon, overheard him and called forest preserve rangers.

Within minutes rangers, state police, county highway police and special details from the Chicago police department were on the scene.

Capt. John Olsen of the state's attorney's police also dispatched a team of men.

Sheriff Lohman arrived at the murder scene to take personal part in the investigation. The forest preserves are his jurisdiction.

About 75 policemen were helping search the woods.

Police Commissioner O'Conner said he had assigned his "best men" to cooperate with county authorities.

"I'll give them everything I've got," he said.

Chief of Detectives James McMahon, two special squads from the homicide unit and Lt. James Lynch, a recent graduate of the FBI Academy, were assigned immediately.

REPORTED SEEN SUNDAY NIGHT

The boys disappeared after leaving the Peterson home about 3 p.m. Sunday to see a movie in the Loop.

They had told their parents they were going to the Loop Theatre, State near Lake, to see "The African Lion," a Walt Disney production.

When their parents reported that the boys had failed to come home, the theater was searched. But it yielded no trace of them.

Mrs. Eleanor Schuessler, mother of two of the boys, reported that Sunday night a boy and a girl—friends of her sons—came to the Schuessler home and said that they had seen the three in a bowling alley Sunday night.

The bowling alley is the Monte Cristo Bowl, at 3326 Montrose, about four miles from the youths' homes.

The alley manager, Edward C. Davis, of 3320 N. Lockwood, viewed pictures of the boys and "positively identified" them as those of youths who visited the alley.

He said they were at his place twice, once about 3:15 p.m.—*apparently before they went to the movie*—and again about 7 p.m.

He said they left the first time after asking how much it cost to bowl.

He told them the price was 43 cents a line, plus shoe rental of 15 cents. They indicated that was too much for them.

When they returned the alley was crowded with league bowlers so they were unable to bowl.

They were seen a little later, about 8 p.m., in the Drake Bowling Lanes at 3550 Montrose.

The manager of the Drake Lanes, Waldorf Lundgren, of 1732 Columbia, is the last person known to have seen them alive.

When they left home, according to Mrs. Schuessler, the boys had only $4 among them.

Young Peterson had been to the Loop many times before, police were told. But it was the Schuessler youngsters' first Loop venture unaccompanied by adults.

MOTHER HAD GIVEN UP HOPE

All three youngsters attended the Farnsworth School. The two older boys were eighth graders and Anton was a sixth grader.

All were clad in blue jeans when they left home.

The Petersons have three young children. Peterson is a carpenter.

The Schuesslers have no other children. The father, Anton, is a tailor.

Mrs. Schuessler had said Monday that she had "given

*up hope" for her boys. She said they had never stayed
away from home before.*

Careful not to disturb his sleeping wife and children, Lavin climbed into bed early the next day, sometime around 3 A.M. He and other reporters had worked the story for more than twelve hours. He knew he would be getting up in just a few hours and would be right back at it, looking to snare that tidbit of information that would lead to the boys' killer. It was a story, a crime and an event that Lavin would live with for the next several years.

CHAPTER 3

As with many homicides, information as to who had murdered the boys made its way to some unlikely people. Earlier on the day the three boys were last seen, brothers Bruce and Glen Carter came across Bobby, John and Tony and spoke to them on the street. As the boys milled about, as boys that age often do, Bobby blurted out that he and the Schuessler brothers were going to the Idle Hour Stable later that day to ride horses. "It's for free," Bobby said, adding with emphasis, "We don't have to pay." The Carter boys immediately wanted to join in on the adventure.

In the 1950s boys of all ages spent long hours playing cowboys and Indians. The heroes of the Old West were many a young boy's role model. Any opportunity to ride horses, *real horses*, wasn't something that was easily passed up. The Carter boys begged to be included in the adventure, but Bobby and Johnny would have no part of it. The Carter boys had been out to the Idle Hour. They knew how much fun it was to go there. The boys' discussion, which was becoming heated, was suddenly interrupted by the blast of a car horn. Glen, fourteen, turned and saw a flashy, lime green 1955 Chevrolet Bel Air pass by, and he noticed the driver waving. Tony saw the car and asked Bobby, "Is that Hansen?" Before Tony could say anything else, John cut him off with "Shut up, we've said enough already."

Bruce, eleven, took a closer look at the car because he wasn't quite sure who the older boys were talking about. He had a cousin named Donnie Hansen and he wondered if it was his cousin behind the wheel of the Chevy. Bruce turned to Glen and asked, "Does Donnie have his license already?" The specific memory of that moment would prompt tears decades later when Bruce Carter testified about the incident before a Cook County grand jury.

The five boys talked a little more. Tony, John and Bobby had been sharing sips from a bottle of Green River Soda. When they finished the soda, Bobby hurled the empty bottle toward the brick wall of a garage. The bottle shattered and the boys scattered.

After hearing of the murders, the Carter brothers went to their mother and told her what Bobby, John and Tony had told them about going to the Idle Hour to ride horses with someone named Hansen. The Carter boys' mother was terrified by this revelation. She feared if her sons went to the police, whoever had committed the horrible crime would murder them to keep them quiet. The boys' mother forbid them from telling anyone what they knew. This was a difficult task for the brothers. The police visited the Carter brothers Boy Scout troop, the same troop that Bobby Peterson had belonged to, and urged the Scouts to keep a sharp lookout for any suspicious persons or clues. But the Carter brothers were dutiful sons. They kept the promise they made to their mother for decades.

Not far from the Idle Hour Stable another drama played out between a husband and wife who had learned the names of those who were involved in the murders. George Jayne sat at a desk and wrote a letter. He planned to put everything he knew about the slayings into the document. In the adjacent room, he could hear his wife moving about. The couple had recently argued. Marion Jayne was upset.

Marion had come to trust George's judgment on most issues, but the subject at hand was not one of them. She had begged her husband to go to the police but he stubbornly refused. Now was their chance, George had told her. Now was their chance to strike back at George's half-brother, Silas Jayne. Silas, who had been threatening to harm George physically and to put him out of business, wouldn't dare touch them now. The letter would protect the family. George boasted that Silas would now leave him alone because he had enough evidence to "put Silas in the electric chair."

George Jayne was convinced he had finally found a way to neutralize his half-brother. There were few secrets between Silas and George. Word about the murders had traveled fast in the gossipy back stalls among the hired stable hands. That's how George had learned that Silas was deeply involved in the crime that had horrified and shocked an entire city.

The two Jayne brothers, along with a third brother, Frank Jayne Sr., and Frank's son, Frank Jayne Jr., were well known in the stable business. George and Silas were two former rodeo riders who had pulled themselves up by their cowboy bootstraps to become movers and shakers in the clubby show-horse world. Once considered from the wrong side of town, the two men now moved equally at ease between the blue-blooded aristocrats who played in the show world and the foulmouthed stable boys who shoveled manure.

Working together, the two men promoted the show-horse industry in the Midwest and had grown wealthy for their efforts. The show-horse business was and is today a hobby for the wealthy, a high-cost, high-stakes endeavor. It is not unusual for enthusiasts to pay tens of thousands of dollars for a horse and then thousands more for maintenance and training. The sport is also as much about bragging rights among the idle rich as it is about beautiful animals trained to work flawlessly with their riders in a ballet of precision and grace. It's also about prize money. In top competitions the winning purse can fetch up to $100,000.

In the show horse world, a "show hunter" is a horse, most likely a Thoroughbred, that is trained to run a course simulating a fox hunt. In competitions, show hunters, which are sometimes referred to as "hunters," earn points. "Show jumpers," on the other hand, compete for cash. A show jumper is conditioned to complete a jumping course as quickly as possible. Speed is the key in show jumper competitions. A show hunter, however, is judged on agility and precision.

Men like Silas and George Jayne staked their reputations and their livelihoods on the performance of their horses and their riders during show-horse events held throughout the country. Potential horse owners look to buy from the stables that produce the winning horses. At many horse shows, animals are bought and sold on the spot, their price directly correlating to their performance that day. There is no standard to determine how much a horse is worth. A horse is worth whatever someone is willing to pay.

Armed with the knowledge of the murders, George had the perfect opportunity to put Silas away permanently with just one phone call to the police. But George knew that Silas was a ruthless criminal who had strong ties to Chicago's underworld and corrupt police officers. George told friends Silas had many spies on various police departments in the Chicago area, and that any tip to the police about Silas would fall on deaf ears.

George put everything he knew about the murders down on paper. He told Marion she was to give the letter to police if anything were to happen to him. George foolishly thought a piece of paper would protect him from Silas. Instead George's decision to do nothing would forever link him to the murders of the boys and touch off a blood feud that would last more than a decade and cost him his life.

CHAPTER 4

Silas Carter Jayne was a cowboy and outlaw. If he had been born in 1807 rather than 1907, he would have rivaled, if not surpassed, Jesse James in notoriety. He was one of the most feared criminals in Chicago. A muscular man with a face as tough as saddle leather, Silas's most remarkable facial feature was his cold, blue-green eyes. He had the ability to strike fear in most people with just a glare. His face was crowned by a shock of white, curly hair. Silas held up well physically as he grew into his senior years; some would note that he appeared at least twenty years his junior.

Silas played the cowboy-mobster role to the hilt. A larger than life villain, on his left forearm he bore a tattoo of a dagger with a snake coiled around the blade. "Si," as he was known, wore a large diamond pinky ring and had a 1907 $20 gold piece fashioned into a belt buckle. He collected $1,000 bills, which he carried in a money belt, and at any given time, he carried up to $10,000 on his person. He traded in a Cadillac every six months for the latest model and accessorized his car with steer horns affixed to the grill.

Whatever demons possessed Silas took hold at a young age. He was the fourth oldest of twelve children raised on a farm near Chicago, and Jayne family lore relayed to law enforcement presented a glimpse of a man who displayed disturbing psychological traits at a tender age. When he was six years old, a goose on the family farm bit Silas. Instead of running off crying, Silas became enraged and retaliated. He grabbed an axe and slaughtered the entire gaggle. Blood-spattered, he then excitedly told family members what he had accomplished.

Born on July 3, 1907, to Arthur and Katherine Jayne, from a lineage family members claimed can be traced back to Colonial times, Silas's unruly behavior could have been a trait conditioned at home. Court and prison documents show that Arthur Jayne was a man of varying occupations. Fanner, truck driver, Chicago stockyard employee and, during Prohibition, a sugar supplier to bootleggers, Arthur Jayne must not have been much, of a father figure. Silas Jayne never got past the ninth grade. Instead he worked on the family farm.

Silas Jayne's mother, Katherine, never divorced his father, although they separated in later years. During the estrangement, Katherine took a liking to a Waukegan attorney named George William Spunner. Spunner owned a campground of summer cottages that Katherine managed for him along the shores of Lake Zurich, in a northern suburb of Chicago. Whatever their relationship had been, on November 2, 1923, Katherine gave birth to George

William Jayne. Though the child's father was William Spunner, Katherine gave the boy the Jayne surname, possibly to avoid any scandalous talk in the tiny town where she and her children lived.

A little more than a year after George was born, Spunner would recommend to a Lake County, Illinois, judge that Silas spend a year in jail following a conviction on rape charges. Earlier that year Silas had asked a young woman to join him for a ride into town for a soda. Instead of a friendly date, the seventeen-year-old Silas raped the girl in the backseat of a car. Spunner apparently didn't mount much of a defense for Silas. Some would later claim Spunner's less than inspired defense set the sour tone for Silas's relationship with his younger half-brother George.

The year in jail did nothing but harden Silas's already darkened heart. When he got out of prison, he took up rodeo riding with his younger brothers Frank and De Forest. Silas's two brothers managed to keep their older brother under control—most of the time. But Silas was a brawler and drinker. He racked up dozens of arrests. In 1927 he married the first of his three wives. A pathological liar, he would later tell a prison psychologist he couldn't remember his first wife's name, but was able to recall that the marriage lasted only six months.

If there was one saving grace for the Jayne brothers, it was the fact that they were born horsemen. Silas, Frank and De Forest, and later George, were adept and skilled in the art of horsemanship and had a natural knack for making money, especially in the stable business. Former neighbors who had a hard time scratching together a nickel during the Depression remember that the Jayne family always lived comfortably.

The brothers and their unruly gang of cowhands came

to be known as the Jesse Jayne Gang in the 1930s, an obvious reference to the famed outlaw Jesse James. At that time, the Jayne brothers were a larger than life posse of cowboys notorious for disturbing the peace. Like the cowboys of yesteryear, the Jesse Jayne Gang would drive a newly arrived herd of horses cowboy-style from the railyard in Woodstock, Illinois, to their farm on the outskirts of town. Those lame horses that couldn't be used as part of the family's rodeo show were shipped out and slaughtered for dog food. The rest were ridden, used as livery horses in the brothers' stable or sold to others.

"They were just a little on the rough side, maybe too much on the rough side," recalled octogenarian Raymond Murphy. Murphy remembers that the Jayne brothers and their cowpoke employees had earned such a notorious reputation that it was a local cattle auctioneer who dubbed them the Jesse Jayne Gang. The name stuck and the Jaynes did nothing to dispel their rough image.

"I didn't mind being around them," Murphy said. "You had to watch your step, though. If you saw them, you said hello. But, man, you didn't want to get mixed up with the Jesse Jayne Gang."

Despite his unpredictable temper, Silas was a shrewd businessman. In 1932 he opened his first stable. Over the years, Silas and his brothers owned a succession of stables. In addition, Silas and other family members would come to acquire some valuable parcels of property. Much of the land was purchased when it was undeveloped. The brothers held on to the property, which became increasingly valuable as the city grew.

De Forest Jayne, who was known as "D," served as the riding instructor at the brothers' stables and earned numerous trophies for his equestrian talents. De Forest also played a calming role in Silas's life, but that came to an end on October 15, 1938. On that day De Forest's fiancée, a telephone operator and former riding student named Mae Sweeney, committed suicide by swallowing a fatal dose of arsenic. Mae killed herself just hours before De Forest was to pick her up to go dancing.

The day after Mae Sweeney was buried, De Forest dressed himself in his Western best, the costume he wore while trick riding in the brothers' rodeo show, grabbed a 12-gauge shotgun and stole away from his family. When Silas and Frank went to console their grieving brother and he could not be found, they feared the worst. The two brothers and one sister set off looking for De Forest. Frantic, they headed for the cemetery. At the cemetery, among the sweet-smelling floral arrangements and fallen leaves, they found De Forest sprawled across his fiancée's freshly turned grave. De Forest had joined Mae Sweeney in eternity after turning the shotgun on himself.

Silas married for a second time in 1938. His marriage to Martha, who later taught him how to read and sign his name, lasted twenty years. Two years after he married her, ten horses died in a suspicious fire at a stable Silas owned. Over the years, members of the Jesse Jayne Gang would become known to use arson as a tool to collect insurance money, rub out competitors and destroy evidence of other crimes. The fire that killed the ten horses was the first time Silas was suspected of this kind of fraud.

In 1941 Silas had one of his first many legal scrapes. One of his riding students, a wealthy debutante named Ruth De War, sued Silas claiming he had purposely frightened the horse she was riding, causing the animal to throw her to the ground. De War suffered a fractured spine in the incident. Following a brief trial, Silas was found not liable for De War's injuries. At the trial, he took turns glaring at each member of the all-women jury. His frightening gaze unnerved jurors and they ruled in his favor.

During World War II, the Jesse Jayne Gang made a handsome profit selling horse meat as beef. Beef was rationed during the war, and many restaurants were forced to deal with seedy characters for a steady supply. To supplement their horse-meat income, the Jayne Gang also rustled cattle from farmers.

The horse business in Chicago in the 1940s and 1950s was a dangerous line of work. Besides the Jayne Gang, there was another criminal element involved in the stable business during that time. The Chicago version of La Cosa Nostra, otherwise known as the Outfit, had an interest in some of the businesses.

La Cosa Nostra translated from Italian means "our thing" or "this thing of ours" and refers to traditional Italian organized crime in the U.S. The designation La Cosa Nostra was used by the mob at the time it was formed in the U.S. to distinguish it from the Mafia in Sicily. Throughout much of the U.S., membership in La Cosa Nostra and the Mafia consists mainly of persons of Italian descent. Each La Cosa Nostra organization has its own rules and areas of control. There have only been a few examples of dual membership known to law enforcement. La Cosa Nostra in the U.S. consists of five New York "families": the Luchese, Columbo, Gambino, Bonanno and Genovese families. Other La Cosa Nostra groups operate in Buffalo, New England, Pittsburgh, Detroit, Kansas City, Los Angeles, Denver, Cleveland, New Orleans and Chicago.

The Chicago "family" has never referred to itself as La Cosa Nostra, although it has always played an important role in the national organization. From the time that Al

Capone was dispatched to Chicago from New York, the Chicago version of La Cosa Nostra has called itself the Outfit and the Mob.

Because there were so many established gangs operating in Chicago, including gangs controlled by Irish, Jewish, Greek and African-American gangsters, Al Capone turned the Outfit into an equal opportunity employer and recruited the best from each group. Those who didn't join forces with Capone were murdered or their influence diminished.

Capone's bodyguard, Anthony Accardo, continued the practice of inclusiveness when he took control of the Outfit in the 1940s. From its inception, the Chicago Outfit has extended its influence to all parts of the U.S. west of Chicago. To perpetuate itself, the Outfit relies on an unholy alliance between itself and corrupt police officers and corrupt public officials.

As Silas Jayne was approaching his zenith as a horseman and criminal, he found himself rubbing shoulders and partnering with members of the Outfit. A typical stable property on the outskirts of Chicago in the 1940s included several barns, a house for the owner/stable hands and maybe a tavern or a restaurant. Some Outfit-connected stables were used as fronts for prostitution, and at least one stable Silas operated served as a front for an Outfit bordello. The stables served various purposes. They were also ideal locations to warehouse stolen goods and gambling houses.

Jayne family members have told investigators Silas committed his first murder in 1947 at a stable he operated south of Chicago. The alleged murder victim was a minor Outfit figure who had gone to the stable to "put the arm on Si" and collect a street tax. Instead of turning over a wad of cash to the gangster, Silas murdered the man and buried his remains on the stable grounds. If Silas did indeed murder an Outfit henchman, he did so either with the blessing of the crime bosses or in defiance of them.

A pathological liar and killer, Silas could be charming as well. To the outside world he was a good ole boy, a harmless hayseed who happened to be a gifted horseman. This chameleon-like personality served Silas well, especially when it came to separating the well-to-do from their cash.

Like all good con men, Silas figured out a new angle. Unlike grifters who prey on a victim's greed, Silas's scam appealed to the paternal instincts of the wealthy men who frequented his stable. Into this world of greed and deceit many an unwitting parent entrusted his or her daughter. Silas often sold his wealthy patrons broken-down, ready-for-the-glue-factory nags at inflated prices. The con was not a one-shot opportunity, but an ongoing process. After a few weeks or months, Silas would tell a girl's parents that their daughter had genuine talent but was being held back because she needed a better horse. In short order many parents purchased a second, more expensive horse.

On top of all his other traits—killer, con man and sadist—Silas was also a pederast. It wasn't something Silas hid from people in the horse business. He often bragged about such assaults as "funning with them."

Silas had little fear that his shady horse scheme would be reported to authorities. He treated patrons that threatened to go to the police over a deal in one of two ways. Silas's direct method included threats of violence or actual violence. One wealthy factory owner who threatened to file a lawsuit against Silas after buying sickly horses from him received a series of anonymous phone calls. When the phone calls failed to deter a lawsuit, a bomb was detonated outside of the man's home. The lawsuit was quickly dropped.

Silas's other method of dissuading unhappy customers with daughters was to threaten to ruin a young girl's reputation by spreading rumors that he and a few of his stable hands had had sex with the girl. Faced with these choices, no one was willing to complain to the police about Silas.

This was the type of man some of Chicago's leading families trusted their daughters to spend hours with. It was into Silas Jayne's world of violence, greed and sex that Tony, John and Bobby had stumbled.

CHAPTER 5

Within a week of the boys' murders, the Chicago Police Department sprung fully into action. A task force of dozens of homicide detectives was pulled together from various units throughout the city. About six sergeants were assigned to the detail. The sergeants would serve as the front-line supervisors. The murder probe got off to a rocky start. The majority of the detectives and sergeants assigned to the case never got a chance to visit the crime scene until weeks after the boys' bodies were found.

After a few days of intensive investigative efforts, police were able to pull together only a few undisputed facts. An autopsy had determined that the three boys had been beaten. Death was caused by asphyxiation due to strangulation. The Cook County coroner determined that Bobby Peterson had "put up a terrific struggle" before he was murdered. There was indication that Bobby had been repeatedly struck in the head with some object, leaving seven wounds on his scalp. Two wounds had cut the boy's head down to the skull. On Bobby's neck there was a finger mark and indications that a belt or some kind of strap had been wrapped around his neck and twisted, resulting in his death. No undigested food was found in Bobby's stomach.

The autopsy showed that Tony Schuessler had received a heavy blow to the left eye. There were also finger marks on his throat and indications that he had been punched at the base of the skull. Tony died from asphyxiation. The killer had taken Tony's life with his bare hands. Tony had eaten chicken noodle soup before leaving home. In Tony's stomach the pathologist found tomato seed, tomato skin, celery and shell macaroni.

The coroner determined Tony's older brother, John, had been beaten on the head with such force that his brain had been disturbed and hemorrhaged. He also had been punched in the right eye. He was struck with such force to his neck that his Adam's apple was crushed and his vocal cords inflamed. This was the deathblow to John. The damage to his throat was such that it closed and suffocated him. On his upper left thigh, a hole was found in the skin. It was assumed a rodent had made this wound after the body had been dumped. Like Tony, John had eaten chicken noodle soup before leaving home. In John's stomach, the coroner also found tomato seed, tomato skin, celery and shell macaroni.

All the bodies bore evidence that the boys' mouths and eyes had been bound with one-inch adhesive tape. The wrists on all the victims also bore marks indicating that they had been bound. The tape on the bodies and the boys' clothes had been removed. No tape or bindings were found with the bodies at the crime scene. A check of the stomach contents indicated that the boys were murdered between 9 P.M. and midnight on October 16, 1955.

The boys' parents were able to provide police with fairly good descriptions of what their sons were wearing on the day they disappeared. John Schuessler was last seen in a navy blue, satin Chicago Cubs jacket. John had been wearing blue jeans with a tan belt. He had on a brown cotton long-sleeved shirt. Both top pockets of the shirt were adorned with a cowboy design of yellow with a dash of red. He wore black-and-white gym shoes with white socks. His underclothing included a white T-shirt and undershorts. In the back pocket of his jeans, John carried his brown leather wallet. Inside the wallet he had a picture of his grandmother and a school bus pass.

Tony had worn a tattered, navy blue Chicago Cubs jacket. The right pocket of the jacket was torn and kept together with a safety pin. The Cubs emblem on the left side of the jacket was missing the letter "U." Under the jacket, Tony wore a white flannel long-sleeved shirt with a black, wavy pattern in the background. There was a pocket on the left side of the shirt. Tony's jeans were tattered but clean. There were two mends on the right knee. He wore black-and-white gym shoes with blue socks. Tony also wore a white T-shirt and undershorts.

Bobby's missing clothes included a black satin Chicago White Sox jacket. Bobby wore a flannel shirt and a pair of blue jeans with two patches ironed on the knees. He also had on a multicolored beaded belt, white boxer shorts and a white T-shirt. His shoes were black canvas high-top gym shoes with white soles. Bobby was also carrying a student bus pass.

Police were able to pull together a chronology of the

events leading up to the gruesome discovery in Robinson Woods. On Sunday, October 16, 1955, John and Anton Schuessler had left their home at 2:30 P.M. and bicycled approximately one mile to Bobby Peterson's home. At 3 P.M. all three boys left the Peterson home bound for the Loop Theater located about eleven miles away. Police assumed the boys made it to the theater and watched the show.

From 7:15 to 7:45 P.M. the three boys were seen at the Monte Cristo Bowling Alley by Ernest Niewiadomski, seventeen, and his two younger sisters Leona and Delphine. Ernie and his sisters had known the Schuessler boys for many years. The police considered the Niewiadomskis to be the sole, undisputed eyewitnesses to last see the victims alive.

A man named Harold Blumfield, twenty, told police that he gave three boys a ride from Kimball and Montrose avenues to farther west on Montrose Avenue around 8 P.M. Blumfield wasn't absolutely certain the three boys he had given a ride were the murder victims, but he said one of the boys strongly resembled Bobby Peterson. Jack Johnson, sixty-seven, told police he saw the three boys at Gordon Bowling Alley at 8:40 P.M. CTA bus driver Bruno Mencarini, 44, told detectives that at 8:47 P.M. he picked up three boys at Milwaukee and Berteau avenues, and drove them to Lawrence Avenue, where they exited at 8:52 P.M. A young man named Ralph Helm, who was walking his sweetheart back from the movies, told police he saw the boys thumbing a ride in the same area. A Mrs. Kimske told police she and her husband, George, saw three boys at the corner of Milwaukee and Lawrence avenues at 9 P.M. attempting to thumb a ride on Lawrence Avenue. Such was the extent of the information that the detectives working the case ever developed.

Never before had the Chicago Police Department investigated such a crime—a high-profile case with multiple young victims who had been abducted, apparently sexually abused, murdered by a stranger and then discarded like garbage in a public place. The department used the latest forensic technology of that day, but it was in the Stone Age compared to the tools used by modern crime scene investigators. In 1955 there was no such thing as DNA fingerprinting. In fact just two years before the slayings, British scientists Francis Crick and James Watson had deciphered the double helix of deoxyribonucleic acid, or DNA.

In the days before computers, e-mail, voice mail and cellular phones, the task force faced a daunting task of keeping all the information gathered about the case in one place where it could be reviewed. All the reports about the boys' murders were typed on razor-thin onionskin paper. Copies were generated by the use of carbon paper. Information most likely did not flow easily between teams of detectives investigating the case. Much must have fallen through the cracks. The Schuessler-Peterson murder task force was an organizational nightmare by today's standards.

The task force was also hampered by the lack of experience of those who were selected to serve as the managers of the investigation. Sgt. John Konen, who had been a veteran of the Chicago Police Department since 1941, was the only sergeant assigned to the task force who had any experience investigating homicides. From the beginning, Konen, who retired from the department in 1975 after thirty-four years of service, knew the police faced long odds.

World had spread quickly among the homicide detectives that Harry Glos had moved the boys' bodies for the benefit of newspaper photographers before any forensic evidence had been gathered. Detectives did get their hands on the film shot by Richard Ritt for WGN-TV before the bodies had been disturbed, but that proved to be of little value.

The public and the press did their best to aid the police. Overnight, the city came alive with tips. Police had asked the press to get word to the public for help in finding the boys' clothes or to volunteer any information that could lead to the suspects. Tipsters were encouraged to call the police directly. Many also contacted the daily newspapers in the city. Some of the tips led detectives to bona-fide pedophiles and resulted in arrests on various charges.

"We got this tip, a telephone tip, from a guy who worked for the gas company. He had been out to a service call and it involved a reported leak in a rooming house," Konen recalled. The utility worker noticed in the room of a young male border a cardboard box filled with blue jeans that would fit young boys. "The public was being encouraged to report anything like that. The clothes had never been found on these kids."

Konen dispatched a team of detectives to interview the landlady to find out everything about the tenant. After the man's name was called in, Konen did a little investigative work himself. "I went to the records section. And found they had a file on him. Not only a file but also a warrant. A warrant for a sex crime against a young boy." The suspect was subsequently arrested on the warrant, but he was cleared of any involvement in the boys' murders when it was determined that the jeans belonged to the suspect, who was of slight build.

Over the next three years, detectives investigating the murders would run down 5,886 leads and interview 43,740

people. Those interviews would result in the interrogation
of 3,270 suspects, resulting in 104 arrests. Of those arrests,
45 persons were indicted, and 40 were convicted of various
crimes. In addition, police would give polygraph examinations to 147 different suspects. Members of the task force
would travel throughout the country to interview them.
Other agencies would give polygraph examinations to another 97 persons across the U.S. The task force would
eventually compile more than six thousand pages of reports in hopes of catching the boys' killer. The Chicago
Police Department did its best to solve the crime. Decades
later, however, it would be determined that the police had
done a poor job of policing themselves.

CHAPTER 6

In the weeks following the murders, *Daily News* reporter Jack Lavin had a front row seat to the anguish and fear that gripped an entire city. A few days before Walter McCarron held a coroner's inquest to determine the boys' cause of death, *Daily News* city editor Clem Lane called Lavin and artist Frank SanHamel over to his desk. Lane announced that he was teaming SanHamel with Lavin to provide daily coverage on the boys' murders. The two were told they were expected to produce a story every day until otherwise notified. Lavin didn't mind working with the artist; SanHamel had proven his worth on several other high profile police investigations.

"He told us we should go down and meet with McCarron because we were being deputized as deputy coroners. This meant we had authority to investigate any homicides in Cook County," Lavin said. The deputy coroner title was legitimate, but Lavin and SanHamel would remain employees of the *Daily News*. The arrangement struck between Lane and McCarron ensured that McCarron would get favorable press from the *Daily News,* and that Lavin and SanHamel would get a leg up on their competition. Lavin and SanHamel had to wait until after McCarron presided over a coroner's inquest to get a look at the evidence that the Coroner's Office had pulled together in the case.

The two were given access to all of the material that McCarron had on the case. "It wasn't a lot," Lavin recalls. "He gave us quite a few photographs and negatives." There was also an understanding that McCarron would receive first word of any break in the case that the reporters developed.

The coroner's inquest was held on October 19, 1955, at the Cook County Morgue, a decrepit building located on the city's west side that reeked of decomposing human remains due to a poor ventilation system. With so much interest in the case, the hearing quickly turned into a media feeding frenzy. Reporters climbed over one another to get a spot in the small hearing room. "It was a circus. An absolute circus," Lavin recalls. The press wanted to hear from the witnesses, especially Malcolm Peterson, Anton Schuessler and Victor Livingston. When Malcolm Peterson and Anton Schuessler walked into the hearing room, the two grieving fathers were almost crushed by the onslaught of news photographers.

"Gentlemen, gentlemen," McCarron pleaded. "Please don't hurt these men any more than you can help. Everybody, please sit down. Please!" McCarron's handling of the inquest was a "disgrace," Lavin said. The coroner was facing reelection and seemed interested in promoting his own importance in the investigation. "McCarron was playing up to the press. It was terrible," Lavin said.

After asking a few preliminary questions, McCarron began walking Malcolm Peterson through the last moments he saw his son alive. The coroner's inquest was the only time sworn statements were taken from the boys' parents:

MCCARRON: When was the last time you saw your son alive prior to this incident?

PETERSON: Just about three o'clock Sunday afternoon.

MCCARRON: That would be October 16, 1955, three o'clock in the afternoon?

PETERSON: Yes, sir.

MCCARRON: Did he say where he was going, what he was going to do?

PETERSON: Yes.

MCCARRON: Will you tell the jury, and tell me what you know about this, what ideas you have?

PETERSON: Well . . .

MCCARRON: We want you to go into the entire affair, it is very important, trace your son's movements as closely as you can, we want to get all the facts in this matter as we can.

PETERSON: We knew that he was going to a show.

MCCARRON: You knew that he was going to a movie?

PETERSON: Yes, with the Schuessler boys. They came over to the house.

MCCARRON: Yes?

PETERSON: We had been working on the garage all the morning, him and I.

MCCARRON: Your son and you?

PETERSON: Yes. He was in the house listening to the Cardinal football game, and he just went away.

McCARRON: Three boys went to the show? You knew they were going Downtown, to the Loop?

PETERSON: Not to the Loop, to a theater.

McCARRON: Now we're getting into Sunday evening, when they didn't come home.

PETERSON: Yes.

McCARRON: You and your wife became very much worried?

PETERSON: Yes, sir.

McCARRON: Who did you call and what did you do?

PETERSON: Well . . .

McCARRON: What time would that be?

PETERSON: We called the police, I don't know, between ten and eleven o'clock Sunday night and they told me if the boys were not home by midnight, we should come down and give a description of the boys.

McCARRON: Yes?

PETERSON: Which we did. We went, gave them a description; before that we got the bright idea that maybe the boys had gone to the show, and eaten up all their money and were walking home from the show. Mr. Schuessler and I proceeded, took a ride down Milwaukee Avenue to the Loop, we left the 33rd District police station, drove our car down Milwaukee, looked in all the hamburger joints, bus stations, in busses and all. We went down to the Loop Theater, which was closing, and then we got the bright idea they went across the street to the State and Lake Theater. We went over there just as it was letting out.

McCARRON: Yes?

PETERSON: We told the manager our predicament, he was very cooperative. We went all through the show, completely; the boys could not be found. We took Elston Avenue back home, went back to the 33rd District police station to tell them we had found nothing.

McCarron: Yes?

Peterson: We got there. The sergeant behind the desk, a very accommodating fellow, he called up the Clark Theater and they searched the lobby and the auditorium. No boys. Then he called the Wood's Theater. The same thing. I then suggested we call several bowling alleys, which we could have done sooner. We called them to ask if they had seen them. We called the 20th Century Bowling Alley. They said, "No boys here." We called the Natoma, it was closed, this was about 3:30 A.M. I took Mr. Schuessler home. And that's about all I can say.

McCarron: Did you call the police by means of telephone?

Peterson: First time, yes.

McCarron: And what time was that?

Peterson: The time element, I'm not sure. I'd say from about 10 to 11 P.M. at night.

McCarron: You said your boys were missing?

Peterson: Yes.

McCarron: They asked you to come to the station, and you men went to the station on your own volition?

Peterson: Sure. They told us to come down at twelve o'clock if the boys were not home. So we went down at twelve o'clock.

McCarron: It was not at 9:30 P.M.?

Peterson: Went down to the police?

McCarron: When you first made the telephone call?

Peterson: No sir. From 10 to 11 P.M.

McCarron: You should know, that's fine.

Peterson: Yes.

McCarron: We know your boy is a good boy, we know that.

Peterson: Yes.

McCarron: Everything has shown that, all that has been said about them has been fine, but. Do you know of any boy or boys, or gangs . . . I don't mean to use this word . . . I don't want to call it, teenagers, gangs, cliques, or group of boys or of men, in this vicinity, or any other vicinity, that your boy had ever, had ever complained to you about such boys or groups at any time that wanted to beat him up, or do anything of that sort?

PETERSON: No, sir.

McCARRON: Your boy never registered such a complaint?

PETERSON: No, sir. He was a home boy sir.

Malcolm Peterson was then excused as a witness. Lavin remembered Peterson looked like a man who hadn't slept in days, but he remained composed during the proceedings. Anton Schuessler, Sr., however, was an emotional wreck. He had fainted in front of the news photographers shortly after viewing the remains of his sons. Moments later, the hearing resumed.

McCARRON: I want to make it easy as I can for you, so I won't go over everything as I did with Mr. Peterson, you heard his testimony?

SCHUESSLER: Yes, sir.

McCARRON: You are the father of these two young boys, Anthony and John Schuessler?

SCHUESSLER: Yes, sir.

McCARRON: As I understand it, your boys also were going to a show last Sunday evening?

SCHUESSLER: Yes.

McCARRON: They did go to a show?

SCHUESSLER: Yes.

McCARRON: You gave them permission to go to a show?

SCHUESSLER: Yes. I didn't know they were going Downtown.

McCARRON: They did go to a show?

SCHUESSLER: Yes.

McCarron: Did John . . . by the way, what grade was he in school, the oldest boy?

Schuessler: Same as the Petersons', seventh grade.

McCarron: Did your boy, at any time, ever tell you of any trouble, difficulty with a boy, or with boys, or a man or men or group, clique or gang, teenage group, ever tried to be nasty, threaten to hurt them or do anything as dastardly as this, did they ever report anything like that to you, or to your wife, that you know of, you know that is so important?

Schuessler: To be honest, no.

McCarron: They never did?

Schuessler: No, my boys have never been Downtown without their parents.

McCarron: Sir?

Schuessler: My boys never left the house without their parents, never. This was the first time.

McCarron: And you don't know why anyone would want to hurt them?

Schuessler: No.

McCarron: I am sorry. You saw the body of your son downstairs and identified it?

Schuessler: Yes.

McCarron: You have identified the body, as the bodies of your sons, Anthony and John?

Schuessler: Yes.

McCarron: Thank you very much, you are excused, we won't bother you anymore, you can go and thank you very much.

McCarron then called Victor Livingston to the stand. When McCarron was informed that Livingston and representatives of the Cook County Forest Preserve Police Department had failed to attend the hearing, he exploded and loudly criticized the police.

"I just want to state, it is a very sad state of affairs when our agencies of government are not here, and these families who have this cross to carry are here, and these others don't think enough of this tragedy, a dastardly crime of this type, they don't think enough of it to be here," McCarron said. Visibly agitated, he raised his voice in anger. "I don't like it. I don't think the people of Cook County like it either," he said.

Shortly after the initial coroner's inquest, Lavin was assigned to cover the funeral of Bobby Peterson. Lavin couldn't help but think about his own children as he and hundreds of others packed the Jefferson Park Lutheran Church. Throughout the ceremony, Bobby's parents, Dorothy and Malcolm, fought back their tears and maintained their composure, right up until the end of the service. Then the tears came. The couple sobbed quietly, holding each other. Bobby's three siblings did not attend the service. Lavin noticed a few plainclothes Chicago Police detectives in attendance. He quickly thought, "They're probably looking for the bastard who did this. Maybe the sick bastard is in the church right now. Whoever did this is still out there." The Reverend William F. Eifrig officiated at the services. A crowd of over three hundred persons packed the church, flowing out onto the steps and into the street.

Not far from the Jefferson Park Lutheran Church, family, friends and schoolmates of the Schuessler boys had gathered for visitation at a local funeral home. The two boys were laid to rest in twin white-and-gold caskets. They were dressed in brown suits, made by their father. A Bible was placed in their hands. As well-wishers gathered to pay their respects, Eleanor Schuessler slumped on a couch, shielding her eyes with her hands. It was as if she could not bear to look at her sons, her only children, lying in their caskets. The boys' father, Anton Sr., sat in an adjoining room. "I'm praying they get whoever did this," he told the press.

More than twelve hundred people gathered for the Schuesslers boys' funeral mass that was held on October 22, 1955, at St. Tarcissus Roman Catholic Church. The boys' caskets were carried into the church by an honor guard of Boy Scouts. Both Tony and John had been members of the same Boy Scout troop as Bobby. As the funeral procession was making its way into the church, a gasp went up through the crowd. Eleanor Schuessler, overcome with emotion, had collapsed on the steps of the church. She was carried into the church.

The funeral service proceeded as expected. As the mass drew to a close, however, a mournful voice cried out. "My boys," Eleanor Schuessler exclaimed. Leaning on the arm of her husband, she stumbled over to the two coffins. She reached out her hand to her sons and brokenly uttered through her tears, "Good-bye, Johnny . . . and Tony." Lavin noted that a few of his hardened colleagues had tears in their eyes. He was among them.

Following the funerals, Lavin spent as much time as possible with the families of the two boys. The Schuesslers proved most accommodating. Every day for several weeks, he stopped by their home to help the family go through the stacks of mail they received. Lavin wanted to be present in case the boys' killer sent a letter or some other item to the Schuesslers. He thought the person responsible for the horrendous crime was some sort of madman, a fiend who had possibly stalked and then murdered the three boys. He theorized that the killer might contact the boys' parents. On a few occasions, a Chicago Police officer went through the mail with the family.

Lavin learned much about the Schuesslers while visiting their home. By 1955 standards, the Schuesslers were doing well for a family of four. They lived in a brick, ranch-style home. Anton Sr., who was forty-two, was a Yugoslavian immigrant who worked hard to make his tailor and dry-cleaning business a success. Anton Schuessler Sr. had been born in the United States but taken back to Germany when he was nine months old. He returned to the United States in 1931 and worked for meager wages as an apprentice tailor. He and Eleanor were married in 1936. Like many first- and second-generation immigrants, the Schuesslers clung to their Old World roots. With other relatives, he and his wife purchased an apartment, and later they sold their interest at a profit. A frugal man, Anton Sr. made the coats and suits that he, his wife and boys wore. Life was good to the Schuesslers.

On the last day with their parents, John and Tony spent some time playing with their cocker spaniel, Penny, watching television and reading the Sunday comics. The family went to Sunday mass at St. Tarcissus and returned home and had lunch of chicken soup; macaroni; and brussels sprouts, lettuce and tomato salad. At some time that day Bobby Peterson and John Schuessler talked to each other on the phone and made plans to go to a movie. John was permitted to go to a movie so long as he took his younger brother with him. Before the brothers headed off, Eleanor Schuessler reportedly consulted the Sunday paper to determine which film was showing that was suitable for young boys. She decided the boys should go to a show at one of several neighborhood theaters. The Schuesslers didn't want their boys traveling downtown on a bus unescorted. Eleanor Schuessler gave John $1.50 and Anton $1. The younger boy only needed a $1 because he could get into a double feature for half price.

Lavin also learned that Sunday morning at the Peterson home followed much the same routine. The Petersons lived in an older, wood frame house a little more than a mile from the Schuessler home. Bobby and his father, Malcolm, forty, a carpenter, were close. Bobby was slight of build for his age but wiry. He was the oldest of four children. His siblings were Barbara, nine, Susan, five, and Tommy, three.

Though Bobby often attended Sunday services at the Jefferson Park Lutheran Church, on that day Malcolm Peterson had decided to keep his son home so the two could work on the family garage. At about 1:30 P.M. they finished their chores and went inside for an early Sunday dinner of fried chicken, mashed potatoes and sliced tomatoes.

"After dinner I sat down with him for about ten minutes and we listened to the [Chicago] Cardinals football game," Peterson would later tell police. "They were playing somebody . . . I don't remember the team. Oh yes, they played New York and I told him I [was] going out to clean up, [that he could] stay and listen to the football game. He stayed in and I cleaned up around the garage and [then] the two Schuessler boys rode in on bikes. One rode Bobby's bike and they went into the house."

Inside the Peterson home, Bobby and the Schuessler brothers changed their plans for the day. Instead of catching a movie at one of the local movie theaters, they would go to a theater downtown. "Bobby said, 'What show should we go to?' I sat down and I looked in the paper with them. I said *The African Lion* was playing at the Loop Theater and they thought that would be good," Peterson later recalled.

A diligent father, Malcolm Peterson called the theater located at State and Randolph streets to find out what time the show started, how long it ran and how much it would cost. The movie admission price was 50¢ and the film ran one hour and forty-five minutes. Malcolm Peterson gave his son $1.50, which would cover the movie, the trip downtown and a few snacks. The trio decided to head off to the theater, planning to take the bus downtown to catch the film. John and Anton had decided to disobey their parents and go to the downtown movie house.

"He went out and kissed his dad good-bye—that's routine in this house," Dorothy Peterson would later say. "And then he kissed all of us and went. When they walked down the street, Bobby was in the middle and the Schuessler boys alongside." The Petersons did not know that the Schuesslers had forbid their sons to travel downtown unescorted.

AFTER WEEKS OF checking the mail with the Schuessler family, it was clear to Lavin that there were not going to be any letters or notes that would shed light on the identity of the boys' killers. During his time with the family, Lavin witnessed the rapid decline of Anton Schuessler Sr. John and Tony's father became consumed with guilt. Anton Sr. blamed himself for his sons' deaths, stating on several occasions to Lavin that his boys might have still been alive if he had only taught them to be more self-reliant and more knowledgeable about the ways of the city. It was especially disheartening for Anton Sr. to learn that his sons had disobeyed him and his wife and had gone downtown to see *The African Lion.*

Anton Sr. was also roughly treated by the Chicago Police, Lavin said. He quickly became a suspect in the case and was grilled numerous times by detectives. It is not unusual for the parents of a murdered child to be considered as suspects. Police usually first look at those who are closest to the victims. Anton Sr. was asked to take a polygraph examination to prove that he had nothing to do with the crime. The intense police scrutiny, however, unraveled the unassuming man. Anton Sr. came to believe the police blamed him. It also became clear to Lavin that it didn't help Anton Sr. that he had spent his younger years in Germany and spoke with a German accent. The elder Schuessler may have reminded some detectives of the Nazis they had been drafted to fight just ten years earlier. "They were pretty rough on him," Lavin would later say. Within a few weeks, Anton Sr., a quiet, unpretentious man, descended into a dark abyss of depression.

Anton Sr. first stopped bathing. He then developed a skin rash. He eventually became paranoid and suspected that his in-laws had played a part in his sons' murders. Anton Sr. also began to hallucinate, imagining that police were secretly filming him and beaming interior shots of his home onto his television set. He did not sleep and began walking the streets of the city, looking for any suspicious character that could have committed the crime. On one occasion, Anton Sr. chased a homeless man whom he suspected was involved in the murders. After he began talking about suicide, Eleanor Schuessler called the family physician. On November 10, 1955, she checked her husband into a local mental hospital, the Forest Sanitarium in Des Plaines, a suburb north of Chicago.

"He was in a very bad way. He became extremely quiet. He wouldn't cry, he just wouldn't say anything and he would hang his head down. He would go into a room and be alone," Lavin said.

At the sanitarium, documents show the physician noted Anton Sr. was "in a state of severe depression and . . . does not want to live without his children. Although he knows the [polygraph] test came out negative, he is worried a great deal about it. He is also given to understand that things are going on that he cannot understand. On the TV screen he saw his furniture and glasses in the room that was being shown on the screen. He talks a great deal about his children . . ."

At 1:05 P.M. on November 11, 1955, Anton Sr. received electroshock therapy, a common treatment for depression at that time. The regimen, in which three hundred volts of electricity were sent coursing through the body, proved disastrous. Two physicians could not rouse Anton Sr. following the treatment. Oxygen, caffeine, coramine and picrotoxin were administered in an effort to resuscitate him. Anton Sr. initially responded to the treatment but quickly faded. After three hours of intensive efforts to save his life, Anton Sr. died. A coroner's inquest later determined he died of a heart attack.

"The poor guy died of a broken heart," Lavin said. "It was just devastating."

In a period of less than one month, Eleanor Schuessler had gone from the married mother of two boys to a childless widow. She was devastated and forever haunted by the events of October and November 1955. Eleanor Schuessler would eventually remarry and raise two stepchildren. But she would go to her grave in 1986 not knowing if anyone would ever answer for her sons' murders and the untimely death of her husband.

Following the death of Anton Sr., Lavin and SanHamel were invigorated in their continued efforts to find some kind of evidence that would help solve the murders. The two journalists, fathers themselves, put in long days reviewing the coroner's materials. They studied dozens of photographs of the boys' bodies for any hint as to who had committed the crime. They were immediately drawn to the four-by-six-inch wound on John Schuessler's left thigh. SanHamel, an artist, didn't believe the wound was caused by a rat feeding on the boy's body as police had speculated.

Using some magnification equipment in the photo department at the *Daily News,* he and Lavin were able to study the negatives in greater detail. It was SanHamel who first noticed that there were impressions made on the surface of the wound. His gifted eye spotted letters spelling out the word "BEAR" and a series of star shaped emblems depicting the constellation Ursa Major, or Great Bear.

The two men consulted with coroner's pathologist Jerry Kearns, who agreed with them that there were impressions on the wound spelling out the word "BEAR." Needless to say, the two journalists and Kearns concluded that a scavenging animal did not cause the wound. Instead, they deduced someone using a very sharp knife had cut away a portion of the boy's skin. The section of flesh had been removed to destroy some "telltale marking," the newsmen concluded.

The journalists went to press with their revelation. "The person had to be handy with a knife. The shallow cut of the depth indicates he had complete control of the knife," Kearns stated in the December 10, 1955, edition of the *Daily News.* He added the development "could lead to a break in the case."

In addition to the markings, Lavin and SanHamel divulged some of the other evidence known to police and the coroner. They reported that a small rake-like tool, something most likely used in a garden, had caused the strange wounds on Bobby Peterson's scalp. In addition, the corpses may have rested against metal stampings or strips, causing the repetitive pattern marks found on some portions of the bodies. The reporters also speculated that brownish stains found on the bodies were postmortem in nature, possibly made by their lying on rubber mats.

Lavin, SanHamel and Clem Lane thought that after they'd presented some intriguing and helpful evidence to their readers, someone would come forward with an explanation that would lead to the boys' killer. Surely, some reader would know the significance of the word "BEAR" and the constellation Ursa Major.

"Anyone who believes he has information about the knife, rake markings, rubber mat, tape or other clues should get in touch with police . . . or call the *Daily News* City Editor," the newspaper urged.

The story fell flat. A few readers called with suggestions as to the meaning of the word and the impression of the stars, but nothing panned out. The Chicago Police brass immediately discounted the theory as untrue. Sensing which way public sentiment was leaning toward the report, McCarron claimed the markings were optical illusions. Lavin recalls that there was one sergeant assigned to the task force who complimented them on their work and told them he thought they might be on to something. Other Chicago newspapers reported that police had refuted the *Daily News* reports regarding markings found on the Schuessler boy's body, and Lavin and SanHamel became the butt of jokes by their colleagues and competitors.

"You guys are seeing things, why don't you have another drink?" Lavin recalls a competitor told him one night at a local reporters' watering hole. "They all thought we were nuts. They gave us the business about that story for weeks." Lavin and SanHamel were no different from the police; they too were grasping at shadows. The two reporters and the police would continue trying to solve the case for the next few years. They would be unsuccessful, though, and the Schuessler-Peterson case would slowly fade from the memories of all but a few.

CHAPTER 7

Fast-forward thirty-six years later. To many the Schuessler-Peterson case had become one of several legendary unsolvable crimes gathering dust in the Chicago Police Department's cold case files. As memories of the crime faded, so did the fear that kept many quiet for decades. The break that came in the case would come from an unlikely source, from a man who was just six years old when the boys were murdered.

A phone rang on Special Agent James Delorto's desk. He was one of the last people in the darkened office that evening, having decided to stay late to catch up on some paperwork. Delorto's office had a surreal look. The Chicago branch of the federal Bureau of Alcohol, Tobacco and Firearms had recently moved into the building, and workmen had been busy erecting drywall. Many offices were without lights, walls and ceilings. Employees had been handed out electric lanterns that cast an eerie glow when used. The ATF's new Chicago digs were located in a high-rise just west of the Loop and adjacent to the Chicago River. From several offices one could view the elegance of the Chicago skyline with the Chicago River in the foreground.

Delorto wasn't that lucky, though. From his desk and those of the arson group he supervised, he had a view of a parking garage. Delorto, who was nearing the end of his career, had joined the ATF at age twenty-five in October 1968 following a brief stint in the U.S. Army. He had been injured five months into his service for Uncle Sam, while running an obstacle course during a training exercise at Fort Ord in California. In 1967 he received a medical discharge.

Delorto, who was called "Jimmy" by his friends, was proud of the fact that he had enlisted in the Army. He most likely would have been sent to Vietnam as a "tunnel rat" had he not been injured. "Tunnel rats" were a special breed of soldier whose job was to bring the fight to the Viet Cong by crawling into their tunnels and planting satchel charges. Soldiers selected to be "tunnel rats" were chosen for their small size and courage. Standing at five feet, nine inches tall and weighing about 150 pounds, Delorto fit the bill. Before he had been injured, Delorto told friends he was the biggest "tunnel rat" in his platoon.

Delorto was wrapping up his career as a federal agent on a high note. Since 1989, he had been part of a task force, made up of ATF and FBI agents and several representatives from local law enforcement agencies, that had been conducting an investigation into questionable dealings in the show-horse industry in Chicago and the disappearance and presumed murder of Chicago candy heiress Helen Vorhees Brach.

Brach, heiress to the Brach candy fortune, was a former hatcheck girl who had married into wealth. She had simply fallen off the face of the earth on February 17, 1977, after checking out of the Mayo Clinic. When she vanished, Helen Brach was one of the richest women in America. She left behind her pink Cadillac, her mansion, numerous pets and $30 million.

Delorto and his colleagues were busy building a federal RICO case against some members of Silas Jayne's inner circle. A RICO case consists of at least two acts of racketeering activity, one of which occurred after the effective date of the RICO Act, which was October 15, 1970, and the last of which occurred within ten years. The act defined racketeering activity as any act or threat involving murder, kidnapping, gambling, arson, robbery, bribery, extortion or dealing in obscene matter or narcotics or dangerous drugs.

As a result of the federal probe others in the show-horse world were being investigated in regards to numerous incidents of insurance fraud. The investigation revealed that several well-to-do show-horse owners had hired a horse executioner nicknamed the "Sandman" to kill their horses in such a manner that it appeared the animals had died of natural means. The owners then filed claims and collected on their insurance policy after having their horses executed.

Shortly before Helen Brach disappeared, she had been keeping company with a man named Richard Bailey, a gigolo and known con man. Bailey was a former dance studio instructor who had once operated a driving school in St. Louis that catered to elderly women. He knew how to turn on the charm. Although he was paid for numerous driving lessons, Bailey taught few women to drive. Eventually authorities in Missouri forced Bailey from the state and he resettled in Chicago.

On the night that the phone rang on Delorto's desk, the Helen Brach investigation was years away from completion. Once the investigation was made public, the indictment of Bailey and twenty-three others would show that the show-horse industry was rife with greed and questionable characters. And throughout the entire investigation, one man's name was raised with regularity. That name was Silas Carter Jayne. Though Silas Jayne had died of leukemia in 1987, his ghostly fingerprints were found on many facets of the Brach investigation. Some witnesses refused to cooperate with federal authorities because they still feared remnants of Silas Jayne's posse.

Delorto had learned that Bailey and Silas Jayne met purely by accident. After he relocated to Chicago, Bailey had intended to open another dance studio. He changed his mind, however, after stumbling upon a more lucrative swindle. One day while on a leisurely drive, Bailey pulled into a stable. On a whim he decided to take riding lessons, and later purchased a horse from Frank Jayne Jr., the owner of Northwestern Stables. Within a short period of time, Bailey learned that he had paid a good sum of money for a worthless animal. Bailey didn't get angry though. Instead, he was impressed. He had met his match in the art of the con.

Intrigued, Bailey began frequenting the stable more often and befriended Frank Jayne Jr., the nephew of Silas Jayne. Through Frank, who was known simply as "Junior," Bailey was eventually introduced to Silas Jayne and became a member of Jayne's criminal organization. Bailey and Junior used the Northwestern Stables as their base of operation. Employees at the stable were instructed to keep an eye out for potentially wealthy customers. If a customer drove up in an expensive car, his or her license plate was jotted down and passed along to Frank Jayne Jr. Junior then forwarded the tag number to a corrupt suburban police officer. The officer, from the northern suburb of Skokie, used his department's police computer to run the customer's plate in an effort to learn where the person lived.

If the computer check indicated that the potential victim resided in an exclusive area, Junior sought additional financial information from a local banker. The banker would conduct an extensive credit check to determine how much available cash the person had on hand. Frank Jayne Jr. and Bailey then used the intelligence to set the price of horses they sold the victim. If a victim had at least $50,000 to burn, the horse would cost $50,000. Bailey also ran personal ads seeking lonely, susceptible, older women, in a newspaper that circulated in Chicago's exclusive North Shore communities.

"There is no Blue Book on horses," he allegedly told one rider, referring to the publication often quoted to price used cars. Bailey was boasting how easy it was to sell worthless animals at inflated prices. "This is the greatest game in the world," he said.

Frank Jayne Jr. nicknamed Bailey the "Golden Tongue" for his ability to woo elderly women. Bailey referred to Brach as his "Golden Goose." The two collaborators often relied on Silas Jayne for advice and direction.

A longtime friend had introduced Bailey to Helen Brach in 1973. Bailey, who had grown up dirt poor in Kentucky, drove a Rolls-Royce to his first date with the heiress. He ordered $200 bottles of champagne, sent flowers and love notes, and wined, dined and romanced the lonely widow. His words of love and devotion paid off. Working with Junior, Bailey and his fellow grifters sold Brach at least ten lame horses for $300,000. But Helen Brach wasn't a love-struck fool. She began to question Bailey, and ulti-mately confronted him. She told Bailey she knew she had been swindled by the smooth-talking Lothario and threat-ened to go to the police.

Bailey told other members of the Jayne Gang that Brach was on to their scam. Delorto and his colleagues would eventually learn that shortly before Brach disappeared, Bailey had solicited several men to kill the millionairess.

The phone chimed again. Delorto picked up the re-ceiver and said hello. On the other end of the line was William "Red" Wemette, a longtime federal informant who had worked with Delorto in the past. In 1990 Red had helped the FBI in Chicago put away one of the Outfit's most feared hitmen, a man named Frank Schweihs. Over a two-year period, Red assisted federal authorities in record-ing eighteen videotapes of Schweihs collecting "protec-tion" money. Schweihs, whom the FBI suspected in the murders of two pornographic film distributors, was sen-tenced to thirteen years for extorting $21,450 from Red. After losing one of its star assassins, the Outfit had put a contract out on his life. Red went into seclusion.

After a few "So how the hell have you been"s, Delorto began running some names past Red, of persons involved in the Chicago Horse Syndicate. Delorto didn't expect Red to know too much; Red was more of an expert regarding the Outfit, not Silas Jayne's gang. But task force investiga-tors had been asking enough people questions that word of a federal investigation was starting to spread. Delorto was pleasantly surprised by Red's response. Red said he knew of the Horse Syndicate, especially Silas Jayne, his brother Frank and Frank's son, Frank Jayne Jr. Plus Red told De-lorto he knew one of the men Delorto had mentioned, a man named Kenneth Hansen.

"What's his claim to fame?" Delorto asked, and Red then dropped a bombshell.

"Kenny told me he murdered three kids back in 1955," Red said.

Delorto was stunned. He knew immediately what case Red was talking about. Delorto had been fourteen years old when Tony, Bobby and John's bodies were found just a few miles from his childhood home. He and his friends pedaled their bikes to the woods soon after the gruesome discovery. Like many children at that time, Delorto's childhood came to screeching halt following the murders. His parents would not let him leave sight of his home for weeks.

Red told Delorto that he had lived with Hansen for about eighteen months. He said Hansen had confessed to him on a dozen occasions that he murdered the three boys and dumped their bodies in a forest preserve.

"Why didn't you tell someone this before?" Delorto asked. "Why wait all these years?" Red responded that he had tried to tell the FBI in 1975 that Kenneth Hansen had confessed to him about the murders. "What did they do with the information?" Delorto asked.

"They didn't seem interested," Red said. "They were only interested in [organized crime] strike force crimes. If it wasn't O.C., if it was a local matter, they didn't want to hear about it. They told me murder was a local crime."

Delorto was shocked by what he was hearing. He knew, however, that there were certain rules regarding confidential informants. Because the FBI had developed Wemette as one, it had no legal authority or obligation to report to any other police agency information that Wemette divulged. The FBI's rules regarding confidential informants are similar to rules in effect in other federal law enforcement agencies. It would have been a violation of those guidelines for Wemette's handlers to inform the Chicago Police Department that they had the name of a man who might have murdered three boys in 1955. Delorto thought, however, that if the FBI had stumbled across the information, they would have found some way to pass it along. How could the FBI disregard the murders of three young boys? It was possible that the agents had not realized the significance of the information.

At that time Red was basically a bird in a cage that the FBI had paid to sing in order to learn as much as possible about the Outfit. Surreptitiously passing along the information about Hansen to the Chicago Police might have tipped off the Outfit that Red was cooperating with authorities. Red's cooperation with the FBI was not made known until after he decided to help the FBI videotape Schweihs. At that point, he became a cooperating witness and his confidential status was stripped since he had agreed to testify in court.

Red quickly added that he had never pursued the matter with the FBI because he thought Hansen's confessions were hearsay, and therefore not admissible in court. Delorto of course knew Red was wrong. Such evidence would be admissible if Red testified about the conversation and subsequent admission of guilt. His conversation with Red continued for about thirty more minutes and then Delorto told Red he would get back to him regarding what was known in Chicago law enforcement circles as simply the Schuessler-Peterson case.

One would expect that Jim Delorto would have taken immediate action after hearing such news—informing his colleagues, a supervisor or any of the assistant United States attorneys he was working with on the Brach investigation. Especially since Kenneth Hansen's name had surfaced in that investigation.

But Delorto did nothing at that time. He would later explain that he was too busy with the Brach investigation and didn't have the agents available to adequately investigate Red's claim. "I needed everyone to concentrate on the Brach case; we were still in the middle of that when Red called. What were we going to lose? Nobody had been arrested or charged in this case for forty years. So I waited. I knew Red was not going to be going anywhere," Delorto said. The case would continue to remain dormant for a few more years, until Delorto had the right man for the job.

CHAPTER 8

John Rotunno smiled at the waitress as he took a seat and ordered coffee. It was shortly before 9 A.M. and Rotunno had been asked by Jim Delorto to meet him and retired Illinois Police Lt. David Hamm at a restaurant to discuss some new aspect of the ongoing RICO investigation into the disappearance of Helen Brach. Rotunno had heard the new development had something to do with some old murders he vaguely remembered hearing about as a child, a well-known horseman named Silas Jayne and another man whose name had come up in the Brach investigation.

Rotunno knew little of Silas Jayne. He had heard the name mentioned a few times around the office in connection to the ongoing Brach case. Rotunno was new to the investigation, having transferred into Delorto's arson group after wrapping up a five-year undercover investigation into one of Chicago's most feared street gangs, the Undertaker Vice Lords. The investigation had been a major success. Rotunno had played the role of a West Coast marijuana dealer so well that he had been asked to join the gang.

The investigation, however, had been stressful for Rotunno and his family. On a moment's notice Rotunno would find himself switching gears from a suburban family man with a wife and three daughters to his undercover persona as a ruthless drug dealer who "moved" truckloads of marijuana. Gang members came to admire Rotunno, nicknaming him "Red" because of the government-issued undercover hot rod he drove, a fully loaded red Mustang. Rotunno infiltrated the gang via a confidential informant who had introduced him to the gang hierarchy. When the investigation concluded, the probe resulted in numerous arrests on charges ranging from murder, extortion and narcotics trafficking to weapons violations.

Sometimes it was in the middle of the night or during family gatherings such as Christmas or Thanksgiving that Rotunno had to break away from his wife, Diane, and his children without notice. Rotunno's beeper would buzz and he would be out the door, perhaps on his way to meet some murderous thug in a darkened alley. Rotunno couldn't tell his wife or family members exactly where he was going or what he was doing. A veteran of Rotunno's undercover work dating back to when he started his law enforcement career with the DEA in San Francisco, Diane knew her husband was dealing with ruthless people. A devout Catholic, whenever he left the home Diane prayed he would return safely, but she expected the worst. She also feared for her children. She was afraid if Rotunno's cover were ever blown, someone might kidnap one of her daughters in retaliation.

Rotunno was looking forward to the meeting with Delorto. He was looking for a new assignment, a new challenge. He was glad the new case didn't involve undercover work. He wanted something different to sink his teeth into and something hopefully with more normal hours.

Within a few minutes of his arrival, Rotunno looked up from his coffee and spotted David Hamm walking into the establishment. The two lawmen made eye contact and acknowledged each other with a nod. Rotunno had seen Hamm in the ATF offices before, so he recognized him immediately. Hamm, who had retired from the Illinois State Police in 1991 after thirty-three years of service, was one of the local police officers assisting in the Helen Brach investigation, a barrel-chested man who stood about six feet tall and weighed about two hundred pounds. He walked over and stuck out his hand.

"Nice to meet you again," Hamm drawled in his distinct accent, which was a mixture of upper Midwest and Kentucky twang. He grew up in the Chicago area.

Within a few minutes Delorto arrived and the three got down to business.

"The best way to tell you everything I know about Silas Jayne and Ken Hansen is to start from the beginning and move forward," Hamm said. "Ken Hansen was one of Silas Jayne's men. He was with Si since the 1950s."

Rotunno asked about Silas's relationship with his younger brother George. He knew that sometime in the early 1970s Silas had been convicted in connection with the murder of George Jayne. The stormy relationship between Si and George had been the topic of many news articles. Before Hamm went into detail regarding that slaying, he first recounted much of the Jayne family history. Hamm noted that Silas's conviction on rape charges in 1924 most likely planted the seed of his hatred toward George.

"We found in the court records remarks by Spunner. He said something like 'Silas is a reckless young man, a year or two in jail would do him good,'" Hamm said. He added that Jayne family members told him that the incident touched off Silas's hatred toward George. "That's where it started, right then and there," Hamm said. "Silas hated George because his father didn't keep him out of jail."

Silas had been trying to kill George for a number of years. Silas's animosity toward George first became public in 1961 after George Jayne's fourteen-year-old daughter, Linda, beat Silas's best horse and took top prize at the Oak Brook Hounds horse show. With dozens of witnesses looking on, Silas stood in the middle of a horse ring and bellowed, "I'll never talk to you again, you bastard."

From that moment on, Silas and others in his employ began harassing George at every turn. In July 1962, George's office at his Tri-Color Stable in Palatine was burglarized. In September 1962 at the Ohio State Fair someone loosened the front wheel lugs of George's truck. After those experiences George hired security guards to watch his business and vehicles. Despite the precautions, the tires on some of George's vehicles were punctured with an ice pick. George naturally suspected Silas was behind the attacks, and he and his close friends started carrying loaded firearms for protection. In March 1963 someone opened fire on the Tri-Color Stables. Police counted twenty-eight bullet holes on the building. A few months later, in May 1963, after George's entry beat Silas's in the open jumping event at the Lake Forest Horse Show, Silas growled, "I'll kill you, you son of a bitch." Later that month Silas threatened George again at the Cincinnati Horse Show.

"One of the first threats was made in front of George's daughter Linda," Hamm said. "Silas was obviously the person who had been gunning for George. He didn't care who knew about it." There were other incidents of violence. Shadowy drivers tried running George off the road at night while he was hauling horses down lonely country byways. George and his wife Marion found sticks of dynamite near their house.

The harassment turned deadly on June 14, 1965. On that day George had asked one of his employees, a young woman named Cheryl Lynn Rude, to move his gold two-door Cadillac. George wanted to drive into town to pick up a trailer that was in the shop for repairs. Rude, twenty-two, was a champion equestrian who had once been Silas's star rider but had quit to work for George. "She was like another member of George's family. I heard she was very close to his daughters," Hamm said.

When Cheryl turned the key in the Cadillac, an explosion rattled the stable. Six sticks of dynamite that had been alligator-clipped to the ignition detonated. The explosion blew off one of the Cheryl's legs below the knee and a piece of shrapnel tore through her trachea. Rude drowned in her own blood.

"The bomb was definitely intended for George," Hamm said. "Everyone knew it." Cook County Sheriff's Police investigating the murder immediately suspected Silas was behind the bombing. George, who believed most police officers were on Silas's payroll, initially refused to cooperate with authorities investigating the murder.

"A few events occurred soon after that and things got

very interesting. The Cook County State's Attorney's Office came very close to convicting Silas on conspiracy to commit murder charges for plotting to kill George," Hamm said.

A break in the investigation came within days after Rude was murdered. Two hit men that Silas had hired to kill George arrived in Chicago from Florida. The hit men, Eddie Moran and Stephen Grod, picked up a Chicago newspaper and read about the murder attempt on George. The two hired killers were confused. Silas had agreed to pay them $15,000 to murder George, not someone else. "So Moran called Si and he said, 'Hey, what's going on? I thought you hired us to kill George. What are you doing?'" Hamm said. "Silas told him, 'It was a mistake. It was a mistake. Keep going, keep trying.' That wasn't unusual for Silas. We later learned he often hired multiple groups of hit men to kill George."

The botched murder attempt, however, made Grod and Moran nervous and they went to George and told him everything. The two suggested that they con Silas out of the money he had promised to pay for the murder. They could call Silas and then put George on the phone. George could then do a little playacting and plead for his life. "They wanted George to scream and then they would shoot off their guns, leaving Silas with the impression that George was dead," Hamm said. The two would then collect their fee from Silas and split the proceeds with George.

George, however, wanted no part of the ridiculous scam. Instead he convinced the two to accompany him to the Cook County Sheriff's Police headquarters where they were investigating the Rude murder. With the cooperation of Grod and Moran, the police set a trap. They tried to record Silas ordering the murder of his brother. Grod wore a recording device and met with Silas at a horse show in

Wisconsin. The police recorded Silas telling Grod, "It's time to buy a horse." Grod later told a Cook County grand jury that the phrase was an agreed upon code meaning he was to kill George. Silas also passed an envelope to Grod that contained $1,000. Based on the evidence, Silas was indicted on charges of conspiracy to commit murder. The case went to trial in March 1966, Hamm said.

"As he was walking into the Cook County Criminal Courthouse prior to Silas's trial, Frank Jayne Sr., Silas's brother, handed Grod a copy of a news article about a key witness in some criminal case being murdered before he could testify," Hamm said. "That killed the case. When Grod took the stand, he suddenly got amnesia. Under questioning, he claimed he couldn't remember what he had for breakfast that morning. The case collapsed. Silas walked out of the courtroom a free man."

Rotunno stopped writing and put down his pen. He had dealt with some brazen criminals in his day, but he was amazed that Silas was bold enough to threaten a witness on the steps of a courthouse on the first day of his trial.

"Did they do anything to the witness?" Rotunno asked.

"He was held in contempt, fined $1,000 and jailed for thirty days," Hamm responded. "George and Marion were devastated. Naturally they were scared to death. Marion later told me that as they were being escorted out of court, they asked the prosecutor what they could do to protect themselves. The prosecutor supposedly told them, 'Kill the son of a bitch,'" Hamm said. The prosecutor in question, now a well-known defense attorney in Chicago, has strongly denied that he made such a comment to George and Marion Jayne.

When Silas escaped his narrow brush with justice, he must have vowed to ruin George. Soon after the trial, the office at George's stable was burglarized and all his business files were stolen. A short time later, George was indicted by the Internal Revenue Service on tax fraud charges. "We later found out Si told one of George's employees, 'Your boss is going out of business soon, because I gave the IRS boys all the dope on him,'" Hamm said. At his tax fraud trial dozens of witnesses were called to testify that George had an income of almost $300,000 from 1959 to 1961, and evidence was introduced showing he had failed to pay taxes on about $100,000. George was found not guilty of the charges.

The continuing investigation of the Cheryl Rude murder went nowhere, Hamm said. Cook County Sheriff's Police, working in conjunction with the Chicago Police, developed several suspects in the case and issued search warrants which turned up blasting caps and wiring at the home of one man, but the investigation screeched to a halt in 1967 when the seized evidence was removed from the Chicago Police evidence room and destroyed.

The violence didn't end with the murder of Rude. A little more than a year after she was killed, three women who knew Rude, Ann Miller, twenty-one, Patty Blough, nineteen, and Renee Bruhl, nineteen, disappeared after spending a day at the Indiana Dunes beach, a popular Chicago area summer destination. The three were last seen climbing into a blue speedboat that had pulled close to shore. It is assumed they were murdered by someone in Silas Jayne's circle, Hamm said.

Rotunno was starting to get a very clear picture of Silas Jayne. He was a fearless, out-of-control sociopath driven by his own unbridled rage.

"Do you know if George ever tried to kill Silas? Did he do anything in retaliation?" Rotunno asked.

"As far as we know George never struck back," Hamm said. "He continued to build a thriving business. He retaliated, I guess, by hurting Silas financially."

The rift between the brothers became a matter of growing concern among their sisters. Despite their animosities, both brothers remained close to their siblings, Hamm said. It was clear that Frank Sr. sided with Silas. Silas purchased homes for some of his sisters, he added. The sisters worked together to end the dispute, and in 1968 a deal was brokered at a family reunion. George and Silas supposedly shook hands. George agreed to quit competing directly with Silas at horse shows. The deal, however, didn't last. A year after backing down from Silas, George started to put together plans to expand his business. If the expansion went through, Silas would be ruined.

Speaking of business, Hamm noted that although the brothers didn't talk to each other directly, they often hired the same professionals to work at their stables, such as veterinarians and farriers. The brothers often heard through the grapevine what each other was doing. That's most likely how Silas had learned that George's oldest daughter was going to be married. George and Marion planned a big wedding for their daughter, and Silas put out the word that he would do everything in his power to ruin the event, including kidnapping the bride. A close family friend later told Hamm that George struck a deal with Silas and paid a hefty ransom to keep the peace. The wedding went as planned.

George Jayne appeared to be a man who feared for his life but wouldn't submit to his brother's will. After Rude's murder, whenever George started his car he positioned himself in the driver's seat in such a way as to leave as much of his body sticking out of the vehicle as possible.

George thought that if there was an explosion, the blast might throw him clear of the car, rather than through the roof. He also rigged a device that connected the ignition to a pole, so that he could stand outside of the car on the passenger side and turn the key. George also asked his friends to follow him, to watch his back. Whenever he was judging a horse show, he had friends in the stands armed with walkie-talkies who kept an eye out for Silas and his henchmen. On one occasion, George's spotters spied a gunman sitting in the cab of a pickup truck taking aim at George with a rifle. George was informed via walkie-talkie and quickly left the ring.

George also purchased a transmitter, and paid a private investigator named Frank Michelle Jr. to attach the device to Silas's car in January 1969. Whenever Silas was within a five-mile radius, the receiver would emit a beeping sound. The problem with the little gadget was that it was battery powered and George knew he would have to pay someone again at some point to sneak up to Silas's car and replace the batteries. The first and last such battery-replacing mission turned deadly.

The task of changing the battery fell on the shoulders of Frank Michelle Jr. He was the son of Frank H. Michelle Sr., the former chief of police of Inverness, a well-to-do suburb where George was residing. George had hired the elder Michelle to provide security for his business and home. "It was a real Keystone Cop operation," Hamm said. The younger Michelle was a convicted felon who had done time for auto theft. Twelve days after it was attached to Silas's car, the device stopped transmitting. Naturally George thought the batteries had died. He didn't know, however, that Silas had traded in his Cadillac and was now driving a car that didn't have a transmitter.

On the day that the younger Michelle was to change the battery, January 19, 1969, he returned to his home during the evening hours slightly drunk and ordered his wife, Evelyn, and two young daughters into the family car. Michelle couldn't drive because of his drinking that day, most likely working up the courage to sneak onto Silas's ranch and change the battery. He asked his wife to drop him off along a lonely country road not far from Silas's home. Michelle told his wife he would change the battery and be back in a few minutes.

"He never came back. Silas caught him and shot him to death," Hamm said. "Michelle was shot nine times with three different guns, a .22-caliber pistol, a .30-caliber carbine and a .38-caliber pistol." Silas claimed the shooting was in self-defense. The local sheriff's police investigated the homicide and Silas was not charged with any crime. "He used to brag that he walked away from it because he put $10,000 in the right hands," Hamm said. The Illinois Bureau of Investigation looked into the bribe allegation but it went nowhere, he added.

"The first time I met him he told me about shooting Michelle," Delorto said, speaking for the first time. "I'll never forget the look on his face. Si claimed he was watching television, heard his dogs barking and then the doorbell rang. He said when he went to answer, he asked who was there and Michelle shot at him through the door.

"So, Si being Si, he pulled out his own gun and fired back a bunch of times through the door. He said he saw Michelle go down. He would have kept firing but he had run out of bullets. He said that Michelle started crawling away, pulling himself off the front porch and leaving a bloody trail across the lawn. Si ran back inside and got a couple of other guns, loaded them up, ran out into the front

yard and started shooting Michelle at point-blank range,"
Delorto said.

"You know what was the most interesting part? When
he was telling me all this, his eyes were sparkling and he
had a grin on his face. He was reliving the whole thing
while he was telling me about it. He then looked at me and
said, 'I did good, I did the right thing, didn't I? A man
came up on my porch with a gun. I had the right to kill him
then, right?' That is what he said to me. I thought, 'Wow,
this guy's absolutely nuts,' " Delorto said.

There were more chilling details regarding the incident.
Before Michelle died, Silas took a pair of vice grips and
crushed his testicles, trying to get him to talk, Hamm said.
State police investigators tried to corroborate that information by reviewing Michelle's hospital records and coroner's report. The effort was unsuccessful because the
coroner's report and medical records disappeared, Hamm
said.

Rotunno cleared his throat and looked up from his
notes. "Are you telling me he had enough pull to deep-six
the coroner's report and hospital records? He could make
that happen?"

"Sure. He could make things happen. He knew people.
He knew Outfit people, but they were a little spooked by
Silas," Delorto said.

"You're kidding me, right? I'm thinking this guy must
have been living some kind of charmed life. How did he
manage to survive? The Undertaker Vice Lords would
have just walked up behind someone like Si and smoked
him," Rotunno said. "You would think the Outfit would
have killed him without batting an eye."

"That's true. But the Outfit gave Silas wide berth. He
was so unpredictable. Everyone knew he had been trying to

kill his own brother for years. He could have easily turned to them to murder George but he didn't. They knew Silas wanted the satisfaction of murdering his brother himself," Hamm said. "And in anybody's book that's pretty twisted. So they steered clear of him and only interacted when they needed to."

The waitress came to the booth and freshened everyone's coffee. Rotunno glanced at his watch and noticed they had been at it for some time and had not yet discussed George Jayne's murder and Silas's connection to Kenneth Hansen. "I know Silas eventually managed to kill George. Tell me about that. You investigated that case didn't you, Dave?" Rotunno asked.

Hamm began recounting details that led to the murder of George. He said George was shot to death on October 28, 1970, in the basement rec room of his home while playing bridge with his wife Marion, daughter Linda and her husband Mickey Wright.

Marion told police her husband was about to deal the cards when she heard a loud explosion and saw his chest "light up red." George fell out of his chair bleeding. Both Marion and Linda screamed, realizing that George had been shot. Police would later determine that the shooter had crept up to the home and spotted George playing cards through a basement window. The gunman snapped off a branch of a nearby shrub to get a better shot. George didn't stand a chance. The gunman took aim at a distance of less than fifteen feet and squeezed the trigger, aiming for the button on George's shirt. The bullet hit George directly in the heart, killing him before he hit the floor. George was forty-seven years old; he left behind a wife, four children and a thriving business that had made him a wealthy man. Hamm was assigned the case within hours.

The investigation would determine that the successful plot to kill George had started to gel in November 1969. That's when a corrupt police officer named Edwin Nefeld, who was the chief of detectives for a police department in a south suburb of Chicago named Markham, approached a man named Melvin Adams and asked him if he was willing to commit a murder for hire. Adams was a local hothead who had a reputation as a tough guy but in reality had never fired a weapon at a human being in his life. He accepted the offer to kill George after meeting Silas for drinks.

Silas offered Adams $10,000 plus expenses and would provide the weapons to kill George. The fee later climbed to $30,000, and with the additional money Adams recruited a coworker, Julius Barnes, to help him with the murder. Barnes agreed to act as the triggerman.

In the days and weeks that followed George Jayne's murder, Hamm and other detectives from the Illinois Bureau of Investigation methodically built a case against Silas and others. A boy who had been pedaling his bicycle past the Jayne home moments before the shooting was able to provide a description of an Oldsmobile Cutlass and a partial license plate number: 936. All of the plates with that number and make were assigned to car owners on the south side of Chicago.

"It was a real heater case. There were news stories every day for a few weeks following the murder," Hamm said.

On November 1, 1971, Chicago newspapers reported that George's lawyer, Edward S. Arkema, had told investigators that George left behind several letters with instructions that they should be opened only if he was murdered.

In one of the letters provided by Arkema, George predicted that Silas would someday be responsible for his death. George provided the names of possible suspects in his own murder. In a letter to his lawyer dated July 16, 1969, George wrote, "I know without a doubt that he plans to kill me and someday will probably be successful. To date I've been lucky, for he persists in hiring only amateurs that he can control and who are frightened of him." The letter concluded, "If he is successful . . . I ask you to guide and protect my family, for they will need help. . . . If there is any way to make this maniac pay for depriving my family of their support and me of the pleasures of seeing them to maturity, I ask that you proceed and prosecute to the fullest."

On November 3, 1971, the late Art Petacque, one of the most colorful mob writers in Chicago journalism history, reported that George was murdered because he had uncovered evidence about the Rude murder. Petacque reported that George had been actively pursuing leads to find out who planted the car bomb intended for him. And later Petacque said that in one of George's letters he wrote that he "knew too much" about the Schuessler-Peterson murders. "George Jayne had written he had knowledge of the killer or killers but had not reported what he knew to police," Petacque wrote.

"We never found any letter regarding the Schuessler-Peterson case," Hamm said. "We found other letters about Silas but nothing about the three boys. Marion told me she looked all over that house for every letter he wrote."

Hamm and his colleagues began putting pressure on Silas. Investigators who had questioned Silas noticed that he had loaded weapons all over his home. As a convicted felon, it was illegal for Silas to own a gun. On January 9, 1971, he was arrested by the ATF on weapons charges after they raided his home and found eighteen weapons, includ-

ing four rifles, two long-barrel pistols and twelve handguns. It was on that day that Delorto met Silas for the first
time and heard Silas describe how he shot Frank Michelle
Jr. to death.

A U.S. Magistrate set Silas's bond at $25,000. He was
able to immediately post bail. Silas took fifteen $1,000
bills out from his money belt and handed them to the
clerk. Silas then turned to U.S. Attorney Sam Skinner,
who attended the bond hearing and would later serve as
President George H. Bush's chief of staff and boldly
stated, "I've got $100,000 more back in a bank in Elgin."
Delorto recalled that Silas walked out of the federal courthouse before he had time to finish typing up his report on
the arrest.

The state police investigation of George Jayne's murder
continued to move forward. Armed with the information
provided from the boy on the bike, Hamm and his colleagues quickly zeroed in on Adams. For several weeks IBI
investigators shadowed him, waiting for him to slip up.

Marion Jayne then played a key role in the investigation. With the blessing of Hamm and his IBI superiors,
Marion approached Adams and his girlfriend and showed
them a briefcase containing the $25,000 in reward money.
She begged the couple to tell authorities who had killed her
husband. The widow's tearful pleas worked. Adams caved
in and began talking to investigators.

On May 22, 1971, Silas Jayne, Julius Barnes, Edward
Nefeld and Joe LaPlaca, who had acted as an intermediary
between Adams and Jayne, were indicted for George
Jayne's murder. Adams was later granted immunity and
testified against the others. Silas hired F. Lee Bailey as his
defense attorney, reportedly for a fee of $250,000. In his
book *F. Lee Bailey for the Defense,* Bailey wrote, "Without

exaggeration, the Jayne case was the most bizarre murder case I've ever had."

After a thirty-day trial in 1973, Barnes was convicted of murder and sentenced to fifteen to thirty-five years in prison. After Barnes was released from prison, he was murdered in an unrelated dispute. Silas and LaPlaca were sentenced to six to twenty years on conspiracy to commit murder. One of the three male jurors who passed judgment on Silas later told reporters, "The verdict should have been first degree murder, but Jayne's icy stares scared the nine women jurors . . . Jayne sat about twelve feet away from us. He worked individually on those women jurors. He looked right through them. And they'd come into the jury room and cry after some sessions."

Silas served seven years in the Vienna Correctional Center in southern Illinois. Before the trial, Nefeld had pleaded guilty to conspiracy to murder and was sentenced to three to ten years in prison.

"Before we went to trial with Silas, we picked up your guy, Kenneth Hansen," Hamm said. "I hear this is the guy you're going to be looking at for the Schuessler-Peterson murders."

Not long after George was murdered, Marion received a collect call to her home from a man named Ancil Tremore. Tremore wasn't a sophisticated individual; he refused to state his name when asked but claimed he could provide information about George Jayne's murder in return for the $25,000 reward. IBI investigators tracked Tremore down through the telephone records. After he was picked up for questioning, he told Hamm his cousin Lawrence Smith had been approached by a man named Kenneth Hansen at a bar in Frankfort, Illinois, named the Valley View Young Adults Klub and offered $20,000 to kill George.

After the initial offer to Smith, Smith recruited Tremore, his cousin, to help him commit the murder. Tremore and Smith later met with Silas Jayne at Ken Hansen's stable. "Si was there and he told them straight out, 'I want George killed.' He showed them $25,000 and told them, 'If you can, I'll give you $30,000 if you can get him and bring him to me alive,'" Hamm said.

The Young Adults Klub, which was owned by Ken Hansen's brother Curt, played a key role in some of Silas's plans. If they could, Silas wanted Tremore and Smith to bring George back to the Klub, where Silas could personally torture and murder his younger brother. Silas gave Tremore and Smith guns, a map, the serial numbers on George Jayne's airplane and George Jayne's photo, in hopes they could get the job done.

Tremore and Smith, however, proved to be more fond of beer than murder. The two men staked out George Jayne's Inverness home on several occasions, but they never came close to killing George. Whenever they lay in wait for George, the two men brought along several cases of beer. Instead of committing the murder, they would get drunk.

"Before we knew about these two, I went into work one morning and my boss Tom Drury called me into his office. Tom was an ex–Chicago police sergeant who had a lot of experience. I walked into his office and he had a cardboard box there. It was full of reports about the Schuessler-Peterson murder. He said to me, 'Dave, I want you to go through this. This is intelligence stuff from Chicago. I want you to go through this and see if there's anything in there that will help us with our case.' So I did. I spent probably a whole morning going through it," Hamm said.

"Nothing really jumped out at me, but there was something that got my attention. Back in 1955 there was a lieutenant involved in the case named Nash. He wrote a lot of reports about the Schuessler-Peterson murders; apparently Nash had the ticket on this case. Nash did a lot of interviews. His reports impressed me. He talked to a guy who was out walking his dog and he had heard screams coming from the Idle Hour Stable. Another lady heard screams coming from the same place. Then there was another witness that saw a car leaving at a high rate of speed, peeling rubber near the stable about that same time as the screams. "The car had a loud exhaust," Hamm said. "I figured the boys were probably murdered at the Idle Hour Stable. Everything pointed there.

"I read through all of this and I thought to myself, 'Who in Silas's circle could do something like that?' It had to be somebody who was a pedophile. I knew everybody at Si's place was chasing the girls and the young women. I didn't know anybody who was interested in boys," Hamm said. "Then I found out that Ken Hansen supposedly liked boys. I immediately figured he was the guy," Hamm said. Six months after Hamm had read over the 1955 case files, Ken Hansen was arrested on June 4, 1971, and charged with solicitation to commit George Jayne's murder. Hamm realized he now had his chance to question a possible suspect in the 1955 slayings.

"I knew it would be a waste of time trying to talk to him about Silas; he would never talk. I decided I would instead try to get information about the Schuessler-Peterson case in a roundabout way. I knew I would have to question him indirectly. When I got him in the office, I told him I had to give him Miranda because I was obligated to do so. I told him we were going to talk to make it look good to the boss," Hamm said.

"We talked a little at first about baseball. I told him that

I had heard a lot about him and that he didn't seem to be a bad guy to me. I was building up his confidence. I asked him to tell me about himself. He responded, 'Well, what do you want to know?' I asked him what did he do after high school? He said, 'I went into the service.' I asked him when did he get out? He said, 'In April 1955.' So I said, 'What did you do then? Go to work for Si?' He said he did, at the Idle Hour Stable," Hamm said.

"I told him when I got out of the service I bought a nice car. He said he did too. I told him I considered myself a car nut and I loved the cars from the fifties. I told him the 1955 Bel Air was one of my favorite cars. I asked him what kind of car did he have. He said he had a 1955 Bel Air. I pointed out that that was one of the first V8s Chevy ever made. I asked him if he had the power pack option. That was the option with a four-barrel carburetor with dual pipes. It would have been a loud car. He told me he had the power pack option with the dual exhaust," Hamm said. "He had no idea what I was looking for. I came away from the interview convinced he was good for the Schuessler-Peterson murders because he worked for Si in 1955, he had a car with a loud exhaust, and we heard he was sexually attracted to boys. It had to be him."

Rotunno was impressed. "So what did you do with that information? Whatever happened to Hansen in relation to the George Jayne solicitation for murder charges?"

Hamm said he told Drury about his interview with Hansen and wrote up a report concerning his suspicions. "The report should be in the George Jayne file, that's where it is," Hamm said. .

After the three shared a little small talk, Rotunno excused himself. As he drove back to his office, Rotunno knew he had to go through the original Schuessler-

Peterson case file and the case files regarding the Cheryl Rude and George Jayne murders looking for everything he could get his hands on about Kenneth Hansen.

"The murders of George Jayne, Frank Michelle Jr., Cheryl Lynn Rude and the three boys are all intertwined," Rotunno thought. "The common link appears to be Silas Jayne and Kenneth Hansen to some extent. Now I've got to talk to Red Wemette to see what he knows."

CHAPTER 9

John Rotunno arrived at the home of a man designated by the Bureau of Alcohol, Tobacco and Firearms as Confidential Informant 33117-34. It was a typical warm Florida morning, shortly before 10 A.M. Rotunno had jetted to Florida just days after his in-depth conversation with David Hamm regarding Kenneth Hansen. He was going to meet with William "Red" Wemette, the man who had telephoned Jim Delorto in November 1991 and was the first person to identify Hansen as the suspect in the murders of Tony, John and Bobby. Which course the decades-old cold case investigation would now take depended entirely on what information Red could provide.

Red lived in a three-bedroom ranch-style home. Rotunno noted that both the interior and exterior of the home were pristine. Red and his housemate, a man named Lenny, were fastidious, and Red was agoraphobic and fearful of leaving his home. No wonder it was so clean. Rotunno heard Red never left his apartment in Chicago when he was an informant for the FBI. But though he sheltered himself from the world, Red wasn't cut off from the outside. He ran several businesses from the home and had multiple phone lines and a fax machine. After the introductions were made, Rotunno and Red retired to the back deck. As with many homes in Florida, Red's deck and in-ground pool were protected by a screened-in enclosure.

Rotunno knew Red was a man with a checkered past who had not innocently stumbled on a dark secret. Red had many secrets of his own. At the time the interview was conducted, there was an Outfit contract on Red's life. The Outfit wanted Red dead for his role in sending hit man Frank Schweihs to jail. Red had been offered a spot in the U.S. Marshal Service Witness Protection Program but took a pass. He had seriously considered assuming a new identity and starting a new life, but after he was briefed on all the rules that went with participating in the program, he decided it wasn't for him. Red turned to the FBI, who helped relocate him. He changed his name but otherwise opted to take his chances on the street. One of Rotunno's first questions to Red was where and when he had first met Ken Hansen.

"I didn't meet Kenny initially. I first met his brother Curt," Red said. "I was introduced to Curt through his sister, Marianne, who was dating my uncle. It was in 1968. I first met Curt at the Valley View Young Adults Klub." Red said he had been introduced to Curt Hansen in hopes of landing a job at the Klub. Curt owned the Klub, which was a roadhouse located in Frankfort, Illinois, a sleepy little farm community about seven miles west of Chicago

Heights, a south suburb of Chicago made famous for its connections to the Outfit and Al Capone.

"Curt Hansen was one mean son of a bitch," Red said. "He was a hit man for Jimmy Catura." He estimated that Curt Hansen was good for seven Outfit-ordered executions. Jimmy "The Bomber" Catura was an enforcer for the Outfit who operated out of the south suburbs.

"There was a mom-and-pop hotel across the street from the Young Adults Klub that Curt and some other Outfit guy extorted from the owners," he said. "They turned it into a brothel. Curt often joked how easy it was to take over the business." On one of his first visits to the Klub, Red said, he was invited to play gin rummy with Curt, his sister Marianne and Curt's brother Ken, who everyone called Kenny. It was obvious the first time that he met the brothers that Curt Hansen didn't treat his younger brother with anything that resembled respect, Red said.

"Curt always called Kenny his 'fag brother' or 'his second sister,'" Red said. "Curt didn't like the fact that Ken was gay. They didn't see eye to eye on a lot of things. Kenny hated him."

Marianne used her influence with Curt to get Red a free room at the Klub, he said. Soon after his initial meeting with the brothers, Ken Hansen asked Red if he liked horses. Red said he knew at that time Ken Hansen owned the Sky High Stable, located in nearby Tinley Park, Illinois, but Ken Hansen also owned a second stable in nearby Hickory Hills that he called the High Hopes Stable. There was a tavern located at the stable in Tinley Park, and Ken operated a brothel on the second floor for his brother Curt.

Hansen grilled Red about his background, he said. Red told Hansen he had been charged in 1967 with selling a machine gun to an undercover federal agent. "He later told me he had a cop he knew named Eddie Nefeld check me out. Kenny told me when he found out I was a convicted felon that he knew he could trust me." Red said he eventually accepted Ken Hansen's invitation to visit him at his stable.

"I'll never forget driving up to that place," Red said. "Kenny was raising Doberman pinschers at the time. They were gigantic dogs. He must have had fifteen dogs there. They surrounded my car and were barking like hell. His wife Beverly came out and pulled them away so I could get out."

Red spent a few hours at the stable with Ken, his wife and two young sons. Red said he and Hansen did not have sex until his third visit to the stable. In explaining the encounter, Red indicated it wasn't something he had willingly participated in. "We had been drinking for several hours. I got so drunk and I couldn't drive back to the Klub," Red said. He passed out and awoke to find Hansen performing oral sex on him.

"The next morning I met Roger Spry," Red said. "He told me Kenny was my 'meal ticket.' Kenny had been having a hard time with Roger, who often got in trouble with the cops."

When he returned to the Klub, Red was told he was no longer welcome there as a guest. Curt Hansen kicked Red out of his rent-free room because he thought Red was now another one of Kenny Hansen's homosexual lovers.

"I had no place to go after that," Red said. "I ended up back at Kenny's stable." Kenny allowed Red to sleep in the barn in exchange for working around the stable and acting as Kenny's driver. Kenny and Roger lived in the trailer while Beverly and the couple's two sons stayed in the house. Beverly Hansen was aware that Kenny slept with young men and desired young boys. "Why she put up with it, I'll never know," Red said.

After he started living and working at the stable, Red was quickly taken into Ken Hansen's confidence and learned of many of the criminal endeavors in which Hansen participated. For example, he was introduced to Silas Jayne's nephew, Frank Jayne Jr. Red claimed Hansen and Frank Jayne Jr. often cruised construction sites and stole heavy-duty earthmoving equipment. Hansen also stole cars. He would use the earthmoving equipment to bury items on his property, including cars. "Eddie Nefeld sold a lot of the hot cars through the Markham Police Department," Red claimed.

It was clear that Hansen and Silas Jayne had been good friends, going back to 1950 or earlier. "When did he first tell you he murdered the three boys?" Rotunno asked. "Do you know an exact date? Go into as much detail about that as you can. Tell me everything, even if you think it's insignificant."

"I wasn't the only person he told about those murders," Red responded. "Roger Spry knew. So did his wife, Beverly, and definitely Curt, Eddie Nefeld and Silas Jayne." Red said his initial conversation with Hansen about the Schuessler-Peterson murders occurred in the house trailer while the two men were seated at a kitchen table. He said they had been drinking, sharing a bottle of Cutty Sark. He said his first conversation with Hansen about the murders was either in the summer of 1968 or 1969, definitely before George Jayne was murdered.

Hansen picked up three boys hitchhiking on a school night and took them back to the Idle Hour Stable. Hansen put the two older boys on a horse and was letting them ride it in the arena while he took the youngest boy back to another room. Hansen said he performed oral sex on the youngest child. Rotunno immediately knew the assault victim must have been Tony Schuessler. When he was finished, Hansen told Red he took the child out into the riding ring and put him on a horse. He then asked the second boy, who Rotunno guessed might have been John Schuessler, to come back into the tack room. Hansen said he was performing oral sex on the second boy when the oldest boy, Bobby, walked into the room.

"The third kid was trying to get them all to leave. The kid said he was going to tell his parents and the police," Red said. "So, Kenny told me, he 'took care of it,' that's exactly what he said.

Hansen further explained that after Bobby Peterson had threatened to go the police, Hansen called out to his brother, Curt, who was also at the stable. Red said he asked Hansen what he and Curt did, and Hansen responded, "What did they teach you in the Marines?"

"I told him they taught me how to be disciplined and how to follow orders. He said to me, 'And they teach you how to kill, don't they? Isn't that the first thing you learn how to do?' He told me that he and Curt choked the three boys to death. He said Curt hit one of the kids over the head with some kind of object, but he wasn't sure what it was. Curt always carried a handgun and blackjack on him," Red said.

Rotunno noted that Red's demeanor was very matter-of-fact. He didn't seem disturbed, distraught or at all affected by the knowledge that he had broken bread, drunk and associated with a man who admitted to molesting children and murdering three boys. Others that Rotunno had talked to about homicide would at least acknowledge, in some small way, the seriousness of taking a human life. There might be an expression on their faces, an inflection in their voices, but it was discussed as an event. Rotunno observed

that Red could have been talking about an everyday occur-
rence. Red, however, was used to the give-and-take. He had
been working with the FBI for almost two decades. For a
large part of his life he had done nothing but associate with
mobsters and federal agents.

The hour was getting late. Rotunno looked at his watch
and noticed that they had been talking for several hours.
"Let's cut it off here for now. I'll be back tomorrow," he
said.

CHAPTER 10

John arrived at Red's home around 9 A.M. the following day. There was no need for introductions this time. Over coffee, Red immediately began providing other details that he learned during the eighteen-month period he had lived with Ken Hansen. He said Hansen had confessed to him on at least a dozen occasions that he had murdered "the Peterson boy" and two other children while working for Silas Jayne at the Idle Hour Stable. Hansen never mentioned the Schuessler boys by name; instead he told Red two of the victims had been brothers. Rotunno thought this was interesting. Perhaps he had forgotten their names? Hansen told Red all of his victims were under the age of fifteen.

Hansen once brought up the slayings with Red while the two were talking about Silas Jayne. Hansen tried to convince Red he should murder George Jayne.

"Silas absolutely hated George, he was very jealous of him," Red said. "Kenny told me he had wanted George dead for years." Red, however, refused to become a hit man. He admitted to Rotunno that at that point in his life there were some criminal acts he was willing to commit, but he didn't have the stomach for murder.

"Kenny handed me an M1 rifle with a flash suppressor to do the job," Red said. "Silas offered me $10,000 to kill George. I turned them down." Red was able to specifically recall meeting Silas on one occasion, because Silas was driven out to Hansen's stable in Tinley Park in a brand-new gold Cadillac El Dorado. Silas's driver was a convicted counterfeiter, a man named Joe LaPlaca, he said.

Rotunno made a mental note that Red had identified one of three men who had been arrested with Silas and charged in connection to the murder of George Jayne. Rotunno knew that Joe LaPlaca had acted as an intermediary between Silas and Melvin Adams. It was LaPlaca who had passed along the payment for the murder of George Jayne.

"Kenny told me to use code words whenever talking about murder. He told me to say, 'The horse was sick and it died.' We were never supposed to say the guy's name," Red said. "I think Si and Kenny were afraid their conversations were going to be recorded."

Red said he figured Silas and Hansen would eventually find someone to kill George. He said he wasn't surprised after George was murdered that Hansen was arrested on charges of solicitation for murder. Red told Rotunno that Beverly Hansen had asked him to accompany her to Cook Country Jail to post bond for Hansen. It was a memorable day. Cook County Jail is a decrepit, dull gray complex of buildings adjacent to the Cook County Criminal Courthouse on Chicago's near west side. Almost every murderer, rapist, stickup man, drug dealer, burglar or auto thief who has been arrested has spent time in Cook County Jail.

Red drove Beverly Hansen to the criminal justice complex, where she posted $10,000 bail to get her husband out of jail. After he was released, Red said he drove Hansen and his wife to Hansen's sister's home on the north side of the city. Red told Rotunno that Hansen's sister, Marianne McGann, was living at that time in the same home where Hansen had been living when he murdered the three boys. The home was located about 8.6 miles from the Idle Hour Stable. Red said he remembered the exact location because he was told that Hansen's father, Ethan Hansen, who had also been in the stable business, committed suicide in the home. Ethan Hansen allegedly shot himself in the head with a .22-caliber rifle sometime in 1956, Red said. Rotunno wrote down the address of the Hansen family home, hoping that he could confirm that Hansen was living not far from the Idle Hour at the time of the boys' murders.

"While we were driving to Marian's, Kenny said he couldn't believe it, but he wasn't even questioned about the George Jayne murder," Red said. "Kenny said the cop only made small talk about cars and never mentioned George." Rotunno knew the police officer who had questioned Hansen was Dave Hamm. Hamm had indeed questioned Hansen about his whereabouts and whom he worked for in October 1955. However, Hansen was visibly shaken from the experience and had literally lost hair over the incident. While he was held at Cook County Jail, he told Red and Beverly, he informed jail authorities that he was homosexual and wished to be segregated from the jail population.

Red then dropped another bombshell. He said Hansen told him there was a third person who had helped him and his brother, Curt, dispose of the boys' bodies in the Cook

County Forest Preserve. During his conversations with Hansen, Red said he was never able to determine if the third person actively participated in the killings or just happened to be at the Idle Hour and witnessed the crime. The third person was a Cook County Forest Preserve employee, possibly a Cook County Forest Preserve Police officer, Red said. Whoever the third person was, he had after-hours access to the parking lot where the boys' bodies were found. The entrances to Cook County Forest Preserve picnic groves, parking lots and bridle paths are closed and padlocked at sunset.

"Whoever this guy was he was able to help them get into the Forest Preserve after hours, where they dumped the bodies," Red said. "He didn't stick around too long. Kenny told me Curt shoved a .38 snub-nose into the guy's mouth and told him he'd blow his fucking head off if he talked to anybody about what happened. Kenny said the guy just about crapped in his pants and soon afterward moved to England. I'd say he probably wanted to get away from Curt."

Red's knowledge of Chicago's underworld ran deep. He knew how Curt operated, and Hansen's story about his brother and the third man was more than plausible. Rotunno knew Red and Curt Hansen had briefly been business partners in a Chicago pornography shop, until Marshall Caifano, one of the Chicago Outfit's most notorious hit men, ordered Curt to give up his ownership in the business. Brutal as he was, Curt Hansen would not refuse Caifano's orders. Caifano was a man to be reckoned with. He was a close confidant of Outfit bosses Anthony Accardo and Sam Giancana. Caifano did most of Accardo and Giancana's heavy work. The tools of Caifano's trade were a shotgun and car bomb.

After the slayings, Hansen told Red, the boys' bodies were moved, using a car from the Idle Hour, to the forest preserve, where they were dumped near a bridal path. Hansen mentioned to Red on more than one occasion that police originally speculated that the boys were murdered near the bridal path. "They weren't hurt there," Hansen said.

Rotunno asked Red once again if he knew the names of any other persons to whom Hansen might have confessed to committing the murders. Red responded that Roger Spry most certainly knew, as well as Hansen's wife Beverly, Silas Jayne, Curt Hansen and possibly Ed Nefeld. Rotunno knew that two of those five persons were dead and he doubted that Curtis Hansen or Ed Nefeld, who was still in the stable business, would be willing to tell him anything about Ken Hansen. Rotunno thought Curtis Hansen was still alive. He didn't know at the time that Curtis Hansen had died just a few days earlier, in a Veterans Administration hospital in Chicago.

Red also provided another useful tidbit of information. He said sometime in 1970, Roger Spry burned down a barn of one of Hansen's competitors in Tinley Park, on Hansen's orders. When Rotunno further inquired as to the whereabouts of Roger Spry, Red told him he hadn't heard anything about Roger in years.

"He could be anywhere. He's probably still working with horses. I don't think he knows how to do anything else," Red said. "I didn't like the guy so I didn't keep track of him," he added. Rotunno knew it would be important to track down and question Roger Spry.

Though Hansen had escaped justice for decades, Red said he had been haunted by a nagging premonition that he would be arrested and charged with the murders. Hansen claimed that in 1955 police had missed an opportunity to link him to the killings based on Curt Hansen having "screwed up" the crime scene. Curt left some kind of evidence on one of the boys' bodies, Red said. "Kenny told me he almost made the headlines himself and spent a lot of sleepless nights worrying police would nail him with this evidence. He said it could hurt him if the police ever figured it out. He said he was very lucky to get away with it."

Red added that during one conversation about the murders, Ken Hansen held up his hand and spread his thumb and finger almost together and added that he "came this close to getting caught."

"Kenny was obsessed that he was going to get caught for the murders," Red said. "He kept telling me it was a botched job. He said he was afraid that someday there was going to be a knock on his door and he would be arrested."

"If he's the right guy, it'll be an ATF agent knocking on his door," Rotunno thought.

Hansen told Red that in the 1950s he was terrified because police had found some kind of trace evidence, possibly either horse manure or some type of grain or fertilizer, on one of the boys' bodies. Hansen feared the evidence could be tied to a particular barn or prompt the police to take a much closer look at the stables near where the bodies were found. Hansen said he removed the boys' clothing because their jeans had become smeared with horse manure during the "scramble" when the three were murdered. Police never recovered the boys' clothing. Hansen also admitted to using adhesive tape to cover the boys' mouths.

To protect himself, Hansen told Red, the back barn at the Idle Hour Stable was torched within a few months of the murders, when police stepped up their efforts to solve the crime.

"Did he ever give you a date or a time of year when this arson at the Idle Hour took place?" Rotunno asked. He hoped there were records regarding this fire somewhere.

Red said he wasn't sure when the arson took place, possibly in 1956. "I guess the fire destroyed the crime scene," he added.

Hansen told Red he had some close calls with the police in 1955. He claimed he had almost been questioned by the police at the Idle Hour Stable. "He told me the police, the sons of bitches, were all over the place. I remember he said, 'They almost got me.' After that Silas made him leave the north side and go to the south side of the city to get away from the police." He said Hansen disappeared from the Idle Hour and started working at a stable Silas ran in the south suburbs, in a town called Hickory Hills. Rotunno figured the Hickory Hills Stable was most likely the same stable where Silas had allegedly murdered some minor Outfit figure in 1947.

"He said it was too hot for him to stay on the north side. He said the cops were questioning everybody and he didn't want to get picked up," Red said. "So he left. He was married, and he and Beverly moved to the south side to avoid police scrutiny."

Despite his brush with police, Kenny didn't stop picking up hitchhikers and molesting them, Red said. "Ken was always talking about having sex with drifters. He called them throwaways, or chicken. He used them for cheap labor and sex. When he got tired of them, he kicked them out."

Rotunno would later learn in the gay community that the phrase "chicken hawk" is a derogatory term used among homosexuals to describe a pedophile. In the mainstream gay and lesbian community, chicken hawks are viewed as child abusers. Rotunno also learned the term "chicken" was used to describe a boy under the age of consent and "chicken dinner" was a term used to describe homosexual sex with a teenager.

Remembering his conversation with Hamm about Hansen's car, Rotunno asked Red if he knew what kind of car Hansen was driving when he allegedly committed the murders. Red said Hansen talked about a 1955 Chevrolet Bel Air he bought when he got out of the service. "Kenny told me he really loved that car," Red said. "It was his pride and joy." Hansen said he bought the car equipped with the power pack option, which gave it a loud exhaust. Hansen, however, had the muffler further modified to make the car even louder. He told Red he often compared the cars he owned to those of a friend of his brother Curt. Curt's friend, who was nicknamed "Big Bob," was envious of Hansen's car, he said. Like Curt, Big Bob was also a hit man.

"He told me he had to get rid of the car after it was mentioned in the newspapers that police were looking for a car with a loud exhaust," Red said. "Kenny told me he learned his lesson about cars when he was young. He said any man who needed a fast car to get away from a job didn't do the job right. He said he needed to make a fast getaway after the kids were killed."

Shortly after Red finished talking about Hansen's car, Rotunno's pager went off. He looked at the number and realized immediately it was his home telephone number. He excused himself and called home. Diane answered the phone, Rotunno knew right away that something was wrong; he could tell by the tone of her voice. His heart sank. It was his daughter Kaitlin, a typical nine-year-old girl who had been complaining recently about severe headaches. Kaitlin is John's middle child. The oldest is

Christine and the youngest is Emily. Diane had taken Kaitlin to a local hospital earlier that day to have her examined. The physicians came back with some very bad news. Preliminary tests had indicated Kaitlin might have a brain tumor.

Rotunno did his best to calm Diane via long distance. He immediately cut off the interview with Red and left, driving straight to the airport. When Rotunno arrived home later that day, he loaded up the family van and he, Diane and their daughter left for the Mayo Clinic. The family would spend a nervous week in Minnesota while tests were conducted. In the end they received good news. Kaitlin didn't have a brain tumor. Instead she was diagnosed as suffering from hereditary migraine headaches and sinusitis.

John and Diane were able to breathe a sigh of relief. It had been one heart-wrenching, emotional roller coaster of a week that the couple would never forget.

Rotunno had a hunch after talking to Red that he was going to solve the case. Up until his conversations with Red, he had thought the case was unsolvable, that he would chase nothing but shadows and fading memories. He knew proving that Kenneth Hansen had murdered three boys almost four decades ago was a longshot, but Rotunno thought it was possible to solve this crime. He wasn't quite sure how it was going to be accomplished, but he had a feeling, a hunch, that the facts were going to fall into place.

CHAPTER 11

John Rotunno took several weeks' leave to attend to his family's needs. While he was out of the office, Jim Delorto assigned an additional agent to the case, one that had experience investigating sex crimes. Delorto transferred Jim Grady from a "gun group" to his arson unit. Grady, who was thirty-four years old at the time, was born more than four years after the murders occurred. He began his law enforcement career in Woodridge, Illinois, where he attained the rank of detective. He had been with ATF for a little more than two years. Before that, Grady had spent four years as an investigator with the DuPage County State's Attorney's Office, where he specialized in investigating sex crimes; especially those committed against children. Grady is a red-haired, freckle-faced Irishman who stands six feet tall and weighs about 210 pounds. He is a marathon runner and well known for his quick wit. He gladly accepted the transfer to the arson group because he was looking forward to a chance to work with Rotunno, a childhood friend of his older brother Tom. Working with Rotunno would be like working with family, Grady thought. The two shared similar roots; both were raised in Niles, Illinois. Rotunno's mother, Jenny Rotunno, had been Grady's third-grade teacher.

Rotunno's earliest recollection of Grady centered on an inconsequential but apparently unforgettable confrontation in the school gym. When Rotunno was in the fifth grade, he was refused entry into the school gym by Grady, who was in second grade. Apparently Rotunno had knocked on the door and Grady, who was inside the gym with his class, opened it and stuck out his head. When Rotunno tried to enter, Grady told him to go away and slammed the door shut in Rotunno's face.

"I'll never forget that he wouldn't let me in the gym. I was shocked he did that to me," Rotunno recalls with a laugh. "That's my earliest recollection of Jim."

While Rotunno was busy attending to his daughter, Grady flew down to Florida to also meet with Red. Delorto wanted Grady to be brought up to speed on the case as quickly as possible. Grady, who was trained to interview the victims of sex crimes and those who commit them, came away from his interview convinced Red's allegations were true but would need to be corroborated by someone else, preferably a witness who didn't carry as much excess baggage as Red. Red's past would be used as a weapon against him. Red would be introduced to the jury as a pornographer. That was a label Red couldn't deny. Using a pornographer as a key witness against a pedophile might be too much for some jurors.

When Rotunno returned from his family leave, the two men compared notes regarding Red. Their meeting took placed in the arson unit located on the third floor of the ATF's Chicago office. It's a good thing the two men were already more than acquaintances because they would be working together in close quarters, with their desks facing each other in a partitioned-off, windowless space about twenty feet wide by fifteen feet deep. There was a third desk, which would eventually be used to stack legal boxes containing the original Schuessler-Peterson case files. On the lone, rear wall of their cubicled work area a bulletin board was tacked up. The two men placed photographs of their wives and children on their desks.

Rotunno and Grady worked well as partners. Their personalities complemented each other. Rotunno, with all of his years of undercover work, had honed his instincts, and trusted them. His intuition had gotten him out of a jam on more than one occasion; sometimes he just knew he was right about a suspect or a theory. Rotunno was edgier than Grady and could convey his anger with just a glance.

Like many lawmen, Rotunno was very good at reading personalities. He often relied on his internal lie detector when sizing up witnesses and informants. Rotunno was also a guarded individual. He rarely shared his opinions or true emotions, and when he did, it was only around those he trusted. Rotunno's guarded demeanor would pigeonhole him as the "bad cop" in an interrogation situation.

Those meeting Rotunno for the first time, especially those who didn't have the benefit of an introduction from someone he already knew, would think he was standoffish. With his jet-black hair, muscular physique, mustache, and icy demeanor, it was easy to see how gang members would buy into the fiction that he was a ruthless drug dealer. But

Rotunno would also unashamedly admit he cried when he saw the crime scene photos of Bobby, John and Tony for the first time. Rotunno's reaction was not unusual, even for the most hardened agents. Crimes against children are the toughest to investigate for police and prosecutors. One has to have a thick skin to investigate those kinds of crimes enough to become an expert in the field. Rotunno, who was already a diligent father, began to follow his children's daily routines much more closely after he was assigned to the Schuessler-Peterson case. He always wanted to know where his kids were and whom they were with.

Grady could view the same crime scene photographs as Rotunno and feel the same revulsion as any police officer or father (Grady had four children—Rebecca, Michael, Christine and Maureen). But Grady had been trained to compartmentalize his emotions. Grady met his wife, Gena, who was a police officer in Woodridge, Illinois, while investigating the drowning death of a child. It was a horrible day for one family, one that Grady will never forget for that reason. But it was also the day he met his wife for the first time.

In an interview situation, Grady would be designated as playing the role of the "good cop." He was quick to crack a joke or make a sly observation. Grady's personality was disarming, but it was a ruse. In actuality, Grady was far more cynical than Rotunno. He was not, for example, as quick to rely on his instincts. Grady's instincts were the same as Rotunno's, but Grady always wanted corroboration. Grady was trained to detect lies. In Grady's book, everyone lied, including victims. A victim of sex crimes will often lie to protect him- or herself emotionally. The trauma of an attack can be so severe that a victim may mistakenly imagine that he or she has done something wrong, so the victim will deny an attack ever took place. Victims also lie because they perceive themselves as "dirty" and don't want anyone to know what happened. As the Schuessler-Peterson investigation progressed, it was going to be Grady's job to draw these victims out. Red had told both men that Hansen had molested dozens, possibly hundreds, of young men over the years. These victims would be sought out because some of them might be able to corroborate Red's story that Hansen confessed to the murders.

Grady's friendliness served him well. In an interview situation, he is perceived as non-judgmental and completely understanding. Strangers open up to him and spill secrets they would never share with others. Grady also rarely forgot a fact or a comment made by a suspect. It was almost as if he had a tape recorder running in his mind and the playback was instantaneous.

When Rotunno returned to work, he and Grady met in Jim Delorto's office to discuss the progress made in the case. The two agents told Delorto they would formulate a game plan to advance the investigation. Rotunno and Grady both agreed that Red had provided key details about their suspect, Kenneth Hansen. Rotunno was hopeful Red would prove to be as good a witness in the Ken Hansen case, should it progress to a trial, as he had proven to be in the FBI case against hitman Frank Schweihs. Grady pointed out that in the previous trial all of Red's allegations against the mobster were backed up by audiotapes. Rotunno and Grady were well aware that some FBI agents didn't trust Red and wouldn't have believed his allegations if his words hadn't been backed up by the tapes. Both men knew they needed to corroborate Red's claims. They needed to find more witnesses.

"We can scratch off Silas and Beverly Hansen," Rotunno said. "I doubt they would have told us anything if they were still alive. I would have liked to meet this Silas character though. He sounds like he was one sick son of a bitch."

Grady suggested they talk to Ed Nefeld and Melvin Adams. "Nefeld probably won't talk either, but you never know. We should definitely talk to Melvin Adams, he cooperated before. There's no reason for him not to talk to us now."

Both men agreed Roger Spry was key to the case. They knew little of him except that Ken Hansen most likely also confessed to him about killing the three boys. Rotunno and Grady had checked all the criminal databases for any links to Roger Spry and had come up empty as to his whereabouts. The agents were able to confirm that there had been a suspicious fire at the Forestview Stable in Tinley Park, Illinois, in 1970 that killed thirty-six horses. That fact added further weight to Red's allegation that Hansen ordered Roger Spry to torch the stable.

Another important arson that they needed to confirm was Red's assertion that one of the barns at the Idle Hour Stable was burned to the ground in an effort to destroy the crime scene and any evidence that could be forensically linked to the boys. The Idle Hour Stable went out of business sometime in the 1960s as development spread to the outer reaches of Cook County. The agents had driven by the location where the Idle Hour once stood and discovered it was a parking lot to an office building located across the street from a hotel near O'Hare International Airport. Where George Jayne's nearby Happy Days Stable had once stood there was now a Baskin-Robbins ice cream shop.

If the agents could confirm there was a fire and probable

arson at the Idle Hour Stable, that would help establish a
pattern of criminal activity on Hansen's part. It would also
give them jurisdiction in the case. One of the tasks assigned to the federal Bureau of Alcohol, Tobacco and
Firearms was to investigate, and assist in the investigation
of, arson, which was considered such a heinous crime that,
like murder, it had no statute of limitation.

"We need to find Roger Spry," Grady said.

Rotunno and Grady issued an arrest warrant for Spry.
They were rolling the dice and hoping that he would be
picked up on some charge somewhere. A simple traffic
ticket could lead to his apprehension. Until Spry crossed a
line somewhere, Rotunno and Grady decided they would
begin to quietly question as many people as possible about
Silas Jayne, Kenneth Hansen and Curtis Hansen.

CHAPTER 12

LATE APRIL TO MAY 1993

As Chicago's spring days grew longer, John Rotunno and Jim Grady found themselves with some time to devote to the case. The agents were just at the beginning of their investigation. All they had were a couple dozen pages of notes from their interviews with Dave Hamm and Red Wemette, and a hunch they were on to something. They needed to find out as much about the boys' murders from the official record as possible. Rotunno reached out to Lt. John Farrell, an old friend in the Chicago Police Department, and requested the voluminous files on the Schuessler-Peterson case. Because Rotunno had worked several drug cases with Farrell, the request didn't raise any eyebrows. It could have; the Schuessler-Peterson murders were one of a handful of legendary cases gathering dust in the department's cold case files. If there was a Richter scale for crimes in Chicago, the Schuessler-Peterson case was of the same magnitude as the legendary St. Valentine's Day Massacre. The case was considered unsolvable.

For decades, the murders had baffled some of the most talented, hard-nosed and experienced detectives in the Chicago Police Department. When it came to murder investigations, Rotunno and Grady weren't as seasoned as some of the Chicago detectives who had busted their chops on the case. Rotunno had investigated about a dozen homicides when he worked for the DuPage County State's Attorney's Office between 1977 and 1982, but he hadn't worked a homicide in over a decade. One of the first murders Rotunno ever investigated involved a college buddy who, in a fit of rage, had thrown his mother off a fifteen-story building. "That was strange talking to him about old buddies from Western Illinois University and then charging him with murder," Rotunno said. Grady came to the case with absolutely no homicide experience. He was strictly a sex crimes detective.

The first place Rotunno decided to begin researching the crime was the public library in Skokie. There he was able to find the *Chicago Tribune* available on microfilm. When he started reading the original news accounts, the stories took Rotunno back to a more innocent era. Though he was only five months old when the boys were killed, the familiar logos and advertisements for businesses that had long ago closed reminded him of his early years. The newspapers offered a snapshot of what nostalgia would recall as a simpler time.

Chicago journalists covering the Schuessler-Peterson murders painted a portrait of a wounded and frightened city. There were stories detailing the arrest and interrogation of many "sexual degenerates," hookers, dope fiends and members of teen "wolf packs" that had fallen under police suspicion. Rotunno chuckled at the term "wolf pack," which was an outdated reference to a street gang. In 1955 the newspapers printed the names of many suspects questioned in the case who weren't charged with any crimes. Rotunno was moved by the somber stories describing in detail the funeral services for the three boys.

There were many stories detailing the investigative efforts. Six months after the murders, the *Chicago Tribune* ran a three-part series taking an in-depth look into the police investigation and the evidence that had been uncovered. The series proved particularly helpful to Rotunno. The first installment, which was published on April 8, 1956, covered what was known about the boys' last hours.

Rotunno read the accounts regarding the last known sightings of the boys at the Monte Cristo bowling alley by Ernest Niewiadomski and his two sisters. After they left the bowling alley, the journalists reported that bus driver Bruno Mencarini picked up the boys and dropped them off not far from a place identified as Henri's Tavern. The writers described Henri's Tavern as "a place frequented by sexual degenerates." In 1955 detectives working the case apparently were also interested in this coincidence. The reporters noted that an "intensive investigation" of the area around the tavern "has produced no results."

Rotunno suspected the phrase "place frequented by sexual degenerates" meant Henri's was a gay bar. According to Red, Hansen was a child molester who satiated his pedophile tendencies in homosexual relationships. Rotunno asked himself if it was possible that Hansen picked up the boys hitchhiking after leaving the bar. Rotunno would later learn from retired police officers who worked the murder investigation that the Chicago Police Department declared a secret war on homosexuals after the boys' remains were discovered. Investigators targeted homosexuals, and many were brought in for questioning. In the days before Miranda, the Chicago Police didn't treat homosexual suspects with anything that resembled respect.

The story went into a few details regarding reports of screams heard on the night the boys disappeared. It said investigators were intensifying their efforts to determine the location of the death scene. One woman living not far from Henri's Tavern told police that on the night the boys disappeared, around midnight her husband went out to buy a bottle of beer. A few moments after her husband walked out the door, she said she heard the screech of brakes and looked out the window. The woman feared a car had hit her husband. When she looked out the window, she saw a westbound car stopped in the street and heard a boy screaming in the backseat of the vehicle. A man in the front seat turned and struck the boy repeatedly. The screaming stopped and the car then sped off. Rotunno realized that the chances of tracking down the unnamed woman decades after the fact were impossible. But he did know Chicago streets and realized that the location of Henri's Tavern was about one and a quarter miles from the woman's location.

The *Tribune* series reported that police efforts to determine the place of death were aided by the volunteer work of scientists at the Standard Oil Company of Indiana in Whiting and the Armour Research Foundation at the Illinois Institute of Technology. Scientists at both facilities were asked to analyze fingernail scrapings taken from the body of Bobby Peterson. The nails on the other two boys had been bitten too short to provide material. The reporters wrote that the analysis of the scrapings had detected several minute fragments of a nonmagnetic stainless steel usually used in aircraft production. The metal fragments apparently could not be explained away, because the story noted "police began an enormous survey of metal working places. They have visited 2,060 shops in a large area." Rotunno also wondered where the steel could have come from. It didn't make sense in light of Red's allegations. The *Tribune* reported that researchers also found material on Bobby's right foot similar to casein glue that contained bits of lime, dolomite, sand and "other materials."

The series reported that Bobby Peterson had played hooky three times in the beginning of the school year in 1955. Instead of going to school, Bobby had spent a day or two hiding in his basement and garage. The school later reported the absences to the Petersons. When questioned about the incidents, Malcolm Peterson told police that Bobby had played hooky because he seemed afraid. The article noted that police had never been able to determine whom Bobby was trying to avoid.

On the Monday before the boys disappeared, the journalists noted a personality aptitude test was administered in John and Bobby's classes. One of the questions posed to the youngsters was, "Do you know anybody who is trying to do you harm or hurt you?" Robert and John were the only students in their class of thirty who answered affirmatively.

Another questioned posed was, "Have you often been punished unjustly?" Robert said no and John said yes. The article described John Schuessler as a less assertive boy than others his age. Eleanor Schuessler told the journalist John's personality had changed as a result of serious injuries he had received in an auto accident. Eleanor Schuessler said John seemed dominated by other boys his age.

One of the series' installments reported that parallel marks found on John Schuessler's back could have come from the trunk mat of a Packard made between 1942 and 1952. The story said police had put together a "check list" of twelve thousand Packards in the Chicago area and were questioning each owner.

The second part of the series focused on the medical clues in the case. Medical examiners found no evidence of sexual molestation, but that had not been ruled out by police. Bits of adhesive gum and skin abrasions found on the boys' faces indicated that tape had been applied and then peeled off in strips. The tape was placed over their mouths, noses and eyes. It may not have been placed over Bobby's eyes. In April 1956 police were beginning to suspect the tape might have been removed before the boys were slain, either before or shortly thereafter. It was also reported that there were no indications the three boys had been bound in any manner.

There was some dispute whether one of the boys (the story did not say which one) had a broken nose and another had a broken jaw. Another controversial matter regarded the so-called "rat bite" or "weird wound" found on John Schuessler's left thigh. Rotunno would read the *Daily News* reports by Jack Lavin and Frank SanHamel at a later date.

The time of death had also become a topic of discussion. The autopsy produced several ounces of partially digested food in the Schuessler boys' stomachs and nothing in Bobby's. The food was determined to be chicken soup which John and Tony had eaten between 1:30 and 2 P.M., before leaving home on Sunday, October 16, 1955. Witnesses saw the boys later that day, between 7:15 and 7:45 P.M., at the Monte Cristo Bowling Alley. The boys were known to be alive beyond the time the food would have normally been digested. Based on the contents of the

Schuessler boys' stomachs, police suspected the Schuessler boys were murdered shortly after they were seen leaving the bowling alley. Bobby Peterson may have been killed at a later time.

The depth of the police effort impressed Rotunno, especially for an investigation in 1955. The *Tribune* story reported that nearly 30,000 people had been interviewed and 1,120 suspects questioned. Of that figure, 319 were determined to be "sex deviates." An estimated 7,000 homes, vacant buildings and businesses were visited by police. Residents living in a large chunk of the city, some sixteen square miles, were questioned in a house-to-house canvas of the area.

The reporters concluded their series with "Instead of waning, the investigation has become much more active in the last two months. Police veterans do not see the pattern of the typical unsolved child killing in this case. They believe the killer, or killers, will be caught, in spite of his care and luck."

Soon after he read the newspaper series, Rotunno struck pay dirt. After hours of reading through news stories and jotting down notes, he was becoming adept at scanning the pages on the screen and moving on quickly. He couldn't believe his luck when he looked at page 2 of the Wednesday, May 16, 1956, edition of the *Tribune*. Centered at the top of the page under the headline "Flames Destroy Big Barn at Riding Stables" was a photo of a building engulfed in flames at night. The caption beneath the photograph stated, "Fire raging thru big hay barns at the Idle Hours riding stables early yesterday."

"This is it!" Rotunno said. "This must be the fire Hansen set to destroy the murder scene."

The photograph is dramatic. It was taken from outside

of the stable, apparently from the other side of a two-rail, possibly white fence that surrounded the property. Set against a pitch-black backdrop, the barn is engulfed in flames. The silhouettes of several doors and windows can be seen. Part of the barn appears to have collapsed.

A news brief underneath the caption reported, "Fire destroyed a hay barn at the Idle Hour riding stables, 8600 Higgins Road near Park Ridge and imperiled 80 horses in a nearby building early yesterday. Cause of the fire was undetermined. Firemen from Norwood Park, Park Ridge, Niles, Franklin Park, River Grove and Elmwood Park fought the blaze under direction of Chief Walter Schoenfeld of Norwood Park."

Rotunno looked at the photograph and recalled the photographs he had seen from the other news stories and was convinced that he was going to solve the crime. He still wasn't quite sure how, but he knew it could be done.

Rotunno didn't realize at the time how unlikely it was that the *Tribune* had even published the picture. In addition to the caption and news brief, a one-sentence blurb underneath indicated that the photograph was purchased from a freelance photographer. The name of the photographer was not mentioned. Some shutterbug got lucky and snapped a publishable photo.

Ten days after publishing the photograph of the fire at the Idle Hour Stable, the *Tribune* reported that the Cook County State's Attorney Office had called a special meeting of the various law enforcement agencies involved in the Schuessler-Peterson case. Also invited to the meeting were the parents of the boys, to discuss the possibility of exhuming their bodies. The story noted that secret talks had been ongoing about a possible exhumation for some time. Coroner Walter McCarron supported the exhumation, as did other officials.

The story pointed out that McCarron was troubled each night by recollections of "the innocent faces" of the victims. He defended the pathologist who'd conducted the autopsy. Dr. Jerry Kearns had been sharply criticized for his work. The story reported that the undertaker who had prepared the Schuessler boys' bodies for burial had found fractures on the boys that had not been reported by Kearns. "I saw those little boys," McCarron was quoted as stating. "No one would obstruct anything which would help in solving this crime."

On May 30, 1956, it was reported that the Petersons and Eleanor Schuessler had agreed to have their sons' bodies exhumed so that further forensic tests could be conducted. The parents asked the Reverend William E. Eifrig, who had officiated at Bobby's funeral service, to talk to the press. "We made up our minds to permit the exhumation because we didn't want it to appear we would impede justice," Reverend Eifrig said for the parents. "But we don't want to be subjected to the harassment we have received since this terrible thing happened."

On June 1, 1956, the boys' remains were exhumed. The Cook County Coroner's Office was assisted in their examination by the Henry Baid Favill Laboratory at St. Luke's Hospital in Chicago and the Standard Oil Company's Research Laboratory in Whiting, Indiana.

Jim Grady also did some research. He was tasked with checking the coroner's reports. He confirmed that the cause of the three boys' death was strangulation, each in a different manner. Tony was strangled manually, John in an apparent choke hold and Bobby with a ligature. In the case of Bobby Peterson, however, his assailant had also picked up some three-pronged rake type of object and struck the boy on the head. The original autopsy had detected the wounds on the left side of Bobby's head, behind the hairline. After the bodies were exhumed, the wounds were measured in detail, and it was determined the person striking Bobby had done so with his right hand. Tissue samples were taken from the five wounds on Bobby's head for microscopic studies at both laboratories.

The studies determined that a substance known as diatomaceous earth, or "black earth" which contains crushed bonemeal, was found in the wounds on Bobby's scalp. The investigation concluded that the rake-like object used to strike Bobby on the head had the material in its prongs and the diatomaceous earth was driven into Bobby's scalp.

This gave authorities in 1956 perhaps their best piece of evidence. The medical experts told police diatomaceous earth was used as filler in certain insecticide powders designed for agricultural and horticultural purposes. Police contacted wholesalers who sold the substance for horticultural use and learned it was used mostly by golf courses, municipalities and cemeteries. The discovery took the investigation in a whole new direction. Police began searching every golf course, cemetery and municipal public works garage in and around where the boys' bodies were found.

When Grady researched the uses of diatomaceous earth, one of the first things he learned was that it is a substance that is deadly to insects and other parasites. The crushed bone in the substance comes from fossils of freshwater organisms and marine life. Ground to a fine powder, under a microscope diatomaceous earth looks like shards of broken glass. This substance is deadly to insects because it pierces their exoskeleton, resulting in dehydration and death. It is totally harmless, however, to animals.

As Grady researched further, he learned that the medical authorities and police in 1956 failed to look into the agricultural aspects of diatomaceous earth. Had they done so, they would have learned it is a substance commonly found around livestock and at stables. Horsemen rub the substance on their animals to treat parasites that attach themselves to an animal's flesh or hair. It is also mixed in with horse feed to clean out any internal parasites in a horse's digestive system.

It all added up, Grady thought. It was there all along but they failed to make the connections.

Rotunno also spent several days at the main branch of the Chicago Public Library checking on the addresses of all the riding stables in the Chicago area in 1955. He was able to confirm the address Red had given for Hansen in 1955 by reading the old phone books kept on microfilm.

Rotunno was growing more perplexed by Kenneth Hansen. He did not comprehend Hansen's alleged sexual attraction to children. Hansen was some sort of sexual chameleon, he thought. He knew Hansen had been married and fathered children. But he also engaged in homosexual acts with men. Rotunno asked Grady about pedophilia one day while the two men were in the office.

Grady said his own experience in investigating pedophiles was that many were married men who had fathered children. In a few cases they had married women who had been divorced and had children. Many pedophiles abused alcohol, he said.

"Pedophilia and homosexuality are two completely different things," Grady said. "The majority of pedophiles aren't homosexuals. If everything we know about Hansen were true, I'd say he's a classic pedophile. He's just participating in homosexual acts to satisfy his pedophilia. I bet a lot of the men he has sex with look young, almost like boys."

Grady explained that there were no absolutes, just generalities when it came to profiling pedophiles. "Many pedophiles are popular with kids and adults they know," he said. "They appear to be people you can trust. They're generally more comfortable around kids than adults."

Pedophiles rarely force or coerce their victim, which is why they prey on troubled kids looking for a parent who will pay attention to them. The pedophile's marriage might be troubled by sexual dysfunction, a result of his true sexual preferences and desires, Grady added. "Hansen might have been abused when he was a kid," he said. "Most pedophiles themselves are victims of sexual abuse. There have been cases where there was a whole cycle of sexual abuse from the grandfather, to the father, to the grandson."

"I bet when we find out more about him we might find evidence he tried to keep his home child-friendly, with toys and stuff lying around to attract kids. The horses he had were certainly kid magnets. That's how he attracted his victims."

After the abuse has occurred, a pedophile will tell the victim that if anyone finds out, he or the child and maybe the child's parents will go to jail. "Sometimes they'll threaten to harm the child, a pet or another family member, like the child's mother or little brother or sister. It's all about manipulation and fear. That's why many victims are afraid to come forward," Grady said. "I'm sure Hansen didn't stop abusing kids after he murdered the three boys. He might have just been getting started. Maybe he's a serial killer too."

CHAPTER 13

SEPTEMBER 20, 1993

The Schuessler-Peterson case was at a standstill for several months. The agents remained hopeful that the arrest warrant issued for Roger Spry would soon bear results. While they plotted their next move, it was decided that one of them should interview Marion Jayne, the widow of George Jayne.

There was an obvious link between the murders of the three boys in 1955 and the murder of George Jayne in 1970. That link took shape in the form of Kenneth Hansen. Neither Grady nor Rotunno was able to determine why the solicitation for murder charges lodged against Hansen in connection to the murder of George Jayne had seemingly evaporated. The arrest on the charges was noted in Hansen's police record, yet there was no indication as to the resolution of the case. Hamm did not recall what happened. One person Rotunno and Grady assumed might know the answer to that question was Marion Jayne. Also, because Marion Jayne had been active in the horse industry for years, the agents hoped she might be able to provide additional information about Hansen.

Rotunno turned to Dave Hamm for help in setting up an interview with Marion Jayne. Hamm had worked closely with Marion and several of her children during the George Jayne murder investigation. The agents were prepared for the possibility that their request would be rejected. After all, Silas Jayne, and Kenneth Hansen to some extent, had put Marion Jayne and her children through an emotional wringer. Any potential conversation about Hansen and Silas could prove difficult for the widow. Hamm told Rotunno he had grown to respect Marion Jayne for the strength and the courage she had displayed following her husband's slaying. "She told me she always suspected George's murder was somehow connected to the murders of the three boys," Hamm said.

When she was contacted, without hesitation, Marion Jayne agreed to an interview and she graciously invited Hamm and Rotunno to her town house in a suburb of Dallas to discuss what she knew.

Rotunno did not walk into the interview unprepared. Several weeks earlier, he had interviewed a woman who was once employed by George Jayne as his rider. The woman recalled events surrounding the murders of the boys. On the day they disappeared, the president of U.S. Steel had held a picnic for George Jayne's employees and other horse people at Cook County Forest Preserve, she said.

She was officially designated as "Cooperating Witness #03" in ATF reports. She told Rotunno that she knew Kenneth Hansen had been a close friend of Silas Jayne since the early 1950s. She also told him that George Jayne had informed her that the rift between him and Silas dated back to 1938 and intensified following the suicide of De Forest Jayne. The animosity between the brothers grew because De Forest bequeathed twenty acres of land and a stable to George. The inheritance apparently freed George from Silas's control.

The woman told Rotunno that George Jayne had informed her that Silas Jayne and Kenneth Hansen were involved in the murders of the three boys. George Jayne dictated a letter to her stating that he knew Silas Jayne was involved in the murders. The woman said she never contacted the police because she feared Silas Jayne would kill her.

Almost three weeks after he interviewed the witness, Rotunno met Marion Jayne for the first and last time. Rotunno's impression of her was that she was indeed a gracious, strong woman. During the course of his conversation, he learned that Marion Jayne had been successful throughout her life. Her competitive spirit became evident at a young age. When she was thirteen years old, she participated in U.S. Olympic springboard diving trials but gave up that sport to concentrate on her other love, horseback riding. As an equestrian, Marion was one of the first riders in the U.S. to jump a horse over a seven-foot fence. Later in her equestrian career she became well known as a show horse judge. Marion's competitive edge proved to be an asset for George. She was a full partner in her husband's business. George Jayne's success and the jealousy that it stoked in the heart of Silas Jayne was due in large part to Marion's strong support and influence on her husband.

In 1965, Marion and George took up flying and both earned their pilot's licenses. Learning to fly gave George and Marion an edge in the horse business. George spent less time driving across the country and more time buying and selling horses. Marion was smitten by the freedom of flight. She continued in her pilot training. In 1969, before George was murdered, Marion became the twelfth woman in the United States to earn her air transport license. In aviation circles, attaining such a pilot classification is considered an honor and an accomplishment. With her air transport license, Marion Jayne was considered a highly qualified pilot, capable of operating commercial aircraft. The combination of Marion's competitive spirit and love of flight prompted her to begin competing in air races. Rotunno learned that she had won more than twenty first place trophies in cross-country speed racing. In 1994, she won a gold medal in a twenty-four-day around-the-world air race.

As the interview progressed, Marion told Rotunno she first met George Jayne when she was eight years old. George, who would have been twelve at the time, met his future wife while she was taking riding lessons at a local YMCA in Chicago. Over the years their friendship budded into romance, and George and Marion were married on February 16, 1944. George was twenty-one years old and Marion was seventeen. The wedding took place while George Jayne was home on leave from the U.S. Army, in which he served in Italy during World War II.

Before they were married, one of George and Marion's close friends said Marion had been invited to take a Hollywood screen test. She was subsequently offered a role in an Esther Williams film. Marion, however, turned down a shot at fame and fortune in order to marry George Jayne.

Marion proved willing to tell Rotunno about everything she knew. She said Silas and George never had a close relationship, even when they were in business together. Marion's recollection was that the feud between them began in the 1950s when Silas asked George to break the leg of a healthy horse for some nefarious reason. George refused and from that point on the two men never saw eye to eye. George was never close to Silas, but he had been close to De Forest, Marion added.

"You have to understand that Si was a very unbalanced man from day one," Marion said. "He was a psychopath. I've never before known anyone with such anger, rage and jealousy. He was an evil man."

In the days following the boys' murders, detectives came calling at the Happy Days Stable and interviewed George, Marion said. The stable was located at Cumberland and Montrose avenues, about one and a half miles from where the boys' bodies were found. Silas Jayne had once owned the Happy Days Stable, but after the chasm widened, he moved out in 1950 or 1951 and started the competing Idle Hour Stable. George Jayne borrowed $90,000 from Silas to purchase the Happy Days Stable, Marion said. She said George was able settle the loan in a short period of time.

"We were popular because we ran an honest business," Marion said. "That's why we were successful."

Soon after the murders, Marion said she had a tense

conversation with her husband. At the time Marion and George were living in a second-floor apartment at the Happy Days Stable. George told Marion that he had learned from a groom named Carl that Silas and three other people were involved in the murders.

Whatever Carl knew about the murders was very upsetting; the groom left the Happy Days Stable for about a week, Marion said. When Carl returned to work, George talked to him and was able to find out exactly what Carl knew. "After he talked to Carl, George came to me and said we didn't have to worry about Si anymore. George was convinced that Silas was involved in the cover-up of the boys' murders and that he also knew who had killed the boys," Marion said.

"Do you remember Carl's last name?" Rotunno asked. "We might be able to track him down."

Marion closed her eyes as if concentrating. "There were so many people that worked for us over the years. I think his last name might have been Smith, I'm not sure. I'm sorry, I can't remember his name." Marion said she had begged George to go to the police with what he knew, but he stubbornly refused. George was convinced it wouldn't have made a difference, because there were corrupt police officers on Silas Jayne's payroll.

Instead, George insinuated the information could be used to their advantage. Silas, who had been threatening George, wouldn't dare touch them because George knew of Silas's role in the boys' murders. George told Marion the letter would protect the family.

After George was murdered, Marion said she searched all over the home and through George's business papers for the letter he wrote about the Schuessler-Peterson murders.

George had been in the habit of hiding things. In an unfinished crawl space of the family home he used to bury coffee cans stuffed with cash. Marion said she eventually found some letters regarding Silas and attempts on George's life, but nothing about the murder of the three boys.

"I've never found it. I looked for it everywhere. He told me once that he decided it would bring shame on the Jayne family name so he ripped it up," Marion said. "But George remained adamant that Silas was involved in those boys' murders and that three other people were involved."

Marion Jayne grew quiet for a moment. Rotunno knew she was lost in her thoughts about her husband and partner. When Marion talked about George, it was clear she still loved him, he thought.

"I know George was murdered because of what he knew about those boys," Marion said. "Silas wanted to keep him quiet. I know I can't prove that, but that's what I think."

Marion also raised the subject of the murder of Cheryl Lynn Rude in 1965. Cheryl Lynn had worked as Silas Jayne's rider but then came to work for George. In 1961, Cheryl Lynn rode one of George's horses to victory at a horse show. Silas was enraged by the victory and accused George and Cheryl Lynn of cheating. Silas threatened to kill George at the show, Marion said.

Marion was familiar with Kenneth Hansen, but she was unable to provide any substantial information about him. She did not know what had happened to the case against Hansen after he was charged with solicitation of murder in connection with her husband's death.

On his flight back to Chicago, Rotunno pulled out his notes and read over what he'd heard during the interview.

He remained convinced that he and Grady would be able to gather enough evidence against Hansen. A conviction was possible, he thought. "But we've got to start getting lucky."

CHAPTER 14

John Rotunno was disappointed. He had hoped Marion Jayne would be able to provide more information regarding Kenneth Hansen. Unlike Marion, Rotunno and Jim Grady weren't totally convinced the murders of the three boys and the slaying of George Jayne were connected. Grady pointed out that Silas and George had been in business together for years and shared many of the same customers. He told Rotunno he needed more than the intuition of a murdered man's wife to accept the theory.

On the same day that Rotunno interviewed Marion Jayne, Grady had interviewed the mother of Beverly Hansen, Kenneth Hansen's wife. Hansen's mother-in-law wasn't interested in talking to Grady and refused to meet with him in person. The interview was conducted by telephone. "I'm an old woman, I don't want to talk about that man," Bernice Carlson said. "I never trusted him. He's one smooth talker."

Beverly Hansen had fallen hard for Kenneth and convinced her parents to give him a loan to start up his first stable, Carlson said. "Beverly told us if she didn't come up with the money she would lose Kenny," she said. Clearly not all had been perfect in the Hansen marriage. A few years prior to Beverly's death, she told her mother that she had found Kenneth in bed with a younger man. Beverly took a photograph of the two and was going to use it as part of her divorce, but she later destroyed the photograph, Carlson said.

Before she committed suicide, Beverly Hansen came to suspect that her husband wanted only her money. Beverly put all her assets in her son Mark's name. Carlson refused to talk about Beverly Hansen's suicide. She had hung herself in her home on July 12, 1989, having allegedly wrapped a white extension cord around her neck and tied the other end to an overhead attic door. She was found hanging in the stairway by Mark. Soon after Beverly died, Kenneth Hansen contacted the couple's attorney and tried to get his hands on Beverly's estate, estimated at $300,000, Carlson said.

"People close to this guy have a habit of committing suicide," Grady said, after filling Rotunno in on his interview with Carlson. "First there was his dad in the 1950s and then his wife. What are the odds of that happening to the same person? We're going to have to take a second look at Beverly's death when we get a chance."

The two men chatted about the interviews while en route to the Cook County State's Attorney's office to meet with Assistant State's Attorney Patrick Quinn. Quinn headed up the state's attorney's Organized Crime Unit, which was responsible at that time for many of the cold cases in Cook County. The agents had approached Quinn a few weeks earlier about a twenty-year-old Outfit murder that Red had told them about. Quinn politely refused to prosecute the case because of insufficient evidence. Grady and Rotunno had scheduled an appointment to meet with Quinn to go over everything the office had relating to the Schuessler-Peterson case and the George Jayne murder.

After a few minutes waiting in the lobby, Rotunno and Grady were escorted into an office. Quinn, a balding, bespectacled, barrel-chested man who stood almost six feet tall, pointed to a mountain of legal boxes stacked on a desk and the floor.

"That's everything we've got on the Schuessler-Peterson case and George Jayne," Quinn said. "I also had them pull the Cheryl Rude case file from the warehouse. I didn't know if you wanted to look at that as well." It was clear to Grady and Rotunno that, although they had already met, Quinn was intrigued that the feds were interested in the cold case. "Do me a favor, don't take anything with you. These are the originals," Quinn said. "If you want copies of anything, we'll have them made." Quinn then left the two men to go to another appointment.

The agents spent the next several hours going over the dusty files. They would eventually read all seven thousand plus pages of the reports compiled by the Chicago Police Department on the Schuessler-Peterson case. While reading, they kept an eye out for the names of Kenneth Hansen, Curtis Hansen and Silas Jayne. The Hansen brothers' names did not appear once in any of the reports. Silas Jayne's name appeared only once.

According to a Chicago Police report written on October 26, 1955, three detectives went to the Idle Hour Stable to question people about screams heard in the vicinity of the stable the night the boys disappeared. The detectives interviewed neighbors Vince Salerno and Stanley Panek, and then went to the Idle Hour to interview a man named Ralph Fleming. Fleming was identified as the owner of the Idle Hour. Rotunno knew from Dave Hamm that this was a factual error. Silas Jayne was the actual owner and Fleming was just one of his underlings. Fleming was described in the report as "very cooperative." He apparently had escorted the detectives through the stable. He told them that the business closed every Sunday at 6 P.M. The detectives wrote that in addition to the night watchman, there was a "huge and ferocious German shepherd" guard dog used to keep watch over the stables.

In addition the detectives interviewed five other persons. Those persons were identified as watchman John Lyda, who said he had heard nothing, and stable hands Lester Beatty, Carl Stout, Jerry Goble and Vincent Dzieski. The stable hands all claimed to have been asleep when the screams were heard.

The name of stable hand Carl Stout jumped out at Rotunno. He wondered if this was the same stable hand that had told George Jayne that Silas and the Hansen brothers were involved in the murder of the three boys. Grady and Rotunno would later try to track Stout down. He could not be found.

Rotunno didn't find Silas Jayne's name anywhere in the case file until he read a report dated December 5, 1955, that had been written by patrolmen designated simply as "N. McGrath and James Kelly." The report listed the names of the persons who boarded horses at the Idle Hour. Silas Jayne's name was mentioned as the person who leased the stable to Fleming. Nowhere else in any other reports was Silas Jayne's name mentioned. Contrary to some of the news clips that Rotunno had read regarding the murder of George Jayne, it appeared that Silas Jayne was never interviewed as part of the police investigation into the murders of the three boys. The agents, however, would later learn that hundreds of pages were missing from the original police case file.

"This doesn't make any sense. They had reports of screams coming from near the Idle Hour and they went out there twice but there doesn't seem to have been a very strong effort to connect the stable to the screams," Rotunno said. "How could they miss this?"

The agents took particular care while reading through the George Jayne murder investigation file. They were on the lookout for Dave Hamm's report detailing Hamm's interview with Kenneth Hansen after Hansen was arrested on solicitation for murder charges. The report was nowhere to be found in the file. There was also little to be found in Kenneth Hansen's arrest file. On the jacket of Hansen's file one of the assistant state's attorneys involved in prosecuting Silas Jayne and his co-conspirators had penned a notation indicating that the case had been dismissed.

"Can you believe this," Rotunno said. "It looks like after they got the conviction of Silas and the others, they dismissed the case against Hansen. Why the hell would they do that?"

"Who knows," Grady responded. "There's nothing in this file. And where's Hamm's report? You'd think a report like that would have set off some alarms. Maybe it got misfiled."

Grady grabbed a stack of the files he had already been through and started going over them again. Rotunno picked up another legal file box and hoisted it onto a nearby desk. There was a layer of dust on top of the box. "Nobody's looked at this stuff in years," he said. Inside the box he found several bound case files pulled together by the Cook County Sheriff's Police regarding the Cheryl Rude murder. When he flipped back the first page, the paper crinkled when it was exposed to the air. The report was in good shape, but it hadn't been handled in decades. Rotunno looked at the other files and determined the box contained several bound copies of the same report, which was several hundred pages in length and contained in three binders.

In a synopsis of the report, Cook County Sheriff's Detective Bernard Singer pointed out the glaring differences between Silas and George Jayne. The report, which was written in 1965, described George Jayne as "an extrovert; [he] has an exceptionally pleasing personality and is able to project an image of polish and good breeding, although there is no doubt that this has been an acquired talent. He consistently wears expensive clothing and presents a rather distinguished and impressive physical appearance."

The report continued, "His general personality traits have undoubtedly played a large part in his professional success as he is apparently well thought of by everyone who has been interviewed in connection to this investigation in direct contrast to his brother Silas who has an unenviable reputation. In spite of the foregoing facts, the contrary notwithstanding, investigation in depth has revealed George Jayne to be not only a liar and a cheat, but a compulsive and almost pathological gambler and professionally and morally unscrupulous." The report concluded that George Jayne showed traits of "sexual perversion" but did not detail what that description meant. Grady assumed Singer suspected George Jayne was homosexual. As the case moved forward, the agents would never develop any information supporting that assumption.

Rotunno read aloud the section describing George Jayne to Grady. He added that he had received no indication from Marion that her husband had a gambling problem or that he was a liar and a cheat.

"It just goes to show you, you can be married to someone and not really know who they are," Grady said with a laugh. The reports also indicated George Jayne had a longtime affair with another woman, a horse judge.

The same report offered a description of Silas Jayne. Of Silas, Singer wrote, "Initial interrogation of this subject and subsequent investigation of him indicates that he may be a pathological liar. He made statements which were easily disproved and which were of no significance whatsoever as far as the investigation is concerned. He even apparently falsified in instances where the truth would have served him better.

". . . In personality this subject is almost a direct opposite of his brother George. He is definitely an introvert, and presents an extremely rough exterior both as to dress, speech and demeanor. He is an extremely large man and his physical condition is that of a man who is twenty years younger."

"I'll say it again, I would have liked to meet this guy," Rotunno said of Silas Jayne. "What a piece of work. Hamm said he could be very charming and had a great repertoire of dirty jokes. But he was no doubt a psychopath who could turn on you in an instant."

The Rude case file contained interesting information and observations. The report, however, could not be accepted at face value. For decades the Cook County Sheriff's Police Department was considered by some to be more corrupt than the Chicago Police Department. The Rude case would need to be looked at more closely at a later date. Since there were several copies of the same report in the box and the day was drawing to a close, Grady decided to borrow the report. "I won't tell if you won't tell," he said. He grabbed the three binders and placed them in his briefcase. "We'll bring it back later. We're going to have to ask for all of this stuff anyway."

As they continued perusing the documents, Grady came across a report in the George Jayne murder file by Chicago Police Lt. John Konen that drew his attention. The report by Konen was submitted to Michael Spiotto, a name Grady recognized. Spiotto, who had retired years before, was well known in Chicago law enforcement circles as a hard-nosed, honest cop. The subject of Konen's report was the relationship between George and Silas Jayne. Grady looked at the title designations on the report and noticed that Konen was assigned to an auto theft unit. Grady asked himself why a lieutenant in an auto theft unit would write a report on a murder outside of Chicago's jurisdiction.

"Konen must have known something about Silas and George," Grady said.

Grady didn't know at the time that Sgt. John Konen was one of the original sergeants assigned to the Schuessler-Peterson case in 1955. The agents would later learn that in 1970, after reading over the press accounts regarding George Jayne's murder, Konen did some research on his own and submitted the report to Spiotto. Spiotto had risen through the ranks to become a deputy superintendent, and had been Konen's supervisor during the Schuessler-Peterson investigation.

Within a few days of George Jayne's murder, Konen pulled out his dusty old reports on the Schuessler-Peterson case and all of the news clippings that he had collected over the years on George and Silas Jayne. He had been keeping an eye on the comings and goings of the Jayne family ever since the three boys were murdered. After rereading his old case files, Konen put together a five-page report theorizing that Silas Jayne had murdered his brother George because George had been blackmailing Silas over his involvement in the murders of Tony, Johnny and Bobby.

"John, you've got to read this report," Grady said, handing the document over to Rotunno. "I think this guy was on to something."

In his report, Konen pointed out that there were numerous press accounts following George Jayne's murder detailing the very public feud between the two men. Some of those stories reported that George Jayne had written letters that may have contained incriminating evidence against Silas. Konen had always suspected that Silas Jayne played some role in the boys' murders. In his report he noted the proximity of the Idle Hour Stable to where the bodies were found and also pointed out that screams were heard near the stable. As well, Konen's report mentioned that the detectives who checked out the Idle Hour failed to interview some unknown stable hand.

A team of detectives was sent out to the Idle Hour ten days after the boys disappeared. The detectives questioned several people at the stable, including a night watchman and four stable hands. In 1955, Konen had assumed that the other sergeants assigned to the task force had been dispatched to fully investigate the reports of screams coming from the Idle Hour Stable. It wasn't until after he read over the Schuessler-Peterson case file following the murder of George Jayne that Konen realized that the task force in

1955 had paid scant attention to one of the most glaring clues in the case: the screams near the stables.

As with Grady and Rotunno, what Konen realized years after the murders when he reviewed the Schuessler-Peterson file astounded him. The team of detectives who had been sent to the Idle Hour came back empty-handed. The agents investigating the case in 1993 had reached the same conclusion as a Chicago Police lieutenant in 1970: "Nobody knew anything. Nobody heard anything," Konen would say decades later. "We should have known better."

"I remember the stables looked good to us," Konen said. "A team of detectives talked to people who lived on the premises and they talked to several stable hands. They never talked to Silas Jayne. That's the thing that always bugged me. Silas wasn't there. Silas was out of town and there was some other stable hand who wasn't around," Konen said.

If he had been supervising the team of detectives that were sent to the Idle Hour Stable, Konen said he would have sent them back to interview Silas Jayne and the missing stable hand. Konen also would have applied more pressure on the employees since the Idle Hour appeared to be the likely spot for the murders.

"With the reports of screams being heard in the vicinity of the Idle Hour, it was one of the most logical places to think the killings had taken place. They should not have sent out one team of dicks, but a half dozen," he said. "If they began to stonewall, I would have told the cops to hold the fort. Get the wheels going to get a search warrant. It might have scared the hell out of them and somebody might have weakened and started talking."

Grady and Rotunno read Konen's summation regarding the two visits to the Idle Hour Stable. "It went nowhere, it just died," Konen would later say. "At no time was Silas Jayne or the missing stable hand ever interviewed by the police."

In theorizing blackmail, Konen relied on Silas Jayne's public pronouncements following George Jayne's murder. Silas told eager reporters that he bore no animosity toward George and in fact had helped set George up in the business in 1955 by giving him a stable. Konen postulated that the gift of the stable—if true—might have really been a blackmail payment to keep George quiet about the three boys' murders.

"The stable hands at one stable might be acquainted with the stable hands in another stable. People have loose lips," Konen said. "Maybe the word got out. If George got wind that Silas participated in the boys' murders, that would be a powerful thing to hold over his brother Silas. Silas would have reason to want to get rid of George from that point on."

Based on Rotunno's previous interview with George Jayne's rider, the theory was starting to look good to Grady and Rotunno. Marion Jayne had told Rotunno that her husband had learned of Silas's involvement in the murders from a stable hand. The rider had confirmed that fact. Unlike Rotunno, Grady didn't have much regard for George Jayne. "He was in business with Silas for years. He had to know enough about Silas to realize he was no good. But he still stayed in business with him," Grady said. Rotunno was of the mind-set that George Jayne was a decent man, the product of a dysfunctional family, who made some inexplicable and very wrong decisions that cost him his life.

The two agents wondered why there was no follow-up to Konen's report in the file. Grady and Rotunno did not know that a few days after reviewing the Schuessler-

Peterson files, Konen had typed up his report theorizing blackmail as a motive for George Jayne's murder and passed it along to Spiotto. Spiotto was intrigued by the report. It also made sense to him, Konen would later say. The two men met to discuss bringing the Chicago Police Department into the George Jayne murder investigation. Spiotto directed Konen to meet with the head of the Illinois Bureau of Investigation, which was the law enforcement agency responsible for investigating George Jayne's murder. Konen was instructed to pass along what he had put together and offer the Chicago Police Department's assistance. On November 12, 1970, Konen met with several IBI investigators, including Mitchell Ware, director of the IBI. The meeting went nowhere.

"Ware didn't even look at the damn report. They said buying into the theory would open a whole new line of investigation and they would have to pursue it. I never heard anything from them again," Konen said. "I'm surprised I'm one of the few people who made a connection like that. A lot of others could have made the same connection between the Schuessler-Peterson murders and George Jayne's murder. But I had the advantage of being involved in the original investigation of the boys' murders."

After reading through the Chicago Police file on the Schuessler-Peterson murders, John Rotunno and Jim Grady found themselves in the position of trying to figure out why dozens of Chicago Police detectives failed to adequately investigate reports of screams coming from the Idle Hour Stable. Looking over the news accounts from that day, the police record and John Konen's report, the two agents were perplexed. They just didn't understand why the Chicago Police Department had failed to investigate the obvious.

"It doesn't make sense," Grady said. "They made all

these left turns. They should have been looking at the stable but instead they went off looking at all the metalworking shops and golf courses. There had to be some other reason for all of this misdirection."

Grady and Rotunno were aware that the boys' murders were one of the first, and possibly the largest, task force type of investigation ever put together in Chicago. Was it possible the left hand didn't know what the right hand was doing? Was it possible this was just an example of a monumental screwup that no one ever caught? The agents could not tell.

For weeks Grady and Rotunno had been in contact with several Chicago Police detectives assigned to the Belmont Area Violent Crimes Unit. During one of several conversations with the detectives, the agents raised the issue. Had the Chicago detectives ever asked themselves about the huge hole in the Schuessler-Peterson case? Had anyone in the Chicago Police Detective Division noticed that the Schuessler-Peterson case should have been solved within a matter of days in 1955? In light of the Chicago Police Department's checkered reputation in the 1950s, what Grady and Rotunno heard in response wasn't all that shocking.

The agents were told that yes, more than a few inquiring minds in the Chicago Police Department over the years had quietly suspected, and raised the possibility, that the Schuessler-Peterson case was somehow derailed back in 1955. Grady and Rotunno were told that at least one high-ranking police officer involved in the case was close to several powerful hoodlums, gambled excessively and was deeply in debt to the Outfit.

At one time, the Chicago Police Department was considered by some to be the most corrupt police department in the country. To this day it has the dubious reputation of

being one of the largest big city police departments in the
U.S. not to have solved one traditional organized crime
murder. As the case progressed, some involved in the investigation would come to believe Silas Jayne influenced
the investigation in 1955. There was no other way to explain the failure of the Chicago Police task force to fully
investigate the screams coming from the Idle Hour Stable
on the night the boys disappeared.

Grady and Rotunno never pursued looking into allegations that the Schuessler-Peterson case was fixed in 1955.
They realized the chance of ever proving such a scenario
was slim. Besides, whoever might have been pulling the
strings back in 1955 was more than likely dead. In the
months ahead, however, the agents would reach a different
conclusion when it came to the Cook County Sheriff's Police investigation into the 1965 car bombing murder of
Cheryl Lynn Rude. Grady and Rotunno would conclude
that the Rude case was definitely thwarted by Silas Jayne
via his organized crime contacts. Those contacts reached
into the Cook County Sheriff's Police investigation, and
possibly the Chicago Police Department's to influence the
case. Once they had wrapped up their case against Hansen,
Grady and Rotunno planned to revisit the Rude murder.

The failure of the Chicago Police Department to solve
the case haunted John Konen. "To this day it really bothers
me that with the flood of information we received, the Idle
Hour Stable never got the attention it deserved. It looked
like the logical area for where the murders occurred," Konen said. "We were trying to muddle along the best we
could. None of us had ever seen a case like this before."

Konen acknowledged that the Chicago Police Department was not a squeaky clean organization during some of
his tenure with the force. He doubted, however, that the

case was fixed. John Lavin, the *Daily News* reporter who was friends with many on the Schuessler-Peterson task force, also doubts the case was derailed by dark design.

Events from the past were clearly dictating how Grady and Rotunno's investigation would proceed. The spirit of Silas Jayne, who had been dead for almost six years, loomed large over the investigation. From the limited number of interviews they had conducted in connection with the Schuessler-Peterson case and from what they knew was occurring in the Brach case, it was clear that many still lived in fear of Silas Jayne and his cohorts. Rotunno was angry that Silas Jayne had cheated justice by dying. He would never answer for the boys' murders in a courtroom. Nonetheless, Rotunno, who was the product of twelve years of Roman Catholic education, began identifying Silas Jayne as Hansen's codefendant in official ATF reports. It was a symbolic measure "just to torment" Silas Jayne's spirit, he said.

CHAPTER 15

Federal agents don't work without supervision. In the Chicago Bureau of the ATF, agents routinely consult with their immediate supervisors, who review their work and make suggestions. In addition to their supervisors, federal agents often work directly with, or report to, an assistant United States attorney. Depending on the prosecutor's management style and the work produced by the agents, an assistant United States attorney may even direct an investigation. It is a collaborative effort between the agent working an investigation and a government prosecutor to build the best possible case against a criminal defendant.

John Rotunno and Jim Grady were confident they could put together a solid case that would result in the conviction of Kenneth Hansen. The agents realized, however, that it would be a purely circumstantial case. The likelihood of

discovering some physical evidence linking Kenneth
Hansen to the crime was remote at best. The case against
Hansen would come down to his word against others. So
far, all they had was Red Wemette's claim that Hansen had
confessed to him that he had murdered the boys. The
agents were hoping human nature had compelled Hansen
to talk about his role in the murders to others. The warrant
that had been issued for Roger Spry had yet to bring any
results. However, if Roger Spry wasn't dead, he'd be
picked up eventually.

The agents were at a crossroads. They needed some indication that their case would be prosecuted if they were
able to gather enough evidence against Hansen. The notion
of going to trial to convict a man of a horrendous triple
murder almost four decades old would give the most gifted
prosecutor pause. The only comparable cases were those
involving allegations against immigrants from Europe accused of being Nazi sympathizers or actual concentration
camp guards who had participated in war atrocities. Before
Grady and Rotunno were going to jump further into building a circumstantial case against Hansen, they wanted to
know if there was anyone in the U.S. Attorney's Office
who had the moxie to take it on. The U.S. Attorney's Office in Chicago has a reputation for issuing criminal com-
plaints that are so airtight, most are dead bang winners. It's
tough to beat a federal rap in Chicago. The U.S. Attorney's
Office there doesn't accept "iffy" cases.

The assistant U.S. attorney supervising the Helen Brach
case was considered brilliant by some legal observers.
Prosecutor Steven A. Miller, who was in his midthirties,
grew up on Chicago's North Shore. Using his expertise developed as a civil attorney, Miller was able to build cases
against defendants that had stumped others.

Grady and Rotunno knew it could be tough convincing Miller to consider prosecuting Kenneth Hansen. But they thought Miller was their man. He had a litigator's swagger about him and the self-esteem of a fighter pilot.

Murder is a crime usually not prosecuted in the federal system unless under special circumstances. Grady and Rotunno thought the only possible angle Miller could use to his advantage was the arson at the Idle Hour in 1956 and other arsons committed or solicited by Hansen. And arson, like murder, had no statute of limitations.

Grady and Rotunno decided to approach Miller one afternoon while he was meeting with Jim Delorto in the ATF offices. Delorto and Miller were sharing a light moment; the two agents could hear them laughing as they knocked on Delorto's door and then stepped into his office.

Delorto was sitting at his desk, leaning back in his chair. Miller was lying back on the couch, his hands clasped behind his head and his legs stretched out. Rotunno spoke first.

"Steve, I'm sure Jimmy has told you about this case we've got going about the murders of the Schuessler-Peterson boys back in 1955. I'm convinced we can nail this guy. It's going to take some work but—"

Miller cut off Rotunno in midsentence. "Get out of here with that case," Miller said with a laugh, waving the two agents off. "I don't want anything to do with it." Rotunno started again, trying to get a word in, but Miller waved him off again. "No way," the crack prosecutor said.

Grady and Rotunno were dumbfounded. They couldn't believe Miller wasn't slightly interested in hearing what they had put together. Some of the same people Miller was utilizing in the Brach case would play key roles in the Schuessler-Peterson case. Kenneth Hansen's name had come up in the Brach investigation. Investigators working that case had learned that Richard Bailey had offered Hansen $5,000 to murder Brach. Hansen refused the offer, stating he didn't murder "little old ladies."

Rotunno and Grady shot each other a glance. They could tell by Miller's demeanor that he wasn't joking. He didn't want anything to do with their case and would never be convinced otherwise. The two men excused themselves and exited Delorto's office. They shared a few choice words between them as they walked back to their cubicle. "We're going to have to reach out to someone in the Cook County State's Attorney's Office," Rotunno said. "If we can't get someone to prosecute it there, we'll go to the Illinois Attorney General's Office."

Over the next few days, Grady and Rotunno contacted detectives they knew in the Chicago Police Department to ask them if they knew of any Cook County prosecutors who had the chutzpah to take on the case. Two names were relayed back to them. One was the name of Patrick Quinn, whom the agents had already met, and the other was Scott Cassidy, who was assigned to the same unit.

Quinn and Cassidy sounded like prosecutors who were willing to give the case a chance. Grady joked that he hoped Quinn had not figured out that he swiped one copy of the Rude case file. The agents called the prosecutors and asked if they could get together for a beer or two. A meeting was set up at an Irish tavern on the south side of the city.

Quinn and Cassidy had no inkling the agents wanted to meet them regarding an old murder case. Quinn thought the get-together was purely a social outing. Joining Cassidy and Quinn were several other prosecutors from their office. The lawmen and prosecutors grabbed a table in the rear of the bar and the suds began to flow.

After a few beers, Rotunno raised the issue. "We've got a case you guys might be interested in," he said. "I'm sure you've heard of the Schuessler-Peterson case. We're pretty sure we can get the guy who did it."

The statement had no effect. Both Quinn and Cassidy, two lifelong south siders, knew little of the Schuessler-Peterson case. It wasn't an unusual admission. Chicago has long been divided along geographic lines. The division has much to do with the city's neighborhoods and the rivalry between Chicago Cubs and Chicago White Sox. True "south siders" and true "north siders" view the opposite end of town as a foreign country and know little, if anything, of their rivals' history and neighborhoods.

If Grady and Rotunno had mentioned the Grimes Sisters case, Cassidy and Quinn would have immediately known what kind of case they were talking about. On December 28, 1956, sisters Barbara and Patricia Grimes, ages fifteen and twelve, disappeared after seeing Elvis Presley's latest movie at that time, *Love Me Tender,* at a south side theater. The girls had been missing for twenty-seven days when their naked bodies were found along a lonely stretch of road in Willow Springs, a south suburb. It was determined they had died of hypothermia. The case was never solved.

Cassidy is considered a no-frills practitioner. He isn't known for being flashy or dramatic in the courtroom. In fact, some would consider his verbal delivery to be somewhat dry. Cassidy is, however, sincere. His closing arguments attempt to re-humanize the victim of a violent crime.

Cassidy was first drawn to law enforcement while in high school. His older brother Jim joined the Chicago Police Department at the age of twenty-two, and Jim often invited his younger brother over when he threw parties for his fellow police officers. At the get-togethers, Cassidy served as the bartender. He was intrigued by the war stories and other yarns told to him by the veteran cops who worked with his brother in some of the toughest neighborhoods in Chicago, and he decided to become a prosecutor based in large part on those stories. After he graduated from college, Cassidy found employment as an apprentice union electrician but also enrolled in night classes at a local law school. Around the time he completed his electrician's apprenticeship, he received a law degree, and immediately went to work at the Cook County State's Attorney's Office.

Grady and Rotunno's recitation of what they knew about the Schuessler-Peterson case piqued Quinn and Cassidy's interest. Quinn was undaunted by the fact that the murder case was almost forty years old. By the end of the night, after Grady and Rotunno told them what they knew, Quinn had agreed to help the agents out, but he wanted to meet with Red face to face to hear his story firsthand.

"I want to talk to this guy to see how solid he is," Quinn said. "We're also going to need something substantial from Roger Spry. That's just the beginning. We'll eventually need more. Red by himself isn't going to make this case." Quinn told the agents he could not get Hansen convicted on the word of William "Red" Wemette alone.

"There's no pressure to solve a forty-year-old murder. Nobody cares, there's literally no pressure to lodge charges in those cases," Quinn would later say. "In fact it's quite the contrary. The pressure is not to charge them, because now when you do, it's going to be a big deal in the press. And unless you win, you're going to look like an idiot, a publicity-hungry hound. People will think you've decided to torment some defendant forty years after the fact. There's no upside in bringing charges in an old case. Unless of course you're convinced you've got the guy who did it."

After meeting the two prosecutors, Rotunno and Grady knew they could work with the Cook County State's Attorney's Office. There was no pretentiousness about Cassidy and Quinn. They were two prosecutors that would see the case to its end.

CHAPTER 16

As the investigation began to gather steam, there was one other person besides Red Wemette who could give John Rotunno and Jim Grady an inside glimpse into the world of Silas Jayne and Kenneth Hansen. That person was Melvin Adams, the hit man with a conscience who couldn't kill George Jayne. Like Red's, Adams's life was intricately enmeshed with that of Silas and George Jayne. Rotunno occasionally called Adams to confer on various aspects of the case.

Before he had earned his fifteen minutes of fame in the eyes of Chicago's media, Melvin Adams was known only by a few people. He had few friends and lived a mundane life. Melvin had his dreams, though. He saw himself as a tough guy and wanted others to think the same. Adams's relationship with Silas Jayne began one afternoon in November 1969. Adams had stopped by a restaurant in Markham, a south suburb of Chicago, to say hello to his girlfriend Patricia Farmer. Patricia worked at the eatery as a waitress. While Adams was reading a newspaper and drinking a cup of coffee at his favorite booth, he was disturbed when a man named Edwin Nefeld slid in across from him.

Adams knew Nefeld was the chief of detectives in the Markham Police Department. He expected he was about to receive a stern talking-to regarding a run-in he'd had a week or two ago. Adams had a reputation for his temper. Otherwise calm and quiet, on occasion Adams would get himself into a situation and lose control. Adams's most recent cork popping incident involved his brother's ex-girlfriend and her new boyfriend. After the young lady had broken up with Adams's brother, she began seeing another man. Adams's brother was upset over the failed relationship. He asked Melvin to accompany him to her apartment to retrieve a few personal belongings. At the apartment the two brothers exchanged words with the new boyfriend. The new boyfriend struck a nerve with Adams and Adams lost his cool and pulled a gun on the man. Word of the incident traveled fast.

Though he carried a badge, many people knew that Edwin "Eddy" Nefeld was a wolf in sheep's clothing. He was one of Silas Jayne's trusted companions. Nefeld figured Melvin Adams was the kind of guy Silas Jayne had been looking to hire to kill George Jayne.

"He wanted to talk to me," Adams told Rotunno years after the fact. "He said, 'Mel, I've got some pictures of you holding a machine gun.' Now, I don't know where he got that. I know I used machine guns when I was in the Army. I don't remember handling one outside of the service. But I was a little wild in those days."

Before Adams could respond, Nefeld continued, "I know you're not one hundred percent upright. And you know I'm having a hard time. I've got a problem. I need a hit man."

Adams, who had been raised by religious parents and considered his upbringing idyllic, was immediately interested. Despite his parents' best efforts, he had led a troubled life. He was found to be a juvenile delinquent for skipping school. He joined the U.S. Army but was dishonorably discharged and served a brief sentence in Leavenworth for forgery. Though he was interested, Adams kept his emotions in check. Nefeld continued trying to convince Adams to accept the job. He told Adams that Silas Jayne had already been involved in a few murders and could be trusted.

"Have you ever heard about the Schuessler-Peterson case? The three boys who were found murdered in the woods?" Nefeld asked. Adams responded that he had heard about the crime while serving time in Leavenworth.

"Those kids were killed at Si Jayne's stable," Nefeld said. "The bodies were later dumped in the woods. You can trust Silas, he's been in these situations before. They tried to pin the murders on him back in 1955, but who knows what happened."

Nefeld continued. He said that Silas had been involved in the car bombing murder that claimed the life of Cheryl Lynn Rude in 1965. He also said Silas was involved in the kidnapping and slayings of three girls who had disappeared from the Indiana Dunes the same summer Rude was murdered. As well, Nefeld boasted that Silas Jayne had murdered a man named Frank Michelle Jr. at his home that January.

"Silas shot the guy through his front door," Nefeld said.

"The guy tried to run away but Si caught him. He shoved the gun into his mouth and blew his brains out. He takes his killing very seriously."

Adams had often wondered what it would be like to kill a man, and the notion of becoming a professional killer seemed exciting. He told Nefeld he was interested. "I wanted to see if I could do it. I just wanted to see if I could cross that line and kill a man," Adams said.

Several days later, Adams met with Silas Jayne, Nefeld and Joe LaPlaca at a tavern in Dixmoor, another south suburb. He told Rotunno he remembered Silas Jayne as a happy-go-lucky, jovial sort of a fellow who didn't seem capable of hurting anyone. "He had a happy smile on his face all the time. But he had the type of eyes that looked through you. You knew you shouldn't bullshit him," Adams said. "But I did anyway. He asked me if I had ever killed anyone. I told him I had."

Adams, of course, had never killed anyone. But he thought he could do it. "I've got everything you need, you know, a string of lawyers, money, anything," Silas told Adams. The grizzled horseman went on to say that he had been trying to kill George for ten years but had been unsuccessful. Silas then offered a few tips to Adams on how to carry out the murder. "Shoot him with a machine gun on the expressway while he's driving down the road, I can get you a gun," Silas said. "Whatever you do, don't leave any witnesses. If you have to kill his wife or his kids, do it." Nefeld and LaPlaca also offered some advice on using a car bomb.

"You need to use at least six sticks of dynamite to make sure the job's done right," Adams was told. "That's how many were used when we tried to get George the last time but that girl got killed instead." From the tone of the con-

versation, Adams got the impression that Silas Jayne, Nefeld and Joe LaPlaca had been friends for some time.

Adams accepted a $20,000 offer to kill George Jayne.

He told Rotunno that Silas provided him with rental
cars and weapons and paid for all of his expenses. For several months Adams followed George Jayne to horse shows
around the country and on one occasion right into his
home. After a few weeks, Adams learned he wasn't mean
enough to kill George Jayne. He had seen George with his
family and his friends. George seemed like a nice guy, he
recalled.

"I was at his house one time and I watched him walk in
the front door," Adams said. "I followed him. I went all the
way up to the door, opened it and walked in. I had the gun
in my hand. There was a dog sitting there. It was a big dog,
a Labrador. The dog didn't do a thing. It didn't bark, it
didn't jump up. It just looked at me and wagged its tail. I
closed the door and I left. I could have gone in there and
killed him but I couldn't do it," Adams said.

It wasn't the first time Adams had had the opportunity
to kill George Jayne and couldn't bring himself to squeeze
the trigger.

"In New Orleans I was right behind him. I wasn't two
feet from him. He was by himself. He was walking out to
his car, from the horse show. It was in the parking lot, it
was dark. I had the gun in my pocket, a .38-caliber,"
Adams said. "I thought of the consequences for myself."

After a few weeks without any result, Adams needed an
excuse. Silas was starting to ask questions. He didn't know
why George wasn't dead. Adams told Silas his brother
took precautions and was an elusive target. Adams never
told Silas, who was paying him about $300 a week, that he
didn't have the stomach for the work. "I had a couple of

opportunities but I just couldn't do it," he told Rotunno. Frustrated by the lack of progress, Silas suggested Adams get an accomplice to help him commit the crime. Silas increased the fee to $30,000. After the fee was increased, Adams asked a coworker, Julius Barnes, if he was interested. Barnes agreed to help Adams carry out the murder.

On October 28, 1970, Adams and Barnes drove to George Jayne's home in Inverness. Adams, who usually drove a rental car provided by Silas, drove his own car that night. That proved to be his mistake.

"I just saw Barnes go up to the house. After a few minutes I heard a muffled shot. I had the hood of my car up, like I was working on it. A kid passed on a bicycle. He got close to me. I was worried about the kid on the bike," Adams said. "I heard that pop and I figured that was it. George Jayne was dead. I got in the car. Barnes ran back and he got in the car. And then I said, 'Did you take care of it?' He said, 'Yeah. It's all done. It's okay. I aimed right in the center of his chest." Adams said the two men then drove back to Chicago in silence after committing the slaying.

Adams received his payment for the crime a few days later. He paid Barnes $10,500 for acting as the triggerman.

The boy on the bike was able to give Dave Hamm and other IBI investigators a description of the car and a partial license plate number. The information eventually led investigators straight to Adams. For several weeks Hamm and his colleagues followed Adams, shadowing his every move. Adams was worried. He knew it was only a matter of time before he was arrested or Silas Jayne had him murdered to keep his mouth shut. When Marion Jayne approached Adams and his girlfriend and showed them a bag containing $25,000 cash and then begged the couple to confess to the authorities, Adams found the guilt unbearable. He caved in and told Hamm everything about the murder plot.

"I was in a bad place. I just didn't know who was going to get me first, the police or Silas Jayne," Adams said.

Adams, Nefeld, LaPlaca and Silas Jayne were eventually charged with George Jayne's murder. Adams was granted immunity and testified against the others. As a result, Barnes was sentenced to fifteen to thirty-five years on a conviction of murder; Silas Jayne and LaPlaca were sentenced to six to twenty years on conspiracy to commit murder. Nefeld, who pleaded guilty before the trial started, was sentenced to three to ten years in prison.

After turning state's witness, Adams told the Cook County prosecutors handling the case everything he knew about Silas Jayne. Adams told Rotunno he informed assistant Cook County State's Attorney Nicholas Motherway about Silas Jayne's involvement in the Schuessler-Peterson murders, the Rude murder, the execution of Frank Michelle Jr. and the kidnapping and murder of the three young women from the Indiana Dunes. Based on Adams's recollections, Rotunno contacted Motherway, who had retired from the Cook County State's Attorney's Office to private practice, to ask him about Adams's claims and also in regards to the disposition of Kenneth Hansen's solicitation for murder case. Motherway, who had gone toe to toe with Silas Jayne's defense attorney, F. Lee Bailey, proved to be no help to Rotunno. He told the federal agent that the George Jayne trial was so long ago he couldn't accurately recall anything Adams had said.

Adams told Rotunno that to his dying day he would regret his participation in the slaying, especially since it occurred on George Jayne's son's sixteenth birthday. The slaying had a profound effect on everyone who loved

George Jayne, especially his son. The murder derailed the young man's life, leading him down a path of drug and alcohol abuse, though he eventually set his life straight through his religious faith.

After testifying against the others, Adams told Rotunno he was reminded by Hamm that he was entitled to the $25,000 reward that had been offered by Marion Jayne for information leading to her husband's killer. "I didn't want it. I didn't deserve it. I should have done the right thing and gone to the state's attorney when Nefeld first approached me," Adams said. "I didn't deserve a dime."

As the investigation against Hansen progressed, Rotunno would find himself occasionally telephoning Adams to ask him about a witness or a fact involved in the case. Rotunno came to appreciate Adams's honesty. "He's the friendliest hit man you'll ever meet," Rotunno would tell his colleagues.

CHAPTER 17

Roger Spry looked up from the bench where he had been sleeping. His head was pounding. He had been arrested the night before following a bar fight in Phoenix, Arizona. Spry, who had been sleeping off the drink in another cell, had been roused moments before and taken to an interrogation room at the Maricopa County Jail. It was about noon. A deputy told him that he had some visitors. Spry couldn't imagine who was coming to see him; maybe it was his girlfriend Colleen.

Spry wiped his eyes. Standing in front of him were four men. Four very serious looking men. Spry didn't know who they were, but he knew they weren't there to talk about the scuffle at the bar.

"Hello, Roger," the tallest man said. "My name is Assistant Cook County State's Attorney Scott Cassidy. With me are ATF agents John Rotunno and Jim Grady and Chicago Police Detective Lou Rabbit. We've been looking for you for some time. We'd like to ask you a few questions about an old friend of yours. A man named Kenneth Hansen."

So began the interview that would determine if the case against Kenneth Hansen would proceed or stop dead in its tracks. Taking one look at Spry, Cassidy wasn't about to bet the ranch that he was going to be able to provide any useful information. Spry was a sorry sight. Sprawled across the uncomfortable looking bench in his dusty jeans, cowboy boots and dirty T-shirt, bleary-eyed and unshaven, Spry looked like one very tired, broken-down cowboy.

The night before, Rotunno had received a telephone call from ATF Intelligence Analyst Deborah Mero. Mero informed Rotunno that she had just received word that Spry had been picked up on the warrant that Rotunno had issued. Rotunno got on the phone to his colleagues right away and they booked the next available flight.

Following their interview with Red Wemette, Cassidy and Quinn had concluded that he was providing truthful information, but like everyone else involved in the investigation, they knew Red's allegations were weak without corroboration. Cassidy viewed Red as he would any other confidential informant. Everything Red said was valuable, but it needed to be supported by direct evidence or another witness. Red also told the two prosecutors he was certain Roger Spry knew that Hansen had murdered the boys. The prosecution team wasn't concerned that Red and Spry were collaborating. By all accounts they hated each other; the two men had not talked in years. Unless Spry was found, Quinn and Cassidy were not very confident that enough evidence would ever be pulled together to charge Hansen. That had now changed.

Cassidy's mention of Ken Hansen's name hung in the

air briefly before Spry grunted and sat up. "I'll tell you everything I know," Spry said. "I've known Kenny Hansen for years. He was like a father to me."

Spry didn't hold anything back. Within minutes, he had confirmed the same allegations raised by Red. Yes, Spry said, Hansen had admitted to him that he murdered three boys at a stable owned by Silas Jayne. During the course of the interview, Grady took down Spry's statement. When the interview concluded, Spry read over Grady's handwritten statement and signed the document.

"When I was ten years old my family moved to Chicago from West Virginia," Spry drawled in a soft voice tinged with a twang. He went on to say that the local coal mine had shut down and his father lost his job. Spry was the oldest of seven kids. When they moved to Chicago, Spry's mother, a former prostitute, found work as an exotic dancer at a local strip club in Calumet City, a south suburb of Chicago well known for its sin strip of whorehouses and strip clubs. Spry's father, an alcoholic, worked as a janitor.

Spry said he had come to know Hansen while working at a relative's gas station in Chicago. A man named Wally Lasowski would gas up a trailer that he used to haul ponies leased from Ken Hansen. Wally asked Spry one day if he would like to lead the ponies around for him. "I said sure, I loved horses," Spry said.

Spry worked for Wally on the weekends. "We'd take the ponies out to the suburbs and people would pay to let their kids ride on them." Spry would go with Wally to bring the ponies back to Kenny's stable. On one of those trips he met Ken Hansen. Eventually Spry started working for Ken Hansen too, he said.

"One day my mother up and left," Spry said. "She took my two younger brothers and dropped me off at my uncle's gas station. I didn't know it then but she left for good. The other kids were split up among my relatives in Chicago."

Hansen approached Spry one day and asked him if he would like to come live with him, his wife Beverly and his two sons. Spry agreed, as did his father.

On his first night living with Hansen, Hansen tried to molest him, Spry said. When Spry fought off the attack, Hansen ordered the tearful, abandoned child to sleep in the kennel with his dogs. The stench of feces and urine prompted the young boy to prop open a window for fresh air. Hansen put a little cot in the room, and the kennel became Spry's bedroom for the next four years. As Spry continued his tale of hardship, the four lawmen occasionally shot each other a glance. The man's story was heartbreaking, but Spry, like many longtime victims of abuse, recited the facts with little emotion.

Spry said his typical day at the stable was far from ideal. Up at the crack of dawn, he had to feed and water about twenty horses and another twenty ponies and clean out their stalls before he had to tend to the kennels that contained up to thirty dogs. Spry was given only food, clothing and a bed in the kennel for all of his work.

"When I was about eleven years old, Kenny began to molest me," Spry said. The first successful attack occurred after a friend of Hansen's started beating Spry, he said. The man in question appeared at Hansen's home one evening and angrily began asking for Spry, claiming that the boy had been bad-mouthing Hansen.

Huddled in his room, Spry could hear the commotion. He heard the man and Hansen arguing loudly right outside his door. He was terrified. Spry stacked up some cases of empty soda pop bottles by the door hoping the flimsy barricade would stop the man from getting inside the room.

The barrier didn't hold. The door flew open with a loud crash and the soda bottles came tumbling to the floor and many shattered. The man barreled his way into the room and began striking Spry. Hansen ran into the room and pulled the bigger man off him. As Hansen dragged the man from the room, Spry fled and wandered around the woods near Hansen's stable for several minutes. Spry wanted to run away, and in the coming years he would do so often. But he had no place to go. So he returned to his room and curled up into a ball under the covers of his bed. He began to cry.

A short time later Hansen returned to the room to console Spry, and he sexually assaulted the youngster for the first time that night. The attacks continued for the next seven years, Spry said.

Spry had been thrown deep inside a pedophile's web. He was an abandoned boy with no place to turn. Grady saw the attack on Spry from Hansen's friend as a setup. Hansen wanted the boy to view him as his protector, a common ploy used by many pedophiles. "Every day of Spry's childhood in Ken Hansen's home was worse than the one before it," Cassidy thought.

Spry told the lawmen that when he was fifteen or sixteen years old, Hansen admitted to him once that he had murdered three boys in 1955. Spry provided as much information as he could recollect. When asked if he had ever told anyone else about Hansen's confession, Spry said he had told his girlfriend once that he had been molested by Hansen and that Hansen had admitted to him he killed the three boys.

During the time he lived with Hansen, Spry said Hansen often picked up young men hitchhiking along the road. Hansen would ask the young men if they liked horses, needed a place to stay or were hungry. Hansen would offer them a job and take them back to his stable, where he would molest them.

"We'd pick them up hitchhiking or they'd come out to the stable to go riding, and we'd tell them if they would help us around the barn cleaning the stalls or feeding the horses, we'd let them go riding for free," Spry said.

"What would Ken Hansen typically say to a boy that he picked up hitchhiking to have him come back to the stable with him?" Cassidy asked.

"He'd say, 'Do you like horses? You know if you come out and work at the barn, we'll let you ride for nothing,'" Spry said.

"Do you know if Ken Hansen ever had sex with these boys that he brought out to the stables?" Cassidy asked.

"He had sex with all of them," Spry said. "There were dozens of them. Maybe hundreds. He did that all the time."

After a few more questions, the interview ended. Before they left, Spry said he would talk to them about Hansen at any time. "If there's anything else you want to know, just ask," Spry said.

On the way back to their hotel, it was decided a follow-up interview would be necessary to ask Spry about his involvement in the arson that destroyed one of Hansen's competitors' barns. The lawmen and prosecutor thought they had struck pay dirt. When he got the first opportunity, Cassidy called Quinn to let him know that Spry had corroborated everything that Red had said. Now they had two witnesses who could testify that Hansen had admitted he murdered the boys.

Two days later another interview was conducted. Once again, Spry was very matter-of-fact, this time regarding his involvement in an arson that put one of Hansen's competitors out of business.

"It was back in 1970. I was living with Kenny and his family at the Sky High Stable in Tinley Park. During the summer of that year Kenny asked me and another guy to burn down the Forestview Stable. He told me he wanted to put them out of business, they were hurting him," Spry said. On August 18, 1970, Spry and his companion went to the Forestview Stable. It was early in the morning. The two men stole into the barn, where they found a pickup truck. They took some clothes and rags and put them behind the seat of the truck, near the gas tank, and then set the rags on fire and pushed the seat back. Spry and his companion walked out of the barn and locked the door behind them. As they were walking back to Hansen's stable, they heard the whine of fire sirens. The resulting fire burned the barn to the ground and killed thirty-six horses. At the time of the arson Ken Hansen was out of town on business.

"When Kenny heard about the fire, he said, 'That's fucking great. Now I'll get some business around here.'" Spry said. Hansen paid Spry $300 for setting the blaze. Spry didn't know what Hansen paid the other man. During the course of Spry's interview, Grady wrote down his statement. At the end of the interview, everyone in the room, including Spry, signed the statement.

Spry was then informed he was going to be charged with the arson and he would be extradited back to Illinois. He was told that if he were willing to testify against Hansen, prosecutors would inform the judge at sentencing that Spry had helped them with another criminal case. Cassidy made no promise that Spry would receive a lenient sentence. Spry agreed to the arrangement.

Before the agents and prosecutor left town, they called on Spry's girlfriend, Colleen Quinn, to see if she knew anything about Kenneth Hansen. Colleen Quinn told the group she had met Spry while working in a bar in Noblesville, Indiana, a town located just northeast of Indianapolis. The two started dating in August 1992, and began traveling throughout the South and Southwest.

One day while on the road, Spry told Colleen that he had been abandoned by his mother when he was a boy and eventually went to live with a man named Ken Hansen. Colleen said she knew it was difficult for Spry to talk about his past. During the conversation, Spry told Colleen about stealing a few bucks from Hansen by pocketing fees paid by riders and being warned by Hansen that he could "end up like the Peterson boy."

The case against Kenneth Hansen was getting stronger. What Quinn and Cassidy had once considered a long shot at best, was now becoming a circumstantial case that they hoped to improve by finding more witnesses.

CHAPTER 18

With Roger Spry's statement, the case against Kenneth Hansen was becoming more viable. The prosecution team now had two witnesses to whom Hansen had admitted killing the boys. As the case progressed, more witnesses were found who supported Spry and William "Red" Wemette's statements. Cook County State's Attorney Jack O'Malley, the first Republican officeholder in heavily democratic Cook County in a decade, directed Pat Quinn to begin pulling together all the loose ends on the case in anticipation of charging Hansen. O'Malley's office had its hands full with several hot cases. Another team of investigators was preparing to file charges against a local Democratic congressman who was facing allegations of having sex with an underage campaign worker.

O'Malley, who didn't micromanage his prosecutors,

trusted the recommendation of his assistants and ultimately approved charges against Hansen. He would later say he was well aware of the public relations risks involved in prosecuting an old case but was bound by duty to pursue the matter once sufficient evidence had been gathered to support a conviction.

"There is no statute of limitations on murder cases," O'Malley said. "In law enforcement many times the police and prosecutors have a pretty good idea who committed a particular murder, but lack the evidence to prosecute a case, much to the chagrin of a victim's family. That happens more often than you like. We had to prosecute this case to send a message to others who have committed a murder and got away with it that you can't rest even after forty years."

O'Malley was four years old when the boys were murdered, and he remembered hearing about the slayings when he advanced to the upper grades in grammar school. "This crime had a profound effect on many people," O'Malley said. "It changed the city."

By late July and early August 1994, the agents had interviewed a little more than a dozen persons. The investigation was still under wraps. Grady and Rotunno had to proceed cautiously. Hansen and other members of the Jayne Gang had friends throughout the horse industry. The investigators didn't want to tip off Hansen that he was the target of their probe. As the investigation proceeded, Rotunno and Grady consulted frequently with Quinn and Cassidy to discuss different aspects of the case.

The agents needed to corroborate two important elements. First, that the murders occurred at the Idle Hour Stable and, second, that Kenneth Hansen worked at the Idle Hour at that time. With the help of Deborah Mero,

Grady and Rotunno were able to find and interview several people who were willing to testify that Hansen was a close friend of Silas Jayne and had worked at the Idle Hour when the boys were killed. The agents also tracked down witnesses who were living near the Idle Hour Stable on the night it was assumed the boys were slain. Grady and Rotunno were racing the clock. Many of the witnesses would be in their sixties and seventies.

Grady first interviewed Delores Wisilinski at her home in suburban Chicago. Wisilinski was one of several witnesses who reported to police in 1955 that they heard screams on the night the boys disappeared. Wisilinski said on the night of October 16, 1955, she and her husband had gone to visit her mother-in-law for Sunday dinner. The couple, who lived more than a mile from the Idle Hour Stable at that time, did not return home until 11 P.M. After putting their children to bed, Wisilinski went into the living room of their home, where she noticed that her husband had fallen asleep while watching television. While preparing to go to bed, Wisilinski said she heard a little boy scream, "No, no!" and then heard an adult man's angry voice grunt, "Get in there." Wisilinski said she looked out a window and saw a car parked just a short distance from her home. She told Grady she thought the car had been already running, because she didn't hear it start up. The driver of the car gunned the auto's engine and the vehicle drove away.

"I should have called the police right away. But I didn't think it was anything important at the time," she said. "After they found those boys' bodies, I told a few friends at work and they told me I should call the police, so I did."

Grady then tracked down and conducted a telephone interview with Hetty Salerno. Salerno, who was living in

Arizona, was the wife of the late Vince Salerno, who, along with a neighbor named Stanley Panek, had reported to police in 1955 that they heard screams coming from the Idle Hour Stable. In October 1955, the Salerno and Panek families resided near the Idle Hour Stable. Mrs. Salerno told Grady she recalled that police interviewed her husband after he reported the incident.

"I remember that evening very clearly. I had never heard screams like that before," Salerno said. She spoke in a British accent and told Grady she was from Liverpool and had driven an ambulance in London during the Blitz. Salerno said during the war she had never heard such bloodcurdling screams as she did on that night. "It sounded like someone beating the hell out of a child," she said.

Salerno said she had been sitting outside with her husband in a screened in breezeway between their house and their garage enjoying some quiet time together when they heard the screams. The Salerno home faced west, toward the Idle Hour Stable, and the screams came from that direction. The screams started up, then died down and then started again and stopped. In addition to her husband, Salerno said Stanley Panek was outside his home at the time and heard the same thing. "We didn't have anyone in the neighborhood who beat their children. It definitely came from the stable," Salerno said.

Leaving no stone unturned, Grady then went out to the area where the Idle Hour once stood to beat the bushes for any possible witnesses. The stable was long gone; what had once been the center of Silas Jayne's criminal empire had faded from the landscape many years ago. Where the investigative team suspected the boys' murders had taken place was now a parking lot. Grady canvassed some nearby homes and, much to his surprise, found Violette and

Leonard Sable, a couple who had been living in the area since prior to 1955.

The Sables told Grady they remembered the Schuessler-Peterson murders because they recalled police officers searching an empty field across from their home and adjacent to where the Idle Hour Stable had once stood. The Sables said on the night of October 16, 1955, they did not hear any screams coming from the direction of the stable. The Sables said they and other couples from the neighborhood had been at a barbecue at the home of Stanley Panek. However, the Sables recalled that Stanley Panek had told them the next day that he and the Salernos had heard screams coming from that area. The Sables also told Grady that Stanley Panek had died several years before and that his wife had remarried and moved from the area. The Sables didn't recall Mrs. Panek's new name.

In late July, Rotunno interviewed a man named Ralph Helm. Helm, who had been interviewed by the police in 1955, may have been one of the last people to see the boys alive. On that cold, rainy October night, Helm said he and a friend were walking Helm's girlfriend home around 9 P.M. when he spotted three boys wearing baseball jackets near the corner of Milwaukee and Lawrence avenues, a little more than four miles from the Idle Hour Stable and a few blocks from the boys' homes.

Helm recalled to Rotunno that he thought it was dangerous at that time of night for three young boys to be trying to hitch a ride. It was raining out at the time and Helm said that the two larger boys sought refuge under a store awning while the younger boy stood on the street corner with his thumb out trying to hitch a ride in the direction of the Idle Hour Stable. Helm told his mother of the incident after the boys' bodies were discovered. She called the police and he was interviewed by detectives. Helm was asked to go to the visitation services for Anton and Johnny to see if he could identify the murder victims as the same boys he saw hitch-hiking on the street that night.

"The younger boy was the same boy I saw that night. I couldn't see the other two because they were under the store awning. I know it was the younger boy because I walked right by him," Helm said. Helm, a former Chicago Police officer, was employed as a police officer for the Metropolitan Water Reclamation District of Chicago at the time of the interview. He told Rotunno he often thought of the incident.

"I didn't see them get in a car. But somebody picked them up," Helm said.

The investigators also spent some time looking into Curtis Hansen's shady past. Grady and Rotunno were able to quickly determine that Red was correct when he described Curtis Hansen as a hit man for the Chicago Outfit. "He was the most vicious, sloppy pig you could imagine," Red Wemette said of Curtis Hansen. "He was into kinky sex." Wemette described Curtis Hansen as about five feet, nine inches tall and weighing over three hundred pounds. "He was a stone cold killer," Red added.

The agents learned Curtis Hansen had once worked as a bail bondsman and was an associate of some of the most vicious members of Chicago's underworld, including Anthony Spilotro, Victor Spilotro, Sam "Mad Sam" DeStefano, Albert "Caesar" Tocco, William "Billy the Irishman" Dauber and James "The Bomber" Catura. Interestingly, out of Curtis Hansen's known associates, DeStefano, Anthony Spilotro, Dauber and Catura had all been murdered.

One of the first murders tied to Curtis Hansen was the November 1963 slaying of an Outfit juice-loan collector named Leo Foreman. Foreman had been reported missing and was found murdered in the trunk of his car. An autopsy showed that Foreman had been tortured, and stabbed and shot multiple times. Chicago Police detectives investigating the case picked up Curtis Hansen. At that time Curt Hansen was an associate of Mad Sam DeStefano. Grady and Rotunno would later learn Chicago detectives tried to beat a confession out of Curt Hansen for Foreman's murder. Curt took the beating and didn't say a word. In his book *Man Against the Mob,* the late William Roemer, an FBI agent turned author, labeled DeStefano as "the worst torture-murderer in the history of Chicago." Roemer described Mad Sam as a "sadistic, arrogant, swaggering thug of the worst order, responsible for scores of killings, almost all by his own hands."

Curtis Hansen submitted to a polygraph examination as part of the Foreman murder investigation. The results were inconclusive. Grady and Rotunno would discover through various interviews that Mad Sam, and his equally nasty brother Mario, enjoyed riding horses at Ken Hansen's stable. The DeStefano brothers' trips to Hansen's stable were special occasions. Mad Sam and Mario didn't arrive decked out in jodhpurs, boots and derbys. Instead, they fulfilled their Hopalong Cassidy fantasies and went riding in full cowboy regalia. Unlike little boys who play cowboys armed only with a cap gun, the DeStefanos came armed with pearl-handled Colt .45s, loaded with live ammunition. The guns did not always stay loaded because the brothers shot them off at whatever target suited their fancy.

The murder of Foreman took place in Mario's basement. In their book *Getting Away with Murder*, *Chicago Tribune* reporters John O'Brien and Ed Baumann wrote that Mad Sam had received permission from Sam "Momo" Giancana to do away with Foreman because Foreman owed $5,000 to DeStefano. Assisting in the slaying were Anthony Spilotro, Charles Crimaldi and Sam's brother Mario. Spilotro would later become the Chicago Outfit's man in Las Vegas. Actor Joe Pesci's role in the film *Casino* was based in large part on Tony Spilotro's life. Unlike the movie, the Spilotro brothers were beaten to death in the basement of a home in a north suburb of Chicago. Tony Spilotro was lured to his death with the promise of being inducted as a "made man" in the Outfit. The brothers were killed because Tony had gambled away millions of the Outfit's cash in Las Vegas. After they were murdered the two men were buried in an Indiana cornfield.

After Mad Sam and Spilotro shot and stabbed Foreman, Mad Sam placed his gun against the dying man's testicles and threatened to pull the trigger. Foreman, who called Mad Sam "Uncle," pleaded, "Oh my God. Please, Unc." The request for mercy worked. DeStefano rolled Foreman over and shot him in the buttocks. Spilotro and Mario then stabbed Foreman a few more times "until he stopped moving." Mario DeStefano, however, wanted his pound of flesh. Mario took a knife and gouged a chunk of flesh out of Foreman's upper arm. "I told you I'd get you for this," Mad Sam said.

Wherever Grady and Rotunno turned, they found that Curtis and Kenneth Hansen had left a trail of bodies and questionable deaths in their wake. Before Kenneth Hansen teamed up with Silas Jayne, he and his father, Ethan, who was a printer by trade, had once operated a stable not far from the Idle Hour. The agents were told that there were several tragic accidents at the stable, resulting in the deaths of two young stable hands. One boy was run over by a car and the other was "pitchforked to death."

Sometime in the 1950s the Hansen brothers teamed up with Silas Jayne and his cohorts. Though Curtis Hansen answered to his Outfit bosses, he maintained a close relationship with Silas and other members of the Jayne family. Curtis leaned on people professionally for the Outfit and apparently freelanced for Silas. One informant told Grady and Rotunno that Curtis Hansen once nearly beat a competing rider to death with brass knuckles because the man had bad-mouthed one of Frank Jayne Jr.'s horses.

In addition to his talents as a thug, for years Curtis Hansen bankrolled cheap, 8mm pornographic films that were shot at Ken Hansen's stable. One informant told Grady and Rotunno they drove with Curtis Hansen to New York City to hand over reels of the films to members of the Gambino crime family. One of Curtis Hansen's more famous 8mm pornographic films was dubbed *The Pony Express*. In the film a woman has sex with a horse.

Rotunno took some satisfaction in the fact that Curtis Hansen had died in the manner he feared most. An associate of Hansen told Rotunno that Curtis had a premonition about his own death. He thought the most horrible manner of death would be to die in a coma, covered with bedsores, with his arms and legs amputated. The angel of death must have whispered that notion into Curtis Hansen's ear, because he died exactly that way on April 15, 1993.

Curtis Hansen had suffered a brain aneurysm while being entertained in the arms of a prostitute. He never regained consciousness. He was hospitalized in a federally funded health care facility. Surgeons at the hospital were forced to amputate all of Curtis's limbs due to diabetes. When he died, Curtis Hansen was covered with bedsores.

"The murdering bastard got what he deserved," Rotunno said. A day of reckoning was also quickly approaching for other members of Silas Jayne's inner circle.

CHAPTER 19

JULY TO AUGUST 1994

For decades, Silas Jayne and his cohorts operated with impunity. Nothing except death itself would stop the Jesse Jayne Gang. When Silas Jayne died on July 13, 1987, the veil of fear that had kept secrets in the dark for decades was slowly lifted and crimes long thought unsolvable began to emerge from the shadows. The first of those secrets came to light on July 27, 1994, when James Burns, the U.S. attorney for the Northern District of Illinois, held a press conference to announce that Richard J. Bailey, a gigolo with close ties to Jayne, was being charged with conspiring to kill candy heiress Helen Vorhees Brach.

Bailey, who faced a twenty-nine-count indictment that included charges of mail fraud, wire fraud and money laundering, was one of twenty-three people charged in a wide-ranging investigation of fraud in the equestrian in-

dustry. Nineteen of those charged faced counts relating to
the killing of fifteen horses to collect insurance premiums.
The accusations of the horse executions enraged animal
activists and equine devotees. Some of the animals were
dispatched by electrocution, others by fire, and at least one
unfortunate animal was beaten with a crowbar. Eighteen of
the twenty-three indicted were convicted.

The driving force behind the investigation headed by
Assistant U.S. Attorney Steve Miller was the presumed
murder of Helen Brach. Not all of those charged as a result
of the investigation were cohorts of Silas Jayne. But much
of the sleaze uncovered in the equestrian community was
first practiced and perfected by Jayne.

Soon after the U.S. Attorney's Office in Chicago made
the announcement, prosecutors Patrick Quinn and Scott
Cassidy received the go-ahead from Cook County State's
Attorney Jack O'Malley to finalize bringing charges
against Hansen. O'Malley told the prosecutors to move
forward on the case when they were ready.

In preparation for Hansen's arrest, Roger Spry was
summoned to appear before a Cook County Grand Jury on
July 29, 1994.

It was the first time Spry would testify under oath about
what he knew of the Schuessler-Peterson murders. Spry
was nervous when he walked into the grand jury room located on the fourth floor of the Cook County Criminal
Courts Building. He was questioned during his appearance
by Scott Cassidy. Several times during his testimony Spry
needed to stop and compose himself. Talking about the
murders of the three boys was emotionally difficult for the
hardened cowboy. Much of what he told the panel of
twenty-three grand jurors was the same as what he had told
the investigative team while in the Arizona lockup. After

he explained how he had come to live under Kenneth Hansen's roof, where he was sexually assaulted, Cassidy asked Spry what he knew about Silas Jayne.

CASSIDY: Did you ever meet a person by the name Silas Jayne?

SPRY: Yes.

CASSIDY: And how did you meet Silas Jayne?

SPRY: Well, he was in the horse business too, up in Elgin, Illinois and we would . . . Kenny would buy horses off of him. He was like friends with him because he was friends with his brother Frank Jayne Sr. Kenny's wife Beverly was friends with Gloria, who was Frank Jayne Sr.'s wife.

CASSIDY: And what type of relationship would you say Ken Hansen had with Silas Jayne?

SPRY: Business, business relationship, personal relationship.

CASSIDY: Was it a close business and personal relationship?

SPRY: Yes, sir.

CASSIDY: Who introduced you to Silas Jayne?

SPRY: Kenny.

CASSIDY: Ken Hansen?

SPRY: Ken Hansen, yes, sir.

CASSIDY: Have you ever been to the Idle Hour Stables?

SPRY: Yes, sir.

CASSIDY: Who owned the Idle Hour Stables?

SPRY: Silas Jayne.

CASSIDY: Did you ever see Kenneth Hansen at the Idle Hour Stable?

SPRY: Yes, sir . . . Quite a few times. We'd go there all the time.

CASSIDY: Now, Mr. Spry, when you were fifteen years old, did anything unusual occur?

SPRY: Yes, sir.

CASSIDY: And what was that?

SPRY: Well, I don't know if you people know anything about it, but what we used to do is repair saddles and bridles. We used to fix them ourselves because it was much cheaper that way. So what we would have, like a repair shop where we'd fix saddles and bridles, and we would do it in the evening after the barn was closed and nobody was around.

So we were working in this repair shop one evening and Kenny asked me to go get some scotch. So I went upstairs and got him some scotch. And we're fixing saddles and fixing bridles and Kenny says—Si Jayne's name came up some way, because my, what I wanted to do was I wanted to show horses and Si had all the top show horses in the country. And Kenny said, "Stay away from Si Jayne. He's crazy." I said, "What do you mean?"

And he says, well, he said he picked up three kids hitchhiking, three boys hitchhiking one time.

CASSIDY: Who picked up the boys?

SPRY: Ken Hansen.

CASSIDY: Ken Hansen told you he picked up three boys hitchhiking?

SPRY: Yes, sir.

CASSIDY: Okay. What else did he say?

SPRY: He said he picked up three boys hitchhiking and he took them to a stable, and he said that his, his thing was to have sex, sex with two boys, two young boys at the same time. So he took these three boys to the stable and there was this one boy. His name was Peterson. He was the older boy. He told . . . he sent the older boy off to brush some horses and get a Coke or something.

CASSIDY: He sent the older boy off?

SPRY: Yes, sir.

CASSIDY: Go ahead.

Spry: So he could have sex with the two younger boys. And so the older kid left to do whatever he was going to do and Kenny was having sex with the two younger boys. And this is kind of hard to say, but while he was having sex with the two younger boys, the older boy came back and caught him having sex with the younger boys.

And so the older boy said he going to tell. So Kenny grabbed the older boy and put his arm around him, grabbed him by the neck like this. He sort of had them boxed in where the only way the two younger boys could get away was to get past Kenny, Ken Hansen. So he had to hold the other boy, the older boy with his arm around his neck, and he was trying to keep the other two kids from getting around him. And in the process he realized that, he said accidentally he killed this older kid, this Peterson kid.

Cassidy: What did he say happened after he, as he said, accidentally killed the older boy or the Peterson kid?

Spry: Well, he said everything had happened so fast, he said, that when he realized he had, he said he accidentally killed this Peterson kid, that he had no choice but to kill the other two boys, which is sad.

Cassidy: Mr. Spry, did he tell you how he killed these other two boys?

Spry: No, sir.

Cassidy: What did he say, if anything, happened after he killed the other two boys?

Spry: After . . . just, I guess, simultaneously after he killed the other two boys, Si Jayne appeared and . . .

Cassidy: What happened after Silas Jayne appeared?

Spry: Well, Si got really upset. He said that he said, "Why do I even got to walk into a situation like this?" You know, he said he said, "I can be ruined for something like this."

Cassidy: Whose stables did this, where did this occur?

SPRY: I don't know, sir.

CASSIDY: Go ahead.

SPRY: We never got into details like that.

CASSIDY: What else happened then?

SPRY: So from what Kenny told me, Si was sort of like in the middle. And so Si, to help cover himself, they took the kids and put them in a car or something and hauled them off and dumped them in a forest preserve.

CASSIDY: Did Ken Hansen ever mention the name of Peterson to you again after that?

SPRY: Yes, sir, he did.

CASSIDY: And in what context?

SPRY: Well, when people come out to go riding, they sign their names on a sheet. Okay. Well, Kenny, he wasn't paying me no money. I mean, I was making nothing. So what I used to do is every so often when somebody would come out to go riding, I wouldn't sign them up. If we were charging, I think at the time, two, three bucks an hour to ride, so what I would do, I wouldn't sign them up and stick the money in my pocket so I'd have a little bit of money in my pocket.

So two people came out one day and they were going to, I put them on the horses and sent them out on the trail and nobody was there. And they went out on the trail, but they hadn't quite gotten to the forest preserve. And Kenny pulled up and he saw them. And he walked over to the sheet and he picked the sheet up, and he goes, "Why didn't you sign these people up?" And I said I forgot. And he goes, "Roger," he said, "You keep it up," he said, "you're going to end up just like that Peterson kid."

Spry concluded his testimony. He wiped his eyes and cleared his throat before stepping down from the witness stand. Over the next few weeks others would be called to testify before the grand jury. The groundwork was being laid to ask the grand jurors for a true bill to indict Hansen with the murders.

Within days of Spry's appearance before the Cook County grand jury, Quinn called Steve Miller to let him know that he would be indicting a suspect in the murders of the three boys within a few weeks. It was a professional courtesy call. Quinn did not know Miller, but he was aware that Miller had been working with the FBI and ATF to investigate Brach's murder and other shady dealings within the horse industry. Rotunno played a minor role in Miller's investigation. Rotunno's immediate supervisor, Jimmy Delorto, was more involved in the Brach probe.

Quinn wanted to give Miller a heads-up because he suspected the two cases would overlap in some regards. After all, Bailey had asked Hansen to murder Helen Brach. Quinn wanted to make sure the Cook County prosecution of Hansen would not negatively impact the federal case against Bailey. How Miller responded surprised Quinn. He never asked his fellow prosecutor who his witnesses were or how they would testify. Instead, the federal prosecutor asked Quinn to hold off indicting Hansen. Miller told Quinn that if Quinn held off on the Hansen case, Miller hoped to eventually bring charges against the person who had murdered Brach.

"I told him there was no way I could do that. Basically he had a theft case and I had a triple murder case," Quinn said. "I would not delay the case." Some of Quinn's witnesses were elderly, and he feared any delay in the start of the trial could jeopardize the entire case. Grady and Rotunno would later hear that Miller wanted to bring in FBI agents to "build a better case against Hansen" than the two

ATF agents had already accomplished. The rumor did not sit well with Rotunno and Grady.

To make matters more tense, soon after Spry appeared before the Cook County grand jury, the *Chicago Sun-Times* reported that the Brach investigation had prompted ATF agents to reopen the investigation into the Schuessler-Peterson murders, the 1956 slaying of the sisters Barbara and Patricia Grimes, the car bombing slaying of Cheryl Lynn Rude at George Jayne's stable and the presumed murders of three women who disappeared from the Indiana Dunes in 1965.

The *Sun-Times story,* written by reporters Tim Gerber, Gilbert Jiminez and Jim Casey, reported, "Investigators believe that the boys, after leaving the bowling alley, found their way to Silas Jayne's Idle Hour Stable . . . It is there, according to information obtained by the investigators, that the three boys were murdered during the course of a sexual assault on one of the three boys by a worker at Jayne's stable."

The next day *Chicago Tribune* reporters John O'Brien and Peter Kendall broke a similar story, that authorities were closing in on a suspect in the Schuessler-Peterson murders as an offshoot of the Helen Brach investigation. The stories sent shock waves through the Cook County State's Attorney's Office. Jack O'Malley was furious. He wanted to know who was willing to jeopardize the investigation into the murders of three young boys by going to the press. The published article contained too much accurate, inside information not to have come from someone with ample knowledge of the investigation.

"Investigators are looking into the possibility that the boys' murders, Brach's disappearance and five other infamous, unsolved crimes are interwoven, somehow connected by a wicked thread that originates in a fraternity of horse traders," wrote O'Brien and Kendall. "The notion is fantastic. Can one investigation divine connections between several of the most intractable criminal mysteries in Chicago history?"

The *Tribune* also reported that the car bombing murder at George Jayne's stable in 1965, the disappearance and presumed killings of three women from the Indiana Dunes in 1965 and the murder of Helen Brach were all related. Other slayings included the murders of the Grimes sisters and the assassination of a Cook County Sheriff's Police officer who had scolded Mad Sam DeStefano while he was being held in the infirmary at the Cook County Jail.

Though the Grimes murder case was as well known in Chicago as the Schuessler-Peterson case, Grady and Rotunno found only one connection to Hansen in that case. The owner of the horse that was used in the pornographic *Pony Express* film, made at Hansen's stable, told Grady and Rotunno that the girls' bodies were found on a parcel of land leased by Kenneth Hansen. The owner of the horse also said he was to meet with Hansen on the day the girls' bodies were found, but Hansen canceled at the last moment. Hansen told the witness he couldn't make it because there were "too many cops around."

Grady and Rotunno studied the Grimes sisters' case file and found nothing in it that connected the case to Hansen or his brother Curtis. In addition, Hansen, who had made a habit of telling others about his involvement in the boys' murders, had been mum regarding any involvement in the girls' slayings. "We knew Kenny liked little boys. We never heard anything about Kenny and young girls," Grady would say. The agents came across nothing in Curtis Hansen's past linking him to the girls' murders. The fact that the girls were found on Kenneth Hansen's leased property was significant, but there was nothing else linking Hansen or any other member of Silas Jayne's posse to the murders.

The newspaper stories were disturbing because only Grady, Rotunno, a handful of Chicago police officers, Quinn and Cassidy knew the investigation was uncovering evidence linking other murders to Silas Jayne and members of the Jayne Gang.

On August 3, 1994, the *Chicago Sun-Times* was delivered to readers' doorsteps with two more stories about the Schuessler-Peterson case. The first story reported that a suspect in the slayings of the three boys would be in custody soon. "The suspect is expected to be arrested by week's end on federal charges for a 1956 arson stable fire at the late Silas Jayne's Idle Hour Stable . . . , sources said."

The story also stated, "The suspect is in his 60s and is still involved in the horse industry, the sources said." The second story reported that retired Chicago Police Detective John Sarnowski was convinced the three boys were murdered by serial killer John Wayne Gacy when Gacy was a teenager. The story by reporter Scott Fornek noted that on the eve of his execution, Gacy denied he had anything to do with the murders of the three boys.

The article brought a chuckle to members of the Schuessler-Peterson investigation. Grady and Rotunno, along with Quinn and Cassidy, thought it was preposterous that Gacy's first foray into murder as a thirteen-year-old would be a triple homicide.

To make matters more difficult, the next day, on August 4, 1994, the *Tribune* also reported that authorities had a suspect in the 1955 slayings.

"According to sources familiar with the renewed Schuessler-Peterson murder investigation, the boys' killer was a stable hand employed by the late horseman Silas Jayne and the crime, one of chance, took place in a barn owned by Jayne on the city's edge," the story said.

"In addition to unmasking the suspected killer, state and federal investigators have informed the Cook County state's attorney's office that other findings in the long dormant case point to a cover-up of the crime by Jayne, according to sources. It was Jayne, who died in 1987, who helped the suspected killer, a man now in his 60s, dispose of the bodies." The story also mentioned that authorities had two informants who "provided information that implicated the stable hand and Jayne in the murders and cover-up."

The Cook County State's Attorney's Office immediately suspected the source of the leak was within the Bureau of Alcohol, Tobacco and Firearms. If the leak did come from the ATF, whoever was talking to the press faced not only the loss of a job but criminal charges as well. Grady, Rotunno and Delorto were called into the office of Rich Rawlings, the special agent in charge of Chicago's ATF unit, for a thorough chewing out. Outside of the SAC's office, Rotunno confronted Delorto and asked him if he leaked the story to the press. Delorto denied doing so. When they met with Rawlings, both Grady and Rotunno denied being the source of the leak. Rotunno offered that all three were willing to take a lie detector test to prove their innocence. Nothing ever came of the offer to take the polygraph examination. To this day, Delorto, who was feeling poorly and was just days away from suffering his first heart attack, does not recall the specifics of his conversation with Grady, Rotunno or Rawlings.

Years later, Rotunno and Grady would confirm their

THE DAILY BULLETIN

HON. RICHARD J. DALEY, Mayor

VOL. 2.   OCTOBER 20, 1955   NO. 206-B

ATTENTION   ATTENTION   ATTENTION

John Schuessler
5711 N. Mango av.

Wore a brown shirt with a ranch design, blue zipper satin jacket with slit pockets trimmed in red; lettering on left side of jacket "CUBS" blue lettering with red trim, blue jeans, black gym shoes trimmed in white with white shoe laces. The above clothing is old and well worn.

Anton Schuessler
5711 N. Mango av.

Wore a white flannel shirt with mixed black design, blue satin zipper jacket with slit pockets trimmed in red; tear on right pocket pinned together with a safety pin; lettering on left side of jacket "CUBS" blue lettering with red trim; letter "U" missing, blue jeans with stiching on right knee, black gym shoes trimmed in white with white shoe laces. The above clothing is old and well worn.

Robert Peterson
5519 Farragut st.

Wore a dark satin zipper jacket with red elastic bands at wrists and waist; red line down each sleeve; White Sox Emblem on left side of jacket white on black, blue jeans, black gym shoes trimmed in white with white shoe laces. The above clothing is old and well worn.

THE VICTIMS IN THE ABOVE PHOTOGRAPHS, WEARING THE DESCRIBED CLOTHING, WERE LAST SEEN ALIVE AT 9:00 p.m., SUNDAY NIGHT OCTOBER 16th, 1955, IN THE VICINITY OF LAWRENCE AND MILWAUKEE AVENUES. ANY INFORMATION RELATIVE TO THE ABOVE SUBJECTS SHOULD BE FORWARDED AT ONCE TO:

Chief of Detectives, John T. O'Malley
Chicago Police Department, 1121 S. State St.
Telephone: Wabash 2-4747, Extensions 253 and 295.

Timothy J O'Connor
Commissioner of Police

The Chicago Police *Daily Bulletin*, October 20, 1955, which includes images of the boys and descriptions of what they were wearing when they were last seen alive.

The crime scene of the Schuessler-Peterson murders. The press and the police are gathered around the bodies.

The coroner's inquest for the three boys. The boys' fathers, Anton Schuessler and Malcolm Peterson, can be seen seated at the table just left of a film camera on a tripod, surrounded by Chicago media.

Anton Schuessler, Sr., grieving at the Cook County coroner's inquest.
AP Wide World Photos.

Anton Schuessler collapsing
at the Cook County morgue
after viewing the remains of
his sons.

*Photograph courtesy of the Chicago
Tribune. Copyright © 2005, Chicago
Tribune. All rights reserved.*

Grieving parents, Anton and Eleanor Schuessler.

Reprinted with special permission from Chicago Sun-Times Inc. © 2005. File photograph, October 19, 1955.

Anton Schuessler and Malcolm Peterson meeting outside of the Cook County morgue prior to the coroner's inquest.

Reprinted with special permission from Chicago Sun-Times Inc. © 2005. Photograph by Merrill Palmer, October 25, 1955.

At the playground dedication for Robert Peterson. His parents, Dorothy and Malcolm Peterson, stand in the center.

Reprinted with special permission from Chicago Sun-Times Inc. © 2005. Photograph by Larry Nocerino, July 16, 1956.

The barn at the Idle Hour in flames, after an arson was set to destroy the place where the boys were murdered. May 1956.

Silas Jayne's brother and business rival, George, riding his Palomino, "Butterscotch," at the Chicago International Amphitheater, December 3, 1952.

Cheryl Lynn Rude, murdered in a 1965 car bombing at George Jayne's stable.

Marla Ryan © 2005

The Cadillac that belonged to George Jayne, pictured here following the car bombing that killed Cheryl Lynn Rude.

Mug shot of James Blottiaux, who was charged and convicted with Cheryl Lynn Rude's murder.

ATF photo.

George and Marion Jayne at the Tri-Color Stables, June 17, 1965, three days after a bomb killed Cheryl Lynn Rude.

Photograph courtesy of the Chicago Tribune. Copyright © 2005, Chicago Tribune. All rights reserved.

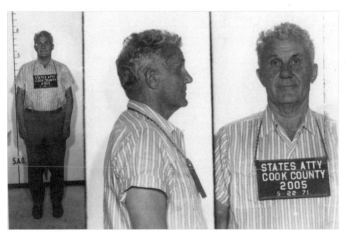

May 22, 1971: Mug shot of Silas Jayne taken after he was charged with the murder of his brother, George Jayne.

Joseph LaPlaca was one of Silas Jayne's henchmen, who was tried and convicted for his role in George Jayne's murder.

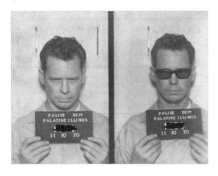

Melvin Adams was the hitman hired by Silas Jayne to murder George Jayne. Adams later cooperated with authorities leading to the arrest of Silas Jayne, and also assisted in the investigation of Kenneth Hansen.

Edwin Nefeld, the corrupt Markham police officer who recruited Melvin Adams to murder George Jayne.

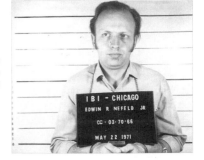

Silas Jayne (far right) in handcuffs accompanied by sheriff's deputies on his way to court in 1978 on arson charges.

Kenneth and Beverly Hansen on their honeymoon.

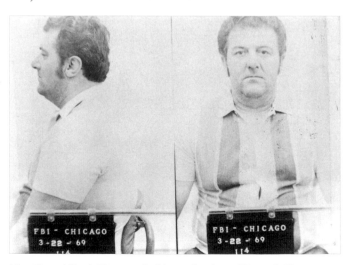

Mug shot of Curtis Hansen, the hitman brother of Kenneth Hansen.

June 4, 1971: Mug shot of Kenneth Hansen taken the day he was arrested on solicitation of murder charges in connection with the slaying of George Jayne.

Photograph of Kenneth Hansen taken following his arrest for the three boys' murders.
ATF Photo

ATF Agent John Rotunno
Judith Fidkowski © 2005

ATF Agent Jim Grady
Judith Fidkowski © 2005

ATF Agent James Delorto
Judith Fidkowski © 2005

Frank and Helen Brach. It was Helen's disappearance that eventually led agents back to this case.

suspicions that someone in the ATF had funneled information to the press. When *Tribune* reporter John O'Brien passed away in October 2003, Grady and Rotunno asked his widow if they could peruse his files. O'Brien was a well-known, well-respected journalist. The agents were working a case and they knew O'Brien had a lot of information that could prove helpful. Mrs. O'Brien agreed to allow them to go through her husband's files. In O'Brien's files, Grady and Rotunno found every report they had prepared as part of the Schuessler-Peterson investigation.

The case against Hansen moved full steam ahead despite the press leaks. On or about August 8, 1994, Rotunno and Delorto drove out to the home of Malcolm and Dorothy Peterson to inform them that charges were going to be brought against a suspect in their son's slaying. Within a few days of that meeting, Jim Delorto suffered a heart attack. He would be out of the loop on the case for months.

CHAPTER 20

For almost four decades no one had answered for the murders of Bobby Peterson and brothers John and Tony Schuessler. The boys' slayings, which had shattered the innocence of one city, had faded from the recollections of all but a few who were intimately touched by the boys' untimely passing. What had once been the focus of hundreds of police officers was now an obscure reference. The boys' murders were all but forgotten and would have forever remained a mystery but for a series of random actions and occurrences—quirks of fate. Destiny brought together two childhood friends at the Chicago office of the Bureau of Alcohol, Tobacco and Firearms and set them on a path toward a suspect. Fate had come close to solving the case once before. Red Wemette had told his FBI handlers in the 1970s the name of a man who had admitted to him that he murdered three boys in 1955. Wemette's tip went nowhere for several reasons. The agents involved weren't from the Chicago area and therefore had no historical knowledge of the case. The FBI also wasn't interested in Wemette's claim because, in their opinion, the case didn't involve the Chicago Outfit. If they had questioned Wemette further, they would have learned of hitman Curtis Hansen's role in the killings.

When John Rotunno first glanced at the crime scene photographs of the three boys, his eyes had teared up and made him angry. He was determined to solve the case. Jim Grady shared that same commitment. If Kenneth Hansen had indeed murdered the three boys, the two Bureau of Alcohol, Tobacco and Firearms agents would see to it that Hansen would have to answer to a jury and judge for the crime.

After months of quietly gathering evidence, Patrick Quinn and Scott Cassidy gave the go-ahead to arrest Hansen. The decision to approve charges came directly from Cook County State's Attorney Jack O'Malley. After the stories appeared in the *Tribune* and *Sun-Times,* the covert investigation had been exposed—Hansen knew he was under suspicion. Rotunno and Grady were looking forward to the arrest for obvious reasons, but they were also looking forward to officially taking the wraps off the investigation.

Because they had been proceeding quietly, Grady and Rotunno had purposely held off questioning numerous witnesses. The equestrian community was already abuzz as a result of the investigation into the Helen Brach murder. Bringing up the Schuessler-Peterson murders with certain parties would have increased the volume. It was also apparent, according to several persons questioned by Grady and Rotunno, that many in the horse world knew or suspected that Hansen and Silas Jayne were involved in the murders. Those persons had been silenced by fear of Silas Jayne and his minions.

One potential witness that Grady and Rotunno had long wanted to question but dared not approach until charges were approved was Edwin Nefeld. Nefeld was the corrupt cop who had been charged in the slaying of George Jayne.

One hour before Hansen was arrested, Rotunno, Patrick Quinn and Chicago Police Detective Lou Rabbit met with Nefeld at the offices of his attorney Matthew Walsh. Walsh was a former Cook County state's attorney who'd assisted in the prosecution of Silas Jayne for the murder of George Jayne.

Nefeld was cagey during the questioning. He told Rotunno and the others that he had known Kenneth Hansen since 1962 or 1963, while he was in high school. Nefeld said he first met Hansen at a stable Hansen owned in Hickory Hills. At that stable, where Nefeld had purchased a horse from Hansen, he heard from others that Hansen was homosexual. Nefeld said he knew Hansen had a "homosexual love affair" with a young man named Roger Spry. "Roger was with Kenny for a long time," Nefeld said.

Nefeld befriended Hansen and his wife Beverly. Like other witnesses, Nefeld said he had heard that Beverly Hansen had discovered her husband in bed with a stable hand and had taken photographs of the two. "Beverly would complain to me about Ken and the young men," Nefeld said. "It caused problems for them."

Nefeld was close to Beverly. So close that Hansen once accused him of having an affair with his wife. The accusation caused a rift between the two men, but the bad blood

eventually passed. Nefeld remained friends with Hansen.
Just three weeks prior to the interview with the federal
agents and prosecutor, Nefeld said, he had spoken to
Hansen. Hansen had told him that Beverly had died of a
heart attack. Nefeld claimed he didn't know that Beverly
had committed suicide.

Nefeld also echoed other witnesses' statements that
Hansen was close to the Jayne family. Nefeld said he was
introduced to Silas Jayne, his brother Frank Jayne Sr. and
his son Frank Jayne Jr. by Hansen. "Kenny used to work
for Silas Jayne at the Idle Hour Stable," Nefeld said. "He
told me that he used to work there." At one time Silas Jayne
had offered to set Nefeld up in the stable business, he said.

The interview with Nefeld didn't produce any surpris-
ing results. Nefeld was aware that Curtis Hansen had ties
to organized crime, but he did not provide much information about Curtis.

In an effort to get Nefeld to offer more information
about Kenneth Hansen, Rotunno showed him a report written as part of the George Jayne murder investigation. The
report was written following an interview Nefeld had with
Cook County Sheriff's Detectives John Boeger and John
Foscoe. In the report, Nefeld fingered Ken Hansen, his
good buddy, as being the likely shooter in the slaying of
George Jayne.

The report was written on January 13, 1971. It said that
Nefeld had failed a polygraph examination. Nefeld had
been reluctant to take the polygraph but volunteered to take
sodium pentathol. The questions that triggered the negative
response in Nefeld were "Do you have any knowledge of
who did kill George Jayne?" and "Are you telling us everything you know about the murder?"

The sheriff's detectives reported that Nefeld was so nervous and frightened talking about Silas Jayne and Kenneth Hansen that it appeared that he was going to vomit "as he had done on previous occasions.

"Finally he regained his composure and tried to answer our questions," the report stated. "All he could say at first was the name Hansen. I asked him if he meant Ken Hansen and he said yes. He was asked if he thought that Ken Hansen was with Melvin Adams when George Jayne was killed. He said yes to this also. We then asked him if he thought Melvin Adams was the man who shot George and he said no. He thought that Melvin Adams had gathered all the information about George Jayne and even obtained the rifle that was used but for some unknown reason, Adams could not or would not go through with it at this point. Ken Hansen took the rifle and finished the job."

The report continued, "When asked what he had based this on, he said that first of all Ken Hansen and Silas Jayne were very close. It was Hansen that Silas went to, to find someone that would follow George in the spring of 1969."

Nefeld's statement to the sheriff's detectives would later prove to be inaccurate, but it showed he was willing to give up Hansen. The report was handed to Nefeld and he read it. Nefeld then stated that in 1969 he was under Hansen's control.

Rotunno hoped that by reminding Nefeld that he had turned on Hansen once before, he might be willing to do it again. After all, Melvin Adams had told Rotunno that Nefeld knew of the boys' slayings.

Nefeld admitted the statement was accurate. The admission, however, didn't prompt him to begin talking about Hansen. He said he had no knowledge of Hansen's involvement in the Schuessler-Peterson murders. Despite the denial, Nefeld's words didn't ring true with Rotunno and Quinn. The two found it hard to believe that Nefeld, who was part of Silas Jayne's inner circle, wouldn't have picked up something about Hansen's involvement in the murders. Before the interview concluded, Nefeld said he would search his memory, and if anything came back to him, he would contact Rotunno with any additional information.

Hours before Nefeld was interviewed, Chicago Police tried to arrest Hansen at his home. Hansen was to initially be placed under arrest on arson charges. Grady and a team of Chicago Police officers, among them Lt. John Farrell, went to Hansen's home around 6:30 A.M., but Hansen was not home. Fearing that Hansen had possibly fled, the officers set up surveillance on the home while a search warrant was obtained. At the same time that Nefeld was being interviewed, Grady and his Chicago Police colleagues served the warrant on Hansen's home. No one was home; the lawmen let themselves in through a side door. Seized during the search warrant were several address books.

After the search warrant had been served, Hansen somehow got word of all the activity at his home and called his neighbor Jim Tynan to ask Tynan if he noticed anything suspicious going on at his home. Tynan, who was cooperating with the police, was instructed to tell Hansen that nothing was amiss. Hansen then told Tynan that he would be coming home soon and would be driving a different car. Hansen added that he was planning to "go south" to a farm he owned in southern Illinois.

Grady and the Chicago detectives trying to pick up Hansen were concerned that he would try to flee. If Hansen was able to make it out of the country, there was no telling where he would go. During the course of the investigation the agents heard rumors that Silas Jayne owned ranches overseas, supposedly in Australia and Argentina.

Tynan had provided Grady and Lieutenant Farrell with several interesting tidbits about Hansen. "When Ken was out of town, he once called me and we had a conversation. I told him I saw an article in the newspaper about Richard Bailey. He had called earlier and asked me to get a newspaper to see if there was anything in it about who had gotten indicted with Bailey," Tynan said. "After I read the list of names to him, Ken said, 'How about that. I didn't make the list.'"

Tynan said he had also read Hansen an article about the Schuessler-Peterson murders. He informed Hansen the article said there was a suspect in the case and that the suspect was still active in the stable business.

A short time after Tynan received the call about Hansen "going south," Grady and Farrell watched as Hansen pulled up to his home in his son's pickup truck. In the back of the truck were several suitcases. The lawmen were positive Hansen was planning to hit the road. Hansen, who wearing blue coveralls, the type that a mechanic might wear, exited the truck and walked into his home.

This was the moment that Grady, Rotunno and others involved in the investigation had been working toward for months. As Grady and Farrell approached Hansen's home, each man drew his service weapon. Grady walked to the front door and opened up the screen door. He silently stepped into the home, followed by Farrell. In the living room of the home, Grady spotted Hansen sitting on a couch, watching television. He pointed his 9mm pistol at the middle of Ken Hansen's chest.

Only a few ounces of pressure on Grady's trigger finger were all that separated Hansen from the here and now and eternity. If Hansen had made the wrong move, Grady would have shot him without hesitation. Hansen, however, raised his hands in surrender.

"Kenneth Hansen, you're under arrest," Grady said as he handcuffed Hansen and secured his weapon. Hansen was read his rights and then driven to the Chicago ATF headquarters, where he would be questioned for the next twelve hours.

Farrell was the first person to interview Hansen. During the interview, Hansen admitted to having sex with boys and men between the ages of eleven and twenty-two. He did not admit to being a pedophile; instead, he claimed he was homosexual. He claimed to have had a "love affair" with Roger Spry since the time Spry was nine or ten years old. He also admitted to picking up male hitchhikers and offering them employment at his stable and having sex with them. "He didn't see himself as a pedophile but a homosexual," Grady would later say. "He was willing to admit to everything except the boys' murders."

Hansen described Roger Spry and Red as "good guys" with whom he had been sexually involved. When told that Spry and Wemette were cooperating with the investigation, Hansen claimed they would "say bad things" about him since he had "spurned" their sexual advances. Hansen also claimed he had been good friends with George Jayne and was only arrested for conspiracy to commit George Jayne's murder because of "guilt through association." Hansen also strongly denied that he was a close friend of Silas Jayne.

Around 11:30 P.M. that night, Grady had an opportunity

to question Hansen. He told Grady he had been in the stable business his whole life, starting before he was drafted into the U.S. Army. Hansen said that over the years he eventually came to know Silas Jayne through the business, but he had never been to the Idle Hour Stable until the late 1950s or early 1960s.

Hansen told the lawmen he purchased a stable in south suburban Hickory Hills with his parents and brother Curtis in 1955. He later took over the business because Curt didn't pay any of the bills. Hansen couldn't remember the exact date of the purchase, but he recalled that October 1955 was a "transitional month" for him.

With Grady guiding Hansen through the interview, Hansen repeated that he was homosexual and routinely had sex with young boys. He said he began engaging in such activities with children after 1955. Hansen repeated that he often picked up teenagers between thirteen and sixteen years of age and took them to his stable, where he would assault them. Over the years Hansen estimated he picked up and had sex with over a thousand boys. Hansen would make the same statement about molesting numerous boys to Assistant Cook County State's Attorney Barbara Riley.

"After pulling together everything we had on Hansen, I wasn't surprised he had molested so many kids," Grady would later say. "He is a classic pedophile."

The next day the Cook County State's Attorney's Office held a press conference to announce that Kenneth Hansen had been arrested for the Schuessler-Peterson murders. The press asked Cook County State's Attorney Jack O'Malley if there was any physical evidence linking Kenneth Hansen to the murders. "After forty years go by, you don't solve a case by physical evidence," O'Malley said.

Hansen's son Mark told the *Tribune* he thought the charges were a "crock." "I think the police are just trying to clean up some old homicides."

CHAPTER 21

The arrest of Kenneth Hansen generated headlines across the country. It remained a page one story in Chicago for several days. Surviving family members of the boys had few words to say. Eleanor Schuessler's stepson told reporters that she had kept a bronzed baby shoe from each one of her murdered sons and their photographs next to her bed until the day she died. Eleanor Schuessler, who died in 1986, was buried next to her boys. "If this was the person and they can prove it one hundred percent, she would be really joyful," stepson Gary Kujawa told the *Chicago Tribune*. "She still would like to know why he did it. She couldn't understand why anybody would want to do that to some young kids like that." Malcolm and Dorothy Peterson did not make any public comment.

Hansen remained mute when he appeared in court for a

bond hearing on the murder charges. He was represented by Attorney Arthur O'Donnell. It was O'Donnell who had represented Hansen when he was charged with solicitation for murder in connection to the George Jayne slaying. Hansen, who was ordered held without bond, was eventually indicted for the boys' murders on September 7, 1994.

That same month O'Donnell and his co-counsel filed court documents indicating Hansen was on his honeymoon in Texas when the boys were murdered. The alibi defense notice stated that Hansen married his wife Beverly on June 27, 1953, but delayed his honeymoon until the fall of 1955. The motion asserted that Hansen's oldest son, Mark, was told by his mother that he was conceived in Texas in 1955. The defense also filed a motion seeking to dismiss the charges against Hansen on the grounds that too much time had elapsed since the murders, thereby denying Hansen an opportunity for an adequate defense because witnesses who could corroborate his alibi had died.

Between the time Hansen was arrested and indicted, Grady and Rotunno kept themselves busy interviewing many more witnesses. One person interviewed by Grady following the arrest was a man named Patrick Mason, a former Chicago Police officer who called the Cook County State's Attorney's office after learning of Hansen's arrest.

Mason, who was fifty-one years old at the time, told Grady he had worked for Hansen at the Broken-H Stable in south suburban Hickory Hills between 1956 and 1958. Like other young men who frequented Hansen's stable, Mason worked in exchange for free horse rides at the end of the day. One day Mason said he went to retrieve a horse for a customer and discovered Hansen sexually assaulting a young boy about fifteen years old in a stall. Startled, Mason walked away. Mason told Grady that Hansen had never approached him for sex.

A few minutes after the incident, Mason said, Hansen approached him, grabbed him by the crotch, threw him up against a fence and jabbed his finger into his face. "You better not say anything. If I hear you mention a word to anybody else about this, you'll end up in the forest preserve like some other boys," Hansen growled. Mason told Grady he had a pretty good idea that Hansen was referring to the Schuessler-Peterson murders.

At the same time, Hansen also threatened to harm Mason's sister, who often accompanied him to the stables, if he breathed a word of the incident to anyone. Fearing for his life and his sister's, Mason didn't give Hansen a chance. He immediately retrieved his sister from another part of the stable and both fled. He told Grady he never returned to the stable.

Another witness who contacted the Cook County State's Attorney's Office was a woman named Judith Mae Anderson. Anderson told Rotunno that she was certain Kenneth Hansen had worked for Silas Jayne at the Idle Hour Stable in the summer of 1955. Andersen said she had met Hansen at the Idle Hour and recalled asking him if he was any relation to a high school friend of hers with the same last name.

Rotunno considered Anderson's information truthful, especially when she recalled that she was smitten by Hansen. Rotunno had heard from several witnesses that Hansen was a good-looking man when he was in his twenties. "He had a curly head of hair and was very attractive," Anderson said. She said it was clear to her that Hansen worked for Silas Jayne. "Silas Jayne began yelling at him about a horse," she said.

The arrest of Hansen also helped clear the memories of some witnesses that Grady and Rotunno had interviewed in previous months. One of those witnesses was a man named Joseph Plemmons, a soft-spoken Southerner whose demeanor helped him considerably in his true vocation as a con man. In 1981 Plemmons was convicted of theft for swindling his girlfriend's family out of $15,000. In 1991 federal charges were lodged against Plemmons for stealing more than $90,000 in two bogus horse deals in California. Grady and Rotunno had first interviewed Plemmons in March 1994.

Plemmons, who was also cooperating with the investigation run by the U.S. Attorney's Office, told Rotunno and Grady that Richard Bailey asked him and Kenneth Hansen to murder Helen Brach. The meeting took place at a restaurant not far from Bailey's stable.

"Bailey said the candy lady wasn't so sweet anymore and he offered $5,000 to Kenny to kill her," Plemmons said. "Kenny told him he wouldn't kill a little old lady for $5,000." Bailey then offered Plemmons $5,000 to do away with Brach, but he also refused. Plemmons told the agents it was common knowledge around the horse business that Hansen was the man to see if you wanted someone murdered. Despite what he had to say about Hansen's involvement in the Brach case, Plemmons was cagey when it came to the Schuessler-Peterson murders. He didn't offer anything about the slayings to the agents. Grady and Rotunno didn't ask Plemmons directly about the boys' murders, but they asked several leading questions about Hansen's sexual preferences.

Plemmons told Grady and Rotunno that he moved to Chicago in 1970 from New Mexico, where he worked as a horse trainer at Santa Fe Downs. He said he met Hansen at a horse show in the Chicago area and the two became friends. Plemmons worked for Hansen for a number of years. He said he soon discovered Hansen's sexual preferences for boys and youngish looking men, but claimed Hansen never approached him for sex.

Before Hansen was arrested, Plemmons had talked to Rotunno on a number of occasions. It was clear to Rotunno that Plemmons was close to Beverly Hansen. Plemmons later said he thought Beverly Hansen was "coming apart at the seams" and was on the edge of a nervous breakdown before she committed suicide. Plemmons, however, didn't think she was capable of killing herself. Beverly never talked of suicide, he said.

The arrest of Hansen for the boys' slayings eventually prompted Plemmons to act. He had decided to come forward not because he wanted Hansen to pay for the boys' murders, but because he was convinced that Hansen had murdered his wife Beverly in an attempt to get to her money and had gotten away with that crime. Plemmons grew suspicious of Hansen after Hansen told him Beverly died from a heart attack and then he learned her death had been ruled a suicide. Plemmons's anger toward Hansen reached the boiling point on November 13, 1994. On that day he paged Rotunno. When Rotunno returned the call, Plemmons was frantic and had some interesting things to say.

Allegations that Hansen had murdered his wife would be taken seriously by the investigative team, especially after they learned that weeks before her death Beverly had sold some real estate for several hundred thousand dollars. Hansen has never been charged with his wife's murder.

"I need to see you as soon as possible," Plemmons told Rotunno. "Kenny told me some things back in 1971 that I've never told anyone." Rotunno pressed Plemmons for details but Plemmons said he didn't want to talk about it over the phone. He said he feared for his own life.

Soon after the conversation, Plemmons flew to Chicago to meet with Rotunno. The two met at O'Hare Airport. Under the watchful eye of Grady, Rotunno drove Plemmons to a local motel where the two talked about Hansen. Grady shadowed both men to protect Rotunno. The agents weren't quite sure what Plemmons had to offer. Plemmons had done such a poor job in previous interviews dancing around what he knew about Hansen that the federal agents didn't trust him and didn't want to take a chance they were being set up.

Rotunno and Plemmons spoke briefly at the motel. The gist of the conversation was that Hansen had admitted to Plemmons that he had murdered three boys in 1955. Plemmons said he had decided to come clean because if Hansen wasn't going to pay for Beverly's death he wanted to make sure Hansen went to prison for the boys' murders.

Following the conversation, Rotunno immediately contacted Pat Quinn and Scott Cassidy to let them know he and Grady had found another witness to whom Hansen had confessed that he had murdered the boys. Two days later, Plemmons was driven to the Cook County State's Attorney's complex and interviewed in Quinn's thirteenth-floor office. Present for the interview were Grady, Rotunno, Quinn and Cassidy. Before he began speaking, Plemmons was read his rights. Rotunno took notes during the interview.

"Kenny told me he killed three boys on at least five occasions," Plemmons said. "He usually told me these things when he was drinking. I figured you two were looking at Kenny for these murders a few months ago when we first talked."

Hansen's involvement in the slayings was common knowledge among some, Plemmons said. Over the years, he said several of Hansen's cohorts and employees told him that Hansen had been involved in the murders of two or three young boys at Silas Jayne's stable.

Plemmons first learned of Hansen's involvement in the crime from a competing rider named Wally Holly that he faced in a "jump-off" in 1971, he said. Jump-offs are held to break a tie after the final round in a show jumping competition. Plemmons said he was positive he first learned of Hansen's involvement at that competition. The jump-off event was reported in an equestrian industry publication. He added that he lost the competition while riding a horse named Saturday's Dock.

Holly first asked Plemmons what he was doing working for Hansen. Plemmons responded that he was working for Hansen as a trainer.

"He looked at me and said, 'No. What are you really doing here?' He then licked his second finger and ran it across his eyebrow," Plemmons said. "Now, you boys may not know it, but that's a gesture indicating someone's homosexual. Holly thought I was Hansen's boyfriend or something. Before I could answer him again, he said, 'Ken Hansen killed three kids on the north side and Si Jayne owns him.' He repeated himself and then asked me to come work for him."

Later that evening, Plemmons joined Hansen and several others for dinner and drinks. During the course of the evening, Hansen had some kind words for Holly. Plemmons told the prosecution team he cut Hansen off in midsentence with the comment of "Wally Holly is not your friend."

"About a week later we were all at the same restaurant

and Kenny must have remembered what I said. The others had gotten up from the table and Kenny asked me what I meant by that statement. I told him I didn't want to talk about it but he pushed me. He said you're either loyal to me or you're not. So I told him that Wally Holly had told me that he had killed three kids and that Si Jayne owned him."

The statement did not sit well with Hansen.

"When Kenny heard that, he gave me this cold stare. He then said, 'Wally talks too much for somebody who's got his own ghost.'" In addition to the comments about the boys' murders, Hansen said he was angry that Holly had tried to steal one of his employees. "I later asked Kenny if he did indeed kill three kids on the north side. He never denied it," Plemmons said.

Hansen also made incriminating statements following a night of drinking at the home of an equestrian devotee in the exclusive suburb of Barrington, Illinois, Plemmons said. As the two men were leaving the party, Hansen spotted several boys' bikes in the garage of the home.

"He said, 'Let's take them. Boys like bikes.'" Plemmons said he reluctantly helped Hansen put the bikes in the back of the station wagon they were driving. The trip back to Hansen's home proved memorable because Plemmons took a wrong turn and drove north into Wisconsin instead of south toward Indiana, he said. During the ride Hansen brought up the boys' murders.

"Kenny started talking about Curtis. He said, 'Curt holds those boys over my head like a club, you know, we're going to have to kill him someday.' He told me to stay away from Curtis. He said Curtis hated anyone who was loyal to him. Kenny said Curtis once killed somebody in Chicago because he was mad." Hansen also claimed Curt Hansen "really was not" his brother but a half-brother.

Plemmons had his own run-in with Curtis Hansen, not long after Ken had suggested killing Curtis. The incident involved a dispute over a $6,000 barn bill Plemmons owed to the owner of a stable who was close to Curt. Plemmons was summoned into the stable owner's office to discuss the bill. When he got there, he saw that Curtis, the enforcer, was going to participate in the conversation. Plemmons got the message. He told the stable owner he would pay the bill in total the next day.

"Curt got up from his chair and grabbed me around the back of the neck and said, 'Don't go running to my fag brother about this or I'll have to kill you like he killed those kids. You know Kenny likes killing people. He plays with them after they're dead.'"

The statement froze Plemmons on the spot. He did not know what to say in response. The awkward moment prompted Curtis Hansen and the stable owner to erupt into laughter. Plemmons said he was deathly afraid of Curtis Hansen. In the summer of 1974 he watched Curtis Hansen use a pair of brass knuckles to beat a man who had made disparaging comments about horses owned by Frank Jayne Jr., Silas Jayne's nephew. "He was vicious," Plemmons said.

On another occasion while at the same stable, Plemmons said he saw the stable owner deep in a conversation with Curtis. The two men were standing near the trunk of Curtis Hansen's Cadillac. During the conversation, Curtis popped the hood of the car to show the stable owner the body of a man in his fifties lying in the trunk. Plemmons immediately looked away just as Curtis and the stable owner turned toward him. It wasn't quick enough. Over the next few weeks the stable owner asked Plemmons probing questions about what he'd seen that day. Plemmons played dumb. He knew that if he said he'd seen a body, he too would end up lifeless in the trunk of Curtis Hansen's car.

Plemmons said he also once considered borrowing money from a bail bondsman associated with Curtis Hansen. Hansen served as the bail bondsman's collector. When Plemmons decided not to borrow the cash, Curtis Hansen slapped him on the back and said, "That's the smartest thing you've ever done."

Plemmons offered additional details regarding Richard Bailey's $5,000 offer to him and Hansen to murder Helen Brach. He said the offer prompted another conversation with Hansen about the murders of the three boys. While on their way back to Hansen's stable following the lunch meeting with Bailey, Plemmons said Hansen expressed disbelief at Bailey's solicitation. He couldn't believe Bailey had only offered him $5,000 for the job. When they reached Hansen's home, the conversation touched on the murders of the three boys.

"I told Kenny I didn't understand why he turned the offer down. It was obvious Kenny was short on cash," Plemmons said. "He was always complaining that he had no money. So I said to him, 'You told me you killed three boys. You told me you helped set up the George Jayne murder. You said you watched Curt kill a man in Chicago. And you need the money. Why did you turn it down?'"

Hansen then shot Plemmons the familiar icy glare, which Plemmons had come to fear. "He told me with those boys 'it was either them or me.' He said in 1955 you couldn't be gay and the law was unforgiving and that it was a sin to be queer." Hansen also told Plemmons he was angry that Bailey and members of Silas Jayne's inner circle had made a lot of money off Helen Brach and were now only coming to him to clean up their mess.

"They must have screwed up," Hansen said. "They must have taken a lot of money from her."

Hansen also complained to Plemmons that he had been cheated by Silas Jayne. He said Jayne never paid him $10,000 for helping arrange the murder of George Jayne. Although the hit team that was recruited by Hansen only managed to kill off a few cases of beer, Hansen was adamant that he was entitled to $10,000 for helping get the job done. Plemmons said with so many people trying to kill George Jayne for Silas it would have been comedic had not one finally succeeded.

Before George Jayne was shot to death, Hansen told Plemmons, he and another member of the Jayne Gang had armed themselves with high-powered rifles and rented a room near the airfield where George and Marion Jayne kept their plane. The two gunmen planned to shoot George as he approached his aircraft on foot or taxied down the runway.

"Murder is not such a bad thing," Hansen said. "Even though I believe in God, if I kill someone I won't go to hell because God sends people to war every day where people get killed." Hansen also mentioned that he believed in reincarnation. "He said there was nothing wrong with killing because we're all coming back anyway."

The next time Plemmons recalled speaking to Hansen about the murders was in 1988 while the two men were having a few drinks at a Holiday Inn. After knocking back a few scotches, Hansen started lecturing Plemmons and accused the younger man of "wasting his life."

"That got me a little hot under the collar," Plemmons said. "So I said to him, 'Look at your life! You killed three kids and helped George Jayne get killed plus one other.'" Later on in the conversation, Plemmons asked Hansen if he worried someday he would be arrested and charged with the boys' murders. "He told me he was worried because too many people knew about it."

Hansen never went into any specific details about the boys' murders with Plemmons the way he had with Red Wemette or Roger Spry. However, he boasted that he was proud of his criminal achievements and the fact that he had never been convicted. Hansen was satisfied with his role in George Jayne's murder and some drug running that he had done between Chicago and Texas.

Hansen collected child pornography as well, Plemmons said. Once when he was at Hansen's apartment, Plemmons said, he noticed an 8mm projector and several rolls of film. When Hansen was out of the room Plemmons started up the projector and saw a film of young boys. Hansen often had young boys over at his apartment.

Toward the end of the conversation Cassidy asked Plemmons if he had spoken to Wemette or Spry recently. "I haven't spoken to either one of them in years," Plemmons said. "I didn't like either one of them. I couldn't tell you where they lived or if they're even alive."

CHAPTER 22

Jim Grady and John Rotunno had their share of lucky breaks throughout the Schuessler-Peterson investigation. After all, the entire investigation began with an off-the-cuff statement made during a single phone call. Throughout, witnesses turned up in unexpected places. One such witness was Roger Hammill, the photographer who took the crime scene photographs in 1955. He was found purely by accident. Grady and Rotunno had concluded an interview with a retired firefighter regarding the fires at the Idle Hour Stable when the retiree suggested they contact a local photographer who might have taken some photos of the blazes. After a few minutes of conversation with Hammill, the agents learned he had taken the crime scene photographs of the boys on that fateful day. Hammill was able to provide additional photographs of the scene and volunteered to testify at Hansen's trial. The ATF agents' luck continued. They hit the jackpot, however, six months after Kenneth Hansen's arrest.

The media's attention toward the case died down considerably once Hansen's case had entered the Cook County Criminal Court system. There were only a handful of reporters who covered every development and attended every court hearing. It was one of those hearings that would generate several news reports and lead to the next big break in the case.

At a status hearing on Hansen's case held on Thursday, March 30, 1994, before Cook County Circuit Court Judge Thomas Cawley, prosecutors Patrick Quinn and Scott Cassidy laid out additional facts of their case that had never been revealed before publicly. Sitting in Cawley's near empty courtroom that day was *Chicago Tribune* reporter John O'Brien and a reporter from the *Daily Southtown*. No other media attended the hearing.

Hansen's defense attorneys Jed Stone and Art O'Donnell had filed a motion seeking to suppress the statements of several witnesses who would testify that Hansen had sexually assaulted and then murdered the three boys. At the same time, Quinn and Cassidy sought permission from the judge to introduce evidence that Hansen routinely picked up and sexually assaulted hitchhikers. The prosecution claimed the evidence should be allowed because it showed a pattern to Hansen's criminal activity. Quinn and Cassidy said the state had several witnesses who would testify that Hansen admitted to them he had sexually assaulted and then murdered the boys.

During the hearing, Quinn revealed that once Hansen was in custody he had admitted to sexually assaulting as many as a thousand boys that he had picked up hitchhiking between 1955 and 1989. "We must be able to show his motive and intent and why he did it and show it through his own words," Quinn said. "Otherwise it would make no sense why he killed the three children. They were killed to silence them."

Jed Stone's reaction to the request offered a glimpse of Hansen's defense strategy. Stone argued that the prosecution wanted to bring in past acts of "homosexual behavior" to inflame the jury. Quinn responded that the state's case had nothing to do with homosexuality but with child abuse. Quinn told Cawley he would be fired from his job if he attempted to base a case on homophobic allegations.

"I'm heartened to hear the state's attorney's office thinks homophobia is dead," Stone said in response. "But that's poppycock. Homophobia is alive and well. Homosexual acts will be the cornerstone of the prosecution." Stone argued that testimony dealing with sex shouldn't be allowed because there was no evidence indicating the three boys were sexually abused. To bolster his argument, Stone showed Cawley a copy of correspondence written by Joseph Morris, who was chief of detectives of the Chicago Police Department in 1958. In the letter, Morris wrote there was no evidence the boys had been sexually abused. Instead, the letter noted, Bobby Peterson had suffered a head injury and had been strangled with a belt. Johnny Schuessler had received a blow to the neck, and his younger brother was manually strangled.

"After you cut through the state's homophobia, there's no evidence of sexual molestation," Stone said. "These boys were not sexually molested."

Quinn and Cassidy argued that they should be given the opportunity to show that Hansen was a pedophile who routinely picked up hitchhikers for sex. In order to do so, they claimed, they would need to bring in evidence showing a pattern to Hansen's behavior. Quinn told Judge Cawley that several of the state's witnesses would testify that Hansen told them he feared he would not survive long in prison if he were convicted of sexually assaulting a child.

"This defendant told three people he molested these children and then killed them," Quinn said. "The reason he killed them was because he was afraid they would go to the police. He decided these children had to die because he had sexually assaulted them."

Judge Cawley made a decision but crawled out onto thin ice. He told the prosecutors he would allow them to explore sex as a motive in the case, acknowledging the potential jury prejudice but reasoning that an attempt to get to the truth had overriding importance in the case. Cawley warned Cassidy and Quinn that they would only be able to broach Hansen's past sexual activities in a limited scope. He granted the defense motion seeking to limit such testimony and prohibit the mention of other crimes in which Hansen or any of the witnesses were involved. Mentioned specifically during the hearing as off-limits was Hansen's involvement in the murder of George Jayne.

Outside of courtroom, O'Donnell claimed Cawley's ruling was a mistake and would lay grounds for an appeal. Any good defense attorney would appeal a conviction born out of a trial in which the prosecution was allowed to present evidence of a defendant's sexual past that would incite a jury. O'Donnell predicted the ruling to allow evidence of homosexual activity would bring a reversal of any conviction.

The hearing generated two news stories, published in the *Chicago Tribune* and the *Daily Southtown*. Those stories prompted other Chicago media outlets to report that prosecutors had claimed in open court that Hansen had molested over a thousand boys he picked up hitchhiking over a thirty-nine-year period. One media outlet that picked up on the story was WGN-TV, a local *Chicago Tribune*–owned television station in Chicago that was carried by many cable systems nationwide.

When WGN broadcast its story, a photograph of Kenneth Hansen was flashed across the screen. The image had a profound effect on one man, a divorced alcoholic sitting in a trailer in the desert about forty miles outside of Tucson, Arizona.

For decades Herbert Hollatz, a retired pipe fitter, had buried his memories of what he knew about Kenneth Hansen under layers of fear and self-loathing. Hollatz saw Hansen's face and immediately made a connection to a past he had tried hard to forget. With the help of alcohol he had been able to drive what he knew out of his mind, but only for a while. The image of Kenneth Hansen brought back the memories that had haunted him for years. Finally he couldn't take it anymore. He picked up the phone and called his daughter. It was Monday, April 7, 1995. Hollatz told his daughter he couldn't believe what he saw and what he heard on the newscast. Kenneth Hansen had been arrested for the murders of three boys in Chicago in 1955. Hollatz thought Hansen had been arrested and charged in the murders decades ago.

Herbert Hollatz choked back his tears. He told his daughter he didn't know what to do. He unburdened himself. Through the tears and sobs it became clear that Hollatz had been harboring a deep, deadly secret for decades.

"Kenny did it. I know Kenny is guilty," Hollatz said. "He told me he did it. I should have done something a long time ago."

Cheryl Zormeier listened to her father empty his soul. Herbert Hollatz told his daughter everything he remembered about Kenneth Hansen. After she hung up with him, it didn't take Zormeier long to place a long distance phone call to the Chicago Police Department.

Zormeier reached a dispatcher and was transferred from one location to another. Eventually she was put in touch with Jim Grady. Since Hansen's arrest, Grady and Rotunno had fielded a number of calls from the public, offering tips. Some of the tips panned out, some didn't. Some just offered an opinion on the case. Grady recalls that Zormeier's call was different from many of the others. As Zormeier relayed her conversation with her father, Grady knew her call was important. Zormeier was familiar with so many details about Kenneth Hansen that Grady was convinced the information had to have originated with someone who knew Hansen. Zormeier said her father wanted to tell the police what he knew but was afraid to come forward because someone named Curt would murder him.

Grady took down all the information Zormeier had to offer. He wrote two pages of notes about the conversation. He then made several phone calls that night to John Rotunno and prosecutors Patrick Quinn and Scott Cassidy. A few days later Grady, Rotunno and Quinn flew to Tucson to interview Hollatz. The three men were in one car and Cheryl Zormeier and her husband were in another when they drove up to Hollatz's trailer. Hollatz was a man looking to get away from the world. His trailer sat alone in the desert.

After exiting their car, Quinn remained near the vehicle while Grady and Rotunno approached the trailer with their weapons held to their sides. Zormeier and her husband stayed in their car. Grady knocked on Hollatz's screen door. The weapons were precautionary; all the agents knew for certain at the time was that Hollatz had some information about Hansen's involvement in the murders. Nobody knew how Herb Hollatz would react to an unannounced visit by federal agents. Was he going to cooperate or come out guns blazing?

Hollatz came to the door and looked out, squinting into the sun. He was a slight man, about five feet, seven inches tall, wearing a T-shirt and a pair of dirty jeans. He was unarmed and obviously didn't pose a threat to anyone.

"Mr. Hollatz, my name's Jim Grady. We're police officers from Chicago. We'd like to talk to you about Kenneth Hansen. We understand that you might be able to help us with a few things," Grady said.

Hollatz invited the three men inside. He was sober but appeared unkempt. He might not have showered in days. Grady spotted gay pornographic photographs taped up on some of the walls, and Hollatz was living with a younger man. He became emotional out of fear, and shame.

He cracked open a beer and said he was afraid to talk to the agents about Kenneth Hansen because he was afraid of Hansen's brother. Hollatz feared Curtis Hansen would find out he had talked to the police and seek retribution. The agents assured Hollatz that Curtis Hansen was dead. When the agents got back to Chicago, they promised Hollatz they would mail a copy of Curtis Hansen's death certificate and a Polaroid snapshot of his grave marker to further assure him that Curtis wouldn't come calling. Hollatz described Curt Hansen as a "big man with no job and lots of money."

Before the interview started, Quinn read Hollatz his Miranda rights and asked him if he wanted an attorney present. At that time, the agents and Quinn did not know what role Hollatz played, if any, in the boys' murders. Hollatz said he was willing to talk to them without an attorney present.

Hollatz said he had known Kenneth Hansen from roughly 1953 to 1957. In the early 1950s he got to know Hansen when he boarded his horse "Baldy" at a stable Hansen operated with his father. In late 1952 or 1953, Hollatz said he ran away from home to escape his father, a Chicago police officer who was a strict disciplinarian. Hollatz had no place to stay. Hansen invited him to move into the stable. During his stay at the stable, Hollatz said Hansen performed oral sex on him. It wasn't something Hollatz desired, but he had no choice. He had nowhere else to stay. The statement fit Hansen's pattern. Hansen's sexual assault of Hollatz was similar to his assaults on Roger Spry and Red Wemette. Hansen was indeed an opportunist with predator instincts who forced himself on others who were in a tight spot.

Hollatz's relationship with Hansen continued after Hollatz moved back home and Hansen was drafted into the U.S. Army in 1953, he said. Hollatz became good friends with Hansen's girlfriend, Beverly Carlson. Before Beverly married Hansen, she and Hollatz actually went on a few dates, visiting Beverly's aunt and uncle in McHenry, Illinois, he said. While Hansen was in the Army, Beverly Carlson told him that Hansen had written a letter home to his parents admitting that he was homosexual. Carlson, who soon would become Hansen's wife, told Hollatz she also knew Hansen was homosexual but was willing to marry him because she thought he had a lot of money. Other witnesses had told the agents that Beverly Hansen knew about her husband's sexual preferences but thought she could change him. Hollatz resumed his friendship with Kenneth Hansen when he returned from his military service in 1955, he said.

At some point in time, the sexual relationship between Herb Hollatz and Kenneth Hansen had become consensual.

Hollatz remembered distinctly the murders of the three boys. Tears then began to well up in his eyes as he recalled the events that had forever changed the course of his life. Within a week or two of the murders, Hollatz said, he met Hansen either in the parking lot of a competing stable not far from the Idle Hour or the parking lot of a local tavern. He wasn't positive of the location. It was at night. He said Hansen was performing oral sex on him when Hansen started talking about the boys' murders. Hansen then confessed to Hollatz that he had murdered the boys.

Hollatz ended his relationship with Hansen immediately following the confession, he said. He faced a dilemma. He couldn't go to his father with what Hansen had told him because that would expose his homosexual relationship with Hansen. "If I went to my father with this, I was afraid he would never speak to me again," Hollatz said.

Hollatz had no choice but to run. So that is what he did. He suppressed his sexual orientation and married in 1956. He moved west and fathered six children. His marriage was doomed to fail; it was marred by his alcoholism and lengthy separations from his family. He later divorced his wife. Hollatz's life was far from ideal when Kenneth Hansen's face flashed across the television screen, and when it did, years of denial came crashing in.

"When I saw him on the television, it brought back all those memories. I was scared because of what I knew. I didn't know if Curt Hansen was out there looking for me to keep me quiet," Hollatz said. "This secret has been bothering me a long time."

Hollatz read over the written report that Grady had

drawn up based on the interview and signed the document indicating it was accurate. He agreed to testify against Hansen. Every member of the prosecution team agreed that Herbert Hollatz was the state's best witness against Hansen. What had once been a long shot was now a strong circumstantial case.

CHAPTER 23

A month before the agents and Patrick Quinn interviewed Herbert Hollatz, con man Richard Bailey made a difficult decision. Bailey was in a tight spot. He could take his federal case to trial and face a parade of women who would testify that he had romanced them and then bilked them out of thousands of dollars. If convicted, U.S. District Court Judge Milton Shadur would have no choice but to follow the federal sentencing guidelines and sentence Bailey appropriately. Bailey faced a long stretch in prison.

But if Bailey pleaded guilty to some of the charges, Shadur would be able to take his admission of guilt into consideration when handing down a sentence. Bailey rolled the dice. He knew he faced jail time but hoped his plea would lesson the severity of the sentence. On March

1, 1995, Bailey plead guilty to sixteen of the twenty-nine counts lodged against him. In entering his plea, Bailey denied having anything to do with the disappearance and presumed murder of Helen Brach. Bailey's defense attorney was Patrick Tuite. Tuite was a former Cook County state's attorney who had tried unsuccessfully to convict Silas Jayne in March 1966 on charges of conspiracy to commit murder. The case against Silas Jayne collapsed on the first day of the trial when the state's key witness suddenly couldn't remember that Silas Jayne had hired him to kill George Jayne.

Though Bailey avoided a trial, a sentencing hearing held by Shadur became a mini version of the trial that Bailey would never have. During that sentencing hearing, which lasted two weeks, prosecutors were able to disclose some details of the state's case against Kenneth Hansen. At the conclusion Shadur issued a forty-one-page decision in which he determined "it is more probable than not" that Bailey "had a powerful motive" to solicit the millionairess's murder after she threatened to reveal he defrauded her in a series of horse purchases.

Shadur found that Bailey had conspired to murder Brach based on a "preponderance of the evidence," a legal standard available to him as a result of the sentencing hearing. If Bailey had gone to trial, a jury would have been required to find him guilty beyond a reasonable doubt. A key witness against Bailey at the sentencing hearing was Joseph Plemmons. Plemmons testified that Bailey had offered him and Hansen $5,000 to kill "the candy lady." On June 6, 1995, Shadur sentenced Bailey to thirty years in prison. For Bailey, at age sixty-six, Shadur's decision amounted to a life sentence.

While Bailey's case was garnering headlines, Hansen's

defense attorneys were doing their best to hobble the
state's case against him before trial. When representing
clients charged with murder, there are only so many strate-
gies available to the defense. For veteran criminal court
watchers, it often seems that many defense attorneys representing alleged killers strategize using the same playbook.
In the weeks and months before Hansen went to trial,
Arthur O'Donnell and Jed Stone filed some of the typical
motions often seen in a murder trial. One of the motions
filed on Hansen's behalf sought to throw out statements he
made to the police that he had molested up to a thousand
boys over almost four decades.

Cook County Circuit Court Judge Michael P. Toomin
was now handling Hansen's case. At the hearing, O'Donnell told Judge Toomin that Hansen's statements should be
disallowed because O'Donnell had informed federal authorities a month before Hansen's arrest that he represented Hansen. If Hansen were arrested, federal agents
were to contact O'Donnell immediately. Judge Toomin
heard arguments on the motion because Judge Cawley had
retired from the bench.

Hansen testified as part of the motion seeking to suppress his statements. He looked frail and thin as a sheriff's
deputy led him into Judge Toomin's courtroom on the fifth
floor of the Cook County Criminal Courts Building. He
had grown a beard since his arrest. Toomin's courtroom
was going to provide a dramatic backdrop for Hansen's
trial. When Hollywood comes to Chicago and is in need of
a location to film a trial scene, it's usually shot in Toomin's
courtroom. The courtroom's twenty-five-foot ceilings are
inlaid with multicolored tiles, and the darkly paneled
judge's bench has been polished to a sheen. Hansen was
dressed in a tan prison uniform. With his pencil-thin arms

and unshaven face, he looked like a confused old man who had lost his way and not the alleged killer of three young boys.

On direct examination by O'Donnell, Hansen claimed he had asked for an attorney every fifteen minutes while he was being questioned over a twelve- to fourteen-hour period following his arrest.

"I asked to see my attorney," Hansen said. "I didn't know I was arrested or charged with anything. I didn't know I was in trouble."

To counter Hansen's testimony, Assistant Cook County State's Attorney Barbara Riley, Chicago Police Lt. Richard Schak and Lt. John Farrell testified that Hansen freely made to them the admission that he had molested numerous young men he had picked up hitchhiking over the decades. "Mr. Hansen never asked to see a lawyer," prosecutor Scott Cassidy told Toomin. "He thought he could talk his way out of this. According to the police and the assistant state's attorney, he wouldn't shut up." A few days after hearing testimony on the motion, Toomin ruled that Hansen's admission would be admissible.

Stone and O'Donnell weren't about to give up. A little less than one month after Toomin's ruling, they filed another motion seeking to bar evidence seized from Hansen's home prior to his arrest. Specifically, the defense team sought to bar much of the evidence pulled together in the case, claiming investigators were led to most of the state's witnesses from two address books seized at Hansen's home by the Chicago Police.

"I can assure you we found no witnesses using what we found in the home," Pat Quinn told the court. "Nothing came from these phone books." Outside the courtroom, O'Donnell and Stone told the press they knew the state's two primary witnesses against Hansen, Red Wemette and Roger Spry, didn't come from the phone books. Stone, however, said he believed the bulk of the state's case did come from the phone books. He pointed out that the investigators had contacted most of the witnesses after Hansen was arrested.

Stone and O'Donnell claimed the address books were the result of an illegal search of Hansen's home by Chicago Police Detective Richard Schak. Schak, however, testified that when police first tried to arrest Hansen at 6:30 A.M. and found that he was not home, Schak made his way into the home via an unlocked patio door. "I was in the home about fifteen minutes. I went from room to room looking for Mr. Hansen," Schak testified. During his time in Hansen's home, Schak said he spotted the address books in the kitchen and living room of the home. The police returned about 3:30 P.M. with a search warrant to seize them. Schak testified that investigators hoped to find Hansen's whereabouts by using the address book.

On August 11, 1994, Judge Toomin ruled that the evidence seized from Hansen's home was obtained legally. Quinn considered the ruling a minor victory. He told the court that after further consultation with the agents, it was determined that one of the state's witnesses came from the address books. Quinn said the prosecution most likely was not going to call that witness to testify.

In other matters, Stone asked the court to require Quinn to contact the various federal police agencies that had utilized Red as an informant to determine when Red first began telling federal agents that it was Hansen who murdered the boys. Outside the courtroom, Stone described Red as a "notorious stoolie" who had been working with federal agents since 1974. "We want to know when he began telling federal authorities about these murders," O'Donnell told the press. "It goes to his credibility as a witness, especially if he told them years ago and they took no action."

O'Donnell and Stone were on to something when it came to Wemette. Red had indeed told several FBI agents that he knew who was responsible for the murders of three boys in 1955. The agents, who were using Red as an informant in organized crime matters, failed to recognize the historical significance of Red's statement. At least one agent told Red he would revisit Wemette's allegations about the boys' murders, but that agent and others failed to look into Wemette's claim.

During the hearing, Quinn gave O'Donnell a letter from the FBI. The letter stated that the FBI had no reports indicating when or if Red ever told agents that Hansen had committed the murders. The defense was informed that Red claimed he had told his FBI handlers on several occasions that Hansen had admitted to him that he murdered the boys, but the FBI wasn't interested in the case. Quinn told O'Donnell he would contact other federal agencies and ask them to check their files and reports to see if Red ever raised the issue with other agencies.

Following the hearing, John Rotunno contacted one of the FBI agents who had been Wemette's handlers for several years. The agent, John Osborne, confirmed vaguely recalling that Wemette had made a statement about the murders of the boys. Osborne said he never wrote a report regarding Wemette's allegation and the accusation was not looked into because Wemette was being utilized purely for "O.C." activities at the time. Rotunno appreciated Osborne's candor.

Grady and Rotunno weren't the only ones who questioned potential witnesses. Quinn did some research on his own. A few weeks before Hansen's trial date, Quinn drove out to a retirement home in a northern Chicago suburb to interview former Chicago Police Sgt. George Murphy, who was in his nineties. Murphy, who was bedridden, but still mentally sharp, congratulated Quinn and the agents for cracking the case.

Quinn wanted to know if Murphy recalled ever hearing the name Kenneth Hansen come up in the investigation. Quinn mentioned that the prosecution team had received a few phone calls from retired police officers who claimed they knew something about Hansen but could provide no details. Murphy said he didn't recognize the name. Quinn was also interested in the 1955 investigation. He asked Murphy why police passed out sheets of paper to hundreds of schoolchildren back in 1955 and asked them to write down what they thought had happened to the boys.

"Well, we knew it was very possible some kid might know exactly what happened but would be too scared to tell the police. So we figured if we asked the kids and gave them a chance to respond anonymously, we might find out what happened."

Murphy said police read over all the compositions they received back. None of the kids' papers offered a solid clue as to the identity of the boys' killer.

As Quinn was about to leave, he noticed Murphy had become emotional. "I knew we'd catch the guy who did it someday. I'm really glad you got him," Murphy said. "I just wish it had been us forty years ago."

As Hansen's date with a jury drew near, O'Donnell and Stone filed a last-minute defense motion seen by some as an act of desperation. The motion, filed just twelve days before Hansen was to go on trial, sought to allow the testimony of a retired Chicago police officer who theorized that it was serial killer John Wayne Gacy who murdered the three boys. Gacy, who was prosecuted for the murders of thirty-three young men and boys in 1980, was executed for twelve of the murders in May 1994. The motion argued that the state waited to bring charges against Hansen until after Gacy had been executed.

The genesis for the defense motion was a 1989 article published in *Chicago* magazine by freelance writer Richard Vachula. The article was based on a theory postulated by retired Chicago Police Detective John Sarnowski. Sarnowski had been assigned to the Schuessler-Peterson case in 1955.

It was Sarnowski and his partner, Edwin Kocinski, who had discovered the last piece of evidence pinpointing the boys' whereabouts hours before they were murdered. According to the article, in June 1957 Sarnowski and his partner had gone to the Peterson home to search Robert's room, when Sarnowski noticed that Bobby Peterson's younger sister was wearing glasses. Sarnowski, who had a child with vision problems, asked Dorothy Peterson for the name of the girl's doctor. Dorothy Peterson told the detectives the eye technician was named Maria Gonzalez, and that she had offices in the Garland Building, located at 111 North Wabash in Chicago's Loop. She said Bobby had taken his younger sister to appointments at the Garland Building.

Because the Garland Building wasn't far from the movie theater where the three boys had gone to see *The African Lion*, Sarnowski and Kocinski interviewed the eye technician and the doorman at the building. On a hunch, the detectives asked to see the sign-in sheet at the building. It showed that Robert Peterson had signed in at 6 P.M. on October 16, 1955, the day he and his two friends were last seen alive.

Gonzalez told the detectives she recalled Bobby escorting his sister to appointments several times. She also recalled that Bobby was sometimes seen in the company of a boy, possibly a fifteen-year-old, who stood about five feet, eight inches high and weighed about 160 pounds. The boy had a large head, puffy cheeks and dark blond hair which he combed straight back. The boy also walked with a limp. Gonzalez told the detectives that she last saw Bobby and his sister on October 12, 1955, just a few days before Bobby and the Schuessler boys disappeared. On that day, the boy, whom she dubbed "Mr. Potato Head," was with Bobby. A friend of Bobby Peterson would later describe the same boy to detectives. He said the boy's name was "John" and he hung around a local candy store.

A police artist interviewed Gonzalez and drew a sketch of Mr. Potato Head. Police searched for the boy but never found him. The Schuessler-Peterson case eventually faded into obscurity. Fast forward to Christmas 1979. Sarnowski had retired from the Chicago Police Department. His wife Rosemary, while busy putting together a scrapbook of her husband's career, came across the sketch of Mr. Potato Head. She looked at the sketch and later told a *Chicago* magazine writer that the sketch reminded her of someone. Soon afterward, Rosemary Sarnowski saw a photograph of serial killer John Wayne Gacy. She told her husband that Mr. Potato Head looked just like John Wayne Gacy.

Sarnowski agreed. Though retired, he began looking into the life of John Wayne Gacy and concluded it was Gacy who murdered the three boys in 1955 at the age of thirteen. Sarnowski based his theory on the fact that Gacy lived not too far from the boys. He also concluded that the boys were murdered in the same fashion as Gacy's known victims—they were tied up and then strangled. Sarnowski was also convinced Gacy murdered the three boys in the garage of his home. The garage had a dirt floor, which Sarnowski claimed would explain the grime found on the soles of the boys' feet.

Thus the Gacy theory was born. Other journalists picked up on Sarnowski's hypothesis. As word began to leak out that an arrest was imminent for the boys' murders, the *Chicago Sun-Times* resurrected the Gacy theory and published an article on August 3, 1994, quoting Sarnowski. Sarnowski didn't think that Silas Jayne was involved in the murders. "Those guys are so off base," Sarnowski told the newspaper. "All three boys were blindfolded. All three were gagged. All three were beaten before and after death. And that was a Gacy trademark."

O'Donnell wanted permission to use the Gacy evidence. The state strongly objected. Toomin took the matter under advisement and told both parties he would rule on it prior to trial.

Reaction to the defense motion was swift. Former Gacy prosecutor William Kunkle said the notion that Gacy was able to pull off the murders of three boys at so young an age was preposterous. Before he left the Cook County State's Attorney's Office for private practice, Kunkle said, two of the Chicago Police Department's best homicide detectives reexamined the Schuessler-Peterson case for any possible link between Gacy and the slayings of the three boys.

"It's silly. The bottom line is there is nothing to it," Kunkle told the *Daily Southtown*. "We found there was no way Gacy could have committed the murders. The sketch doesn't even look like him." The investigation by the Chicago detectives determined Gacy didn't limp and wasn't overweight when he was thirteen. Gacy also had no means to dispose of the bodies in the forest preserve. Sarnowski theorized that Gacy secretly borrowed the family car to dump the bodies. "Even if you believe Gacy was evil to the core, it's tough to believe the very first time he killed someone he did a triple and then didn't do another one until 1975," Kunkle said.

Three days before jury selection was to begin for Hansen's trial, Toomin ruled that Sarnowski's testimony was inadmissible. It may not have mattered. Sarnowski, who was being treated for cancer, was too ill to testify. The prosecution had objected to a defense request to admit Sarnowski's theory via an affidavit. The prosecution would never stipulate to such a request and deny itself the opportunity to cross-examine Sarnowski. Toomin agreed.

"None of what you have said here or what Sarnowski could say connects Gacy to this crime," Toomin said. "The jury would hear the name John Wayne Gacy and that would set them off."

Kenneth Hansen's defense would be limited to testimony from a friend from his Army days that he had visited in Texas while on his honeymoon. The defense would also rest on the stringent cross-examination of the state's witnesses. The stage was set and the curtain was about to rise on Act One.

CHAPTER 24

Soon after Kenneth Hansen was charged with the murders of Bobby, John and Tony, Assistant Cook County State's Attorney Patrick Quinn received a telephone call from an attorney who represented Malcolm and Dorothy Peterson, the parents of Bobby. The attorney had a simple request. He asked Quinn if Hansen could be tried without any involvement from the Petersons. During the course of the conversation, it was relayed to Quinn that Malcolm and Dorothy Peterson didn't have the emotional strength to endure a trial and relive their son's murder. Quinn told the attorney he would do his best to keep the Petersons off the witness stand. In court filings, however, Malcolm Peterson was identified as a potential witness. Quinn and fellow prosecutor Scott Cassidy never planned to call Malcolm

Peterson as a witness, but they didn't want to close the door on that possibility if his testimony were needed.

The day before the trial was to begin, after a jury of seven men and five women had been selected to hear Hansen's case, both the prosecution and defense stipulated that an interview of Malcolm Peterson that had been conducted in 1955 could be presented as uncontested evidence in the defense's case. Though the murders of the boys would be the focus of one city for the next week, Malcolm and Dorothy Peterson would be spared the anguish of a trial.

The eve of the trial was hectic for John Rotunno and Jim Grady. Neither man got much sleep. Rotunno was nervous, his mind raced. He and Grady had spent most of the evening prepping witnesses for the next day. As a result, Rotunno found himself replaying many of the interviews with dozens of witnesses. Over the past two years he and Grady had taken statements from forty-six individuals and interviewed almost one hundred persons. The witness list that the state gave to the defense included ninety-nine names.

Rotunno was confident that Hansen would be convicted but was plagued by doubts that maybe he had missed something along the way. It wasn't unusual for Rotunno to experience the jitters. He was a perfectionist and would only have been completely satisfied if Hansen had offered a full confession, signed and court recorded, when he had been arrested.

Grady, on the other hand, was not as nervous. Grady had other things on his mind. His mother, Mary Rose, who had been diagnosed with terminal pancreatic cancer, had moved in recently with his wife and children. Grady's time was divided between his wife, children and the demands of his job and his dying mother. He had little time to obsess over what he might have missed. He was more confident than Rotunno that their case was a winner, that the jury would reach the same conclusion: that Hansen was guilty. In any event, he and Rotunno had given the case their best effort. Rotunno was also concerned about Grady's mother. He had known Mrs. Grady since he was a boy. Rotunno's mother, Virginia, and Grady's mother had socialized over the years and played bridge together.

In addition to prepping witnesses, Rotunno and Grady were busy acting as chauffeurs and porters for the state's witnesses. Many of them were put up at a hotel in a western suburb of the city. The Bureau of Alcohol, Tobacco and Firearms took no shortcuts when it came to providing security for the trial. As far as the ATF knew, the Chicago Outfit still wanted Red Wemette dead. Rotunno requested assistance from the ATF's Special Response Team. The SRT unit cordoned off an entire floor of the hotel and set up motion detectors plus video surveillance cameras throughout the building. No one could get to the witnesses unless they were cleared by security. No one ever tried to breech the security perimeter. The trial was to proceed without any outside interference.

Before opening statements were heard on September 6, 1994, Judge Toomin had to dispense with several pretrial motions filed by the defense and the state. Arthur O'Donnell and Jed Stone tried one more time to improve Hansen's case by seeking to prevent the state from mentioning the name of Silas Jayne throughout the trial. O'Donnell and Stone claimed that the mere mention of Jayne's name in connection to Hansen would inflame the jury. In addition, in a separate motion filed by the prosecution, Quinn and Cassidy sought to limit testimony about Hansen's past, specifically that he had never been convicted of any crime.

The defense argued that it was fundamentally unfair that defense witnesses could not be called to testify about Hansen's lack of any convictions while prosecution witnesses could raise allegations that Hansen had committed dozens, if not hundreds, of illegal acts of molestation against children. In deciding the matter, Toomin noted that previous court rulings supported the state's motion to limit the scope of what defense and state witnesses could say about a defendant's past.

"When do we start limiting virtue but we emblazon sin when the evidence is all condemning?" O'Donnell stated in protesting the ruling. "It strikes me as being distinctly disingenuous [that the] state can announce to the press that this man had sexual contact with over one thousand people . . . Now virtue is going to be covered over. The fact that he's never had trouble with the law at all cannot be mentioned. Isn't there something fundamentally off balance with that?"

O'Donnell further questioned the veracity of the state's claim that Hansen admitted he had molested one thousand boys. "You'd think if there were that many boys out there, one of them would have come forward by now," O'Donnell said. He was joined by Stone, who added, "We deny that the statement was ever made. It makes him the Wilt Chamberlain of pedophiles. A ridiculous statement, hyperbole on the part of the prosecution."

Judge Toomin, who was considered by many to be a no-nonsense judge, refused to budge. He pointed out that Judge Cawley had previously ruled on the evidence regarding Hansen's sexual past, and while he might not have made the same ruling, he would not overrule Judge Cawley's decision. Judge Toomin also ruled that Silas Jayne's name could be used during the proceedings as long as the prosecution did not connect Hansen to the murder of George Jayne.

After the motions had been addressed, the jury was led into the packed courtroom. Hansen was already seated at the defense table, facing them. He looked frail and thin, very much like a helpless old man, dressed in a blue suit that appeared several sizes too big, a white shirt, a blue tie and white gym shoes.

The atmosphere in Toomin's courtroom held an added touch of solemnity that day. Hansen's trial was going to be part of history and everyone in the room knew it. The sixteen long, wooden, graffiti-scarred benches in the courtroom were filled to capacity with reporters and attorneys. In all, there were about one hundred fifty people packed into the room.

The testimony that was heard on that day would take spectators back to a different era, one colored by nostalgia and happy memories. Back to a time when children roamed the city's neighborhoods freely and without fear; when high school boys walked their sweethearts home from a date and when it seemed strangers were kind to one another. The city that had waited decades for an explanation as to why a terrible crime had been committed was now about to get some answers.

It was clear from the opening statements that Kenneth Hansen's sexual appetite was going to play a crucial role in the trial. The prosecution wanted the jury to understand that the trial of Kenneth Hansen wasn't an indictment of the homosexual lifestyle. It seems absurd that in 1994 the public could easily confuse homosexuality with pedophilia.

The defense, on the other hand, would argue that the case was all about sex. As a result of that posture, it was important for the prosecution to get out in front of the sex issue and to distance itself from any perceived anti-gay position. Months prior to Hansen's trial, homosexuality had played a role in the trial of a man charged with the murder of his homosexual lover's then wife. The man was acquitted of the crime, due some said in part to the defense's strategy in and outside of the courtroom of attacking the state's case as homophobic.

"Ladies and gentlemen of the jury, let me start by telling you what this case is not about. This case is not about homosexuality," Quinn said in his opening remarks. "What this case is about is child molestation and murder." Quinn than gave a brief synopsis of the state's case against Hansen. He said over the past thirty-nine years Hansen had made statements to several people either confessing to the boys' murders or indicating his involvement in their slayings. Quinn pointed out, though, that Hansen had lived as a free man for decades while the boys lay in their graves. The time for justice had arrived, he said.

"Every witness you hear from that stand will tell you how they were touched by this case and how they have never, ever forgotten it. And, ladies and gentlemen, I assure you as I stand here now that you will never forget this case either," Quinn said. "And at the end of the case you will find that justice delayed is not justice denied."

In his opening statement, O'Donnell claimed the state's case had little to do with the actual murders and more to do with Kenneth Hansen's homosexuality. "We will not deal with the question of homosexuality in the same sense that Mr. Quinn does. We will deal with the question of murder that took place forty years ago and you will see the emphasis between the defense case and the state's case by that and that alone. . . . I have to beg you, do not make this a whole case of homosexuality."

The state's case was nothing more than fabrication, woven from the lies and stories of paid witnesses who were working hand in hand with federal agents to rebuild the tarnished reputation of the Bureau of Tobacco, Alcohol and Firearms, O'Donnell said.

"An unholy alliance was created a few years ago, that alliance was between William Wemette, a man who has to please people who pay him money, provide him housing, give him free telephone service, and a unit of government called ATF," O'Donnell said. "The ATF in 1993 was probably the most discredited law enforcement agency on the face of this earth after the Waco disaster and Ruby Ridge. They desperately needed to seek to rehabilitate their image before the public."

O'Donnell added that the case was unique in that it had taken so many years for the state to charge a suspect. He admitted he and Stone were hobbled in their defense and faced a daunting task in defending a man for a crime that took place decades ago. The grandfatherly defense attorney likened the case to those in which former Nazi concentration camp guards were charged with war crimes after being found living in the United States.

Although Toomin had ruled earlier that the defense could not use the John Wayne Gacy defense, O'Donnell just barely skirted the issue when he told the jury the only hard evidence ever uncovered in the case was developed by Chicago Police Detective John Sarnowski and his partner when they had determined that Robert Peterson had signed the visitor's log at the Garland Building on the day the boys disappeared. O'Donnell theorized that Robert, Tony and John went to the building to meet someone. The person that they met was the boys' real killer, he said.

"If you listen carefully to the evidence, you will see that

there is no physical evidence, no scientific evidence, no fingerprints, no eyewitnesses, nothing but a few isolated circumstances plus the testimony of . . . paid witnesses and another pathetic character by the name of Hollatz. None of these people who heard [about] these horrible crimes ever told another single human being about it. And you have to ask yourself why? Because ladies and gentlemen, that is the quality of the evidence that they have here . . . [The state] is hoping your prejudice and emotion . . . clouds your sense of direction and keeps you distracted from focusing on the one thing that not only is there a total lack of any evidence against Kenneth Hansen for forty years. The evidence that has been produced on this case by indicates that somebody else committed this crime."

A total of eight witnesses were called on the first day of the trial. One of the first was what prosecutors term a "life and death" witness. The only living relative of Anton and John Schuessler, an aunt named Beatrice Blane, was called to the stand. Blane, who would sit through the entire proceedings, testified that she recalled the murders and had attended her nephews' funerals.

The most dramatic testimony on the first day came from Hetty Salerno and Roger Spry. In a typical British accent not often heard by many Midwesterners, Salerno told the jury that on the night of October 16, 1955 between 9 and 10 P.M. she and her husband and a neighbor heard screams coming from the direction of the Idle Hour Stable. "I heard two screams. The first scream was loud, piercing, it was a young voice and it was a frightened scream. It scared me. Then a little while later the next scream came lower than the first scream," she said. Salerno said she had never heard a scream like the one she heard that night. She added that it sounded as if it came from a young boy.

Cassidy attempted to get Salerno to say she had never heard screams like that even when she worked as an ambulance driver in London during the Blitz. Stone objected to the line of questioning before she could answer. Salerno also said that after the boys' bodies were discovered and her husband had talked to police, she spotted a group of about thirty police officers searching the field near the Idle Hour Stable.

Following Salerno was retired photographer Roger Hammill. Hammill testified that he was called to the scene that day to take photographs of the boys' bodies. His testimony was also important, because it laid the foundation for the state to enter his photographs into evidence. The black-and-white photographs were powerful images. They showed the boys' naked, bruised bodies lying in a ditch. Others showed the press gathering near the scene, within feet of the boys' remains. Some members of the jury reacted visibly when they saw the images. Several turned pale, one appeared to wipe a tear from her eyes. Hammill, who acted as the crime scene photographer for several police departments until he retired in 1982, said the crime scene was not protected in any way.

Roger Spry was then called to testify. Every juror appeared to hang on his words, especially after he explained how he had been abandoned as a boy and come to live with Hansen. The soft-spoken cowboy said he had initially spurned Hansen's sexual advances but eventually acquiesced to the demands. Over strong objections raised by Stone and O'Donnell, Spry was allowed to tell the jury that Hansen had molested him for seven years. Spry also testified that Hansen made a habit of picking up young men hitchhiking whom he would take back to the stable and sexually assault. "He called them chicken," Spry said.

In the most chilling testimony that day, Spry recounted Hansen's explanation for killing the boys. As he had told Grady, Rotunno and Cassidy months earlier, Spry said Hansen had gotten drunk one night while the two men were repairing saddles and begun reminiscing about the murders after Silas Jayne's name came up in a conversation.

"He said that he was having sex with the younger boys and that the older boy showed up and caught him. . . . So Kenny said he grabbed him and he had a hold of him around the throat and that he was watching the other two boys so they couldn't get away," Spry said. At the request of the prosecution, Spry stood up in the witness stand and demonstrated how Hansen had showed him how he choked the boy in the crook of his arm.

"He said he grabbed him like this," Spry said, showing the jury, his arm cocked as if it held a young boy by the neck. "With his right arm to hold him so he could have his arm free so the other two boys couldn't get away . . . He said the other two boys were trying to get away. He said . . . the other kid was screaming and . . . he had accidentally choked the kid to death." After he had murdered the boy, Hansen told Spry, he had no other choice but to murder the other two.

As Spry testified about the attack, Hansen shook his head as in disbelief and muttered audibly, "That's stupid." The jury didn't hear Hansen's comment, but several members of the media did notice his remark.

When Silas Jayne came into the barn and discovered the murders he went "crazy, he was really mad," Spry testified. He added Hansen had told him that Jayne feared the murders would ruin his business. "He said that he and Si took and loaded the kids in the car because Si figured to cover himself up he'd help Kenny and they would take them and they dropped them off in the forest preserve."

Over the next few days the state would call twenty-two witnesses plus five rebuttal witnesses to the stand. Herbert Hollatz and Joseph Plemmons were called to testify on the second day of testimony. Hollatz proved to be the state's star witness. As he recounted the events that had changed the course of his life, tears began to fill Herb Hollatz's eyes and his voice weakened. He told the jury it was during a consensual sexual encounter with Hansen that he first learned of Hansen's involvement in the murders.

"He asked me for a favor," Hollatz said. "He was going to tell me something and to promise that I wouldn't say anything to anybody."

"Did you promise not to say anything to anybody?" Quinn asked.

"Yes," Hollatz responded.

"What did he tell you?" Quinn asked.

"He told me he had just killed three boys," Hollatz said, almost choking on his words. Hansen's confession to him came about one week after the boys were killed, he said.

"When Ken Hansen told you that he murdered these three boys that you knew about, what did you say?" Quinn asked.

Hollatz answered, "I said, why?"

"What did Ken Hansen tell you when you asked him why?" Quinn asked.

"He said that somebody told him to do it," Hollatz testified.

In further testimony Hollatz explained that Hansen told him he picked up the three boys hitchhiking. In addition, Hansen threatened Hollatz and told him if he breathed a word of the murders to anyone, his brother Curtis would come looking for him. The threat worked. When police interviewed Hollatz at a stable where he was boarding his horse several weeks after Hansen's confession, he said, he remained silent. "I told them I knew nothing about anything," Hollatz testified. Hollatz kept quiet for so many years also because he feared revealing his homosexual relationship to his father, a Chicago police officer.

During cross-examination O'Donnell attacked Hollatz's credibility. He raised the possibility that Hollatz was lying and asked Hollatz if it was true that he had been hospitalized for alcoholism treatment. O'Donnell also raised the possibility of jealousy as a motive behind Hollatz's testimony. He asked Hollatz if he too had fallen in love with Beverly Carlson while Hansen was serving in Korea.

O'Donnell's cross was blistering; on more than one occasion, Hollatz, who was visibly upset, did not respond to his questions.

"Now after you heard this horrendous statement by Kenneth Hansen within a week or so of the bodies being found, you didn't even talk to your father, your mother, your sister, right?" O'Donnell asked.

"Nobody," Hollatz said.

You didn't go to your father's friends on the police force and tell them what you knew, did you?" O'Donnell inquired.

Once again, Hollatz responded, "Nobody."

"There's no question that you knew about the Peterson-Schuessler boys. It was the biggest thing that happened in that area at that time, right?" O'Donnell said.

Hollatz responded, "Yes."

"It was in every newspaper, every radio, every program,

but you never ever contacted anybody to let them know what you heard?" O'Donnell said.

Once again Hollatz responded, "No."

"After your father died in 1980, you didn't have to worry about what your father would think. Didn't it occur to you to go to one of his friends on the police force or somebody?" O'Donnell asked. Hollatz did not respond to the question.

"Didn't you know this man, this murderer, was loose on the street?" O'Donnell said. Once again Hollatz remained mute.

On redirect examination, Hollatz told the court he had never before publicly admitted his homosexual past. Hollatz was essentially coming out of the closet at the murder trial, he said.

Other testimony that day came from Bobby Stitt and Joseph Plemmons. Stitt, also a former stable hand who was sent to live with Hansen at a young age because his family could no longer care for him, said that Hansen had tried unsuccessfully to sexually molest him on several occasions. The first time was after Hansen returned to the stable drunk following a polo match. Though he spurned Hansen's advances, Stitt told the jury he willingly provided sexual partners for him by stopping to pick up every young male hitchhiker he came across and bringing him back to the stable. Stitt estimated that he provided thirty to thirty-five victims. Like the others, Stitt said he too feared Curtis Hansen.

When he testified, Plemmons said that Hansen had told him on three occasions, specifically in 1972, 1976 and 1988, that he had killed the three boys. Plemmons said Hansen admitted he killed the boys because "it was either them or me. He said in 1955 to be gay was unacceptable. Society wouldn't tolerate it. It was unforgivable."

Plemmons's testimony proved to be disjointed and somewhat confusing. Later Quinn admitted he had not done a very good job of prepping the witness. Quinn, however, was in precarious straits while questioning Plemmons. Much of what Plemmons had to say, he had learned from Hansen while conversing with him about other crimes in which Hansen had been involved. Those crimes included the murder of George Jayne and Richard Bailey's attempt to find a hit man to murder Helen Brach.

Quinn did his best to guide Plemmons through those conversations without raising anything about Brach or the George Jayne slaying. Judge Toomin had specifically forbidden the state from mentioning anything about George Jayne's murder. During one exchange, however, Plemmons crossed the line. Under direct examination Plemmons let it be known that Hansen was involved in George Jayne's murder. Stone moved for an immediate mistrial. Toomin denied the motion following a brief discussion away from the jury.

Plemmons also admitted he had cut a deal in exchange for his testimony with the federal government to slash his prison term on a fraud conviction. He said he faced a sentence of three years in prison but that was reduced to seventeen months. He also testified that he received $5,800 in various forms of compensation, including a hernia operation, from the government.

Testimony on the third day of the trial was dominated by the appearance of William "Red" Wemette. Before he was ushered into the courtroom, about a dozen athletic-looking men and women took up strategic positions throughout the room. These were members of the ATF's

Special Response Team. Four men, two on the inside and two on the outside, covered the door of the courtroom. At least another eight were scattered about the room. One man stood in each corner and several were seated among the spectators. Though no weapons could be seen, it was obvious the security detail was armed, judging by the bulges underneath their suit coats.

Jurors heard a third version of the murders from Wemette. He said Hansen had admitted to him on at least a dozen occasions that he had murdered the three boys. The first admission came in 1968, while Hansen and Wemette were sharing a bottle of scotch in a house trailer that Hansen kept at his stable. "He said he wanted to tell me about a very famous case. He said he almost came that close to getting caught," Wemette said, holding his thumb and forefinger about half an inch apart.

"He said he strangled the three boys," Wemette said. "He said he picked them up hitchhiking and took them to a barn . . . the Idle Hour Stable. He said he asked his brother for assistance." Wemette said Hansen's brother, Curt, helped him commit the murders. "I believe he said his brother injured one of the kids with a blunt instrument of some type." Wemette also testified that a third person, possibly a Cook County Forest Preserve District employee, was involved in the slayings.

Hansen, Wemette said, first sexually assaulted Anton Schuessler while the other two boys were distracted by riding a pony. After he had finished assaulting Tony, he sent the youngest boy out of the barn and told John Schuessler to come in. Little Tony apparently told Bobby what had happened and the two walked back into the room and confronted Hansen. "There was a scramble," Wemette quoted Hansen saying. "And he asked his brother for assistance.

He told me his brother botched the job. That there was a piece of evidence left behind. He seemed plagued by that and was afraid he would get caught."

Soon after the murders, Hansen moved to the south side of the city to avoid police scrutiny. A few months after, when the case began to heat up, Hansen arranged for a barn at the Idle Hour, where the murders had occurred, to be burned down to cover his tracks, Wemette testified.

It was up to Jed Stone to cross-examine Wemette. Stone zeroed in on Wemette's long history as a federal informant from 1971 to 1989. Stone wanted to know why during that period of time Wemette never told a Chicago Police officer about Hansen's involvement in the boys' murders. Stone didn't ask Wemette if he had ever told any FBI agents about Hansen's role, because during the course of pretrial preparation, Stone had been informed that Wemette had told the FBI about Hansen's involvement in the murders but the FBI had ignored the claim. Stone did ask Wemette if he'd ever told any assistant United States attorneys about Hansen when debriefed about other matters.

"It wasn't even on any of our minds at the time," Wemette said in response.

Wemette proved to be a cagey witness. During one tense exchange with Stone, in which it was clear Stone was trying to trip Red up on his response, Wemette broke into a wide grin and chuckled. The laugh didn't sit well with Stone. "Mr. Wemette, there's nothing funny here. Am I mistaken about that as well?" Stone asked.

Wemette responded, "The only humorous part is you're trying to confuse me."

Other testimony came from Cook County Medical Examiner Edmund Donoghue. Using a pointer and several enlarged photographs of the boys' corpses. Donoghue pointed out various forensic details. He said that each of the boys had been strangled but that Bobby Peterson had been murdered with a belt or a rope.

The state rested its case on Monday, September 11, 1994, following testimony from Chicago Police Lt. John Farrell and Assistant Cook County State's Attorney Barbara Riley. Both Riley and Farrell testified that following his arrest, Hansen denied murdering the three boys but admitted to molesting hundreds of young boys he picked up hitchhiking over decades.

During his cross-examination of Farrell, Stone asked him if he had obtained Hansen's employment records from the Internal Revenue Service to determine if Hansen had worked at the Idle Hour when the boys were murdered. Farrell replied he had not. Following the questioning, Quinn asked for a sidebar. In the sidebar conversation he pointed out that the defense was barred from bringing up the issue of IRS records. "IRS records reflect this defendant has never filed a return," Quinn said.

Riley told the court that Hansen had informed her that he was bisexual. "He stated that if he were to pay attention to the women around the stables, his wife would become upset. He stated that his wife never seemed to know or pay attention if he were hanging around with the stable boys." The state rested its case without presenting one shred of physical evidence tying Hansen to the crime.

O'Donnell and Stone had little ammunition in mounting a strong defense for their client by way of witnesses. Prior to the trial, the defense had claimed it would be impossible to mount a defense because many of those who could fill in the blanks for Hansen by providing alibis were dead.

The defense would call six persons to the stand. The

first witness called was John Rotunno. Rotunno was questioned for less then five minutes about two witnesses he had interviewed who had both said they could only recall one sexual indiscretion on Hansen's part. Rotunno was called apparently to show that not everyone who knew Hansen considered him promiscuous or a pedophile.

The next person called was perhaps the strongest defense witness. Frank M. Jayne, the last surviving brother of the infamous Jayne Gang. Jayne slowly made his way to the stand. He was the brother of both Silas and George Jayne. Jayne, who was hard of hearing, provided the only humorous moment during the proceedings.

"Frank, how old are you?" O'Donnell asked him.

"Seventy-four going on seventy-five. Oh, my . . . nuts. I am eighty-four," Jayne said.

"Eighty-four?" O'Donnell repeated.

"I was thinking, I was thinking of your age," Jayne said. Members of the jury and the spectators then erupted in laughter.

Jayne testified he had been in the stable business with his brother Si in the 1950s. He claimed Silas ran a top-notch operation and stabled thoroughbreds and taught only English-style riding. He added that he knew all of his brother's employees and Kenneth Hansen wasn't one of them. Jayne also pointed out that Hansen was a Western saddle rider, not English.

"We taught English riding and hunting and jumping so that customers when they graduated from that, they could go in better competition. And we had much better horses," Jayne said. He added that Hansen was just starting out in the business at that time and was familiar with only livery horses. He said he did not meet Kenneth Hansen until sometime in the early 1960s, sometime between 1961 and 1963.

Jayne also testified that there was a night watchman and about eleven other people, including a caretaker, his family, a cook and four stable hands who were living at the Idle Hour Stable in 1955. In addition the night watchman, a man known as Big John, would let four Dobermans loose on the premises after hours to guard against prowlers. Jayne's testimony suggested that if the three boys had been murdered at the Idle Hour, someone would have heard a commotion. Jayne added that his brother Silas owned the Idle Hour Stable from 1952 until about 1970, when he sold it.

The next defense witness was a man named Edwin Thomas. Thomas testified that he had known Kenneth Hansen most of his life, having worked for him or lived at the stable since he was a young boy. Thomas said that, although he came to suspect Hansen was homosexual when he got older, he never once approached Thomas for sex or asked him to pick up male hitchhikers. Thomas added that Roger Spry was a liar who couldn't be trusted.

On the second day of testimony by the defense, Hansen's son, Mark, was called. Mark Hansen said he didn't realize his father was homosexual until he was in his twenties. He said he never saw his father attempt to sexually assault anyone.

The defense presented its final witness on September 13. Called to testify was Dan Strong, a former Army buddy who had served with Hansen in Korea. Strong testified that Hansen and his wife, Beverly, had come to visit him in Texas in the fall of 1955 for a period of several weeks. Strong, a residential home builder from Texas, said he and the Hansens traveled to the Gulf Coast and to Mexico. He told the court he wasn't positive, but he thought the visit might have been in October 1955. Strong could not provide any documentation to pinpoint the exact time. He spent about fifteen minutes on the witness stand.

The prosecution then put on five rebuttal witnesses. The gist of their testimony was that they knew Kenneth Hansen worked at the Idle Hour Stable in 1955 and that Hansen was a pedophile. One witness, Robert Milliken, said he had gone to live with Hansen after he had run away from home. Milliken said Hansen had sexually assaulted him in 1985 when he was fifteen years old.

The trial them moved into closing arguments. Closing arguments are the last chance to drive home the important aspects of a case, but they're a double-edged sword. In a criminal case an impassioned closing argument may convince a potential holdout to convict a defendant or strengthen the juror's resolve that the defendant is not guilty. As the prosecution and defense were about to deliver the final words in Kenneth Hansen's case, Judge Toomin's courtroom once again filled with spectators. Throughout the proceedings, the trial had been well attended. It was overflowing, however, for the opening and closing statements.

Patrick Quinn was given the first opportunity to speak. For about forty-five minutes he went over the state's case, offering thumbnail sketches of the testimony of each witness and pointing out why he believed certain facts were important to the state's case. Quinn once again argued that the state's case was not a prosecution of homosexuality. "Counsel keeps hammering that I'm sort of Neanderthal about homosexuals," Quinn said. "I don't give a tinker's damn what adults do in their bedrooms. But it changes dramatically with children . . ."

Quinn urged the jury not to make the same mistake that the Chicago Police Department did in 1955 and ignore the screams that came from the Idle Hour Stable. Going into the trial, Quinn and Cassidy theorized that Silas Jayne used his influence to turn the investigation away from the Idle Hour, possibly though a corrupt influence in the Chicago Police Department.

"The police were right the first day. It was at the Idle Hour, it was the Jaynes. It was Silas Jayne and his men," Quinn said, pointing at Ken Hansen. "They [the police] bought into their stories and left it alone, never to come back. Don't you make the same mistake . . . The first day the police had the right place. We know that from the witnesses. If they had followed up those leads the first day, this case would have been solved forty years ago."

The fact that Roger Spry, Red Wemette, Herb Hollatz and Joseph Plemmons testified differently of what they knew about the same crime showed that the witnesses had to be telling the truth and did not collaborate, Quinn said.

"Counsel would have you believe that this case revolves around ATF coming in to protect themselves after Waco. Do you honestly believe for a moment there was any pressure in 1991 or 1993 or today to solve the Schuessler-Peterson triple murder from 1955? Do you think for a moment that anybody outside of the families themselves lost a second of sleep about these cases in the early 1990s? There was no pressure on anybody to solve these cases. This case was put away in the attic to collect dust. There was no pressure to solve it."

Defense attorneys are given only one opportunity to address the jury before deliberations begin. It's their last chance to plant a kernel of doubt in the jury's mind. Every defense attorney hopes his or her case is strong enough to sway the jury. But in the end all a defense attorney needs to do is cause one juror to doubt the state's case.

Jed Stone took his best shot. He hammered at the fact that the state had presented no hard evidence that Hansen had committed a crime. He argued that the testimony of Wemette, Spry and Plemmons had to be discounted because those witnesses had cut deals to stay out of prison or, in Red's case, the testimony came from the mouth of a professional snitch. Herbert Hollatz was a pathetic figure, Stone said. Hollatz was a drunk who couldn't be trusted to tell the truth. In the end the state's case was nothing more then an exercise in character assassination. The state had used Hansen's bisexual orientation coupled with unfounded allegations of pedophilia to pin the murder of three boys on him four decades after the fact. The only physical evidence in the case came from the defense, in the form of a stipulated copy of the sign-in registry at the Garland Building. The sign-in sheet proved the three boys had gone to that location to meet someone after the show. That unknown person was the real killer, not Kenneth Hansen. Besides, Hansen was in Texas on a delayed honeymoon when the murders occurred. That's why Hansen's son was told he was "Texan by conception," Stone said. In addition, he said, Kenneth Hansen didn't get to know Silas Jayne until the early to mid 1960s, and if the murders had indeed occurred at the Idle Hour Stable, why didn't any of the almost dozen people living there not hear a commotion and report it to the police?

"This case, this case is a mystery," Stone told the jury. "It's made no clearer today than it was in October 1955. Forty-one thousand people interviewed later, attempts to retrace the boys' steps, combing of the forest preserves and the fields with police officers looking for clues and now after seven days of trial and forty years, the deaths of Anton Schuessler and John Schuessler and Robert Peterson are still shrouded in mystery. Dr. Kearns and Dr. Hirsch, who performed the autopsies and re-exhumation autopsy, are dead. Beverly Hansen is dead, Coroner Glos is dead, many of the police officers who investigated the case in 1955 are dead. Silas Jayne is dead, Curt Hansen is dead. Their contributions to the mystery, to the solutions, to the answers, to the defense are forever taken away from us."

Cassidy was the last person to address the jury before they began deliberating. In a brief rebuttal argument, he criticized the defense case as based on speculation and no evidence. He said claims by the defense that Kenneth Hansen was in Texas on his honeymoon at the time were untrue. He said Ken Hansen's medical records indicated Hansen was most likely in Texas in late September 1955. Cassidy also claimed the screams that Hetty Salerno had heard most likely came from the mouth of Bobby Peterson, who had made it out into the field but was hunted down like an animal and murdered. The forensic evidence indicated two persons most likely committed the murders; one of the killers strangled the boys with his hands, and the other used a ligature, possibly a bridle or leather strap. Cassidy also likened Hansen to a murderous, inhumane beast.

"When you consider Ken Hansen, he looks like a human being, he talks like a human being, he eats, he drinks, and he walks. But you know now that he is not human. There is not one ounce of humanity about Ken Hansen. You must realize that by now. He is a person all right. He produces children. He has the bodily functions of a human. But now you know his personae . . . He is a predator, simply an animal, and he preys. And who does he prey upon? He preys on the weak, the weak of the litter, our children, those eleven-year-old and twelve-year-old boys or those with no place to go, no homes, no families.

"What does he call these kids? He calls them chickens, as if they were animals, something he can devour. And what does he do with the bodies? He throws them into a ditch, then off the pavement, like garbage. Don't let this destroy your faith in mankind. People like Ken Hansen come along few and far between in our lifetime. And you had the misfortune of not only being in the same world with him but in the same room," Cassidy said.

Cassidy continued going over the state's case for a few more minutes. He used the gruesome crime scene photographs to make a few points and then pulled them off the easel and turned the grisly images away from the jury. He then concluded his argument.

"I'm about to finish, ladies and gentlemen, and I will not use those photographs. I will use this one," Cassidy said, which showed the three boys in life, smiling for what appeared to be their school portraits.

"The boys have waited too long for today for it not to be done the right way, so I will not try to prejudice you in the end with those [crime scene] photographs. No, I will not. They would not like that, and they have waited too long. Those boys were trailblazers in a sad sort of way. The path that they took, they did not choose. It was chosen by the man behind me, and they had no choice but to follow that path. They are smiling now, like they do in that photograph. And they welcomed others, welcomed others where they're at now similarly situated as them. Taken from this world at much too young an age, taken by no reason of their own. And they said to them be patient, be patient, your time will come on that unjust world you left. You will receive justice.

"Well, right now, ladies and gentlemen, they're up there having a party and everyone is around. They're the oldest kids on the block. Justice is due them today. That is what they seek, just justice, simple justice. The justice they seek is in your hands. On behalf of Tony, Bobby and John, thanks."

After Toomin read instructions to the jury, the panel of seven men and five women were led from the courtroom to begin their deliberations. The prosecution team retired to their offices and the defense team did as well. Members of the media gathered in the press room. Many of the journalists assumed the jury would deliberate at least one or two days before reaching a verdict. That estimate was very high. Within one hour and forty minutes the jury sent word that it had reached a verdict. The prosecution, defense and others quickly gathered in Toomin's courtroom to hear the decision.

The moment was tense as the judge and the defense and prosecution teams took their places. Grady and Rotunno, who weren't allowed inside the courtroom during the trial in case they were called back to testify, found seats near Beatrice Blane. No one was quite sure what to expect.

The jury was led into the room. Not one of them looked up to gaze at Hansen as they made their way into the jury box. That was not a good sign for him. The jury foreman stood when instructed by Toomin and announced the verdict the jury had reached. Kenneth Hansen was found guilty of the boys' murders.

Beatrice Blane, who had attended every day of the trial and did not miss one word of testimony, was overcome with emotion. Tears ran down her cheeks and she hugged Quinn, Cassidy, Rotunno and Grady. "When I heard guilty, guilty, guilty, all I could think of was 'Thank God,'" Blane told the press afterward. "I've waited forty years for this." When he got back to his office, the first phone call that Cassidy placed was to Malcolm and Dorothy Peterson. Malcolm Peterson had little to say to Cassidy and offered no comment to reporters who called his home.

In the days following the verdict there were several news stories recounting the agents' efforts. One news report revealed that the night before opening statements were heard, Quinn and Cassidy decided they would not call former *Daily News* reporter Jack Lavin to the stand. The prosecutors had known weeks before that Lavin was right on the mark when he reported in 1955 that a chunk of skin had been cut away from John Schuessler's body to hide the fact that the word "BEAR" had been imprinted on the boy's left thigh. John Rotunno and Jim Grady found several witnesses who said Hansen had owned a favorite horse named Bear. Hansen also hand-tooled leather and made himself a small stool that he kept around the stable and in the trunk of his car which he used while shoeing horses. He had emblazoned the stool with the word "BEAR" and decorated it with several stars in the shape of the Big Dipper. The agents learned that many in the horse industry decorate their saddles and other leather gear with images of the Big Dipper. The constellation is known as Ursa Major, which is Latin for "greater bear." Mizar, which is a cluster of stars in the Big Dipper's handle, is referred to in Greek mythology as a horse and its rider. Quinn and Cassidy decided not to use the "BEAR" evidence since it was too tenuous, even though the story had appeared in the *Daily News* following the slayings.

On September 15, 1995, the *Chicago Tribune* published an editorial entitled "The Murder of Innocence" which captured the sentiments of many. "If it were possible to put a date to the end of a generation's innocence, it would be, for many in the Chicago area, Oct. 18, 1955. That's when the nude, battered bodies of Robert Peterson, 14, John Schuessler, 13 and his brother Anton, 11, were found in a ditch near a bridle path in the Robinson Woods forest preserve . . ."

CHAPTER 25

OCTOBER 20, 1995

Exactly forty years and four days after brothers Tony and John Schuessler and their friend Bobby Peterson were last seen alive by their parents, Kenneth Hansen was brought before Judge Michael Toomin to be sentenced for their murders. Bearded and disheveled, Hansen was dressed in the tan-colored prison uniform issued to the inmates at Cook County Jail.

Despite the severity of the case, Hansen never faced the death chamber. Under Illinois law a defendant is allowed to be sentenced under the existing law of any year from the time of the crime to the date of sentencing. Hansen chose to be sentenced under Illinois' 1973 statutes. At that time, the death penalty was not on the books in Illinois. Prior to sentencing, Toomin dealt with several post-trial motions filed by the defense. Jed Stone and Arthur O'Donnell reiterated their arguments that they should have been allowed to present testimony from retired Chicago Police Detective John Sarnowski, who had theorized it was the notorious serial killer John Wayne Gacy who murdered the boys in 1955 at the age of thirteen.

Toomin listened quietly to the arguments and immediately rejected them. "There is no evidence, no hint, no scintilla that John Wayne Gacy killed these three boys," Toomin said. "There's no evidence he even knew them."

At a sentencing hearing, the prosecution and the defense are allowed to call witnesses to testify to the defendant's character or other criminal acts. The state and defense each called five witnesses to testify about Hansen. The rules of evidence are more lax during a sentencing hearing. As such, the prosecution took the opportunity to inform the judge via witnesses of a few more dark chapters in Hansen's past.

The state's first witness was Lawrence Smith. Smith was a heating and air-conditioning tradesman who had been approached by Hansen in 1969 at the Frankfort nightclub owned by Curtis Hansen. Smith testified that Hansen recruited him to murder George Jayne. He testified that Hansen showed him a small travel bag containing $20,000 and said it would be his if he killed George.

"He gave me a picture of him, gave me a complete schedule of where he was, at what times of the day and where he went. Descriptions and license numbers of his cars . . . and the numbers on his plane. A complete dossier on him," Smith said. In addition, Smith testified, Hansen gave him a .30-caliber carbine and asked him to demonstrate his marksmanship. The two men walked back into the woods behind the nightclub, and Smith showed Hansen he could hit a beer can at one hundred yards without a scope. Hansen was impressed and hired him on the spot.

Smith further testified that he and his cousin Ancil
Tremore staked out George Jayne's Barrington home on at
least two occasions. The two men, however, came to the re-
alization that they weren't cut out to be killers. "I just
couldn't do that," Smith said. "He wanted me to go back
again. He offered another $5,000 to kidnap him on a Satur-
day when he was visiting his country club." If Smith managed to kidnap George Jayne, he was to bring him back to
the nightclub where Silas Jayne would personally "take
care of it," he said.

Another witness, who testified in aggravation, was a
forty-year-old married father of several children, who told
the court Hansen raped him in 1975. In an emotional recounting of the incident, the man broke down and began to
weep. The witness said he had been working in a jewelry
store at the time and was also making jewelry "on the side"
when he met Hansen and Hansen told him be wanted to
purchase a ring. The witness said Hansen lured him to an
apartment in order to size the ring for him. At the apartment, the witness said Hansen gave him a large glass of
scotch and he became inebriated.

"He was telling me how handsome I was and I was getting very uncomfortable. And then he took me into the
bedroom and undressed me," the witness said. The man
held a handkerchief wadded up in his hand, which he used
to wipe the tears while he explained the rape in stark detail.

Another witness, a man named Robert Lee Brown, testified that Hansen told him he was deeply involved in efforts to murder George Jayne. "He told me he had three hit
squads out to kill George Jayne." Brown testified that
Hansen claimed he was being paid $25,000 by Silas to
have George murdered. Silas would pay Hansen $50,000 if
Hansen captured George alive and brought him out to Si's

farm. Silas Jayne apparently wanted to torture and murder George and then bury the remains on his farm.

Brown said he was at the coroner's hearing held in Lake County in 1969 to determine the cause of death for Frank Michelle Jr. Frank Michelle Jr. was the ex-con hired by George Jayne to change the batteries on the transmitter affixed to Silas Jayne's car. Michelle was discovered by Silas Jayne and murdered in cold blood. Grady and Rotunno later developed information that Silas Jayne made a $10,000 bribe payment to ensure that he wouldn't be charged with murder. Brown said he had brought along to the coroner's hearing a new camera that he had purchased and took several photographs. In one of the photographs, he captured an image of George Jayne. Brown testified that Hansen purchased the negative of that photograph and had copies made which he handed out to the hit teams he had recruited to murder George.

The defense also called several witnesses to testify to Hansen's supposedly good character. Among them was Mark Hansen, who testified that Hansen never abused children left in his care or mistreated his horses.

The other witnesses offered similar testimony. Ken Hansen was not a pedophile but a loving father and husband. It was then Scott Cassidy's chance to present a heartfelt closing argument to Toomin. Before he began, Cassidy had decided to use photos of the crime scene to drive home his point. He put several large photographs of the three boys on an easel. The photos depicted three smiling young men. Next to those photos was an enlarged shot of the crime scene depicting the three in death.

"During argument to the jury, Your Honor, we stated that the only injustice surrounding this trial was the fact that Ken Hansen was allowed to live forty years as a free man. And that is true. However, with his freedom other injustices have occurred. He has, as you know, destroyed many other people's lives. He has sexually and psychologically molested an untold number of young boys. The impact felt by these acts will never be known.

"How do you measure a boy's lost innocence? How do you measure a boy's fear when being molested and the scars that are left due to that fear? How do you measure the pain a young boy goes through after he has encountered Ken Hansen in his predatory role? Will these boys ever be whole again? Will they ever feel right about themselves and recognize that they didn't do anything wrong? Will they ever escape their personal nightmare known to them as Ken Hansen? Some may not be able to deal with it and they themselves would become the abusers and perpetuate the cycle begun by him."

Cassidy used one of the grisly photographs taken of the crime scene to illustrate what he called Hansen's disregard for human decency.

"He is certainly not one of us," Cassidy said, pointing in Hansen's direction. Hansen sat emotionless at the defense table. "He cloaks himself in the body of a human being, offering little boys the opportunity to ride horses and then he molests them, brutalizes them, destroys them and sometimes murders them. He solicits other people to kill someone who has done nothing to him. He refers to kids without homes as throwaways . . . If the man who sits over there, who is void of human emotion, ever develops a conscience, he would become a madman at the thought of what he had become."

Using the various photographs of the three boys and the crime scene, Cassidy laid out his version of the crime.

"That photograph, the second photograph to your left,

Your Honor, is a photograph of Tony Schuessler, the inno-
cent one. That is how he looked when he first met Ken
Hansen. The photograph to your far right is of Tony
Schuessler and how he looked after he met Ken Hansen,"
Cassidy said, pointing to the photograph of Tony's corpse.
"Tony was the youngest of the three. He was eleven years
old and he weighed ninety pounds. He was forced to submit to sexual molestation and faced real fear for the first
time in his young life. Like a deer frozen by car lights,
Tony watched as Ken Hansen moved from him to John, his
older brother, who had walked in on Hansen.

"The photograph, Your Honor, next to Tony is John.
And that is how he looked before he met Ken Hansen. The
photo the second from the right on the end, Your Honor, is
of John after he met Ken Hansen. He was one hundred
pounds and he was thirteen years old. He saw Hansen attack his brother and he tried to protect him. This was his
little brother and he was ready to give his life for him. And
that, sir, is exactly what he did.

"I cannot describe nor articulate the fear that little Tony
faced at that time. I'd only ask you, Your Honor, to consider what Tony was thinking about at that time. He had
just been sexually molested and just watched his only
brother, his only sibling killed. And now he was next.
Hopefully, for his sake, death soon followed.

"The remaining photograph, Your Honor, as you know is
of Bobby Peterson. The photograph in the middle is of
Bobby Peterson. One is of life, one is of death. Bobby is the
courageous one. You can see he fought the good fight. He
made it outside of the barn and into the fields. For some moments he had escaped evilness and death. His screams would
be heard forty years later through the testimony of Hetty
Salerno. God bless you, Bobby Peterson, you tried your best.

"Your Honor, that photograph to your far left," Cassidy said, pointing to a grim black-and-white photograph of the crime scene. "The closest one to you, shows Tony, Bobby and John. This is how Ken Hansen left them. Lying beaten to death, naked in a dirt field. Anything that illustrates best Ken Hansen's view toward mankind is in that photograph. He sees mankind as pieces of meat to be discarded by him after having been given to this world for his pleasure and his alone. God help us, to think of the audacity of this fiend, this creature. He actually lived and breathed in the same world as us, sharing with our families and our children.

"Tony, Bobby and John are all gone. And now their killer awaits your justice, the justice by law. Your Honor, on behalf of the boys and the rest of the humanity of this world, please sentence him to a long prison term. Place him behind bars inside the same cage he has built with his own hate and lust. Let him rot. Let him waste away. Let him never, ever hurt another child again," Cassidy said, wrapping up his remarks.

O'Donnell delivered his closing statement in less than five minutes. He said the state's case was fantasy, that there was no physical evidence that Kenneth Hansen had committed the crime.

"Up until about thirty days ago or thereabouts, Kenneth Hansen had never been convicted of a single crime. Not even a traffic ticket. He has lived his sixty-two years by every conceivable standard known that we could measure without trouble with the law. Even if he were to have committed this crime, and we sure as hell don't admit that, it has been forty years since these crimes were committed, and he has not even committed any offense at all," O'Donnell said.

"He talks about Bobby Peterson putting up a good fight.

With whom?" O'Donnell asked. "He didn't put it up with him. We don't deny Peterson is dead, the Schuesslers are dead. They've been dead for forty years. The question is, who did it?" Before he concluded his statement, O'Donnell questioned why no one from Bobby Peterson's family had attended the trial. "I think by the deliberate fact that Mr. Malcolm Peterson or any member of his family hasn't attended this trial at any time, I don't believe they think he did it either," O'Donnell said. Quinn immediately objected to the statement. Toomin let it go as "mere argument."

Before Toomin was to hand down his sentence, he asked Hansen if he had anything to say. Hansen stood and addressed the court. He spoke with no emotion.

"I'm an innocent man. I did not commit these crimes," Hansen said. "If anybody's a victim, it's me. The character assassination has been conducted with the highest magnitude. I did not kill those children. I did not run hit squads; I did not burn stables. I did not do any of those things. I'm innocent. Thank you." Hansen then took his seat and awaited his fate.

Before he rendered his sentence, Toomin noted that the murders had forever changed Chicago. He said for many, their innocence had been destroyed.

"The court, counsel and I suppose all in attendance here today would recognize and concur in the observation that grief and suffering is wrought by all senseless killings such as these. Nonetheless, amplified here in that for some of the material submitted even as of today, that grief and suffering literally consumed the life and the lives of the Schuessler boys' parents, resulting in the untimely death of Anton Schuessler Sr.," Toomin said. "And while the grief and suffering are of course the vestige of all murders, from the totality of the case, from its inception, even down to today, the effect of these murders, I think it can be safely be said, transcends the immediate families . . . For those of us who lived before and during these times, all calling to mind perhaps the sounds, visions of yesterday, muted in detail perhaps by the passage of years gone by. Recollections aptly named and described by authors and commentators as the 'age of innocence' that came to a rather abrupt end with these three murders. Recollections of a city where parents such as the Petersons and the Schuesslers could and did allow eleven-, twelve- and thirteen-year-olds to roam freely by foot, by streetcar, by bus, through its back yards, lots, alleys, traveling to different places of amusement and education without fear of harm or injury or molestation. Recollections of neighborhoods, even then populated by people of different races, ethnic groups, but nonetheless were places of community . . . recollections of an age of unlocked doors, civility and respect that ended all too abruptly, replaced by an age that we're all too familiar with."

Toomin noted that it was unfortunate that Hansen had escaped the ultimate penalty. "There is no death penalty for Kenneth Hansen," he said. "Had his acts, had his conduct, had these horrendous crimes been discovered earlier, there is little doubt as to what his fate would have been. Little doubt that it would have been richly earned and deserved. Fate works in strange ways. And because of the passage of time, because of the changes and evolutions in the law, Kenneth Hansen escaped the hangman's noose and he escaped the electric chair. Though he has beaten the executioner, what lies ahead may not be much better today, tomorrow or in the evening of his twilight. Nor should it be.

"A just sentence," Toomin said, "would insure that Hansen would never again be given the opportunity to harm anyone again or be allowed to walk free among civilized individuals." He sentenced Hansen to a term of not less than two hundred years and not more than three hundred years for each murder, to be served concurrently. Hansen did not react visibly when he heard the sentence, and he was led out of the courtroom by two Cook County sheriff's deputies. Toomin's courtroom erupted in activity.

Beatrice Blane breathed a sigh of relief. She had been on edge through all of the trial testimony and the five-hour sentencing hearing. She thought she now had closure.

"After forty years it's been a long time," Blane said. "I'm just glad it's over."

John Rotunno could now rest. The case against Kenneth Hansen was over. He had kept his silent promise that he would solve the boys' murders.

CHAPTER 26

Beatrice Blane spoke too soon. Kenneth Hansen's case was far from over. In Cook County, a conviction on a murder charge is only considered a done deal when a defendant has exhausted all his appeals. Many defendants convicted of murder in Cook County receive a long sentence, and most file an appeal. No one gives up without a fight. After he was convicted, Kenneth Hansen had the good fortune to find himself allied with some well-known and well-qualified attorneys who took it upon themselves to represent him pro bono in the appeal process.

Hansen's case was destined to become one of many studied, researched and ultimately handled by the Northwestern University School of Law's Center for Wrongful Convictions. The Center for Wrongful Convictions, under the guidance of NU law Professor Lawrence Marshall, has become synonymous with exonerating wrongly convicted defendants. Marshall has led the charge in Illinois and other jurisdictions to repeal the death penalty. In January 2003, Marshall's efforts paid off in Illinois when outgoing Illinois Governor George Ryan commuted the death sentence of every inmate on Death Row in that state to life in prison. At that time Ryan claimed the justice system in Illinois was flawed and he wouldn't risk putting an innocent person to death.

Marshall does not fight his battles alone. Many in Chicago's legal community work with him, as do students at Northwestern University's Medill School of Journalism. Journalism students at Northwestern have an equally impressive track record exonerating defendants who have been wrongly convicted. NU Journalism Professor David Protess, who is the founding director of the Medill Innocence Project, has spearheaded efforts contributing to the exoneration and release of eight innocent men and women from prison. Three of those cleared by journalism students working under Protess's guidance were on Death Row.

Shortly after Kenneth Hansen was convicted, attorney Leonard Goodman was contacted by Marshall and asked to take on Hansen's case. Goodman, a graduate of Northwestern's law school, was informed that the Center for Wrongful Convictions had been contacted by a woman who claimed Hansen was innocent and she knew who had killed the three boys. As a result of that telephone call, on September 12, 1997, a post-trial petition was filed on Hansen's behalf seeking to present new evidence at a hearing that would implicate another man. Goodman hoped Judge Toomin would order a new trial for Hansen based on the evidence presented at the hearing.

Specifically, Goodman's motion stated that family members of a man named Jack Reiling had come forward to claim it was Reiling who had committed the murders. Reiling had admitted to his wife in 1955 or 1956 that he had murdered the three boys and also admitted to another family member prior to his death in 1980 that he was responsible for the boys' murders, Goodman said.

Joyce Saxon, Reiling's ex-wife, and his daughter, Margie Mack, had contacted Goodman and described Reiling as "cruel and violent." Goodman noted that Reiling's prison records from the California Department of Corrections indicated he was an antisocial sociopath prone to outbursts of violence. Other evidence included the fact that Reiling was often in the area where the boys were last seen alive. Reiling also drove a Packard, which the Chicago Police suspected was the vehicle used to transport the boys' bodies.

In addition, Goodman claimed he had evidence that would discredit the testimony of Herbert Hollatz, whose powerful words represented the heart of the state's case. Hollatz was the only state witness who the defense could not claim received compensation in some form for his testimony. Goodman knew discrediting Hollatz would improve Hansen's position considerably. Following Hansen's conviction, one juror told *Chicago Sun-Times* reporter Neil Steinberg that it was Hollatz's testimony that had swayed the jury to convict Hansen. The juror said that when the panel began deliberating, the first vote taken was nine to convict, one to acquit and two undecided.

Goodman's motion claimed that two members of Hollatz's family had provided affidavits claiming that Hollatz had admitted to them following the trial that he had committed perjury. Goodman hoped the hearing would show that if the evidence had been available for Hansen at trial, it would have changed the verdict. In the end, Goodman hoped Judge Toomin would order a new trial.

On April 9, 1998, Judge Toomin granted Goodman's request for a hearing. Toomin said he was acting in the "interest of justice" and would give Goodman a chance to present the so-called new evidence. Toomin predicted that his decision whether or not to grant a new trial would hinge on the "trustworthiness, reliability and credibility" of the witnesses.

Judge Toomin's ruling put the Schuessler-Peterson case and Kenneth Hansen back into the media spotlight. Hansen underwent a transformation of sorts for some in the electronic media. Goodman, Saxon and Mack appeared on *The Oprah Winfrey Show* to claim Hansen had been wrongly convicted. Hansen appeared on the show in a videotaped segment and described the mother and daughter as angels who had answered his prayers and come to his aid. Saxon and Mack also gave interviews to Chicago television news stations. As a result of the exposure, on the day of the hearing, Judge Toomin's courtroom was packed.

Prior to the hearing and the storm of publicity, Jim Grady and John Rotunno had visited Margie Mack to interview her concerning what she knew about her father. The two agents listened to Mack and told her that the last thing they wanted was for the wrong man to be convicted for the crime. The mother and daughter lived on the same street in a western suburb of Chicago, and after hearing Mack's story, the two agents decided they would walk across the street to visit Joyce Saxon. As they walked up to knock on

Saxon's door, Goodman greeted them. He informed the ATF agents that he represented Saxon and that she did not wish to speak to them. To this day, Grady suspects that the entire Mack interview, which was planned in advance, had been a setup. He suspects that Goodman thought the agents would not take Mack's story seriously and would leave without asking her many questions or talking to her mother. If the agents had left without trying to talk to Saxon or Mack, Goodman would use that against them, Grady thought. Goodman denied that he set a trap for the agents to stumble.

The agents also thought it was peculiar that Goodman just happened to be in the western suburb on the same day that they had arranged an interview with Mack. Saxon, who would express a strong desire in subsequent interviews with the media to right a grievous miscarriage of justice, was never interviewed by the state prior to the hearing. The media buildup to the case would prove more successful than the actual "new evidence." Over a period of two days Assistant State's Attorney Thomas Gainer took a wrecking ball to Goodman's case.

It was clear during one and a half hours of testimony that Joyce Saxon was an unreliable witness. Saxon testified that her ex-husband, whom she described as "very tall, heavy built, big shoulders . . . with nice teeth" was an out-of-control bully. Reiling had once punched her in the face, causing her to lose her teeth. Saxon added that her ex-husband, who died in 1980, was a compulsive gambler and an unreliable breadwinner.

Reiling's marital abuse led to a separation, Saxon said. Soon after the boys were murdered, Saxon said she began to suspect Reiling was involved in the crime. She testified that when they were separated, Reiling failed to show up for his weekly Sunday visit with his one-year-old daughter on the same day the boys disappeared. A week later, when Reiling did visit, Saxon asked him to drive by the murder scene. Reiling refused. "I remember he was strange, nervous, uptight . . . He was terrified. He was shaking. He wouldn't go there."

Her suspicions roused, Saxon tried to get a look in the trunk of her husband's car, which she claimed was a green Packard. At the time, Reiling worked for the McCormick spice company and was provided with a car, she said. Goodman made a point of raising the fact that Reiling allegedly drove a green Packard. News accounts published weeks after the boys were murdered reported police were searching for a green car seen in the vicinity where the bodies were discovered. Within six months of the crime, the press reported that Chicago Police had questioned owners of Packards because the pattern found on Bobby Peterson's body appeared to come from a trunk mat of a Packard. Saxon testified that when she tried to get a look in the trunk of her husband's car two weeks after the murders, Reiling suspiciously drew her attention away from that area.

Saxon and her husband eventually reconciled and began living together again, she said. The marriage, however, was doomed. Saxon testified that her suspicions about her husband were realized in February 1956 during a fight with Reiling about money. "We had this heated argument, and in the process I said, 'And you killed those three boys, didn't you?' I screamed that out. And he said, 'Yes, I did.' Then it just kind of calmed down, and I went to bed."

After what may or may not have been a good night's sleep, Saxon testified, she left her husband the next day. They were divorced and Saxon remarried. She rarely saw Reiling again. He remarried several times and moved to California. Saxon testified that she kept her suspicions to herself for decades because she feared that her daughter would be branded as the daughter of a mass murderer. Saxon eventually told her daughter under unusual circumstances of her father's alleged involvement in the crime. Saxon's version of her ex-husband's involvement in the murders came out one night during a mother-daughter spat. On that particular night Joyce Saxon interrupted her sixteen-year-old daughter necking with her twenty-six-year-old boyfriend in a car parked in front of the family home. Saxon said she knocked on the window and interrupted the couple because she was concerned her daughter was going to run off to California in search of the father she never knew. At that time Saxon told her daughter that her father was the killer of three boys in 1955.

Gainer's cross-examination of Saxon was intense. He questioned why Saxon was willing to give her ex-husband visitation privileges with her daughter during their separation and divorce if she had suspected he was the boys' killer. Gainer also asked why Saxon was willing to go on a nationally syndicated talk show and grant interviews to the press but then refuse to meet with prosecutors regarding the allegations she raised against Reiling.

"Do you remember what this crime did to the city of Chicago?" Gainer asked. "Do you remember what it did to people like me and a few others that were eight and nine years old, what our parents had to do? Do you remember that? Do you remember the city was gripped with fear? Do you remember this was the time they said the City of Chicago lost its innocence?" Saxon responded yes to most of his questions.

Saxon said it wasn't until Hansen was charged with the boys' murders that her daughter began an "investigation" to learn more about her father. Her daughter Margie wanted to determine if Reiling had ever confessed to committing the murders to any other person. Saxon proved combative during her cross-examination and was also testy when Judge Toomin posed a few questions. Her demeanor did little to help Hansen's case.

Margie Mack was Goodman's next witness. Mack testified that she contacted Jed Stone prior to Hansen's trial with her concerns that an innocent man was being prosecuted. She said Stone referred her to Larry Marshall at the Center for Wrongful Convictions. Mack's memory proved as faulty as her mother's. She could not pinpoint the exact year she first contacted Hansen's defense team and Marshall about her suspicions. It could have been in 1994, 1995 or 1996, she said. "I don't want to see somebody go to jail for something they didn't do," Mack said. "I don't believe Ken Hansen is guilty." Mack testified that she and her mother went on *The Oprah Winfrey Show* and other news shows "because we wanted the truth to come out."

As part of her attempts to research the case, Mack said Goodman gave her the entire Hansen case file and asked her to go through the documents to search for anything that could be connected to her father. Mack testified that she obtained her father's prison records from California, which she claimed showed he had been diagnosed as a passive-aggressive psychopath. Reiling had served two stretches in the California penal system for writing bad

checks after he remarried and moved west. Reiling's psy-
chiatric evaluation was a key component to the motion for
a new trial.

On cross-examination, however, Gainer pointed out that
the diagnosis discovered by Mack was in error and she had
actually read the diagnosis of another prisoner named
Ristler. Ristler was a convict who had torn up his cell in
San Quentin on several occasions. Mack had read the records incorrectly and her faulty assumption had made its
way into Goodman's case. When Mack's error was pointed
out to her, she was surprised, as was Judge Toomin. At one
point Mack testified she had completed her investigation of
her father in the spring of 1995. The admission prompted
Toomin to pose a few questions.

"You had it all together in the spring of 1995 and you
knew Mr. Hansen had been arrested in the fall of 1994 for
the heinous crime. Why didn't you do something with it?"
Toomin inquired. Mack responded that she was concerned
that if she came forward the information could lead to the
end of her marriage and hurt her son.

"So you waited until he got convicted and sentenced to
two hundred years, is that what you did?" Toomin asked.
Mack tried to answer Toomin's question. She claimed she
tried to talk to the state's attorneys but then went to Jed
Stone and Larry Marshall.

"You waited until October 20, 1995, which was the date
I sentenced Mr. Hansen to two hundred to three hundred
years. You waited until that date. You heard about the sentence, and you still didn't come forward, did you?" Toomin
asked.

Mack replied, "No, I did not." It was clear from her response that she knew Judge Toomin wasn't finding her testimony credible.

At a break in the hearing, outside of the courtroom, Mack denied news reports that she and her mother tried to sell their story to several television news organizations for $10,000. Representatives of three Chicago television stations who participated in a question-and-answer session outside the courtroom told their colleagues in the press that their stations had indeed been approached and asked to pay $10,000 for the story.

After Mack was dismissed, Goodman put on several more witnesses who testified that Herbert Hollatz was a pathological liar. Hollatz's ex-wife, Arlene Zielke, testified that Hollatz had admitted to her during a telephone conversation at the home of her daughter Cheryl Zormeier that he had lied when he testified against Hansen. Zielke also said her ex-husband carried a photograph of Beverly Hansen in his wallet for years and had admitted to her that he loved Beverly. Zielke claimed her daughter was present and heard a portion of the conversation. Zormeier, however, was called to testify by Gainer and she denied any knowledge of the alleged conversation.

Another family member, Herbert Hollatz Jr., told the court he hated his father for what he had done to his family. The younger Hollatz admitted he signed an affidavit that claimed he had confronted his father about his testimony regarding Hansen and that his father had admitted he lied on the stand. On cross-examination, however, Hollatz's son admitted that he had signed a second affidavit when an assistant Cook County state's attorney had interviewed him. The second affidavit claimed that the first affidavit was false. "You have to understand I have a lot of anger toward my father," Herbert Hollatz Jr. said in explaining his efforts to discredit him.

In additional testimony, Gainer also questioned a representative of the McCormick spice company. The company representative testified that salesmen working for the company in the early to mid 1950s drove Chevrolets and not the more expensive Packard. The testimony was offered in an attempt to disprove that Reiling, who was habitually short of cash, ever drove a Packard, considered a luxury car at that time. Following closing arguments, Toomin said he would rule the next day.

When he issued his ruling, Toomin stopped short of branding Margie Mack and Joyce Saxon as liars who had injected themselves into a well-known case purely for notoriety. During a forty-minute oral ruling explaining why he would deny Hansen's request for a new trial, Toomin concluded that the so-called new evidence "approaches zero." Toomin found Saxon and Mack's testimony contradictory and inconsistent. He expressed amazement that the two women were willing to go on national television and grant interviews to news shows, but refused to meet with prosecutors. He suspected they did so to "enjoy their own fifteen minutes of notoriety and fame." In addition, Toomin noted that Arlene Zielke sounded more like a "vindictive ex-wife" than a credible witness and that Herbert Hollatz Jr. admitted his father had never told him he lied.

"In the final analysis the story does not stand up to scrutiny," Toomin said of Saxon and Mack. "Maybe it's good enough for the 10 P.M. news, favorable sound bites, and maybe it's okay for a well-rehearsed direct examination, but when it's subjected to the type of cross-examination demonstrated here by the assistant state's attorney, by Mr. Gainer, it simply . . . is a story that taxes the gullibility of the credulous."

Hansen sat stone-faced as he listened to Toomin dash his hopes for a new trial. Before he was led back to the lockup to be returned to the Pontiac Correctional Center, Hansen turned to Goodman, smiled and shook his hand. It wasn't, however, the last time Hansen would appear in a Cook County courtroom.

CHAPTER 27

John Rotunno was driving on Interstate 55 somewhere between Chicago and Bloomington, Illinois, when his cell phone rang and brought him some unexpected news. Jim Grady was on the other end of the line. Rotunno then learned that in a split decision just made public the Illinois Appellate Court had ordered a new trial for Kenneth Hansen.

"You're BS-ing me, right?" Rotunno said, half-joking, half-serious.

"I wish I was," Grady said. "But I'm not. I'm getting the opinion faxed to me. When I know more I'll call you." For the rest of the dull drive back to Chicago over the flat, unremarkable Illinois landscape, Rotunno began to question where the case could have gone wrong. Rotunno was aware that Goodman had filed an appeal seeking to overturn Hansen's conviction, but he hadn't thought it would succeed. The only issue that Rotunno could pinpoint as possibly problematic was testimony about Hansen's sexual history. He was right.

In a twenty-seven-page opinion, the court found that Judge Michael Toomin erred when he allowed Patrick Quinn and Scott Cassidy to present testimony that Hansen routinely molested young men that he had picked up hitchhiking over a twenty-year period. Specifically the court found that testimony on that subject by Roger Spry, Bobby Stitt, William "Red" Wemette, Lt. John Farrell and Assistant State's Attorney Barbara Riley should not have reached the ears of the jury.

"Clearly evidence that the defendant routinely picked up young boys hitchhiking and sexually assaulted them could not be used to directly establish that the defendant killed the victims. Rather, it is apparent that the state sought to establish that the defendant was more likely than not also the person who killed the victims, having both the opportunity and motive to do so," the majority wrote.

"Most of the evidence in question pertains to incidents which occurred well after the victims' murders. The defendant can hardly be said to have been motivated to kill the victims in 1955 to prevent the discovery of acts of pedophilia he committed in the 1960s and 1970s," the opinion stated.

In addition the court noted much of the testimony about Hansen's sexual activity with hitchhikers was sketchy at best. "Due to the complete lack of detail regarding the defendant's activities, we find the evidence is more in the nature of character evidence intended to demonstrate that the defendant has a propensity to commit bad acts. Specifically a propensity to pick up male hitchhikers for the purpose of engaging in sexual activity," the opinion said. "Therefore, we cannot say that the evidence that the defendant sexually assaulted innumerable young boys over a twenty-year period did not influence the outcome of his trial. Accordingly, we reverse the defendant's conviction."

Some testimony by Spry and Herbert Hollatz that they had sex with Hansen was deemed relevant because it established Hansen's close relationship with both witnesses, the court said. The testimony by Stitt that Hansen attempted to molest him and the testimony of Patrick Mason, who told the jury that he saw Hansen having sex with a fifteen-year-old boy at the stable, was also deemed permissible by the appellate court.

In her two-page dissent, Appellate Justice Shelvin L. M. Hall stated that she believed the "other crimes" evidence in the Schuessler-Peterson case should have been admissible as evidence of Hansen's modus operandi. "Moreover, the strong evidence in this case including the defendant's admission to four witnesses that he killed the boys renders harmless any error that may have occurred in admitting this other crimes evidence."

Leonard Goodman enjoyed his victory. He told the press that Hansen, who was incarcerated at the Pontiac Correctional Center, was also caught unaware by the decision and was speechless when informed that his conviction had been overturned. "He thought I was kidding him," Goodman said. Goodman acknowledged he had a long road ahead of him in clearing Hansen's name. He pointed out that Hansen faced the possibility of dying in prison without getting a chance to prove his innocence. Hansen had had a heart attack in 1999 and had recently undergone triple bypass surgery. "We've got a tough fight in front of us," Goodman conceded. Hansen would not taste freedom while awaiting a new trial, since he had been ordered held without bond following his arrest.

In response to the ruling, the Cook County State's Attorney's Office quickly appealed the decision to the Illinois Supreme Court. Hansen's case remained at a standstill until the Illinois Supreme Court weighed in on the matter on October 5, 2000. On that day the court denied a petition filed by the Cook County State's Attorney's Office to reconsider the appellate court ruling.

Though the appellate court decision was a blow to the ATF's investigation of Silas Jayne's Chicago Horse Syndicate, Grady and Rotunno had been successful in solving the Cheryl Lynn Rude murder. After they had wrapped up Hansen's conviction, the two agents reopened the murder investigation into the June 1965 car bombing that claimed the twenty-two-year-old equestrian's life.

The car bomb that killed Rude was intended for George Jayne. In July 1999 the Cook County State's Attorney's Office tried a man named James Blottiaux for Rude's murder. Prosecutors presented evidence that showed Blottiaux had accepted a $10,000 fee from Silas Jayne to murder George Jayne. Blottiaux was sentenced in September 1999 to one hundred to three hundred years for the murder.

Within days following the appellate court decision, Hansen's case was assigned to Cook County Circuit Court Judge Mary Ellen Coghlan, a former assistant Cook County public defender and assistant Illinois attorney general. Handling the prosecution of Hansen's case the second time around was Scott Cassidy and fellow prosecutors Thomas Biesty, Linas Kelecius and Jennifer Coleman. Hansen's defense team included Goodman and attorney Steven Weinberg. Cassidy's partner in Hansen's first trial, Patrick Quinn, had been elected Appellate Court Judge.

Almost two months after the Illinois Supreme Court let stand a new trial for Hansen, Arthur O'Donnell died of leukemia in Concord, California. It was O'Donnell who had predicted in April 1995 that Judge Cawley's decision to allow the state to use sexual incidents from Hansen's past would result in a reversal of any conviction of his client.

When the case landed in Judge Coghlan's court, a tentative trial date of a May 21, 2001, was set. As the case inched its way toward trial, Judge Coghlan dropped a bombshell on the prosecution. In response to a defense motion, the judge ruled from the bench on March 27, 2001, that the testimony of Joyce Saxon would be allowed at Hansen's second trial. Judge Coghlan's ruling came despite the fact that Judge Michael Toomin had found Saxon's testimony without merit in 1999 following a two-day hearing. In issuing her ruling, Judge Coghlan reasoned that "justice demanded" a departure from the general rule that third-party confessions were inadmissible hearsay. The ruling was a blow to the prosecution team. Rotunno was concerned that Hansen was not going to be convicted at the second trial if Saxon took the stand and told the jury her preposterous story about her dead ex-husband Jack Reiling.

"It's the blame-it-on-the-dead-guy defense," Rotunno would later say.

As a result of the Saxon ruling, Cassidy decided he would go into court with every weapon he had at his disposal. He gave the defense notice that he would call Bruce and Glen Carter as witnesses. At Hansen's first trial, Glen Carter had testified that he knew Robert Peterson when he was fourteen years old and that he and Bobby Peterson had been in Boy Scouts together and attended the same church.

Glen Carter also testified he had been to the Idle Hour Stable on almost a dozen occasions between 1954 and 1955 and that he had seen Bobby at the Idle Hour riding horses.

At Hansen's second trial, the state wanted to call the Carter brothers to testify that they saw the three boys in an alley near their home on October 16, 1955. Bruce Carter would testify that Glen introduced him to the three boys and that Bobby Peterson told him, "We're going to the ice cream parlor on Lawrence Avenue and then we're going to get a ride out to the horse stables to ride." Bruce Carter would also testify that a short time later a car drove by and honked its horn. In response to the honk, Bruce Carter heard Tony blurt out, "Is that Hansen?" to which John Schuessler replied, "Shut up, we've said enough already." The conversation with the three boys continued and Bruce Carter was told, "We're going to get a ride out to the stables with Hansen." At trial the brothers would say the conversation took place around 2 P.M.

When he received notice of the prosecution's intent to call the Carter brothers, Goodman objected that the information was not truthful and could not have occurred at 2 P.M. on that day because the evidence showed the Schuessler brothers didn't arrived at the Peterson home until 3:15 or 3:30 P.M. The prosecution countered that the statements should be admissible under the "state of mind" exception to the hearsay rule. The statements were not being offered to show the truth of the matter but to illustrate the victims' state of mind at the time of the conversation and to explain their subsequent actions. On May 11, 2001, Judge Coghlan ruled in the defense's favor, finding that the testimony of the Carter brothers would be hearsay and inadmissible.

The prosecution team was disappointed. Judge Coghlan found there was no nexus of truth to the Carter brothers'

statements. She pointed out that the statements made by
the three boys were not made to family members, close
friends or neighbors and did not indicate any sincerity. In
addition, the evidence in the case showed that the three
boys did not go to the ice cream parlor at 2 P.M.

Hansen was scheduled to go on trial within a few weeks
of the ruling. A few days prior to jury selection, the Cook
County State's Attorney's Office decided to appeal Judge
Coghlan's ruling regarding the Carter brothers. Hansen's
retrial would be put on hold for a little more than a year
while the appeal worked its way through the system. Goodman expressed displeasure at the prosecution's decision,
noting Hansen's poor health and that Hansen could die behind bars waiting for his second trial to resume.

On February 1, 2002, the Illinois Appellate Court issued its decision upholding Judge Coghlan's ruling. The
court found that Coghlan did not abuse her discretion when
she ruled that there was not a reasonable probability that
the victims' statements to the Carter brothers were true. In
its ruling, the court pointed out the state's contention that
the conversation occurred around 2 P.M. did not fit the facts
of the case. Malcolm Peterson told the police his son did
not leave home until 3:15 or 3:30 P.M. that day. In addition,
Robert Peterson signed the registry at the Garland Building
at 6 P.M. and Ernest Niewiadomski had testified at the first
trial that he saw the boys at the Monte Cristo Bowling Alley at 7:30 P.M. The court noted that the state maintained
that the victims didn't tell the Carter brothers they were
going to the stables immediately. The court noted that the
state had no other evidence indicating Hansen knew the
victims prior to picking them up that night.

Hansen's case was once again back in the Cook County
criminal court system. Hansen was slated to be retried on

July 29, 2002. Before the trial began, Rotunno and the Cook County State's Attorney's Office moved against another member of the Jayne Gang. On May 3, 2004, Frank Jayne Jr., the nephew of Silas Jayne, was indicted on a seventeen-year-old arson charge for torching his stable and collecting the insurance proceeds. Frank Jayne Jr., who was known as "Junior," was an associate of Kenneth Hansen. He had been accused by prosecutors at Richard Bailey's sentencing hearing of scheming with Bailey to solicit Helen Brach's murder. Junior was never charged with any crime in connection to the Brach probe; instead he slipped through the cracks due to a technicality in the RICO statute.

Junior's attorney immediately accused the ATF and prosecutors of bringing the charges against his client because he was scheduled to testify on Kenneth Hansen's behalf at Hansen's second trial. The Cook County State's Attorney's Office denied the allegation, stating that Frank Jayne Jr.'s arrest on the charges was an outgrowth of the ATF's ten-year investigation into the horse industry.

About three weeks before Hansen's trial, Goodman asked Judge Coghlan to hold the state and the FBI in contempt because the FBI had refused to produce documents about William "Red" Wemette and Roger Spry. Goodman told the court he had been seeking the documents since March 2002 because he wanted to be able to show that Red never once told his FBI handlers about the Schuessler-Peterson case during his eighteen-year career as an FBI informant.

Goodman had heard that Red claimed he had attempted to tell the FBI about the boys' murders on several occasions but that the agents in question weren't interested in his story. Goodman refused to believe that in order to pursue organized crime figures an FBI agent would choose to ignore a tip that could solve the murders of three children. "That was a story the prosecution spread around before the second trial," Goodman would later say. "I didn't believe it at all."

On July 22, 2002, prior to attending a meeting with Judge Coghlan regarding the FBI documents, one of Wemette's former handlers, FBI Agent John Osborne, admitted to members of the prosecution team that Wemette had mentioned to him that he knew who had murdered three boys in the 1950s. Osborne said he never documented the conversation with Wemette. Osborne also told the prosecution team that he never pursued the tip because such action would have compromised Wemette as an informant and possibly led to his murder. After some wrangling, the FBI and the U.S. Attorney's Office agreed to release redacted versions of Red's FBI reports.

A week before Hansen's second trial was to begin, Goodman requested that Joyce Saxon's previous testimony, from the 1999 hearing before Toomin, be presented to the jury, along with the testimony of Frank Jayne from the first trial. Attached to the motion, Goodman presented an unsworn letter dated June 19, 2002, from Saxon's psychiatrist, Dr. Michael Brilliant, that stated Saxon's physical and mental health had deteriorated over the past several years. The letter said Saxon had been treated for a major depressive disorder since 1997 and that her testimony would not be accurate due to her memory impairment. A second unsworn letter from Saxon's physician, Dr. Reinhold Lierna, said Saxon might be able to endure some time in court but not a full day of testimony. The state argued that Goodman should have given notice of Saxon's mental condition before the 1999 evidentiary hearing before Judge

Toomin. Judge Coghlan denied Goodman's motion to use Saxon's previous testimony. She did, however, grant the request to use Frank Jayne Sr.'s testimony because Goodman provided detailed sworn affidavits from Jayne's physicians attesting to Jayne's physical and mental condition.

Hansen's second trial began on August 12, 2002, after a jury of eight men and four women had been selected. Rotunno hoped that, whatever the outcome, after he had finished with Hansen and Frank Jayne Jr., he would no longer have to sift through the Jayne Gang's crimes.

CHAPTER 28

There were few surprises at Kenneth Hansen's second trial. The tactics, however, changed. At the first trial the prosecution did everything it could to distance itself from appearing to attack Hansen's sexual orientation. At that time Hansen's defense beat a drum that Hansen was prosecuted because of his homosexuality. Pedophilia was a term that was mentioned only once or twice at Hansen's first trial. In his opening statements at the second trial Assistant State's Attorney Linas Kelecius designated Hansen's pedophilia as the driving force behind the murders.

Kelecius told the jury that on the night of October 16, 1955, as Hansen was "cruising" in the vicinity of Lawrence and Milwaukee avenues, "He saw a stunning sight, he saw three objects of his sexual desire" in the form of three boys hitchhiking. Hansen's recent honeymoon with his wife "just didn't quite do it for him," Kelecius added, because Hansen "was a man with a fantasy." Hansen wanted "a threesome, not with men, not with women" but with young boys. As Kelecius spoke, the photographs of the three boys were displayed on a television monitor facing the jury. Hansen, who appeared much older and about thirty pounds heavier than at his first trial, shook his head in disagreement.

In response to Kelecius, the defense team informed the jury that they would hear many disturbing stories about Hansen but would not see one piece of evidence linking him to the murders. Physical evidence in the case, the defense said, would show that the crime couldn't have occurred in the manner theorized by the state. In addition, the state's case would be based solely on the testimony of unreliable witnesses, several paid informants and an alcoholic.

"You will enter the world of the Chicago horse industry. You will see the players that were involved in the Chicago horse industry," Steven Weinberg told the jury. "And I assure you, you're not going to like them and you know what? You're not going to like the defendant either."

Though Weinberg did not tell the jury what evidence the defense would present to counter the state's case, it became apparent during the cross-examination of the state's first few witnesses that the defense was going to claim that the boys had died earlier than the time proposed by the state. Members of the press that had covered Hansen's pretrial hearings knew that the defense had secured an expert witness who was going to testify that the contents found in the stomachs of the Schuessler boys suggested the boys died much earlier than the 9:30 P.M. time frame proposed by the Cook County Coroner's Office in 1955.

If the boys had died earlier than 9:30 P.M., the defense needed to attack the testimony of Hetty Salerno and Ernest Niewiadomski, who were among the first witnesses presented by the state. Both Salerno and Niewiadomski had testified at the first trial and were able to pinpoint almost an exact time when certain events had occurred.

Hetty Salerno moved slowly to the witness stand. She had grown hard of hearing and her eyesight was failing. The seventy-nine-year-old grandmother once again told the court she and her husband had a nightly routine in 1955 in which they shared a few quiet moments together every evening between 9 and 10 P.M. after putting their children to bed.

While being questioned by Scott Cassidy, Salerno once again told the jury of the anguished screams she had heard on the night of October 16, 1955. She said the screams came from the direction of the nearby Idle Hour Stable. The screams sounded like someone was "beating the hell out of a kid," Salerno testified.

On cross-examination, Weinberg tested Salerno's short- and long-term memory. To many of the questions, Salerno answered no, or stated she could not recall the specific event. Salerno was steadfast, however, that the screams came from the Idle Hour Stable.

When he testified, Ernest Niewiadomski was questioned similarly. Though the jury didn't know it at the time, Niewiadomski's seemingly innocuous testimony was the most serious threat to the defense case. As he had testified in the first trial, Niewiadomski, who was a neighbor of the Schuessler's, told the jury he knew John and Anton Schuessler because the brothers had often participated in neighborhood pickup baseball games. Niewiadomski testified that he saw the brothers and their friend Bobby Peterson at the Monte Cristo Bowling Alley around 7:30 P.M. on October 16, 1955. Niewiadomski talked to the Schuessler brothers, who said they had been to a movie downtown and didn't have any money to bowl, he said.

When Weinberg cross-examined Niewiadomski, he insinuated that Niewiadomski had been lying about his testimony for almost fifty years. After Niewiadomski testified that he had told his story several dozen times to the police, Weinberg asked, "And you knew with each time the officers came back to you, they were puzzled, they were baffled, about this case, correct?"

Weinberg and Cassidy also went toe to toe regarding Niewiadomski's refusal to meet with investigators for the defense. Weinberg tried to portray Niewiadomski as a man who was trying to hide the truth.

The state's final witness on the first day of testimony was William "Red" Wemette. Red's testimony was much the same as at the first trial. During cross-examination Goodman tried to pin him down about whether or not he had ever told the FBI about Hansen's involvement in the Schuessler-Peterson murders during his almost two decades as a FBI informant.

"During this period of time, these eighteen years, you were interviewed by the FBI three hundred and thirty times, is that correct?" Goodman asked.

Red responded, "I don't know how many times. They were mostly phone calls."

"Well," Goodman said, "during these approximately three hundred sessions with the FBI, is it true that you never once told them about Kenneth Hansen confessing to the Schuessler-Peterson murders?" Goodman asked.

"I attempted to tell them several times about different murders and they said if they were local crimes they didn't want to hear about it unless it was organized crime, O.C.," Red answered.

Red also testified that the FBI agents who had served as his "handlers" were John Osborne, Scott Jennings and Hank Schmidt. Red said he also talked to many other FBI agents who had contacted him about various organized crime individuals.

Over a period of three days the state presented largely the same case it had in 1995, minus all references to Hansen's penchant for picking up and then abusing male hitchhikers. The testimony of many of the witnesses included additional, minor details that were not heard in the first trial. The testimony of Roger Spry and Herbert Hollatz was largely the same and the questions posed to them under cross-examination were similar. The defense tried to portray Hollatz as a forgetful alcoholic and Spry as being motivated to lie in order to cut a deal regarding his arson charge. Joseph Plemmons's testimony caused a bit of a stir when he told the jury that he decided to come forward with what he knew about Hansen after learning that Hansen had lied to him about the death of his wife Beverly. After the jury was escorted from the courtroom, Goodman moved for a mistrial, claiming that the jury might infer that Hansen was somehow responsible for Beverly's death. Judge Mary Ellen Coghlan denied the motion.

The state's most important witness to counter the defense was Chief Cook County Medical Examiner Dr. Edmund Donoghue. He was called to testify about the manner of death for each of the boys. The prosecution already knew the defense case was to be built largely on the testimony of Dr. Shaku Teas, a forensic pathologist. Therefore, the prosecution elicited more details from Dr. Donoghue than it had during the first trial.

Donoghue testified that Anton Schuessler died as a result of manual strangulation. He said that abrasions found on the backs of little Tony's hands were consistent with the boy punching something or someone. John Schuessler died of asphyxia, as if he had been held in a chokehold, a manner of death that matched the testimony of Roger Spry. John Schuessler also had a large incise wound on his left thigh that was inflicted after death. Donoghue also testified that Bobby Peterson had been struck on the head with some sort of pronged object and strangled with a ligature, most likely some sort of belt or strap which was wrapped around his neck.

Regarding the exhumation of the boys' bodies, Donoghue testified that a substance known as diatomaceous earth was found in several of the lacerations on Bobby Peterson's scalp. Against the objections of Weinberg, he added that diatomaceous earth is an insecticide that could be found at a stable. He also testified that a minute shard of stainless steel found under Bobby's fingernail could have come from a horseshoe.

When Weinberg cross-examined Donoghue, he zeroed in on the partially digested food that was found in the stomachs of Tony and John Schuessler. Weinberg wanted to know if Donoghue ever estimated a person's time of death by examining the contents of their stomach. "Not really, no," Donoghue responded when asked. Donoghue later added that he didn't think using the gastric contents was a reliable way of determining the time of death. On

further cross-examination, Donoghue testified that there
were no traces of horsehair, oats, hay, barley or horse feed
found on any of the boys' bodies.

Before the state rested, Dr. Richard Ritt was called to
testify about the film he shot for WGN-TV on the day the
boys' bodies were discovered. Ritt, who was seventy-nine,
told the jury he had spent two and a half hours at the crime
scene that day filming the area. His film was edited down
to a five-minute clip that was used by WGN. Ritt's testimony was used to introduce a two-and-half-minute portion
of the clip to the jury. Goodman objected to the videotape
being shown as inflammatory and prejudicial. Coghlan,
however, ruled that the tape was admissible.

The stark, black-and-white videotape first showed the
Robinson Woods Forest Preserve sign and then cut away to
show the three boys lying in the ditch. The boys' lifeless
bodies appeared pasty-white compared to every other object seen in the film. Ritt panned the crime scene, capturing
the chaos as the press began to gather around the remains.
Police and reporters were shown scribbling in notebooks,
smoking cigarettes, grim faced. There was no audio ac-
companying the tape. The videotape appeared to have a
profound effect on some members of the jury. A few exhaled deeply; others clenched the fists that they held over
their lips. Every member of the jury looked at the film.
Some watched every second; others turned away quickly
after a few moments as if they had seen enough. Not one
juror looked toward Kenneth Hansen or the defense table
after the tape was played.

The defense began its case shortly after the tape was
shown. One of the first witnesses called by the defense was
Dr. Teas, a former Cook County medical examiner who

had once worked with Dr. Donoghue. Teas testified that she had reviewed the same material that Donoghue had at his disposal and concluded that the contents of the Schuessler brothers' stomachs, described as partially digested macaroni, would indicate the boys died much earlier than 9:30 to 10 P.M., as theorized by the prosecution.

During her testimony, Teas pointed out that the Schuessler boys' parents had told police their sons ate chicken soup with macaroni and vegetables around 1:30 P.M. on the day they disappeared. Teas also testified that the boys' bodies would have consumed the pasta, a quickly digestible carbohydrate, within three hours. She placed the boys' time of death no later than 4:30 P.M. The state attacked the opinion on cross-examination. Teas, who testified that she had read over the transcript of the coroner's inquest held in 1955, was asked if she placed more credence in science than in the testimony of Ernest Niewiadomski, an eyewitness who had seen the boys alive after 4:30 P.M. Kelecius pointed out in the transcript of the coroner's inquest that Ernest Niewiadomski had testified that he spoke to the victims at the Monte Cristo Bowling Alley between 7:30 and 7:45 P.M. Teas told the jury she had read the same transcript.

"According to you, was he talking to three ghosts?" Kelecius queried. Weinberg immediately objected.

"Are they dead at that time, according to you?" the prosecutor asked. Weinberg again objected.

"Doesn't that shoot down your opinion?" Kelecius asked. After some give-and-take between Weinberg and Judge Coghlan, the judge said the witness could answer the question.

"No, it does not in my opinion, because eyewitness ac-

counts can be very erroneous in a lot of instances and they
need to be evaluated," Teas said. Later she further explained her position, testifying that "I am looking at the
scientific evidence that's there, rather than something that I
know can be unreliable."

The following day several more witnesses were called
by the defense. The testimony of Frank Jayne Sr. was stipulated and allowed into evidence. Another Jayne, however,
took the stand to testify on Hansen's behalf. Dorothy
Jayne, the widow of Silas Jayne, testified that Kenneth
Hansen did not work at the Idle Hour Stable in the 1950s.
Jayne testified that she worked as Silas Jayne's chief rider
starting in 1952 and that she never once saw Hansen at the
Idle Hour. On cross-examination by prosecutor Jennifer
Coleman, Jayne testified that as the stable's top rider she
rarely mixed with the hired help. She also testified that she
might have been out of town at a horse show when the mur-
ders occurred. The defense rested following Dorothy
Jayne's testimony.

Called as rebuttal witnesses for the state were David
Hamm and Dr. Donoghue. Hamm testified that Hansen
told him he had begun working for Silas Jayne at the Idle
Hour in 1953, before he went into the U.S. Army. Hamm
said Hansen informed him that when he was discharged in
1955 he returned to his job. Donoghue was called to further discredit Teas's testimony. He took the witness stand
and told the jury that partially digested pasta could have remained in the boys' stomachs more than three hours because it was ingested in soup and was not chewed. The
boys may also have been excited about their first trip to
downtown Chicago and that would have slowed down the
digestion process, he said.

Before concluding its rebuttal, the state asked for and

received a stipulation from the defense regarding the registry at the Garland Building. A stipulation is an agreement between parties involved in legal matters that certain evidence or facts are accurate and true and not in dispute. It was stipulated that Bobby Peterson had signed the registry at 6:05 P.M. on October 16, 1955. The registry was discovered by Detective John Sarnowski and his partner, Edwin Kocinski, in 1957. At Hansen's first trial, his defense had entered the registry evidence via stipulation. Goodman and Weinberg had agreed to the stipulation as part of a tradeoff with the state. In exchange for the Garland Building registry, the prosecution had agreed to stipulate that partially digested macaroni was found in the boys' stomachs.

In his closing arguments in the first trial, Arthur O'Donnell claimed that the registry exonerated Hansen. O'Donnell theorized that the three boys went to the Garland Building to meet someone who, he said, was the boys' real killer. If it hadn't been for Judge Michael Toomin's pretrial rulings, O'Donnell had hoped to tell the jury that the person that the boys had met at the Garland Building was none other than budding serial killer John Wayne Gacy, age thirteen.

In his closing arguments at Hansen's second trial, Scott Cassidy noted that the Garland Building stipulation destroyed the defense's claim that the Schuessler boys died around 4:30 P.M. To believe Dr. Teas's testimony and also accept the uncontested introduction of the Garland Building registry evidence would mean that Bobby Peterson had abandoned his friends and possibly knew they had been kidnapped but did nothing to help them. The Garland Building registry also strengthened Ernest Niewiadomski's testimony because the Garland Building is near the Loop

Theater, where the boys had told Ernie they went to see *The African Lion*. Goodman's closing arguments pointed out that there was no evidence linking Hansen to the murders and that the state's case was born out of the testimony of paid informants and an alcoholic.

Three and a half hours after hearing the closing arguments, the jury convicted Kenneth Hansen for the boys' murders. *Chicago Tribune* reporter Jeff Coen interviewed several jurors who told him the first vote taken was eleven to one to convict. Following the vote, the jury spent their time going over the trial, witness by witness. One unnamed juror said the panel had little difficulty believing the state's witnesses despite the minor inconsistencies. "Sleazy witnesses are sleazy witnesses, but can they tell the truth on their best day?" The juror later added, "Hansen was controlling the information. Everybody got a piece."

The verdict not only brought a measure of solace to the remaining relatives of the boys, but it also just about closed the Chicago Horse Syndicate/Jayne Gang case files for John Rotunno. Over the next few months, Rotunno would work closely with prosecutors from Cook and DuPage counties to eventually bring about three convictions on arson charges against Frank Jayne Jr., the one man many said had escaped charges in the Helen Brach investigation.

On October 1, 2002, just fifteen days shy of the forty-seventh anniversary of the boys' murders, Kenneth Hansen was sentenced by Judge Coghlan to two hundred to three hundred years in prison, the same sentence Judge Toomin had handed down in 1995 at Hansen's first trial. Had they not taken that fateful ride offered to them by a monster named Kenneth Hansen on a rainy October night decades earlier, Anton, John and Bobby would have been middle-aged men approaching retirement age, possibly with grandchildren of their own.

Hansen appealed his second conviction. He was unsuccessful. The Illinois Appellate Court affirmed Hansen's second conviction on August 25, 2004.

EPILOGUE

Following Kenneth Hanson's second conviction, John Rotunno and Jim Grady were moved on to other investigations. Rotunno knew he wouldn't be completely free of the Chicago Horse Syndicate for a few more months because Frank Jayne Jr. still faced trial on arson charges, but he could see the light at the end of the tunnel.

Rotunno was amazed by the amount of human misery that Silas Jayne, Kenneth Hansen and other members of the Jayne Gang had caused to satiate their desires for money, power and sex. Silas Jayne and Kenneth Hansen were both cut from the same bolt of cloth. Both men were pedophiles and ruthless killers. They felt no remorse when hurting others. Throughout the Schuessler-Peterson investigation, Rotunno's one regret was that he never had the opportunity to arrest, charge and convict Silas Jayne for the boys' murders. Death had robbed him of that opportunity.

Fate, however, was not about to let Rotunno go after he wrapped up the Frank Jayne Jr. cases. There were other murders that members of the gang had yet to answer for. There was the presumed slaying of the three girls abducted from the Indiana Dunes in 1965, the cold-blooded execution of Frank Michelle Jr. at Silas Jayne's farm in 1969 and the murder of candy heiress Helen Brach.

Several weeks after Hansen was convicted and sentenced for the second time, Rotunno received a telephone call at his office. The voice on the other end of the line was familiar. It was Joe Plemmons. Plemmons knew many secrets of the Jayne Gang and Rotunno would soon learn that he had been keeping some of his own.

Plemmons was inebriated. He told Rotunno he had information that had been weighing heavily on his heart. "I'm being chased by ghosts," Plemmons said. He wanted to unburden himself, to come clean. Plemmons told Rotunno he had seen Helen Brach's body in the presence of several of Silas Jayne's minions. As a result of the admission, for the next two years Rotunno found himself investigating the unsolved murder of Helen Brach.

Rotunno worked the case almost nonstop, and it led him deeper into Silas Jayne's criminal organization and further exposed Silas's ties to the Chicago Outfit.

On November 5, 2004, in a hotel room in Philadelphia, Plemmons provided an in-depth statement to Rotunno, Assistant Cook County State's Attorney Thomas Biesty and Cook County State's Attorney Investigator John O'Connell. What was different this time was that Plemmons, who had been cooperating with the investigation all along but had changed portions of his story on different occasions, was about to tell everything he knew, under the cloak of immunity.

Because he would not face prosecution if he told the truth, Plemmons told the three lawmen much of what he had been holding back. In February 1977, soon after Brach checked out of the Mayo Clinic, Plemmons said he had been summoned to Kenneth Hansen's stable in Tinley Park. When he got to the stable, he met with Hansen and was present when a relative of Silas Jayne's drove a Cadillac into an indoor riding ring at the stable. The passenger in the car was Hansen's hit man brother, Curtis. The two men exited the Cadillac and popped open the trunk of the vehicle. Lying in the trunk wrapped in a blanket was Helen Brach. Her face was poking out of the blanket. It was discolored purple and blue. Plemmons recognized Brach because he had met her once at a horse show in Racine, Wisconsin. He assumed Brach was dead.

Plemmons later learned that Brach had been driven from Minnesota and beaten at her home in Glenview by a corrupt law enforcement officer who might have been paid up to $1 million by Silas Jayne to murder the heiress. Brach was murdered because she had threatened to go to the police. She had been conned out of millions of dollars in untraceable bearer bonds and not the few hundred thousand dollars alleged at Richard Bailey's sentencing hearing in 1995. The Chicago Outfit played a role in the con and in Brach's murder.

Curtis Hansen ordered Plemmons and Kenneth Hansen to move Brach from the trunk of the Cadillac to Kenneth Hansen's station wagon. Plemmons grabbed the body by the feet and Kenneth Hansen picked Brach up by the shoulders. The two men had begun moving what they thought was a corpse when Kenneth Hansen suddenly dropped it and exclaimed, "She moaned!"

All four men then stepped back from the body, looked down at Brach and then at one another. Nobody moved for a moment. Curtis broke the silence, blurting out, "Bullshit!" He then pulled a pistol from his waistband and handed it to Silas Jayne's relative. The relative, who looked petrified, said nothing. He handed the gun back to Curtis. The hit man then tossed the gun to Plemmons.

"Put holes in the blanket or there will be two in the station wagon," Curtis said. "Shoot her or you'll be in there," he added, motioning toward the station wagon. Plemmons hesitated. He thought about running away but knew that if he tried to escape Curtis would shoot him in the back. He did not want to kill Brach. Curtis then pulled out a 12-gauge sawed-off shotgun from underneath his jacket. It was Curtis's favorite weapon. He had nicknamed it "Mother's Little Helper." Curtis cocked the weapon and pointed it at Plemmons.

Facing certain death, Plemmons fired a shot into the prone torso. Brach's body "jumped" underneath the blanket. "Do it again!" Curtis growled. Plemmons fired one more round into the body. "Now we don't have to worry about Joe," Curtis said. "He's one of us." Afterward, when Plemmons walked away from the others, he felt ill. The others loaded Brach's body into the station wagon. Approaching the spot on the ground where he assumed he had murdered her, Plemmons noticed a ring lying in the dirt. It was a white gold band that held one ruby. It had apparently fallen off Brach's finger while her body was being moved. Plemmons picked up the ring and pocketed it. The ring, which was the only piece of physical evidence he had that tied him to Brach's murder, would later be stolen from Plemmons. Curtis and Silas Jayne's relative climbed into the Cadillac. "Follow us," Curtis snapped.

Plemmons said he and Kenneth Hansen followed Curtis and the other man from the stable to a steel mill in Gary, Indiana. Curtis drove up to the gate of the mill and both cars were waved through. It appeared as if they were expected, Plemmons said. Both cars were allowed to drive up to the building containing the blast furnace. Several steelworkers were waiting there and waved them inside. The steelworkers used long metal poles with hooks to open two large doors to the blast furnace. The heat was intense. Plemmons and Kenneth Hansen then removed Brach's body from the station wagon and threw it into a pit containing molten steel. The blanket burst into flames and Brach's body was consumed before Plemmons's eyes. The resulting stench was terrible. To this day Plemmons is reminded of the horrible moment whenever he sees smokestacks off in the distance while driving along an interstate.

During the course of the investigation, Rotunno would determine that there were others involved in Helen Brach's murder. Among those who participated but were now deceased included Silas Jayne and mobsters Anthony and Victor Spilotro. The Spilotro brothers were close to a member of Silas Jayne's inner circle and were able to provide access to the steel mill through their corrupt organized labor contacts. There were five others who were living who participated in the murder. Of the five, two were in prison on other charges.

Because Brach's disappearance generated so much law enforcement scrutiny, Silas Jayne did his best to frame Richard Bailey for her murder. Bailey had indeed solicited Kenneth Hansen and Joe Plemmons to murder Brach. But when he failed to accomplish the job Silas was forced to take matters into his own hands and saw to it that Brach was murdered as a favor to the Outfit. Bailey was made the fall guy in order to protect Silas Jayne and his interests.

Despite Plemmons's statement, in February 2005 the Cook County State's Attorney's Office told Rotunno it would not bring charges against any of the other co-conspirators whom Plemmons had identified as participating in Brach's murder. Cook County prosecutors would later tell the Chicago media they were reluctant to press charges because Plemmons's statement could not be corroborated by other witnesses or physical evidence. Plus, Plemmons carried a lot of baggage as a witness. He's a convicted con man whose best friend is a pedophile who murdered three children. A jury might not find him believable. Cook County prosecutors also found the confession hard to believe. They were incredulous that as many as ten persons, including an untold number of mobbed up steel-workers, could be involved in Brach's murder and the disposal of her body and it remain secret for twenty-eight years. Also, how come it took Plemmons so long to tell authorities what happened to Brach? Why did he give conflicting accounts of what happened?

When ATF attorneys learned that no charges would be filed by Cook County prosecutors, they were duty bound to report Plemmons's confession that he had murdered Brach to the United States Attorney's Office, which had been responsible for prosecuting Bailey. Federal prosecutors then passed along Plemmons's exculpatory statement to Bailey's attorney, Kathleen Zellner. She then filed documents with the Seventh U.S. Circuit Court of Appeals seeking a resentencing hearing for Bailey. Zellner sought the resentencing alleging that Bailey had not participated in Brach's actual murder and therefore should receive a reduced sentence. The motion filed by Zellner added some momentum to the case put together by Rotunno.

Zellner's court filing, which included many of Rotunno's redacted case reports, generated quite a few news stories in Chicago. Kenneth Hansen's attorney, Leonard Goodman, said that his client played no role in Brach's murder. As a result of the renewed interest in the case several reporters tracked Plemmons down and tried to interview him. The notoriety also attracted a death threat.

In early February 2005 while at a horse show in Wellington, Florida, Plemmons was going about his business when he heard a man yell out to him. "Hey fuck head," Plemmons heard the man say. "You better have a memory loss. You better forget your story. If you don't, you'll be dead." The man fled before Plemmons could stop him.

On March 22, 2005, the Seventh U.S. Circuit Court of Appeals denied Bailey's motion in a two-paragraph order. The judges wrote that the new evidence did not prove Bailey wasn't involved in Brach's death. The judges noted Bailey's petition did not challenge his conviction for racketeering, which was based on his fraudulent horse deals with Brach. The new evidence was irrelevant, the judges said.

Rotunno's Brach investigation, which had been on life support with barely a heartbeat, was now, as far as he was concerned, officially dead.

Rotunno breathed a sigh of relief. He was finally done with the Chicago Horse Syndicate. The conclusion was bittersweet for Rotunno. He remains convinced that he and others solved the Brach murder. The Cook County State's Attorney's Office said the case would remain an open investigation, but spokesmen told the press charges most likely would never be approved based on Plemmons's confession.

The investigation also carried a personal toll for Rotunno. In the course of conducting it, he had fallen out with some prosecutors whom he had once considered as friends.

After hearing that Bailey's appeal had been denied, Rotunno boxed up his case reports detailing everything that he'd learned about Brach's murder and shipped the reports out to be archived in a federal warehouse. He doubted anything new could be added to his investigation that would prompt prosecutors to approve charges. But he hoped someday they would change their minds.

Although Helen Brach's murder touched off a federal probe which eventually resulted in the conviction of Kenneth Hansen for the murders of Bobby, Johnny and Tony and also the conviction of James Blottiaux for the murder of Cheryl Lynn Rude, Rotunno is convinced no one will ever answer for the heiress's brutal murder. Rotunno, however, took some solace in the fact that Helen Brach's brutal death had not been entirely in vain. Instead it resulted in others being brought to justice for the senseless murders they had committed.

CHRONOLOGY

The following chronology was developed using law enforcement records and reports; trial transcripts and depositions; published media reports and interviews with some participants.

July 3, 1907: Silas Jayne is born in Cuba Township near Lake Zurich, Illinois. He is one of twelve children born to Arthur and Katherine Jayne.

November 2, 1923: George Jayne is born. His father is George W. Spunner, a Milwaukee attorney who owns a campground that Katherine Jayne manages on the shores of Lake Zurich, Illinois.

November 12, 1924: Silas Jayne is convicted of rape and sentenced to one year in jail. He is represented in court by

George William Spunner. Spunner recommends that Silas serve a year for the sentence. "He's a wild young man. A year in jail won't hurt him," Spunner reportedly tells the sentencing judge.

1927: Silas Jayne marries for the first time. The couple is divorced within six months. Forty years later Silas tells a prison psychologist they were incompatible.

1930s: Silas Jayne along with his brothers Frank Sr. and De Forest earn reputations as a rowdy posse of cowboys. Well known as brawlers, they're dubbed the "Jesse Jayne Gang" by a local cattle auctioneer.

1932: Silas Jayne opens the first Idle Hour Stable at Lincoln and Peterson avenues in Chicago.

December 7, 1932: Kenneth Hansen is born. His parents are Ethan and Lucille Hansen. He is the youngest of four, which include an older brother, Curtis, and two sisters. His father, Ethan, is a printer and his mother a piano teacher. Ethan Hansen would later commit suicide circa 1955–1956.

1934 to 1940: Silas Jayne and his brother operate a succession of stables on Chicago's north side and nearby suburbs. Among them are the Green Tree Stable in Norridge, Illinois, and the Elston Avenue Riding Academy in Chicago.

October 15, 1938: De Forest Jayne's fiancée, telephone operator Mae Sweeney, twenty-five, kills herself by drinking arsenic.

October 20, 1938: One day after the funeral of Mae Sweeney, De Forest Jayne commits suicide with a 12-gauge shotgun at the foot of Mae Sweeney's grave. His brothers

Frank and Silas and a sister discover him. In his will De Forest Jayne leaves twenty acres of land to his half-brother George Jayne. The gift of the land to George enrages Silas Jayne.

1938: Silas Jayne marries for the second time. Silas Jayne's second marriage, to Martha, lasts twenty years. He tells a prison psychologist his second wife divorced him because she grew tired of him traveling the show horse circuit. Martha Jayne would later open a stable down the street from Silas Jayne's second Idle Hour Stable near Park Ridge.

1940: Ten horses die in a suspicious fire at a stable Silas Jayne owns in River Grove, Illinois.

1940: George Jayne is forced to kill a Doberman pinscher owned by Silas Jayne. George Jayne beats the dog to death with a cane after Silas Jayne lets the dog loose on him while he is walking up to the Green Tree Stable.

1941: One of Silas Jayne's riding students, Ruth De War, sues Silas Jayne, claiming he frightened the horse she was riding, causing the animal to throw her to the ground and fracturing her spine. An all-woman jury finds in Silas's favor at trial.

1941–1945: Silas and other members of the Jesse Jayne Gang are key players in what became known as the horse meat scandals in Chicago. During World War II the Jesse Jayne Gang sold horse meat to restaurants as beef. Members of the gang also rustle cattle from farmers in the Chicago area.

February 16, 1944: George Jayne marries Marion Pollard. Marion would later tell an investigator she had known

George since she was eight years old, having met him at a YMCA stable.

1947: Silas Jayne allegedly commits his first murder at a stable in Hickory Hills, Illinois. The victim, who was buried at the stable, was a minor Chicago Outfit figure who tried to collect a street tax from Silas to operate the business.

1951: Kenneth Hansen graduates from Amundson High School in Chicago.

January 28, 1952: A fire destroys George and Marion Jayne's seven-room home in Morton Grove, Illinois. Some would later speculate this fire represents the opening salvo in the feud between Silas and George Jayne. However George Jayne would later testify the fire was caused by a faulty freezer.

January 3, 1953: Kenneth Hansen is drafted into the U.S. Army. While in the service, he is assigned to the 40th Infantry Division, Headquarters Staff.

1952–1953: Herbert Hollatz, the son of a Chicago Police officer, begins boarding his horse at a stable at the Park Ridge Riding Academy. The stable is owned by Kenneth Hansen, his brother Curtis Hansen and father Ethan Hansen. Hollatz is sexually assaulted by Hansen. The relationship eventually becomes consensual, but it is put on hold when Hansen enters the Army.

June 27, 1953: Kenneth Hansen marries Beverly Rae Carlson.

1952–1955: George Jayne borrows $90,000 from his brother Silas to purchase the Happy Days Stable in Nor-

wood Park, Illinois. The stable has three barns, known as
A, B and C barns. Silas Jayne uses Barn C for his business.

1954: Silas Jayne purchases the Idle Hour Stable, moving
out of George Jayne's Happy Days Stable. The two brothers are now competitors. Kenneth Hansen goes to work for
Silas Jayne.

October 16, 1955:

2:30 P.M.: John and Anton Schuessler, ages thirteen and
eleven, leave home at 5711 North Mango Avenue in
Chicago on bicycles, bound for the home of their friend,
Bobby Peterson.

3:00 P.M.: After consulting with Bobby Peterson's father and mother, John, Anton and Bobby, thirteen, leave
the Peterson home at 5519 Farragut Avenue to travel to
the Loop Theater at 165 North State to see the Walt Disney movie *The African Lion*.

Sometime that afternoon: Bruce Carter, who was
eleven years old, and his brother Glen Carter, fourteen,
meet the Schuessler-Peterson boys in an alley on Milwaukee Avenue between Edmund and Gayle streets. All
five boys converse about their plans that day. Bruce
Carter would later tell ATF agents that he recalled that
Bobby Peterson and the Schuessler boys were sharing a
bottle of Green River Soda. Bobby Peterson said the
trio was going out to a stable to ride horses. At some
point in the conversation a car drives by and honks.
Carter recalls Tony stated, "Is that Hansen?" To which
John Schuessler replied, "Shut up. We've said enough

already." Carter recalled the event because he had a cousin named Hansen and wondered if the cousin had his license. Upon leaving, one of the three boys tosses the bottle of pop against a brick wall, breaking it. All the boys run so they won't get in trouble.

3:55 P.M.: National Weather Service climatological data indicates it began raining at this time and continued to 4:50 A.M. on October 17.

7:15–7:45 P.M. The three boys are spotted at the Monte Cristo Bowling Alley by Ernest Niewiadomski, seventeen, and his two sisters. Ernest, who knows the boys from neighborhood pickup baseball games, asks them what they've been doing. They tell him they went to see *The African Lion*. He asks if they plan on bowling and they tell him they have no money.

8:00 P.M. Harold Blumfield, twenty, tells police he gave three boys a ride from Kimball and Montrose to 4444 West Montrose.

8:40 P.M. The three boys are seen by a man named Jack Johnson, sixty-seven, at the Garden Bowling Alley, 4074 Milwaukee Avenue.

8:47 P.M. Bruno Mencarini, forty-four, a CTA bus driver on the Milwaukee Avenue route, tells police he drove three boys on his bus from Berteau Avenue to Lawrence Avenue. The three got off bus at 8:52 P.M.

9:00 P.M. According to Chicago police reports, a Mrs. Kimske and her husband, George, see three boys she later positively identified as the Schuessler-Peterson kids, trying to thumb a ride at Lawrence Avenue. Around the same time Ralph Helm, a high school friend and his date are walking home from an outing. Helm spots Tony Schuessler hitchhiking. He would later positively identify him.

9:00 to midnight: The boys were murdered during this time frame.

9:15 P.M. Mr. Stanley Panek tells Park Ridge Police that he heard strange noises coming from the rear of the Idle Hour Stable. Panek would tell police he heard screams coming from the stable around 9:30 P.M. while walking his dog. He also tells police he thought he heard someone yelling for help. Stanley Panek's story is corroborated by neighbors Vince and Hetty Salerno. Hetty Salerno would later describe the screams as like "someone beating the hell out of child."

11 P.M.: Mrs. Delores Wisilinski tells police she heard a boy screaming, "No, no!" She then heard an angry male voice say, "Get in there!" and saw a car pull away at a high rate of speed. A Mrs. Walter Grzybowski tells police her dog became very agitated around midnight on the October 16. The dog kept looking toward the same spot in the field near the Idle Hour Stable where Wisilinski heard the screams. A Mrs. Sinarski also tells the police her dog became agitated at the same time and was disturbed about something going on in the field.

October 18, 1955, 12:20 P.M.: The three nude bodies of Anton Schuessler, John Schuessler and Bobby Peterson are found lying in a ditch alongside the east side of a road leading into the Robinson Woods Forest Preserve. The bodies are found by Victor Livingston. This location is a little more than a mile from the Idle Hour Stable. Meteorological reports indicate it had rained Sunday night and Monday morning. When the bodies are found, the grass underneath them is wet but the bodies are dry, indicating they were kept somewhere before being dumped.

Days after the murders: Bruce and Glen Carter tell their mother what they know about the boys' plans that day, but she refuses to allow them to come forward for fear of their lives.

Within a week of the murders, 1955: Marion Jayne would later tell ATF Agent John Rotunno that her husband, George Jayne, told her that Silas Jayne and three others were involved in the boys' murders. George also told Marion he had enough information to put Silas and the others in the electric chair. George wrote down what he knew about the murders in a letter. The letter was hidden and never recovered. George Jayne would later tell Marion he destroyed the letter because it would bring universal "shame" on the Jayne family name. Marion urged her husband to go to the police with the information, but George believed the police were on Silas Jayne's payroll. On November 2, 1955, when police visit George at the Happy Days Stable he tells them nothing. On December 16, 1955, the police request a list of names of all those who work or board horses at Happy Days. George Jayne refuses to supply the list.

Within a week of the murders, 1955: While having relations with Herbert Hollatz, Kenneth Hansen tells Hollatz he murdered the three boys. "Herb, can I trust you? . . . I killed the three boys that everybody is reading about in the newspapers." Hollatz asks why and Hansen says, "Somebody told me to do it." "He looked at me with a cold icy stare," Hollatz would later say. Hansen warns Hollatz that his hit-man brother Curtis will kill him if he tells anyone. Hollatz is later questioned by the police and remains silent.

October 26, 1955: Chicago Police Officers V. McAleer, R. Fivelson and C. McCarthy interview Stanley Panek. The officers then interview Ralph Fleming, the manager of the Idle Hour Stable. Fleming provides the police with a list of employees. Kenneth Hansen's name is not on the list. "Mr. Fleming was very cooperative and personally escorted us through his stable area," the officers' report states. The stable was closed on Sundays, and a night watchman patrolled the premises with a "large, ferocious" German shepherd. According to the report, at the time of the screams, the night watchman, John Lyda, was asleep. Other stable hands, Lester Beatty, Carl Stout, Jerry Goble and Vincent Dzieski, were also asleep.

December 5, 1955: Chicago Police Officers H. McGrath and J. Kelly of the Special Investigations Unit visit the Idle Hour Stable. Ralph Fleming gives them a list of people boarding horses at the stable. Fleming tells them other officers have been by to question him.

April 1956: *Chicago Tribune* news articles indicate authorities plan to exhume the bodies of the three boys to look for more evidence possibly indicating the location where the murders took place.

May 14, 1956: The back barn at the Idle Hour Stable burns to the ground. Kenneth Hansen later admits to a witness that the barn was destroyed to cover up the crime.

June 1, 1956: The bodies of the three boys are exhumed for further study.

1956: In fear of his life, Herbert Hollatz decides to leave Illinois. He heads west, marries and fathers six children. A pipefitter by trade, he becomes an alcoholic.

1958: Stable hand Patrick T. Mason, fifteen, catches Kenneth Hansen having sex with a young boy at the Broken-H Stable in Willow Springs, Illinois. Hansen later threatens Mason, warning him not to say anything about what he saw with the comment, "If I hear you mention a word to anybody else about this, you'll end up in a forest preserve like some other boys."

May 21, 1961: Silas Jayne exchanges gunfire with four men during a home invasion at the Idle Hour Stable. Later Silas fingers four mob-connected henchmen with the robbery. Weeks later, following an intensive manhunt, the four mobsters are spotted in Wisconsin and a local policeman is killed in the ensuing shoot-out. Later it is learned that Silas Jayne had intentionally fingered the wrong people for some unknown reason.

1961: George Jayne's fourteen-year-old daughter takes top prize at the Oak Brook Hounds Horse Show, beating Silas Jayne's best horse and rider. Enraged, Silas yells to his brother, "I'll never talk to you again, you bastard!"

September 1961: George Jayne warns the parents of his star rider, Cheryl Lynn Rude, that he believes his brother Silas Jayne is trying to kill him.

Sometime in 1962: Roger Lee Spry is abandoed by his mother, a stripper, and his father. He eventually goes to live with Kenneth Hansen, his wife Beverly and two young sons.

July 1962: George Jayne's office is burglarized.

September 1962: At the Ohio State Fair, the tie-rods are damaged and front wheel lugs loosened on George Jayne's truck/trailer.

October 1962: George Jayne hires security guards. Despite precautions, the tires on his cars and other vehicles are ice-picked.

1963: George Jayne's horse Silouette wins the open jumping event at the Lake Forest Horse Show at Onwentsia. Linda Jayne would later testify she heard Silas Jayne yell at her father, "I'll kill you, you son of a bitch!"

March 1963: The office and clubroom at George Jayne's Tri-Color Stable in Palatine are peppered with an automatic weapon's fire. Twenty-eight bullet holes are found on the building.

1962–1963: Edwin Nefeld befriends Kenneth Hansen and buys a horse from him. At this time Hansen is the owner of the High Hopes Stable in Hickory Hills, Illinois. Nefeld later tells the ATF it was Hansen who introduced him to Silas Jayne, Frank Jayne Sr. and Frank Jayne Jr. Nefeld later becomes chief of detectives for the Markham Police Department.

May 1963: At the Cincinnati Horse Show someone sets fire to George Jayne's tack room.

July 1964: George Jayne's chief rider, Cheryl Lynn Rude, is seriously injured in a riding accident. She is almost killed when a horse falls on her, crushing her chest. She remains in critical condition for twelve days.

April 29, 1965: Chicago Police Detective James Houtsman receives a tip from a man that there is a murder contract out on a man who lives in a house on a hill near Palatine. The target is supposedly one of three brothers involved in the horse business. The target drives a gold Cadillac. The informant claims one of the three brothers wants to kill the target because the target had threatened to turn the brother in to the Internal Revenue Service.

May 1965: At the Cincinnati Horse Show, Silas Jayne is once again beaten badly by George Jayne. George Jayne's rider is Cheryl Lynn Rude. Silas Jayne publicly threatens to kill George.

June 10, 1965: Blue Island resident James Blottiaux, twenty-two, and Chicago resident Haladane Cleminson purchase twenty-one sticks of dynamite and twenty-one electrical blasting caps from Ludwig's hardware store in Lemont, Illinois. Blottiaux tells an old woman working the counter that he works for the Genson Construction Company in Tinley Park. There is no such company. The explosives are purchased on consignment, no cash paid. The two also order a case of dynamite, which they never pick up.

June 14, 1965: Cheryl Lynn Rude, twenty-two, is killed at George's Tri-Color Stable when a car bomb wired to George Jayne's gold Cadillac explodes. The two-door sedan's hood, left fender and left front tire are blown completely off. George Jayne had asked Rude to move the car so he could drive to a welder's shop to pick up a trailer, which was being repaired. Police determine the bomb went off exactly at 2:20 P.M.

Earlier that day, June 14, 1965: Two men, Stephen Grod and Eddie Moran, fly into Chicago from Florida. They were hired by Silas Jayne to murder George Jayne.

Within minutes/hours of the Rude murder: Police investigating the murder threaten to arrest George Jayne for obstruction. George would not allow investigators into his office at the stable and refuses to go with them to the station. "At the time of the initial investigation George Jayne was extremely uncooperative and impeded the investigation," reports state.

June 17, 1965: After they hear of the bombing, Stephen Grod and Eddie Moran contact Silas Jayne. When they ask him about the Rude bombing, Silas Jayne responds, "They missed. Keep going." He offers them $15,000 to kill George Jayne. Grod and Moran instead go to George Jayne and he convinces them to go to the police. Moran admits he fired the twenty-eight shots into the Tri-Color Stable in 1963. Silas is eventually arrested on charges of conspiracy to commit murder.

June 29, 1965: George takes a lie detector test as part of the Rude murder investigation. He passes.

July 12, 1965: Haladane Cleminson is picked up by Chicago police as part of the Rude bombing investigation. Police find bomb making equipment in his home. Cleminson tells Chicago detectives James Blottiaux had asked him how to wire a car bomb.

July 13, 1965: Chicago police pick up James Blottiaux and search his home, where they find bomb making equipment. He passes a polygraph examination regarding the purchase of dynamite but handwriting experts later tie him to a receipt for the explosives.

August 12, 1965: James Blottiaux is questioned by Cook County Sheriff's Detective Sergeant Bernard Singer. Blottiaux admits he's friends with Eddie Moran and that in early May he was present at the Idle Hour Stable when Silas Jayne offered Moran $10,000 to place a bomb in George Jayne's car. Blottiaux says Moran informed him Silas wanted George killed over something to do with "income tax." Blottiaux says he refused the offer. But a telephone check conducted on calls made from Blottiaux's home shows he called a number at Silas Jayne's stable nine times between May 17 and June 30, 1965.

1966: Edwin Nefeld joins the Markham Police Department.

March 1966: As he's walking into the Cook County Criminal Courthouse at Twenty-sixth Street and California Avenue prior to Silas Jayne's trial on murder conspiracy charges in connection to the Rude murder, Frank Jayne Sr. hands Stephen Grod a copy of a news article about a key witness in some criminal case being murdered before he could testify. Grod takes the witness stand and cannot remember anything. He claims he cannot recall anything about Silas Jayne's $15,000 offer to kill George Jayne. "I can't even remember what I had for breakfast this morning. I'm sick," Grod testifies. He is held in contempt of court, fined $1,000 and jailed for thirty days. Silas Jayne walks out of court a free man. The charges against him are dropped on May 3, 1966.

Spring to Summer, 1966: George Jayne's office is burglarized and his business files stolen. A short time later he's indicted by the IRS on tax fraud charges. Silas Jayne later tells one of George's employees, "I will see to it that your boss is out of business soon, because I gave the IRS boys all the dope on him."

July 2, 1966: Three women with ties to Cheryl Rude, Ann Miller, twenty-one, Patty Blough and Renee Bruhl, both nineteen, are last seen getting into a blue speedboat at the Indiana State Dunes park. They are never seen again and presumed murdered. Silas Jayne later brags to an Oklahoma lawman that he has three bodies buried in his basement. When a state police investigator goes to question the lawman, in hopes of securing a warrant to search Silas Jayne's home, he finds that the sheriff has been killed in a freak tractor accident.

October to November 1966: The tax case against George Jayne goes to trial. With testimony from fifty-seven witnesses, the government claims he underreported his income from 1959 to 1961. The government claims George made a total of $270,000 in those years but only reported making $100,000. He's acquitted of the charges.

1967: The evidence collected as part of the Rude investigation implicating James Blottiaux, including a receipt Blottiaux signed and items found in his home under a search warrant, are destroyed by the Chicago Police, possibly at the direction of Silas Jayne or the Outfit. With no evidence, the case against Blottiaux is dropped.

1968: ATF Confidential Informant #34 (William "Red" Wemette) is introduced to Curtis Hansen and Kenneth Hansen by the brothers' sister, Marianne McGann. Red is introduced at a card game at the Valley View Young Adults Klub in Frankfort, Illinois.

1968: George Jayne sells his one-hundred-acre Tri-Color Farms to William Rainey Harper Junior College.

January 1969: Frank Michelle Jr. is gunned down outside of Silas Jayne's Our Day Farms in Elgin, Illinois. Silas claims the shooting is in self-defense. ATF agents later learn Michelle was first tortured by Silas, who took a pair of vice grips and crushed Michelle's testicles. Michelle was then shot to death by Silas Jayne. Silas Jayne brags to many people that he bribed an official $10,000 to dodge a murder rap charge.

July 31, 1969: Ancil Earl Tremore and Lawrence Smith are recruited by Kenneth Hansen to murder George Jayne. They're instructed to lie in wait for George Jayne at his home. If the two men could not kill him, they're told to kidnap George Jayne and take him back to the Young Adults Klub in Frankfort, Illinois, where Silas Jayne can personally murder his brother.

November 1969: Markham Chief of Detectives Edward Nefeld approaches Melvin Adams at a local restaurant and asks Adams if he knows anyone willing to commit a murder for hire. Adams volunteers. Nefeld tells Adams the hit is being commissioned by Silas Jayne and the target is George Jayne. Melvin Adams later meets with Silas. Silas tells Melvin he's been trying to kill his brother for ten years. Silas Jayne makes several suggestions, such as machine-gunning George on the expressway. He also urges Adams not to leave any witnesses, instructing him to kill George's wife and family if need be. Silas promises that after George is killed, he wants several other murders committed. "I've got everything you need, you know, a string of lawyers, money, anything." Adams begins stalking George Jayne.

Summer of 1970: Melvin Adams continues surveillance on George Jayne. When Adams expresses doubts about committing the murder, Silas Jayne offers him $20,000. Adams then recruits his coworker from his day job, a man named Julius "Jake" Barnes. The price for the hit climbs to $30,000. Adams's girlfriend borrows a .30–06 rifle from a Markham police officer, claiming her boyfriend needs the weapon to go hunting. Barnes test-fires the gun at Jayne's stables in Kane County.

October 28, 1970: Julius Barnes fatally shoots George Jayne to death, firing one shot through a basement window while Jayne is playing bridge with his wife, daughter and son-in-law. It is George Jayne's son George Junior's sixteenth birthday. The fatal shot comes just as George picks up the deck of cards and begins to shuffle. When he's hit, George cries out and falls to the floor moaning. Marion screams and rushes to his side. Witnesses spot a red car with a black top fleeing the murder scene. One witness, a young boy riding by on his bicycle, provides the first three digits of the plate, 9, 3, 6, to the police.

October 29, 1970: Marion Jayne walks to the end of the driveway of the family home and meets with newsmen. She makes a very brief statement. "A $25,000 reward is being offered by the family for information leading to the arrest and capture of those responsible," Marion announces. She then takes a few questions from reporters. "What about Silas?" one reporter asks. "Had he and George had any quarrels lately" Marion responds, "Not to my knowledge . . . We were just sitting there playing bridge in the basement. We were all there and we were having a family get-together." A radio reporter blurts out, "What was the occasion?" Marion responds, "It was our son's sixteenth birthday. And now if you'll excuse me . . ." She turns and walks away.

October 29, 1970: Joe LaPlaca gives Melvin Adams $15,000 for the hit. "This is all Si has around the house today," LaPlaca says when he gives Adams an envelope stuffed with tens and twenties.

October 30, 1970: Joe LaPlaca gives Melvin Adams the second $15,000 installment. Adams pays Julius Barnes $12,500 for his role in the murder.

October 30, 1970: Silas Jayne tells reporters his brother was murdered most likely because he owed gambling debts. Silas tells *Chicago Today* that George was a degenerate gambler who played craps and bet on the horses. "I feel very badly about the murder. We had our difficulties over the years but they have never been violent. We are a very close family. We spend every Christmas together." Silas tells *Chicago Today* that he was "like a father to George . . . In 1950 I gave him Happy Days Stable at Cumberland and Lawrence avenues. I started him out in the business. Then in 1958 and 1959 I helped him financially to get Tri-Color Stable. He paid me back . . . Our personalities just didn't click. George always wanted to be bigger and better." On the same day Silas tells the *Chicago Tribune* he and George patched up their feud in 1968. "We shook hands. We've always been good to each other but we haven't visited each other's homes. I feel very bad. I plan to go to George's wake and his funeral although I haven't talked to his widow." Silas also tells the *Tribune* the brotherly feud was blown out of proportion by the media. He describes George as a "nice fellow who worked hard" and that George was the "jealous type."

October 31, 1970: George Jayne is buried at Mount Emblem Cemetery.

November 1, 1970: The Chicago media reports that George's lawyer, Edward S. Arkema, has revealed that George left behind a letter which was written in July 1969. George wanted the letter opened if he should be murdered. On the same day Silas Jayne tells reporters he'll take a polygraph examination to clear his name. In the *Chicago Today* late edition, a story reports that George Jayne had agreed to get out of the horse business at a family reunion in 1967 to end the feud with Silas. Silas also offers a reward, but the amount was never specified. He tells the *Daily News,* "Sure we had problems but that was all straightened out years ago . . . George was a big gambler and maybe he was behind in payments on a juice loan." News reports note police have questioned an ex-convict and bodyguard of Silas Jayne, a man named Joe LaPlaca. LaPlaca is arrested on gun charges when police find three pistols at his home.

November 3, 1970: *Chicago Sun-Times* reporter Art Petacque reports that George Jayne may have been murdered because he had uncovered evidence about the Cheryl Lynn Rude murder.

November 4, 1970: The *Daily News* interviews Marion Jayne. She admits George and Silas shook hands. "They did finally shake hands but George had to pay a price for it," Marion said. "George had to stop entering horse shows to end the feud. He did."

November 17, 1970: Marion Jayne demands that Silas take a polygraph examination. Marion also renews the $25,000 offer to catch the killers. In a *Tribune* article Silas Jayne says he was counseled against taking a polygraph by his attorney. "I offered to take one earlier but my lawyer advised me not to. The lawyer said it would be bad for the family. You know, one brother against another," Silas is quoted as saying.

November 24, 1970: Chicago Police Sgt. John R. Konen writes his five-page report linking the murder of George Jayne to the murder of the Schuessler-Peterson boys. Konen theorizes that George Jayne blackmailed Silas concerning the murder of the three boys.

December 12, 1970: The *Daily News* reports that indictments are expected in the George Jayne murder.

December 17, 1970: A story in the *Sun-Times* by Art Petacque lays out a lot of the factual information leading to the arrest of Melvin Adams. The story also says George Jayne left letters. One of the letters said George "knew too much" about the Schuessler-Peterson murders. "George Jayne had written he had knowledge of the killer or killers but had not reported what he knew to police."

January 1971: Beverly Hansen files for divorce after finding Kenneth Hansen in bed with a stable hand. She later drops the matter.

January 6, 1971: The *Chicago Tribune* reports that Melvin Adams and Patricia Farmer have been indicted on charges of trying to coerce a grand jury witness into giving false testimony about the George Jayne murder. The indictment alleges that the two had wanted Farmer's coworker, Kathy Beaver, to lie about Melvin's whereabouts on the night of the murder.

January 9, 1971: Silas Jayne is arrested by the ATF on weapons charges after police raid his home and find eighteen weapons: four rifles, two long-barrel pistols and twelve handguns. At a hearing before U.S. Magistrate James T. Balog, Silas's bond is set at $25,000. Silas takes fifteen $1,000 bills out of his money belt to pay the bond. He turns to U.S. Attorney Sam Skinner and states, "I've got a $100,000 more in a bank in Elgin."

January 11, 1971: The *Daily News* reports that Silas Jayne's police files concerning the Cheryl Rude and Frank Michelle Jr. cases have disappeared.

April 1971: Illinois Bureau of Investigation investigators go to the home of a Markham Police officer to question him about the George Jayne murder. In his house they find a .20-mm Swedish antiaircraft cannon which authorities later assume Silas planned to use to shoot George Jayne's plane down. Also found are several other weapons and dynamite. The officer, a former bodyguard for Silas Jayne, is arrested on weapons charges.

May 22, 1971: Silas Jayne, Joe LaPlaca, Julius Barnes and Edward Nefeld are indicted for the murder of George Jayne. Silas surrenders at the Elgin Police station. He is accompanied by his brother Frank Sr. At the group's bond hearing on May 23, 1971, Judge Wayne Olson disqualifies himself from hearing the case, stating, "I have been personally acquainted with Silas Jayne and his family for many years." Judge Robert J. Sulski then gets the bond hearing and orders all of them held pending a hearing on June 2, 1971.

May 27, 1971: News accounts reveal Melvin Adams and Patricia Farmer have been cooperating with the prosecution. Melvin Adams has confessed and also agreed to testify against the others. One news report states Silas wanted George dead because George had refused to pay him $25,000 that Silas loaned him to set up his business. It is never reported what business or what year the loan was made.

June 2, 1971: At a preliminary hearing for Silas Jayne, Melvin Adams takes the stand and testifies Jayne paid him

$30,000 to kill George Jayne. Adams says he paid Barnes $12,500 to act as the shooter. Barnes's fingerprints are found on the site of the gun taken from a sewer near Adams's home. In addition, Silas Jayne's fingerprints are found on $50 bills given to Adams for the hit. "Silas said he was a man of means and that he had plenty of money and he could help me if I got in trouble. He also said if I did a good job he had two other jobs for me."

June 4, 1971: Dave Hamm arrests Kenneth Hansen for solicitation to commit George Jayne's murder. During questioning, Hamm develops a strong suspicion that Hansen killed the three boys in 1955. Hansen is indicted a few days later on charges of conspiracy to commit murder. The charges are eventually dropped.

June 6, 1971: Kenneth Hansen is released from Cook County Jail.

July 14, 1971: Silas Jayne, Joe LaPlaca, Julius Barnes and Edwin Nefeld are indicted for George Jayne's murder.

August 10, 1971: Silas Jayne pleads not guilty to George Jayne's murder. Chief Cook County Circuit Court Judge Richard J. Fitzgerald sets a September preliminary hearing date.

September 27, 1971: Murder conspiracy charges are dropped against Melvin Adams. Witness tampering charges are also dropped against Adams and Farmer.

November 1971: Kenneth Hansen moves back in with his wife, Beverly.

1972: Joe Plemmons moves to Chicago from Santa Fe. He befriends Ken Hansen.

April 5, 1972: Edwin Nefeld pleads guilty to conspiracy charges. After he enters the plea, he's sentenced to three to ten years in prison by Judge Richard Fitzgerald.

September 24, 1972: F. Lee Bailey signs on as Silas Jayne's attorney.

December 4, 1972: Patricia Farmer testifies at a bond reduction hearing for Silas Jayne that Marion Jayne offered her and Melvin $25,000 "to tell the truth." Before Marion made the $25,000 offer she showed the couple a $10,000 bundle of cash to urge them to cooperate.

December 5, 1972: At the bond reduction hearing Melvin Adams testifies he tracked George Jayne through several states before the fatal shot was fired. Adams testifies that he and LaPlaca "tried thirty or forty times" to kill George. Adams followed George to one horse show in San Antonio. "I was watching George, seeing what characteristics I could memorize. I had never seen the man before. I sat in the bleachers watching him and seeing if I could get close enough to kill him . . . I was going to try and kill him there if I could." At a horse show in New Orleans Adams passed up a chance to kill George. "He walked right by me. I followed him and in my mind I thought it was a good chance to get him. But I couldn't do it. I just didn't have the courage or whatever it takes to kill him." On the night Julius Barnes shot Jayne, Adams testified, Barnes ran back to the car and said, "I hit him dead center." Barnes told

Adams Jayne's wife was in the way but "finally I got a bead on him." Barnes told Melvin, "I tried for a long time to get George in my sight but the lady [Marion] was in the way. After the shooting I heard the old lady say, 'George, George.'" Melvin also testified that Silas Jayne described the execution as a "real beautiful job." During the entire hearing Marion is present in the courtroom. Several news accounts say she quietly wept while Adams testified. The hearing lasts seven hours. Adams also testifies that after he met with Silas, Silas asked him to kidnap George so he could murder his brother himself. "I'd like to get at him. I could bury him right here on my place."

December 12, 1972: Chief Cook County Criminal Court Judge Richard J. Fitzgerald refuses to grant Silas Jayne bail while awaiting trial.

April 1973: Silas Jayne, Julius Barnes and Joe LaPlaca are tried for George Jayne's murder. Barnes takes the witness stand and retracts a confession he had given earlier. Silas also testifies, denying everything. Barnes is convicted of murder and Silas and LaPlaca are found guilty of conspiracy to commit murder. One of three male jurors later tells reporters, "The verdict should have been first degree murder, but Jayne's icy stares scared the nine women jurors. Jayne sat about twelve feet away from us. He worked individually on those women jurors. He looked right through them. And they'd come into the jury room and cry after some sessions." Barnes is subsequently sentenced to fourteen to thirty-five years in prison on a murder conviction; Jayne and LaPlaca are sentenced to six to twenty years in prison on conspiracy to commit murder.

April 1976: Fire destroys a stable in Oconomowoc, Wisconsin. It is set by Charles H. Johnson. He later tells the FBI that Silas Jayne paid him $30,000 to torch the stable. The fire killed thirty-three horses at Nimrod Farms, causing a loss of $750,000 to Homer Adcock.

1977: Marion Jayne sues Silas Jayne for $7.5 million in a wrongful death suit for George Jayne's murder.

February 17, 1977: Candy heiress Helen Vorhees Brach, whose fortune is estimated at $30 million, checks out of the Mayo Clinic and disappears. Before she vanished, Brach had been keeping company with a man named Richard Bailey, a con man and known associate of Silas Jayne.

June 6, 1978: IBI investigator David Hamm interviews Nick Guido at the Vienna Correctional Center. Guido, head of a torture robbery gang and cellmate of Silas Jayne, tells Hamm that Si admitted he was behind the Cheryl Rude killing. Silas also admits he killed Frank Michelle Jr. Silas told Guido he caught Michelle on his property, tortured him and then killed him. "I chased the guy and caught him. I made him tell me who sent him. After he told me who sent him I killed him." Guido also said Jayne hired jailed Outfit hit man Mike Gargano to kill Joseph LaPlaca. Guido told Hamm Silas was allowed to keep his horses at the prison stable and ride unescorted into the nearby town of Simpson to buy whiskey for himself, Gargano and Outfit honcho Joe Lombardi. Hamm also learns that Silas's brother Frank Jayne Sr. regularly transported prostitutes from Chicago to downstate Vienna to have sex with Silas.

December 1978: Marion Jayne is awarded $1 million in damages in her wrongful death suit against Silas Jayne.

February 27, 1979: *Chicago Tribune* reporter Bob Wiedrich reports that Silas Jayne has a hit list. Those on the list include Marion Jayne and her daughter Linda; Melvin Adams and Adams's wife, Patricia. Also on the list are Eddie Moran and Stephen Grod. "He always said he wants everybody he hates to go before he does," the article quotes arsonist Charles Johnson as stating. "But he always used to tell me, 'If you see one of those people I don't like fall down, help them up.' He didn't want anything to happen to anybody before he made parole."

May 23, 1979: Silas Jayne, seventy-two, is paroled from prison after serving six years for conspiracy to commit murder.

December 13, 1979: Silas Jayne is arrested on arson charges for plotting the Wisconsin fire while behind bars. Charged with conspiracy to commit arson. The FBI reports he was arrested at his house in Elgin. Jayne told the FBI he was an "animal lover" and would never do anything to harm horses.

1980: One year after he's paroled, Silas Jayne offers Marion $250,000 as payment in the wrongful death suit. She refuses.

April 1980: Silas goes on trial in Benton, Illinois, for the Wisconsin arson fire. He is found not guilty.

July 13, 1987: Silas Jayne dies of leukemia.

1989: The U.S. Attorney's Office begins investigating the disappearance and assumed murder of Helen Brach. Persons who fall under suspicion are members of Silas Jayne's inner circle.

June 12, 1989: Beverly Hansen commits suicide.

November 1991: ATF supervisor James Delorto has a conversation with longtime FBI mole William "Red" Wemette regarding the ongoing investigation into the disappearance of Helen Brach. During the course of the conversation Wemette tells Delorto that a man named Kenneth Hansen confessed to him that he murdered three boys in 1955.

April 14, 1993: ATF Agent John Rotunno meets with his supervisor James Delorto and former IBI investigator David Hamm to discuss Kenneth Hansen and the Schuessler-Peterson murders. As a result of that conversation, Rotunno begins investigating Kenneth Hansen for the boys' murders. Rotunno is later joined in the investigation by James Grady.

April 15, 1993: Curtis Hansen dies in a VA hospital.

July 27, 1994: Richard Bailey is indicted on twenty-nine counts as part of the investigation by the U.S. Attorney's Office for the Northern District of Illinois into shady dealings in the equine industry. It is alleged Bailey conspired to murder candy heiress Helen Brach.

August 11, 1994: Ken Hansen is arrested and charged in the Schuessler-Peterson murders.

March 1, 1995: Richard Bailey pleads guilty to sixteen of the twenty-nine counts lodged against him.

March 1995: James Blottiaux is picked up for questioning by the ATF and the Chicago Police Department regarding the Rude murder. He is interrogated for twelve hours and is released.

April 1995: While watching WGN-TV from his trailer in Arizona, Herbert Hollatz sees a news report about Ken Hansen being arrested for the three murders. He becomes emotional, calls his daughter and tells her he thought Hansen had been arrested and convicted of the crime years ago.

June 6, 1995: U.S. District Court Judge Milton Shadur sentences Richard Bailey to thirty years in prison following a sentencing hearing. For Bailey, who is sixty-six, the term is a life sentence.

September 6, 1995: Kenneth Hansen goes on trial for the murders of the three boys.

September 13, 1995: Kenneth Hansen is convicted by a Cook County jury for the murders of the three boys.

October 20, 1995: Cook County Circuit Court Judge Michael P. Toomin sentences Hansen to two hundred to three hundred years in prison for the murders of the three boys.

December 16, 1997: James Blottiaux is arrested and charged with Cheryl Lynn Rude's murder.

July 1999: James Blottiaux is tried and convicted of Cheryl Lynn Rude's murder. Evidence shows Blottiaux was hired to kill George Jayne. Rude was the unintended victim of the car bombing.

September 10, 1999: James Blottiaux is sentenced to two hundred to three hundred years for Cheryl Rude's murder.

May 12, 2000: Kenneth Hansen's conviction is overturned by the Illinois Appellate Court. Two of three justices find that Judge Toomin erred when he allowed evidence to be submitted that showed Hansen routinely picked up hitchhikers and sexually abused them.

August 19, 2002: Kenneth Hansen is retried and convicted for the boys' murders.

October 1, 2002: Kenneth Hansen is sentenced to two hundred to three hundred years in prison for the boys' murders.

November 2002: Joseph Plemmons contacts John Rotunno and tells him he knows who murdered Helen Brach. Rotunno begins investigating Brach's murder and other members of the Jesse Jayne Gang for their involvement in that crime.

September 2003: Frank Jayne Jr., Silas Jayne's nephew who some law enforcement officials say slipped through the cracks in the Brach investigation, is convicted of arson in connection to a 1984 stable fire. He is sentenced to six years in prison.

July 9, 2004: Frank Jayne Sr., the last of the original Jesse Jayne Gang, dies at age ninety-three.

August 25, 2004: The Illinois Appellate Court affirms Kenneth Hansen's conviction.

October 21, 2004, to March 2005: Joseph Plemmons gives a statement to the ATF and the Cook County State's Attorney's Office confessing to his role in Helen Brach's murder. The statement is offered under immunity. The statement and other materials are turned over to Richard Bailey's attorney. Bailey's attorney files court papers seeking a re-sentencing hearing for Bailey based on the provided materials, which show Bailey was not involved in Brach's murder.

March 22, 2005: The Seventh U.S. Circuit Court of Appeals denies Bailey's request for a re-sentencing hearing based on Joseph Plemmons's statement to the ATF detailing who was involved in Helen Brach's murder. The court finds that although Bailey may not have been involved in the actual murder of Helen Brach, he nonetheless remains guilty of conspiring to murdering her.

The Definitive History of the Phenomenon of Serial Murder

SERIAL KILLERS
THE METHOD AND MADNESS OF MONSTERS

PETER VRONSKY

THE FORENSIC SCIENCE OF C.S.I.
Katherine Ramsland

The facts behind the forensic drama of TV's smash hit *C.S.I.: Crime Scene Investigation*

From DNA typing and ballistics, to bitemark and blood pattern analysis, here are detailed accounts of the actual techniques used in today's crime investigations. Go behind the crime scene with prominent experts in the field for rare glimpses into cases ranging from missing persons to murder.

0-425-18359-9

A Berkley Boulevard paperback

Also Available:
THE SCIENCE OF COLD CASE FILES
0-425-19793-X

Available wherever books are sold or at penguin.com

B875